PROJECTION

by Alan Boyce

A CIP catalogue record for this book is available from the British Library.

ISBN 978-1-916294-9-9

Published by Sea Cucumber Ltd

www.sea-cucumber.co.uk

PROJECTION

For Kate, Evan and Rory

DEATH 3

I

I can see a light in the distance getting closer. I'm speeding towards it, or it's speeding towards me - I can't tell. My soul has broken free again, but the street we were in a moment ago has vanished. This is different from the other times I left my body behind. I'm in a tunnel and I can't make out any features on the walls. There is a great rushing wind noise, but I don't feel anything on my face. Am I moving up or down? Backwards or forwards? I don't suppose it matters now. Through and towards. That's all I know.

It's a new sensation and I've always found new things very stressful. But I wouldn't say that I'm afraid - that would be the wrong word. If anything, I'm happier than I have been for a long time. Well, maybe not "happy". I'm satisfied. Satisfied and calm, wherever that light leads to.

The only thing that's bothering me right now is him. The other person with me. We are clinging to one another, as much as the newly-disembodied can at any rate - me, to make sure he doesn't get away; him, because he's in a state of abject, shrieking, pleading, pissing-himself terror.

It's ironic Nigel thinks he's going to hell. To hear him begging for forgiveness, for another chance, saying he'd made a mistake. Obviously, after everything he did, he'd be a prime candidate if there really is a hell. He'd get priority boarding. I suppose I would too. In a way, I was just as much to blame for what happened as Nigel was.

I wonder where Keith is. It's only been a few minutes. But then I'm not really surprised he's not here. I've never seen anyone else while travelling before today, and I've never been anywhere like this. Anywhere that looked so much like a metaphor for something else. But then, I'm not really travelling this time, am I? This is different. This feels like the way to a final destination. I would have liked to see Keith one last time and tell him he's forgiven. Even after everything, he was my only friend.

Whatever that light is - or whatever it signifies - it seems like we're both heading out of this phase of existence. It's even closer now but I still can't make out any details. If it's just nothing, why would it be lit up like that?

Well, no point in worrying about it and upsetting this lovely feeling of satisfaction. I guess I'll find out in a minute or two when I'm properly dead for good. I might as well tell you how I got here while we're on the way - no point keeping it to myself now. Actually, when I think about it, it was secrets and keeping my mouth shut that caused all this trouble in the first place. It will do me good to open up about it at last.

LIFE I

2

Let me start off by telling you about myself. Yeah, that's probably best.

My name is Shaun Strong. Was Shaun Strong. Whatever. I'll use the present tense to keep things simple.

I am 33 years old. I live in Woking in Surrey, in the house I grew up in. I inherited it from my parents when they died three years ago. I haven't had a proper job for just under a year. At university, I studied English - so I've read a lot of books. I like books. When I left, I got a job in the local library. And that's where I stayed, until I gave up work.

I don't have a car because I can't drive. I've never had a real girlfriend, although I do think I've been in love a handful of times. Birdwatching is my only real hobby, but I just do it casually. I know a lot about birds, but I'm not a twitcher or anything like that. I mean, I like spotting birds and recognising them, but I don't go out of my way to find them.

Sport doesn't interest me and I'm not a big one for adventure either. What do I like?

I'm quite a homebody really. I enjoy watching TV ... listening to most kinds of music. I don't really get passionate about it like Keith does though. I can't really imagine caring as much about he does about genres and bands, loving them one day and despising them the next.

It's very hard to describe yourself to someone else. It's especially hard for me because I've never really had to do it, or

3

even think about doing it until now.

The main thing people would say about me is ... well, the main impression I make is no impression at all. I am a very quiet person. I blend in. People don't really notice me, but that suits me fine. Yes, that suits me just fine. Would I say I'm shy? Yes, probably. When I'm actually talking to someone, the words don't come easily or quickly enough. In my head, I am a master of witty repartee.

I am a thinker of deep thoughts and I hold some very interesting points of view. But I find getting that across to anyone else very difficult. The speed I can work at in my mind and the speed my tongue and body can work at are just completely out of tune with one another.

When people think about me at all, it's to take me for granted or to assume that I'm boring or stupid. They make their minds up without my input. I don't mind though. It's much better to be underestimated than overestimated.

When Keith moved out of his mum's and came to live with me, it felt very strange. Even when they were alive, my mum and dad didn't seem to notice me around the house. Keith was totally different. He was the only person who ever took a real interest in me. In fact, he was so interested it unnerved me at times. Maybe I should have seen what was coming then, but it was oddly satisfying to be the centre of attention for once.

Because, you see, I have an unusual gift. I am what you might call an "astral traveller". I can leave my body behind and roam free, invisible and intangible, like a ghost. Well, not like a ghost really - if nobody notices it, it's not a ghost, is it? By definition, a ghost has to be detectable. If there's nothing to see, hear or feel an observer couldn't point to any difference between "a ghost" and "not a ghost". I do like to be precise when I can. When I travel, you would never know I was there. I leave no trace. The difference is I know I'm there.

For as long as I can remember, when I go to sleep I have been able to rise up out of my body and go out into the world.

I realise that's quite a big deal. I didn't mention it

earlier because I don't really like to talk about it. I don't want it to define me, you know? I'm not just an astral traveller - I'm a human being with other qualities and interests. Like birdwatching. There's more to Shaun Strong than just the unique thing about me. I call it a gift, but it's hard to look at it as a blessing now. The gift, and talking about the gift to other people, are what got me here: dead, for the third time.

You probably have a lot of questions about my ability, or "The Thing" as I call it (shorthand for "The Thing I Do"). Well, before you ask, let me stop you. I'm a bit embarrassed about it now, but I never really took much of an interest in the mechanics of The Thing - why it happened, what was going on and so on. I kind of always meant to learn more about The Thing, but - well, as I'm confessing I might as well confess everything - I am not good at getting things started. Tomorrow always seemed like a much better day to begin than today. Tomorrow and tomorrow and tomorrow creeps in this petty pace from day to day to the last syllable of recorded time, doesn't it? From my point of view, that is right about now.

As for what it's like, I can tell you plenty about that, but I think you might be disappointed. Everything is normal. It's a little bit greyer perhaps. Your peripheral vision fades to a blur a little bit quicker than in the real world.

The best comparison I can give is that it's like seeing the world through someone else's slightly greasy glasses. Someone who doesn't have a particularly strong prescription, obviously. It all looks normal, but you feel just a little out of kilter. You know that feeling, when you're drifting off to sleep and suddenly it seems the things around you are actually withdrawing hundreds and hundreds of metres away? Like your eyes have dropped backwards into some other spatial dimension?

That's how it feels - you're there and you're far away at the same time.

That's probably a let down for you, isn't it? There are no mystic portals, no talking animal spirit guides, no wise old men - nothing you could call symbolic or archetypical. Everything

I've heard about the astral plane, shamans, out-of-body experiences is bollocks. Or rather, it's not like that for me. And as I've never seen anyone else there, perhaps I'm somewhere completely different from those places, if they exist at all.

Yeah, you'd expect to meet some spirits in the spirit world, wouldn't you? For me, there's none of that. I can see you, I can hear you, I can follow you but you can't tell I'm there. When I go into this state, it's like I am retuned to a new frequency that the material world's receivers can't pick up. I'm still there in the normal world - I'm just undetectable.

Now, you might think that The Thing is pretty cool, but it's not without its drawbacks and limitations. For a start, the quid pro quo of being out of one's body is that - first and foremost - you don't have a body. I'm just a sort of floating consciousness that can see and hear. No touch, no smell. I cannot interact with the rest of the world. I can only observe. It's like fully immersive TV, and everyone else's lives are the plotlines.

I've got into the habit of situating my centre of consciousness where my eyes would usually be: that is, about 5 feet 11 inches off the ground. Everything is in its normal scale and perspective then. Don't get me wrong. Sometimes I enjoy being able to float thousands of feet in the air or down among the blades of grass with the creepy crawlies. Eventually though, it starts to feel unnatural and I drift back to human size. I guess my sense of self - whatever that is - just involves having a body of this shape, in this arrangement, with two hands and feet and a nose and all that.

Flying is not as much fun as it sounds, and that's because I just can't go very fast. I can move about as quickly in this travelling state as I can on foot when I'm awake. That is to say, walking pace most of the time, with occasional bursts of running. I've got more or less the same amount of stamina when I'm in my ghostly form as I do when I'm running for real. That's not a lot. I've never been bothered about exercise. My body has never been a priority.

Yes, I can walk through walls. And doors and windows

and cars and sheep and other people. I wouldn't say it feels any different passing through solid objects than it does passing through thin air as such, but if I'm in the middle of - say - a two-foot thick brick wall, I can't see or hear. Same as you probably wouldn't be able to. I don't like that sensation, so if there's an open door where I'm headed, I'll use that in preference to the wall. I don't like that sensation of my faculties switching off. Once, I stayed inside a big rock for a whole afternoon to see if anything changed or if I could get used to it. Eventually, I just woke up because it was so fucking boring.

That's how I get back. I wake up. I'm conscious the whole time, so if I want to I can just immediately send my mind back to my body and - bang - I'm back in the real world. I never had any problems getting back before all these recent events. Any time I wanted to, I could return and there I would be, back behind my own eyeballs once again.

And how do I get there? I go to sleep. When other people go to sleep, they often experience a "hypnagogic state". In that state, dream images and sensations start to impinge on their consciousness. If they go along with the dream narrative, they fall unconscious. If they recognise it for what it is, they wake up and start the process all over again.

It's not like that for me. My parents always said I was a sleepy child - I could doze off while walking up the stairs. And I've stayed that way ever since. If I want to fall asleep, I can pretty much do it at will, whenever, wherever. It's nothing to do with being tired so I'm guessing it's a sort of corollary of The Thing. Anyway, what happens is always the same. I feel like I'm sinking. Not straight down, but down and forward, head first - like I'm on a kid's slide in nylon tracksuit bottoms. Sooner or later, I reach a fork. It's not something I can see, but I know that I can go left or I can go right. If I go right, I begin to experience that hypnagogic imagery and soon fall asleep and dream, same as anyone else. But if I go left, the slide gets faster and faster and steeper and steeper until ... well, I come round and find myself looking down on my body. And off I go. At walking pace.

I don't make the rules. That's just how The Thing works for me. Maybe there are real psychics out there and it's different for them. Maybe they're not stuck with a maximum speed of about five miles per hour, and maybe they like walking through solid objects. Maybe they can materialise themselves when they've got to where they're going or communicate with other people. That fraud Dr Claudius said a lot of stuff about what he could do, but I don't believe he really could. It was just another scam. But if I can do it, surely other people can? Because if not, why me?

Why would God or the universe or the Secret Masters or whoever give me this power? I call it a "power" but what good is it really? What could I ever do with it? What else could I have done but turn into a voyeur, when all I can do is watch? That's not a power - at best, it's a feature or a characteristic. Or maybe I was always like that and The Thing just chimed in with quirks and flaws that were already there. Certainly, I keep my head down and don't attract attention when I'm awake. And I watch and listen, and people forget I'm there.

I always thought I would have a chance to use The Thing for good. I knew I was special, but in the end, I only managed to make things worse for a lot of people.

Yes, so those are the rules as far as I know. There may be others, and that's why I'm always very careful where I go. I stay away from government buildings, because they might have psychic detection and extermination equipment installed to prevent ethereal spies from getting in. Keith had read about that sort of thing. Apparently there was a lot of it going on during the Cold War. But as Keith liked to say, just because you're paranoid doesn't mean they're not out to get you. I think he got it from a book, but he never admitted it. Anyway, at the end of the day, you never know if the person you're watching is going to turn around, look you in the eye and say "I can see you."

Jesus ... I can still hear it now. "You weren't there a moment ago. Where did you come from? Yes, you. I can see you."

I can see you.

3

I always thought that I would end up using The Thing to make the world a better place. Superhero stories have always attracted me - that was one of the things me and Keith had in common. Hell, I've even got an alliterative first and last name: Shaun Strong. Just like Peter Parker, Reed Richards and Bruce Banner. But, you know, all those classic heroes got their powers through some kind of traumatic experience - radioactive spider, space accident and so on. They had all been ordinary people and so appreciated that "with great power comes great responsibility" stuff.

And most heroes have a tragic flaw - a weakness like kryptonite or some defining trauma. Well, the last few months have shown me what my fatal flaw was all along. I am hopelessly weak-willed. Others lead, I follow. I'm not a hero. At best, I'm a sidekick.

I've never been ordinary. And yet, what I am has always been ordinary to me. As far back as I can remember I have been doing what I do. I started off thinking I was a sleepwalker, but when I told my parents that I had watched them watching TV, they just laughed. If I had been in the room, my dad said, we would have seen you. You must have been dreaming, my mum said.

So I accepted that explanation for while, until other kids at school started talking about their dreams. They were wild, sexy, disturbing. My dreams apparently consisted exclusively of watching my parents watching TV until they went to bed. That was when I first started keeping secrets. I didn't tell the truth about my mundane dreams and nor did I lie. I just kept quiet and let everyone else speak.

Like all kids, I assumed that the difference between my dreams and the dreams of others proved that something was wrong with me - so from about the age of twelve, I tried to avoid this kind of dreaming. That was when I discovered the choice between the right hand slide and the left hand one. I found that I could dream normal dreams - dreams about turning up for exams without having revised, dreams about my teeth dropping out, dreams about urinating for hours without end, dreams about being chased by giant naked grandmothers. Dreams like everyone else's. That was when I began to understand that something else was happening if I went left. I wasn't dreaming - this was something else.

Was it real? How could it be real when my consciousness was leaving my body and wandering the streets, gardens and houses of suburban Surrey - in defiance of all the laws of physics? But it was real. I could have been a pioneer of 21st century spiritual sciences, or at least a key piece of evidence for the explorers doing the legwork. Yes, I could have changed the course of history if I had just not drifted through my parents' bedroom wall that night in 1992 (June 17th) and discovered them having sex.

I knew what I was seeing, of course. I might have lived a fairly sheltered life up to that point, but I listened to what the kids at school who hadn't said they had seen and heard. This did not look exactly like I had heard sex described. I had seen a few pictures of it in magazines as I strained to look over older boys' shoulders. Both my mum and my dad seemed to find the whole thing very uncomfortable and a great strain. It looked more like two injured elephant seals flapping around a beach on South Georgia than what I had been led to believe sex looked like. However, the resemblance in terms of structural fundamentals was unmistakable.

Projection

Most children who catch their parents at it only steal a fleeting glimpse before they are noticed and either bollocked for sneaking around or fobbed off with some unconvincing explanation as to how daddy was just giving mummy a "special cuddle". But my parents would never notice me. I was invisible, intangible, undetectable.

So I stayed. I was transfixed. Something compelled me, I could not leave. I was disgusted by what I was seeing and by the fact that I couldn't tear my eyes away. I got closer. I changed viewing angles. All the time, I was appalled, but more by what I was doing than what they were doing.

So that was it. That was that. From then on, I could never say anything about it to anyone. That was the moment when I started down the grubby path of the voyeur. That was when my gift and all the potential that had come with it became something shameful, my dirty little secret instead of the frontier of a new science. Sorry mum. Sorry dad. Sorry human knowledge.

After that first time, I didn't stay around the house as much, awake or asleep. I couldn't look my parents in the eye. They assumed it was just typical teenage behaviour, but I was by no means a typical teenager. Something had changed in me. If you will, I had found my vocation - spiritual dogging. I was an otherworldly peeping tom. Neighbours' and school friends' parents' houses, alleyways behind pubs and clubs, recreation fields and waste grounds, isolated lay-bys. Through trial and error, through nights wasted in unfulfilled expectation, I learned where people became intimate and I joined them unnoticed, undisturbed and undisturbing there.

I would like to tell you that I discovered something profound about the human condition from all that - from what I shared with those people. But I can't. I was a teenager. I masturbated. I masturbated a lot. Lacking a body while in situ, as it were, I had to memorise what I'd seen and ... well ... you know. The more I did it, the more I needed to do it. I didn't go blind, but it made me blind to a lot of things. My secret obsession,

11

my double life - normal teenage life passed me by. Why talk to girls and risk rejection and ridicule when you could watch them, critique them, compare them, all from a position of safety? Safety from rejection, from mockery, from risk. With great power came great opportunities. Well, at the time they felt like great opportunities. Looking back now, I can see just how pitiful it was.

Obviously I'm not telling you this because I'm proud of it. It is shameful. I'm ashamed of it, really. But it made me what I was, and what I was led me to the choices that got people killed. Including me - repeatedly. This is my confession and much as I'd like to be the hero of this story, I can't. There is no hero in my story and no one comes out of it well.

I didn't just watch people having sex. I eavesdropped too. I spied and listened in and entertained myself by knowing all sorts of things I shouldn't have known, and that nobody knew I knew. The whole drama of other people's lives entranced me in a way that my own life paled in comparison to. Indeed, it never occurred to me that these opportunities for closeness, intrigue, action were available to me just as much as to the people I followed. Life was something that happened in front of me. I was not a participant.

So that, in a nutshell, is why I never used my powers for good. The whole thing was too tied up with shame and guilt. I hated being the subject of attention, let alone the centre of it. I still do. And what good can a watcher do anyway? I regret not doing better, but I don't think I ever really had the right opportunities. Even a superhero needs an opportunity, right? Still, not every origin story deserves a movie.

4

It certainly was good fun at times. I would follow angry drunks around until they started fights in pub car parks. I know what women talk about when they go to the toilets in big groups. I could whisper my neighbours' most intimate conversations back to them - those they have with their husbands and wives, and those they have with people who are not their husbands or wives.

I know what the vicar does when his parishioners have gone home. I know what really goes on in the big school store cupboards. I rarely, if ever, need to pay to see new films.

Of course, I am limited in the sorts of things I can observe by virtue of where I live and what is within walking distance of my bedroom. There are no opportunities for firsthand experience of life in a warzone, of the bustle of a Moroccan souk, of high political drama when you live ten miles outside the M25. There are shocking moments - car crashes, police sieges, even murders - but if you don't know about them in advance, how can you be there when they happen, in spirit form or in body?

Obviously, I ventured into London every so often, but the sheer scale of the place overwhelmed me. London was too dense. Too many people going in too many different directions. Layer upon layer of stuff, action, history. I just never found it possible to get into anyone's plotlines in London. Back home, the pace and depth of life were manageable for someone like me.

Plus, it was only towards the very end that I had even remotely enough money to think about living in London seriously, once the business I set up with Keith was running smoothly but before Nigel came into the picture and people started dying.

I'll tell you though - one of my most memorable out of body experiences happened in London. Although I was dedicated to watching strangers and people I vaguely knew having sex, there were times when it felt more like a duty than something I really wanted to do. I carried on doing it, at least in part, because it was the thing I did, that I'd been doing since I was a boy. I almost resented the trouble I had to go to so as to fulfil my obligations. But what else was I going to do in Woking? Eventually, faces blurred into other faces, arses into other arses, tits into other tits, cocks into other cocks. Only particularly unusual cases really engaged my full attention. So it's not really those nights that stand out in my memory.

No, this was a night when I went to a premiere. It was one of the Harry Potter films in Leicester Square. I went to sleep in my hotel room and wandered out into Covent Garden. I walked up the red carpet, sat behind the stars, went to the after show party. I always liked Harry Potter - always felt we had something in common. Misunderstood everymen in the Muggle world - that's us. Only he got his Hogwarts letter and I never did. Anyway, after that I went on to London Zoo.

It was about midnight and, after the crowds of the movie premiere, I was looking forward to some solitude - and to seeing what the animals get up to when they think they're not being watched.

So I'm walking through this big open enclosure on my way to the lion pen, when I feel a presence all around me. It's the first time I've ever felt that while travelling and I'll never forget it. I thought maybe it was another person. Maybe, finally I would have someone I could confide in. But I quickly realised that this was not a human presence. I turned around - metaphorically speaking, of course. I rotated my centre of visual perception and out there, in the darkness, were what looked like hundreds of tiny red eyes - all fixed, looking straight at where my eyes would have been.

There was a swishing, a shuffling and the occasional muted plop as things dropped onto the grass. The eyes came closer. Emerging out of the gloom, I could now see long grey arms with black five-fingered hands, staring eyes with constricted, pinprick pupils, coiling, bristling black and white striped tails. There were what seemed to be hundreds of cat-faced, long-legged monkey-beasts creeping towards me. They were looking at me. They could see me.

Of course, I knew that ring-tailed lemurs are harmless to humans - but was I human at that moment? What was it that they could see? I didn't wait to find out and began to drift upwards. In unison, black pointed muzzles tilted upwards to follow me. I flew to the nearest solid pathway, outside the fence of the enclosure. I looked back, and there they all were - on the grass, in the trees, clinging spread-eagled on the chainlink. As I moved away, one lemur began an eerie, barking cry - and then the others joined in, like a colony of mournful seabirds.

That spooked the gibbons who started whooping and brachiating furiously, and the wolves who started howling. Spider monkeys rattled the bars of their cages in impotent rage and the birds in the great aviary all took flight at once, as if caught in a giant tornado.

As you can probably imagine, the whole experience was deeply disturbing. I've always thought lemurs were a bit creepy, but when I knew those spooky little bastards could see me - well, I've avoided zoos ever since and I thank my lucky stars I wasn't born in Madagascar.

I look back on that now as a kind of epiphany - a sublime experience, combining both beauty and terror. I was scared out of my wits at the time, but there was something very moving about it as well. I woke myself up and I was soaked in sweat but relieved as well. It was nice to know that I wasn't completely alone. At last, I could be sure it wasn't all just in my head.

Right now is the first time I've ever seen another human being here.

No, London life was not for me. I lived my whole first life in the house my parents bought when they first got married.

It came into my hands when they died, three years ago, when a pigeon collided with their windscreen on the M180. Dad lost control of the Toyota, swerved into the side of a Schmitz Cargobull and flipped over the central reservation. Dad died instantly, I was told. Mum lasted a couple of days in intensive care on a respirator, but then she died too.

I never did justice to my parents. They loved me, but by the time they died, I think they had more or less forgotten about me. I was so distant - impossible to talk to, absorbed in my own world. The morning they left to go on that fatal trip, I didn't even say goodbye to them as they lugged their suitcases out of the front door.

It wasn't that I didn't like them. I loved them, kind of. I think that between us, we'd just got to a point where no one quite knew how to start a conversation and so it was easier not to. Maybe there would be a better opportunity tomorrow? And so silent hours became silent days, silent weeks, silent months. We would walk past one another around the house - me on my way to the library, dad on his way to his office or the garden, mum on the way to the shops or to a friend's house - with only the barest of acknowledgement.

I always wanted to say something to them, to bring us close together again. I say "again", but my childhood before I saw what I saw is kind of a blur to me now. Were we ever that close? I'm not sure if I'm remembering my happy childhood or one I read about or saw on TV. By the time they died, my parents and I were virtual strangers. My Uncle Len - mum's brother - even took care of the funeral arrangements. He just sorted it out without even speaking to me about it. On the day, I stood at the back and listened to their friends pour out their grief.

Anyway, how could I talk to them? I had gone through my sexual awakening by watching them doing it. Over and over again. By choice. How do you start that conversation?

But why do we estrange ourselves from our parents? And why does it seem so hard to make the first step in bridging that gap when all it would take is a word ... Ah, but I'm getting off topic here and I have no idea how long we're going to have for me to tell you what happened. Has the light got any closer?

5

I need to tell you about Keith. He changed the direction of my life.

It was about six months after my parents died that I met him for the first time at the library. I was pushing a trolley-load of books along an aisle for reshelving and my mind was elsewhere when there was a thump, followed by a cry of "THE FUCK!?" and the trolley went tumbling to the ground, dumping its cargo over the floor.

Two skinny, black denim-clad legs were sticking out from under the fallen trolley. I had run a customer over.

"I'm sorry, I'm sorry," I mumbled as I picked the trolley up. Underneath was a scrawny man clad in an enormous black t-shirt emblazoned with some kind of incomprehensible satanic inscription. He was grubby-looking, and as I righted the trolley, a gust of stale air – hints of cumin, urine, filthy hair - wafted over me.

Keith.

No one could describe Keith as attractive. He had long, lank, blond hair which he tied back into a pony tail with a leather string. "Rat-like" would be the conventional way of describing Keith's physiognomy, although that would be to do something of an injustice to rats. I have always thought that real-world rats have rather kind faces. But you know what I mean. Small, narrow, suspicious eyes. Sallow, greasy skin, his cheeks pock-marked with acne scars. Attempts at facial hair that qualified as neither beard nor moustache. All told, he was odd-looking but not significantly more so than many of our regular customers.

"What the fuck is the matter with you? You fucking idiot!"

Other customers and library workers had started drifting towards the noise. As he saw them approach, Keith hesitated for a second, then began clutching his knee.

"My knee! My knee! Aaargh! You'd better find yourself a good lawyer. You've broken my knee!"

A well-dressed lady strode over and knelt beside Keith. Although he was still holding firmly onto his knee, his face had assumed an expression of horrified anticipation.

"I'm Mrs Chen and I'm an orthopaedic surgeon. Let's take a look at this knee. Now, what's your name?"

"Keith Pardew," he replied, simultaneously frozen and cringing away from Mrs Chen as she reached out towards his knee.

"Can I have a feel please Keith?"

His hands were clamped to the affected area.

"Um ... I'd rather you didn't. But did you see this idiot? I was just bending over minding my own business when he ran this trolley into me."

"I'm sorry," I muttered again, as I picked the last few books up off the floor.

"No, Keith I didn't see it. May I?"

As soon as Mrs Chen reached for Keith's leg, he leapt to his feet like a startled cat.

"I'm alright! I'm alright. Thank you, doctor. What are the rest of you looking at? You," Keith jabbed a finger towards my face. "I want to speak to your supervisor."

I led him over to Mrs Hardcastle's office. I looked through the glass door and saw my boss on the phone. She glanced up, caught my eye and made gestures to indicate "I am on the phone".

"Please take a seat," I said.

We sat down next to each other. It soon became apparent that Mrs Hardcastle was on the phone to her sister and had no intention of winding the conversation up any time soon. Gales of laughter could occasionally be heard through the door.

"Haven't you got anything else to do?" Keith asked, after we had been sat there for ten minutes.

"Not really. Shelving books."

"I'm going to take you and the council to the cleaners over this," he spat back maliciously. "My knee may not be broken - and yeah, that was very clever of you having a doctor lurking around like that - but there's underlying trauma. And you assaulted me."

"I didn't see you."

"Negligence."

"I'm sorry. I really didn't mean to."

"Why is she taking so long? I can hear it's not a work-related call. Why is she taking the piss out of us like this?"

I shook my head, shrugged and gestured fatalistically.

"I will sue you all, so badly."

We lapsed into silence for several more minutes. Finally, Keith stood up.

"I can't be arsed waiting here all day. It's just insulting. My time is worth just as much as your boss'. I'll let you off this time, because you're just a working drone in their system. But you owe me."

"OK," I mumbled.

"What's your name?"

"Shaun."

"Shaun what?"

"Shaun Strong."

"You owe me Shaun Strong."

I looked up. His gaze was like a red-hot scalpel. I shifted my eyes to the floor, to the left, to the right.

He coughed once and hobbled away. I think he really had hurt his knee a bit.

As Keith walked away, Mrs Hardcastle opened the door.

"What did he want?"

"I knocked him over with a trolley."

"For Christ's sake Shaun ... does that require you to sit outside my office for half an hour instead of getting on with your work?"

I didn't see Keith for a couple of weeks after that and I had begun to forget all about the trolley incident. And then, one morning when I was working on the issue desk, there he was.

"I need this gentleman to help me," he said to my colleague Derek, whose eyes looked in opposite directions.

"Shaun, this gentleman has requested your assistance," boomed Derek. Derek was the sort of person who would buy a beer in a pub by proclaiming "a foaming flagon of your finest ale, stout yeoman!" I know this, because I had seen it. Several times.

Keith led me away down an aisle to the back of the library. Eventually, we stopped.

"Which section would I find books about Jesus in?"

"Religion - last aisle on the left."

"No, no, no" Keith replied theatrically as if I had said something idiotic: "The historical Jesus".

"I'm not sure what you mean ..."

"Not the official stories, but the real Jesus. You know."

I looked up. Keith was smiling. His teeth were crooked and yellow and even from this distance, I could see they were encrusted with plaque.

"I'm writing a book. Well, it's more of a multimedia art project than a book. I could use your help. Mate."

The word "mate", coming out of Keith's mouth, sounded artificial, as if it were not a part of his native vocabulary. Like a high court judge saying "bruv" to a defendant.

"Remember, you owe me."

"OK."

"Good. Now, show me your microfiche."

6

Keith tended to visit the library around the end of the day when it was even quieter than usual. He would come and find me, make me help him find something or other and then sit reading graphic novels until we closed.

After the third visit, I found him waiting outside for me.

"Let's go for a beer," he said. "I'm going to let you in on something big."

That evening, he explained "Fist of God" to me.

It turns out that Keith's multimedia art project was destined to be the next international TV phenomenon, or so he said.

It was to be a series of stories about the historical Jesus' bodyguard. Keith wanted to cast Idris Elba in the role when it was inevitably picked up. The bodyguard (as yet unnamed) was endowed with awesome fighting skills. Jesus, in turn, was a spoiled prick who was quite content to go along with people imagining him to be the son of God, and who got himself into all sorts of scrapes, which Idris' fists would have to get him out of. Each episode would see some story or other of the Gospels reinterpreted along those lines. It would be a kind of Roman-era Kung Fu, a Biblical Western.

Obviously, the crucifixion was going to be the big cliff-hanger - ideally we would hold that back for "Fist of God - The Movie". Keith was adamant that it had to be made in the USA, because "only American TV production values can do justice to my vision".

Projection

I was appointed as a script consultant that evening. After a few weeks, I was promoted to executive producer.

Of course, we never wrote any of it. It was all just Keith bullshit. He was the master of starting things he would never finish. It became clear to me pretty quickly that I was never going to get that executive producer credit for my CV. And yet we quickly became friends, due to lack of alternatives on both our parts. By default. I didn't care that all Keith's schemes were destined to come to nothing or that he constantly threatened to sue me for shattering his knee. I was just flattered to have been picked as his accomplice.

Being Keith's friend required me to pretend to like – or at least tolerate - and understand his many niche interests, chief amongst them being extreme metal music: black, death, blackened death, the list goes on. At the time we met, Keith was obsessed with a pagan black metal band, called Bloody Flux. Indeed, Keith was wearing a Bloody Flux t-shirt the day we met. What distinguished the bands that were the focus of Keith's enthusiasm was that they were entirely works of his imagination. Bloody Flux was not so much a band as an idea of band, whose history, discography, stylistic evolution, internal dynamics and - for that matter - nationality (Latvian) were manufactured by Keith in a series of notebooks.

Styles of music (within the narrow parameters of the extreme metal genre) and individual bands fluctuated wildly in Keith's estimation. The last band he had invented, Keith told me, was extremely slow and heavy and went by the name of Terminal Moraine. They had ceased to be a priority when Keith's preferences moved on. Frequently let down by the actual output of real musicians and the displeasing characteristics of other metalheads, Keith developed ideal archetypes whose perfection subsisted in their unreality. Plus, he could boast of quite literally being the only person who had ever heard of them.

Before we met, Keith's primary outlet for his views on music was the internet, where on many forums he was a feared and usually reviled troll, known only by the name of Aldous Fuxley.

Although I never participated in the online debates myself, my expertise was frequently referred to in support of Keith's points of view under the pseudonym he bestowed upon me - Honoré de Ballsack.

Despite his encyclopaedic knowledge of metal, we never went to gigs even when they were taking place very nearby. Keith believed that people were out to get him, which may well have been true had anyone known that he was the notorious Aldous Fuxley. Of course, they did not. However, we did watch a lot of videos on YouTube so that Aldous would be able to give the impression online of having been present at a lot of places he had never in fact been.

Keith's talents lay in the field of ideation rather than execution. If Keith had an idea that he thought was good (such as "Fist of God"), he would usually make some sort of preliminary effort to realise it. This would typically involve extensive planning, wild speculation about how to spend the proceeds of success, followed by an ever-expanding amount of time wasting.

If Keith had an idea that was bad by his standards, he would declare that it was mine. Hence, we went through the motions at one point of working on a TV show telling the story of Robin Hood from the perspective of his horse ("Dobbin of Sherwood") – a concept which had, it turned out, been mine all along.

When Keith had an idea he thought was brilliant though, he would keep very quiet. Out would come a small hardback notebook which Keith carried with him at all times, bearing the legend "Historical Jesus". Keith would furtively scribble down whatever flash of self-assessed genius it was that had inspired him.

Anyway, whichever way you cut it Keith was creative. Compared to me, at any rate. He asked questions when ordinary people took things for granted.

"Have you ever met a horse called Dobbin, Shaun?"

I replied that I was not sure that I had ever "met" a horse.

24

"So why do we call horses Dobbin? Have you ever come across a dog called Fido? Or Rover? Or a cat called Tiddles, for that matter?"

I had to admit that I had not.

"And yet ... And YET Shaun ..." (we had been drinking during this conversation, I should add) "these are the names we automatically, unthinkingly associate with these animals, following the herd. Like the fucking mentally penned-in sheep that we are."

"Larry the lamb."

"What?"

"A name for a sheep."

"Shaun ..." Keith leaned forwards, exhaled heavily and closed his eyes as if he was talking to a particularly exasperating child. "Shaun ... the point is not to come up with a name for a sheep. It's to recognise how ... how our thought patterns, our very language is not derived from our own original thoughts. Power ..." (there was a long pause) "Power ... creates our world."

Usually when Keith was heading off in this direction I would nod and grunt in agreement - however much I questioned the idea that "Power" had any pressing interest in nicknames given to horses. Suffice to say, Keith believed that "Power" - also known as "The System" - exercised more or less complete totalitarian control over every aspect of his life and the lives of those around him. What made Keith special was that he was aware of this while everyone else was not.

Nevertheless, Keith bore the burden of this knowledge very lightly. In fact, it would be hard to differentiate how Keith lived at that time from the manner of living of any other elitist, self-obsessed, social outcast. What I came to understand was that in believing himself under the thumb of Power, Keith had found true freedom - which was being responsible for nothing. Interview goes tits up? The System. Parking ticket? Power exercising its crushing force. Blackmail plot goes horribly wrong and leads to a series of brutal murders? Well ...

He also had one very long fingernail, on the ring finger of his left hand. It was maybe half an inch longer than the others, which were themselves longer than is conventional for men. Keith's hands were white and slim, with delicate skin. With this nail, Keith would habitually stroke a spot just to the left of his chin. Whenever he was pensive, listening, watching TV ... dab dab dab, there he'd go. Hands being what they are, extending the ring finger so as to apply the nail to the skin patch (Keith called it a beard, but this description would not have been corroborated by many independent observers) required the little finger to be projected outwards. This gave Keith an even more effete look whenever he was engaged in this activity. I never knew why he had that long fingernail.

To anyone who noticed either of us, I must have seemed quite normal compared to Keith. He always wore black jeans and trainers, and an oversized metal band t-shirt. His trousers were always marginally too short. As a keen observer of people, I know that this is the universal callsign of the outsider.

I had a variety of clothes, most of which fitted adequately. Polo shirts, chinos, shoes, a coat - the full set. I had to dress "smart casual" for work, so I dressed smart casual outside of work. It saved the energy of making decisions. I was like Steve Jobs in that respect. When I left the library, I just carried on dressing as if I was still there.

Keith lived with his mother. He was a few years younger than me, and he had moved to Surrey from Lincolnshire when his father had been relocated for work. "Best financial move my dad ever made - he got three times what he paid for it in '92," Keith said in one of the few references he made to his late father, who had died a few years later.

To tell you the truth, I'm not 100% sure how old he was. When we met, we were past the age of grading people according to whether they had been in a higher or lower year than oneself at school. We just didn't talk about that sort of thing. I suppose if we'd both ended up having families and things like that, we might have had those conversations. But Keith was a man of esoteric tastes bordering on the obsessive, who believed that everything conventional or normal was a conspiracy against him - while I ... what was I? I was just a mirror for anyone who took the trouble to look at me. Keith only wanted to talk about the things that interested him. The details of our lives outside the little universe we had fabricated were not on that list, and I was ok with that, being very used to never talking about myself.

Keith simply assumed that I shared his interests, views and quirks - chief amongst them being a profound hatred of his fellow human beings. I was never entirely sure how much of this was an act and how much of it was real. Nor could I tell precisely how much of it was really directed at himself. For all his ideas and the effort we put into them (sort of), Keith's greatest scorn was reserved for the doers, the achievers, the "men of action". Only people who are too stupid to consider all the possibilities, to weigh up all the possible side-effects, to take on board the irrecoverable costs of committing to an irreversible decision can be "men of action". Keith would say that people like that are simply less conscious than us, the thinkers. Quite how I qualified as a thinker, I don't know.

Keith considered himself a great intellectual and innovator, who chose to spite the world by denying it the fruits of his genius when they were not immediately recognised and acclaimed. And yet at other times he would declare how much he loved the world - how much he was IN LOVE with the world - and blame himself for its dreadful state. From time to time, he would wallow in despair about world hunger, poverty, the environment, whatever had fixated him at the time. He held himself to blame because he had failed to convince "Power" of his exceptionality (to convince anyone, in fact) and the ability he and he alone had to make a difference to all these problems, singly and collectively. This took place in the intervals between Keith hating everything, most of all "Power" and the ovine masses controlled by it.

You're probably wondering how I ended up being friends with someone who sounds like such a prick. What you have to bear in mind, is that no one had ever selected me like that before. On the few occasions when I had been picked, the choice had quickly been regretted. People who made conversation with me usually realised their mistake in under a minute, once the awkward silences began. I don't mean to be rude or uncommunicative. A few minutes after a conversation has ended, I am the soul of wit. I come up with all sorts of great replies, fascinating questions and entertaining anecdotes. I just can't do it when someone is actually speaking to me. Overwhelming self-consciousness makes me nauseous whenever I am the centre of any attention. I never feel that when I'm travelling - it's definitely one of the upsides.

Keith never minded awkward silences, taking them only as invitations to carry on filling the gaps with more of his own thoughts. I think he saw me as seeing him in the way he wanted to be seen. He saw me as someone who appreciated his brilliance. As a disciple. As a dog.

I stuck around because Keith decided to be my friend and then he never abandoned me - until the very end. We needed each other. I needed him to give me the reasons to do anything other than follow the same routine, day after day, month after month, year after year. He needed me as an appreciative audience for his performances. I validated Keith's perception of himself. I was lonely, and it was only when someone took an interest in me that I realised I preferred having a friend, no matter what his flaws were, to not having anyone. Although he betrayed me when he could have saved my life, so - yes - I do think he's a prick.

7

A year ago last May, Keith arranged for us to go camping in Northumberland. He had become convinced of the need for us to harden ourselves so as to be able to endure physical challenges of an unspecified nature and a camping trip seemed like a minimally uncomfortable introduction into the world of survivalism.

One afternoon, we found ourselves heading to the indoor swimming pool (it was quite a nice campsite) when Keith stopped dead. He had seemed nervous all day and I gathered that we had now reached the crisis point.

"Look at them ... Jesus Christ ... "

A couple in their mid-sixties were walking along the edge of the pool, with that over-cautious, stiff gait that everyone has to adopt when traversing wet tiles.

"You see the real scum here, Shaun. Have you seen that film? 'The Name of the Rose'?"

I had, but I wasn't quite sure where he was going with it.

"That woman - fuck. She looks like Ron Perlman with a flat top. A six-titted squat beast. Why would anyone choose to carry on looking like that?"

I didn't think Keith was being quite fair, although the woman in question did bear a certain resemblance to the prosthetically-enhanced actor, now he mentioned it.

"And the other one looks like a half-starved Brian May. With his little medallion. How can she be so fat and he be so thin? Do they eat separate meals? Or does she just eat for both of them? Jesus, I can smell the tobacco reek from here."

He was right about that.

"Can you imagine them fucking?"

The tendons in Keith's neck contracted as he said this and his Adam's apple bobbed violently down and then up. My brain leapt, as I tried to keep that image from taking root.

"I can't get in that water. It's a soup of scabs, plasters and tampon seepage. It's a menstrual infusion. It'd be cleaner in a sewage outlet. Look at them all ... my God, look at that beer gut. Do you think his tattoo goes all the way under the flap? Could you imagine being a tattoo artist?"

I said that I could not. It was true that we were pretty much the only adults present without at least a couple of tattoos.

"Handling that white, sticky flab? Wiping his sweat off your hands? Carving 'Kieran' and 'Savannah' onto ... that?"

A succession of bony children jumped into the water in a group, splashing water in Keith's face. He flinched, screwed up his eyes and wiped them with the back of his hand.

"Why do they all have so many fucking kids? That one - how can a child get so fat in - what? Ten years? Like a human fucking shar-pei. The scum breeds so fast. What are these little animals going to do when they group up? Fuck each other the second they're physically able and create more and more... so many... dirty children... everywhere... they... they... it's just disgusting. I can't. They make me ..."

He had started to shudder convulsively as his sentences became incoherent. Keith turned on his heels and scuttled back to the changing rooms (the only way to run safely in the vicinity of a swimming pool). I took another look at Ron and Brian, who were now gingerly walking down the steps in the shallow end holding hands. Yes, they were ugly but not horrifically so. And they couldn't help it really, could they? I turned around and followed Keith.

Keith didn't just hate humanity in the abstract. He hated every single person individually, by dint of their humanity -

every person except Nigel, it turns out, the one person who really deserved it. I think he liked having me to talk to because it gave him an outlet for his passive-aggression, the cold, malignant fury that the treatment unwittingly meted out to him by others provoked. I never saw him lose his temper to anyone's face. But you could see the rage in his eyes whenever he was jostled in a doorway, whenever anyone jumped a queue in front of him, whenever a parent failed to control their child in his vicinity. Anything Keith didn't like was not an inconvenience, but a calculated insult. If it involved physical contact, the rage mingled with something verging on nausea.

Sat outside our tent - fully-clothed and eating soup from a tin with his Swiss army knife's spoon - Keith elaborated.

"They're just ridiculous things, bodies. Take noble souls like us Shaun. Look at the sick jokes we're forced to convey ourselves around in. These things," Keith prodded himself at various points around his chest "This isn't what we are. We're in here," now jabbing his forefinger into the side of his head.

"We're minds, stuck dragging these bloody burdens around with us. Chests that give out, knees that wear out, joints that seize up. Can you think of any less-physically well-adapted animal than the human animal Shaun? Pretty much everything can outrun us, outclimb us, out-fight us. We can't fly, we can barely swim. Even the best human bodies are an embarrassment to the human spirit.

"And they pollute our minds!" Keith was unstoppable now. "Where do you think fear, attachment, self-destructiveness ... all that ... where does it come from? Emotions and desires, Shaun - the body encroaching on the mind."

I disagreed on this point. I might not be what is known as a particularly well-rounded individual in an emotional sense, but I've seen enough people to know that it's the emotions that come first. That's the blind spot of human rationality. It can't see the lengths it will go to in order to accommodate and justify its pre-rational givens. Watching the human mind at work is like watching someone trying to fix a light by rotating the room around the bulb.

"You may not think it Shaun, but I am full of compassion. Really. Those people today? I don't hate them. I pity them. Pity the minds trapped in those revolting, ridiculous carcasses."

Keith shuddered, the afternoon's images replaying in front of his mind's eye. I didn't take a word of it seriously - I just nodded and smirked as usual - but somehow Keith's words had planted a tiny seed in my mind.

I would never have got into this trouble if it hadn't been for Keith. It was his idea to use The Thing for gain. He did the planning, worked out how to approach the targets and collected the money. But I can't blame him really. He'd never have done any of it by himself, any more than we'd ever have seen "Fist of God" on the big screen. We enabled each other to do something terrible and we paid the price.

That trip to Northumberland. It was when all this really began. It was when I told Keith about my power.

8

Once Keith heard that I had never been in an aeroplane, he insisted that driving up north was out of the question. We would fly to Edinburgh, hire a car and drive down to the campsite. I had plenty of savings, having basically nothing to spend money on, so I paid. Although I was convinced that we were going to die, I was secretly a little pleased. Hadn't I wanted someone to take me outside my daily routine? Wasn't that why I wanted some company? Even if it was company that was clearly taking pleasure in my discomfort.

We were horribly delayed. We sat for two hours on the taxi-way and it had gone dark before we took off.

After the 'fasten seatbelts' sign went off, Keith examined me with a mixture of fascination and revulsion.

"You're sweating."

The fingernail stroked the bumfluff beard quasi-erogenous zone. He was looking at the sweat beading on my forehead.

"Are you scared? I'm not scared." A voice piped up from the seats in front. The head of small boy followed it.

"I'm not scared of planes. I was scared once because I thought I was going to die, but I didn't and now I'm not scared."

Keith's hand dropped from his face. He looked appalled and shrunk back in his seat, pretending he could not see our new friend.

"Are you best friends? My best friend is Tyler. I'm three months older than him because Tyler is a baby."

At this point, Tyler's best friend's mother instructed him to sit down and he continued the conversation with her. Keith was still recomposing himself after being spoken to by a child. I closed my eyes.

Immediately, I had that sinking feeling. Words and phrases flashed upwards past me - "filing cabinet", "that's not my", "where is". I was falling asleep and I could sense the fork approaching. When I got there I went left ...

My body, Keith, the family in the seats in front and the plane exploded away from me. There was an all-consuming rushing sound, a pressure wave, a frequency that resonated inside and outside of me as every seat in the Airbus A321-100 followed by the toilets at the back (which were thankfully unoccupied at the time) passed through my face.

I found myself suspended in the night sky over northern England, a moth-eaten blanket of cloud below me, a forest of stars above, the illuminated aircraft receding into the distance ahead of me. I started to run after it by instinct. Don't leave me behind! But soon it was gone, and I was alone.

I felt my heart - by now fifteen, twenty, twenty-five miles away - racing. How far away from my body could I go without being cut off? I started to panic. Which way was Edinburgh? Which way was home? What would happen to me up here?

Gradually as I looked around and took in my situation, I began to feel peaceful. How small everything down there looks. How the clouds churn in the wind like vapour around a chemical beaker. I was seeing something hardly anyone has ever seen, it occurred to me. I dived through the clouds. There was the North Sea, black but lit up along its coast. There was a V-formation of airborne Canada geese headed to wherever it is geese go at night. There was a town, there was an isolated farm, there was a quarry. It's beautiful I thought. Just like Google Maps, but animated.

To be above it all, to be detached, to view everything in its full perspective without the constraints of proximity ... surely this is ... what? Freedom? Or is it the opposite of freedom? The sense of weightlessness released me from all my burdens, all my discomforts, all my hurts. A euphoria was rising in me but at the same time I felt like I was sinking back into myself - it was majestic and cosy all at once. Although I was all alone, I no longer felt separate from the world. I felt like I encompassed it.

Would it really be so bad to stay here until the sun rose? Could that moment last forever? But if it did would I be alone forever? I didn't realise it then, but something changed in me at that moment. I didn't want to be alone forever.

But then I woke up. The stewardesses had banged my dangling arm with the refreshments trolley. I was back in my seat. Keith was looking at me. He had the "Historical Jesus" notebook in his hand and discretely tucked it away when he saw me wake up.

"We're just about to start coming in to land," he said.

I grunted acknowledgement and sat up in my seat. I felt incredibly peaceful, and even the realisation that I was back on the aeroplane (which was about to drop out of the sky, deliberately) did not disturb that sense of calm.

"Better put your seatbelt on Shaun. Apparently it's thick fog over the Firth of Forth" - his tongue lingered over the words "thick fog" like he was savouring them, delighting in my discomfort. I told you he was a shit. He also burred the words "Firth" and "Forth", rolling his r's in an absurd approximation of Sean Connery. Keith continued looking at me after he finished this sentence, a barely-detectable smile on his lips. His finger rose to his chin and the stroking began again.

9

I was still thinking about that moment in the sky when I zipped myself into my sleeping bag a few hours later. Like I said, we had hired a car at the airport and then driven 80 miles or so down the A1 to the campsite. The car was a Honda Civic. Keith frequently expressed respect for Japanese culture, manufacturing standards and what he imagined to be their hair- and fat-free cleanliness.

The campsite contained static caravans, mobile caravans and tents – all clustered more or less concentrically around a one-story building housing the swimming pool, shop, washing machines and toilets. As tent-dwellers, we inhabited the outermost circle, near enough to the main road for passing traffic to be disturbing.

As I settled down to sleep, I wondered what it was that had struck me that moment of solitude among the clouds. An epiphany, no doubt - but what exactly had I grasped? Being there in the sky, miles above the comings and goings of the world, halfway between heaven and earth, I had felt elated and melancholy in equal measures. The elation came from the wonder of the spectacle, the vertigo of having nothing close to me in any direction and the knowledge that it was mine and mine alone to see. But so too did the sadness. I realised that I wanted to share what I'd seen with another person. But how?

And who?

Keith?

NYEEEEOOOOOWWWW.

A southbound motorcycle snapped me back to a state of alert sleepiness. Did I want to tell Keith about The Thing? Would it be so bad to let him in on it? Surely he would be pleased. Keith had never seemed jealous of me in any way.

But what about the rest of it? He was bound to ask me what I've been doing with this ability all these years. I couldn't tell him about the watching. About the spying and the eavesdropping. Even though I'd never spied on Keith, he would surely be paranoid and assume I had been. And if he thought I had been watching him in the past, what was to say I wasn't watching him right now - now being any time at all.

No, I couldn't possibly tell Keith about all that. It would be the end of our friendship and that would defeat the object of sharing. I might even get into trouble with the law if he took it really badly. But I hadn't used my powers for anything much, just nosing around and getting off. Who would ever believe that was all someone who could do what I could do would do if they had the chance?

I felt shame, but not the shame I had expected to feel. I had always just assumed that the sexual side of my secret life was the part that tortured me. I thought I would feel like an evil bastard, treating friends, neighbours, strangers - hell, even my parents - like nothing more than porn. That seemed perfectly reasonable and so I put the idea out of my head. If I didn't think about it and if no one ever knew how could I be hurting anyone? It was all just a video game, just an elaborate, non-interactive virtual reality.

I thought I would feel ashamed for the way I had treated other people if I ever let the cat out of the bag. I had betrayed everyone. But I didn't. At that moment, I regretted all the times I had not made the most of my chances to see wonderful and unusual things, to go to exotic places, to meet powerful and intriguing people and make a good impression on them. I felt ashamed because I'd betrayed myself by being satisfied to be nothing more than a spectator in my own life.

In retrospect, I just can't see how being able to move around like a pedestrian ghost centred on his parents' house in Surrey would actually have enabled me to do any of those things. I'm just not a creative thinker like Keith and Nigel. But at that moment, I was filled with a realisation of all the time and opportunities I had wasted, time and opportunities I might never have again - and the determination (if I could be said ever to have felt determined) not to squander any more of my life.

I'd tell Keith in the morning. And I'd tell him that it had only started a couple of weeks ago, to get round the whole "what have you been doing with it until now?" issue. After all, that was no more implausible than the truth.

10

I didn't tell Keith in the morning. I told him three days later, which was the day after the incident at the swimming pool I mentioned earlier. We had driven to Lindisfarne and the tide had come in, so we were stuck for at least six hours. After we'd looked at the castle, the abbey, the lime kilns, the Northumbrian coast and vast expanses of grey North Sea merging into grey northern sky, we found ourselves still with hours to kill.

We found our way to the only pub in the village. The place was deserted, except for a huddle of craggy old men with the scorched faces and bleached eyes of real-life fishermen sitting at the bar, accompanied by two scrawny-tough, younger labourers in hi-vis jackets. Most tourists had the sense to read the tide tables and get off the island before the causeway floods each day, and the locals had supposed that they would have their pub to themselves. Imagine their horror at the sight of Keith and me.

The landlord was chatting to his patrons as we approached the bar. He made no effort to interrupt his conversation. In fact, the harder Keith stared at him the more intent he became on the detailed critique of local bus routes that was underway. I could see Keith's jaw twitching as the delay continued.

Eventually the bar man sauntered over to us.

"Gentlemen," he drawled in a tone that conveyed nothing but bottomless scorn. He managed to make the word sound almost exactly like "wankers".

An orange juice...please," Keith paused for half a beat before the final word, trying to emulate the landlord's feat of being outwardly polite while making sure that the message "fuck you" was clearly conveyed.

There was a snort of hastily stifled laughter from the group along the bar. Faces were turned over shoulders, sidelong glances were cast our way. One mouthed silently "orange juice" and the laughter burst out once more, this time in full flow.

Keith's face was glacial. His gaze could have withered plant matter. But it had no effect on these rugged, self-assured men-of-action, with red hands like joints of salted meat, black hair like barbed wire sprouting bountifully from their ears and nostrils. Keith suddenly appeared like a petulant boy. The younger locals eyed him with predatory intent. One of them smacked his chewing gum over and over like a slow handclap.

"And two pints," Keith's voice was louder, deeper and hoarser as he tried to salvage some self-respect from the situation. His voice was just like the one he'd put on the day we met in the library. He planted his hands on the bar. I could see the carpal bones grinding against one another as Keith gripped its brass rail. The laughter subsided and the men returned to their discussion. The landlord pulled up two pints of the local ale and slapped them down on the bar in front of us. A large gout of beer slopped out of each, soaking Keith's hands.

"Seven fifty."

The bar man turned his back to get the orange juice out of the fridge.

While he was facing away from us, Keith picked up the pints and walked into the beer garden. I assumed this meant that I was supposed to pay - which I did. I followed Keith, bringing the orange juice and a wine glass full of ice which the landlord had presented me with, along with a threateningly victorious smile.

The beer garden was perhaps better described as a car park with a collapsing picnic table dumped in it. Keith was sat at the table and had apparently regained his composure. He had, however, drunk his own pint and about three quarters of mine in the thirty seconds or so for which I had been absent.

"Shall we get another drink?" I said.

"Not here," Keith hissed. We got up leaving the fateful orange juice behind.

I I

Having picked up a couple of bottles of vodka at a local mini-mart, we wandered out of the town, past acres of car parking and up onto the dunes overlooking the still-sunken causeway. There we sat, looking west to the mainland and the setting sun. We drank the vodka as Keith decompressed from his ordeal at the hands of the people of Holy Island. In the distance, I could see a couple of foraging oystercatchers and what might have been a dunlin.

"Fuckers..."

After his initial calmness, Keith had become more and more incoherent with repressed anger as we walked further and further away from the site of his humiliation and (let it be noted) all opportunities for him to do anything directly about it.

"Fucking...fuckers...dirty...fucking...scum bastards..."

As the anger wore off the vodka picked up the baton, keeping Keith unable to string a meaningful sentence together. Or maybe it was me? Maybe I couldn't make out the meaningful sentences. I was matching Keith swig for swig out of sympathy or comradeship or whatever so I was pretty drunk too.

It was only when Keith leapt unsteadily to his feet and declared that he was going to swim back to the campsite (because Lindisfarne was "for cunts") that I remembered I had something important to tell him.

I got up shakily and followed him down to the water. Keith was sat on a rock, trying to undo his shoelaces - looking for all the world like a dog that has been presented with a tin opener instead of its dinner.

"Keith, I don't think you should swim."

"Fucking..."

"It's a couple of miles. Probably. And we're both really drunk."

"Not...staying...fucken...island."

"I don't want you to die Keith."

I really didn't. Not then, not now. I didn't want Keith to die, because if he died, I'd be alone again.

"What? Faaaah...bastard."

"I have something..." a hot wet combination of belch and heave burst from my digestive tract and into my mouth. I sucked it back in and continued: "...to tell you."

Keith had got one of his shoes off. He stood up, swayed from left to right, hurled it towards the sea and sat down heavily again. The shoe made a sad, lonely little plip as it landed in two feet of water.

"Keith, I have a secret power. I can leave my body when I'm asleep and walk around but people can't see me or hear me and I can float in the air..."

I had presumed it would be easier to describe. I felt like I was not doing myself justice.

"I'm an astral traveller."

"An asshole traveller?"

Keith spluttered violently as he laughed at his own joke.

"I can become a ghost - I can walk through walls and no one knows I'm there."

I paused, then added: "Only lemurs."

Arsehole..." Keith was now muttering to himself and smiling, delighted with his pun.

"I only discovered it a few weeks ago," I lied - although I couldn't be sure that Keith was taking any of this in. To be honest this was not going as I had imagined it at all.

"Keith, I've never told anyone this before."

Keith looked up. His eyes were pointed at my face but his gaze was empty.

"I am going...to sleep here. Combat-ready...survive... endure...survival," he stammered. He stood up, looked at his feet and sat down again.

"My shoe is gone."

12

Seeing Keith that drunk had given me a measure of self-possession back and so (against his protests) I supported, dragged and carried him back to the car park. I slept in the back seat and Keith slept under the car. By that time, I was not able to resist his demands to sleep rough any further.

You know how a computer switches on? You hold down the on button, which starts one system. That switches on the next one, and so on and so on, until the whole thing is up and running. So: I woke up the next morning, and my brain was running DOS as it began to boot up. It's always one of my favourite moments of the day, before my higher functions come online and remind me where I am, who I am, and all the subroutines of another day of life begin to play out again.

As I came round, I felt that same sense of euphoric calmness that I had experienced outside the aeroplane. I felt so warm and quiet. But no, I quickly realised that it wasn't warm. Although I had a coat over me, those parts of my body that were exposed to the air were damp and freezing cold. And no, it wasn't quiet. There were the sounds of cars pulling up, of families and dogs disembarking from them, and of Keith banging on the window.

That wasn't the only banging. My head was pounding. I could hear the blood in my ears and I could feel its pressure inside my eyeballs. As my mental Windows (updates pending) started up I realised that I was horribly hungover, if not still drunk. I hoisted my pelvis around and turned my head. As I did so, the whole universe continued to spin around me. My stomach spasmed.

Keith was still tapping on the window. I pulled the coat down so I could see out. He looked worse than I did. I sat up to open the car door. That was fatal. Instead of spinning on one plane only as I manoeuvred to the vertical, I found the interior of my head now rotating on several axes simultaneously. Not even astronauts can put up with those sorts of forces. I vomited over the car door just before I managed to open it.

Keith didn't look surprised, but doubled over and retched violently himself. His eyes dripped steaming tears onto the packed earth of the car park. I gathered that Keith had already deposited his stomach contents elsewhere. I saw that he had only one shoe on.

"We need to get ... " Keith gulped hard to bring his breathing under control: " ... a new parking ticket."

One shoe.

Did I ... ?

He was going to swim off the island.

I didn't want him to die.

I'd never told anyone ...

It came back to me. I had told Keith last night.

But did he remember? He had been completely paralytic, and at the best of times Keith was a poor listener. He hadn't commented on it at the time ... had he?

Then what did we talk about on the walk back to the car? I couldn't remember any of that. Not even a single thread of a memory I could pick up and start pulling on.

I was still sitting upright and I looked at Keith walking slowly to the ticket machine, fumbling through a handful of change. If he remembered, he'd never take any of it seriously. Life would carry on as before. I felt deeply relieved as I puked again over my feet.

13

The drive back to the campsite was quiet. We had scraped out the worst of the vomit, but a car is never the same after an experience like that, is it? The smell suffuses it irreversibly. We had both slept (in the car this time) for most of the rest of the day. I woke up to find Keith driving us along the causeway, the waters of the North Sea uncomfortably close to the road.

"I'm not staying on this fucking island for another night," Keith said when he saw I was conscious. "The tide's coming back in."

He yawned hard, almost convulsively. I yawned too. We didn't say anything else all the rest of the journey, and we went straight to our tents when we got back.

The next morning, I stuck my head out of my tent flap to glorious sunshine, mist and dew on the grass. Keith was sat outside his tent on an upturned bucket, smiling. He had already opened all the car doors and was holding the "Historical Jesus" book.

"Morning! So, tell me about astral travel, Shaun of the lemurs. Did you know that in Roman mythology a lemur is a restless ghost?"

I didn't say anything. I was completely thrown. I had been sure he wouldn't remember that conversation. I laughed weakly and climbed out of my tent, hoping the subject would change.

It didn't.

"We'll have to run some experiments. See what you can and

can't do. If someone who knows you're there can detect you. Stress test it all ... " Keith carried on talking, but I didn't hear what he was saying. What the hell had I done? All I wanted in that moment was for everything to go back to how it had been before.

"You did the right thing telling me Shaun," had Keith put his hand on my shoulder? "We are going to be able to do some amazing things."

He sat back and looked into the distance. He sniffed back a clot of phlegm (Keith had caught a terrible cold from his night under the car) and started to stroke his chin with his fingernail.

"Amazing things."

14

It turns out that I had filled Keith in on more or less everything (several times) as we made our way back to the car park two nights ago. Keith had been gaining in lucidity as I lost it. I guess our metabolisms just worked differently or something.

I was pleased to discover though that I had stuck to my pre-arranged cover story, when Keith asked me what had happened two weeks ago to bring on the discovery of my until-then-hidden abilities. I said nothing special - that one night, I had just found myself outside my body and things had gone on from there. Keith looked sceptical, probed a little on the precise date, but left things there. I was just relieved not to have revealed myself completely. I vowed never to get so drunk again - a vow I did in fact keep for what it's worth. Which is nothing really.

We drove back from Northumberland in virtual silence. I don't know if you've ever driven from the far north of England to the south-east, but it really does take a ridiculously long time. If you're like me, you think of "the north" as centred somewhere around Leeds or Manchester - but there is a hell of a lot more north beyond those places.

I could tell Keith's mind was working overtime as he drove. His jaw was twitching and he stroked his chin nervously as we sped monotonously down the A1. Mostly, I stared out of the window. Endless vistas of fields, clumps of pine trees and in the distance bald humps of hills. Flyovers, anonymous warehouses, boarded-up and crumbling roadside diners. All these places, no more real to motorway travellers than sights on a television screen. What is over the top of that ridge? Who is working in that windowless building? What is the hovering kestrel about to dive onto? What was the last thought that went through the mind of that fox on the hard shoulder, before unnoticed speeding metal transformed it into a steaming pile of mangled flesh, fur and bone splinters? Again, I'm an observer and a passenger - life goes on here, indifferent to my presence, unaware of my attention.

I stare up into the faces of impassive East European truckers as we glide past them. What is he transporting? Has he really driven here from Romania? Europa endless… What does he do at night? Who does he talk to? Would he rather be here, or back in Bucharest? He looks round and catches my eye. Instinctively, I look away and pretend to be doing something else.

The traffic ebbs and flows. We overtake a car. Five minutes later it overtakes us. We drop down to 45 miles per hour as a car towing a caravan decides to overtake a motorhome. Keith is making a clicking noise at the back of his throat. Even with both back windows open, the car stinks of sick. 240 miles to London. I shut my eyes but sleep won't come.

After we got back home, I didn't see Keith for a couple of days. I was starting to worry that my only friend had abandoned me, convinced I had gone insane. Just when I was beginning to despair, he turned up at my house one evening after work.

As we sat down to a cup of tea, Keith looked more excited than I had ever seen him about any of his many projects.

"So, are you ready to start the tests?"

"The tests … ?"

"We need to see what you can do. And how you do it."

"I don't know how I do it. I just sort of choose, and then I'm either doing it or I'm asleep."

"Don't worry about the how side of things at the moment," Keith sat forward in his chair.

"If we're going to take advantage of whatever it is you've got, we've got to know the limits ... the parameters we're working within."

I asked what Keith meant by "take advantage".

"Shaun, if you can do what you told me you can do, then we are laughing. I've made up these experiments. We're going to test you and once we know what you can do, we'll get on to how. So you can teach me ... "

The significance of those last few words didn't strike me until much, much later.

The tests began as ways for me to prove to Keith that this was not all complete bullshit. He was remarkably patient, which was out of character.

"So, I have written a message on a piece of paper in my bedroom at home. I want you to tell me what it says."

"Where is it?"

"It's in my bedroom."

"No, your house."

I'd never been to Keith's house. Gradually we narrowed the location of the message down.

"So, you know how to get there?"

"Yeah."

"It's in my room, which is the one at the top of the stairs. You should be able to tell if you look in the others ... "

"Where in your room?"

"On a piece of paper in my desk drawer."

"I won't be able to see it if it's in a drawer. I can't open drawers and if I put my head in it will be too dark to see."

Keith sighed. He took out his mobile phone.

"Mum ... ? It's Keith. KEITH. Yeah ... no I won't. No ... Mum, just listen. LISTEN. I'm at a friend's house. Yes him. The library. LIBRARY."

This continued for some time, as Keith requested that his mother go to his room and remove an envelope from his desk drawer, while looking at and touching nothing else.

"Can she take it out of the envelope as well? Because I won't be able to," I pointed out. This led to more discussion.

"Yes, it's a white envelope on the top - just open it and put the note on the desk. Yes, a scrap of paper. NO DON'T READ IT OUT! Mum, you've messed it up. For Christ's sake I just said not to read it."

He hadn't actually said that until after she had read it out but I thought it best to stay out of it.

"Just write something on the envelope. I don't know - anything! I can't tell you what to write or it will defeat the object again. Ohhhhh ... that's Power conditioning your language, Mum ... What? Nothing. Anything! OK, now leave it on the desk. Face up. Now, go out of the room and shut the door. No, it's just an experiment. Alright, thank you. Yes. About eight. I don't know ... peas?"

The conversation ended. Keith exhaled heavily, and turned to look at me with expectancy.

"You want me to do it now?"

Keith snorted with laughter.

"If you wouldn't mind! After I've just had to get my bloody mother to go into my desk and open the envelope for you! Jesus, it's a good job she has no curiosity about anything in the world beyond her TV!"

"You want me to go to sleep now?"

"Can't you go to sleep?"

"I'm not really tired. It's six thirty."

"CAN YOU JUST FUCKING TRY TO GO TO SLEEP?" Keith exploded, shaking his hands like claws, as if he were strangling the memory of his mother.

Usually I have no problem dropping off, but the fraught situation was making me anxious - and Keith had told his mum he'd be home by eight for his dinner. We agreed that I'd go and have a look overnight, and ring Keith when I'd done it.

"I'm going to put the note on top of the fridge in the kitchen. I'll leave the light on in there for you. My mum goes to bed around ten, so don't come before then. Don't go upstairs, alright? I trust you not to spy on me, Shaun. I'll know if you do.

I'll be able to see it in your eyes. Don't go in my room ... I will wait in the kitchen until you call me. And then we will know what this all means."

Keith was a little nervous, having just realised some of the implications of what I could do. But he trusted me - I don't think he thought I was capable of betraying him really. And I wasn't.

15

I went to bed about 11pm so as to be sure Keith's mum was out of the way. I'll be honest, I did not find it easy to drop off. I had a very bad feeling about where this was heading. I can't really say it was a premonition, because I don't think anyone could have expected things to pan out precisely the way they did, but I was very nervous about the level of change that every single course of action open to me at that moment was going to bring into my life. I wasn't unhappy with my life really. And now I was heading irreversibly into the unknown, because of a mad skyborne epiphany and a bottle of vodka. But if I didn't do it ... what would Keith say? I had to do it because he'd told me to. Like I said, I'm a follower.

I tossed and turned. It was hot that night. My urethra was itching, deep down to my prostate gland. I tried to sooth it away by having a wank, but even with my vast collection of suitable memories, I just could not get it up - all I could think about was Keith. And his mum. Neither of them were in the least bit sexually attractive to me.

Where was this all going to take me? Why had I just not stayed quiet that night like I had done every night, every day of my life before? I had been drunk before, of course. But no matter how hammered I'd been on other occasions, my brain knew to keep my mouth shut just the same as it knew the way home from wherever I found myself. That's another gift of mine. I always wake up in my own bed even if I have no idea how I got there.

It wasn't the booze. It was the nagging, subterranean desire for a change that made me do it. The heightened feelings of those few days had tipped me over the edge, but I realise now that I'd been yearning for someone to tell for years. And that day when he approached me in the library, my unconscious mind had settled on Keith. Settled for Keith. So it was just a matter of time until I did it. Why worry now? This was always going to happen.

Eventually I dozed off. Sometimes, you have to try to get to sleep. You have to work at switching your mind off. But sometimes it sneaks up on you. Plenty of times, I had been taken so suddenly by it that I hadn't noticed the fork in the road until I'd passed it, and I woke up the next morning having been nowhere at all. It was quite a relief when that happened.

Tonight though, I managed to keep my wits about me enough to notice it coming on. I went left and there I was, looking down on my sleeping body from the ceiling of my childhood bedroom. I used to have Thundercats wallpaper and a Fraggle Rock bedspread, then later black ash furniture with red handles, and a red and grey striped carpet. Now, my bedroom was decorated in the timeless manner of spare rooms everywhere - off-white walls, orange pine furniture, unisex green soft furnishings, beige carpet. Redecorating it in this tribute to "visitor impersonal" was one of the last projects my father undertook before he died. I don't remember being asked what I wanted, but what they did was fine. I'd gone off the teenage look a few years earlier, but I hadn't really thought about what I'd rather have instead.

So there I was on the ceiling. I drifted down to the floor, passed through the door (I can't sleep with the door open), down the stairs and out of the living room window onto the street. The cul-de-sac was quiet. Cars were parked on every drive and across the fronts of most of the gardens as well. A couple of my neighbours' houses still had lights on behind their curtains. Bernard and Maureen, they'd probably be doing it on the living room sofa by now, it being Bake Off night. Mr Tirpitz (like the battleship) annotating his Bible as usual while his dog whined at the back door. Suburban nightlife in all its mundane glory. A tawny owl hooted in the woods over towards St Johns. I set off for Keith's house over the other side of town. I had never been there before. My mind was elsewhere and I found myself automatically heading for the bridge before I remembered that I could glide over the canal anywhere I chose to. Funny how your brain works completely differently when someone's expecting you.

Keith lived in a Victorian terrace house over towards West Byfleet. He didn't have a front garden - he had a yard. None of the houses had driveways here, and practically the whole road was double-parked with cars (and vans) ramped up on the pavement. There were lights on downstairs and upstairs at Keith's house. I took a deep breath and went through the front door.

The house was very brown. Even the things that weren't brown seemed brown. Nothing had the appearance of having been bought in this or either of the two previous decades. The hall carpet was heavily patterned (primarily red, but a brownish greenish red) and had a transparent plastic runner over the centre to protect it, leading from the front door to the kitchen at the back of the house. The kitchen door was half open and a dim light shone through into the darkened hallway. There was a staircase to my left. At the top of the stairs was the door to Keith's room - from which he had explicitly banned me. The staircase (carpeted in the same paisley psychedelia) was dimly illuminated by a dull brownish-blue glow from under Keith's bedroom door, casting banister shadows fit for a creeping Nosferatu onto the opposite wall.

I went into the kitchen. There, sat at the breakfast bar on a brown stool, was Keith. He looked very jumpy. He was eating something brown with peas in it out of a steaming orange Tupperware container. His head flicked from left to right as the house creaked and sounds of nocturnal Surrey broke the silence.

I set myself opposite him, but of course he was completely un-aware that I was there. I drifted up to the ceiling and floated above the fridge freezer. There was a crumpled piece of paper there, and it said "Green milk, onions, Bovril, toothpaste".

I had completed the test. Now what? I went back to the bottom of the stairs and looked up at the forbidden door. No, Keith trusted me and I didn't want to start my new life with more lies and secrets. I woke up.

I reached out for my phone, and I texted Keith the fateful words: "green milk onions bovril toothpaste". I was pleased to note that the itching had relieved itself. Seconds later, he replied: "I will be round at 10am tomorrow." Keith was one of those people whose texts were always correctly and fully punctuated. He would always close with a full stop.

No turning back.

16

Keith was indeed at my house at 10am the following morning. He looked excited, the same as when he was making "Historical Jesus" notes.

"Shaun, we have a tremendous opportunity here. A tremendous opportunity."

He stressed the second "tremendous", as I was putting a mug of tea down in front of him. Keith sat forward in his armchair (formerly my dad's favourite) and looked at the floor, furrowing his brow. I adopted a similar posture and an identical expression of serious thought, although I was actually just wondering what Keith was going to say next.

"I don't need to see any more evidence Shaun. You have a miraculous gift, and it must have been destiny that brought us together. Because I know how we can monetise you. You and I need never work again."

I was not sure Keith had ever worked in the full sense of the word, but I stayed quiet.

"If you had to sum up your power in one word, Shaun, what would it be?"

One word?

"Errr ... astral travel?" I suggested, tentatively.

"That is two words Shaun. Come on. Think harder. You have the power to ... what?"

I wanted to say "leave my body" but of course that was three words. Fly? That was only part of it. Walk through walls? Again, not a complete description and too many words. I looked at Keith and shook my head.

"The power to watch, Shaun. The power. To watch. And what do people do when they're being watched?"

Clearly, I was not going to offer any answers from my own experience here. What was Keith driving at? I shrugged and turned up my palms. Keith sighed elaborately. Of course, he was delighted at being able to explain all his thinking to me, but the dramatic game we were playing required him to act as though it was an exasperating chore.

"They behave themselves. When people think they're being watched, they behave. They only do things that the watchers will find acceptable, even if they want to do something completely different. That's why there's CCTV everywhere. And speed cameras too. Chances are they're not watching you at any given time or place, but they want you to feel like you're being watched, so you behave 'acceptably' don't you?"

The speech marks Keith placed around that final word were virtually audible.

"Let me tell you a story, Shaun. Once I was sat in the square outside the library - before your time, this was - and there was a bunch of pigeons walking about, squabbling, pecking each other; you know what they're like."

I did. The pigeons were there every day without fail, just like me. They usually make the bare minimum of movement to get out of my way. Once, one of them flew straight into my face - just like how my parents died, sort of.

"I'd been watching them for about fifteen minutes and I started to wonder if I could catch one. I thought about it logically. One of the pigeons was definitely slower than the others. Maybe it was old or injured or had eaten something poisonous. It kept sitting down, while the others stayed on their feet the whole time.

"Even when people walked close by and the other pigeons scuttled out of the way, this one made the least effort. Sometimes didn't move at all. I thought, rationally, that one will be the easiest to catch. The test was 'can I catch a pigeon?' remember - so going for a sick one wasn't cheating.

"I was pretty sure I would be able to get it. And then I thought 'well, what would I do with it if I caught it?' What would you have done, Shaun?"

I didn't like it when Keith kept using my name over and over again. It felt a little bit like he was patronising me.

"Let it go?" I said.

"Yeah ... " Keith dropped his eyes and laughed, apparently to himself. "Yeah, you probably would have done. And maybe I would have done too. But at that moment, when I asked myself that question, the answer that came back to me was 'I will bite its head off'."

I wasn't expecting that.

"I really wanted to catch the pigeon and bite its head off. To spit out the head and the feathers and the blood, to see what the good people of Woking, going quietly about their business, made of that. What they made of something like that happening right there in front of them."

"Did you ... ?"

"No of course I didn't. I wouldn't touch one of those fucking disgusting things. They're filthy! God! But that's not the point. The point, Shaun, is that we hold back from what our inner selves tell us we want to do because of what society might think of it. Does it matter what bodies do? Surely it's only souls that matter? People only give in to their real selves when they don't think they're being watched. And let me tell you this Shaun - people are not saints. Everyone has something foul they keep hidden. Everyone. But they let it out when they think they're alone."

Now, I must acknowledge here that Keith's story didn't really hold together. He had said that he wanted to bite the pigeon's head off because he wanted to provoke a reaction from other people, hadn't he? He didn't resist that desire because he was afraid what they'd think - he resisted it because the thought of putting a pigeon's head in his mouth made him feel queasy. He didn't want to catch the pigeon at all. He wanted to be noticed, by shocking people. He didn't achieve that because the way he'd dreamed up of being noticed was something he realised he couldn't actually bring himself to do. Keith's stories didn't always strictly illustrate the point he was trying to make, but I usually understood what he was on about.

Anyway, Keith seemed convinced that his story not only made sense but also that it proved his point. And his confidence gave me confidence that it did.

"When you're doing your thing, Shaun, you can watch people who think they're not being watched. Privacy is valuable, isn't it?"

I was back on solid ground here, so I nodded vigorously.

"And people will pay to keep things private, won't they? Why shouldn't we benefit from their failings?"

I nodded harder. This was building up to some sort of important conclusion, I could sense. I looked up at Keith to see he was sitting back, looking me straight in the face. After a couple of seconds of silence, he raised his eyebrows in invitation. I gingerly raised mine, mirroring his gesture with my own RSVP.

Keeping his eyes fixed on me, Keith cocked his head and turned his hands palms up. There was a pause that seemed to last hours. I was about to speak and I'm fairly sure that I was going to offer, "I don't know what you want me to say". Fortunately, he interrupted me before I got the first syllable out. Keith's desire to finish his monologue outweighed his hope that I was keeping up.

"Shaun, you can find out things people would rather nobody knew about them. And then, they will pay us not to tell. And you can go anywhere and you can never be caught. We can't lose."

Keith sat back, triumphant. So that was it. Nobody was going to have to eat a pigeon after all. We were going to become blackmailers.

17

We found our first victim or our first client, depending on your point of view, through a neighbour of Keith's who was well known to be playing away. Her name was Nerys Shirley. She lived on the same street as Keith and his mum, and her husband worked on oil rigs in Scotland. That meant he was away for weeks at a time, and Nerys (who was on "chatting when they bumped into one another in the street" terms with Karen Pardew) took advantage of this to party the weekends away with a succession of different men, as she had no qualms telling any of her acquaintances.

She was a big woman. "Buxom" you might say. Nerys was always immaculately made-up and coiffeured, and wore very nice clothes, most of which were at least one size too small for her. She was in her mid-40s, had an infectious laugh, worked on the pharmacy counter in Boots and had a wide circle of female friends. Keith hated most people, but he seemed to have a particular dislike for her.

Shortly after we came up with the blackmail idea, Keith put her forward as a good starting point.

"My mum's friend Nerys is having at least three ongoing affairs. That bloody woman is always shooting her mouth off about her fellas and the presents they buy her. I don't know what she does with them. Her husband's a bit of a mad bastard. If he ever found out, he'd probably kill her. But then who knows what he gets up to on shore leave in Aberdeen?"

"Are we going to blackmail her then?" I asked.

"Shaun, please. You've seen where I live - do you think people with money to spare live down there? Anyway, she might be a mouthy slapper but we don't want anyone getting killed."

I do remember him saying that. We don't want anyone getting killed.

"No, she's always telling my mum about these different men she's seeing regularly and she never misses a chance to point out that they're married and well-off. We're going to find out who they are and then see if they want their good ladies at home to know about the Holiday Inn and the town bike."

Keith spat the last two words out with unexpected venom.

"We're going to find their weak points and leverage them to the hilt. We're going to gather some data from this pilot so that when we roll out the plans on a large scale, we've learned the important lessons."

That Friday night, Keith and I went to the pub: Shunters, by the station, which is the opening venue for hundreds of people's Woking nights out or the first preloading stop on a trip to London's nocturnal attractions.

Keith knew that Nerys and her squad would be there, having picked up intel from a reliable source (his mum) earlier in the week. Under no circumstances were we to make contact. Our mission was strictly recon. We were to observe, map her movement patterns and determine her final destination. Then I would go home, go to sleep and see what happened next.

Keith insisted on sitting in a corner, facing the door. Apparently, he had once read a book about the IRA and believed that this was the safest position to adopt, should someone be coming to assassinate you in a pub. I got a pint for me and an orange juice for Keith (the whole "orange juice" thing had gone unremarked since our camping trip). I was coming back from the bar when Nerys and her friends burst in. They were already drunk. It was 8pm.

There were five of them, all of similar proportions and

appearance to Nerys. They were laughing uncontrollably.

Keith froze like a rabbit in the headlights of an oncoming fake-tanned, perfumed, chiffon transit van. Nerys spotted him immediately.

"Eeeey! It's little Keith! How's your mum?"

One of the other women said something I couldn't hear and they all burst out laughing again. Keith looked like he was having a stroke. His temples were pulsing and sweat dribbled through his eyebrows and onto his cheeks. Beyond that, nothing on his face moved at all.

"Say hello to your mum!" Nerys bellowed over her shoulder as the female tide swept her away towards the bar.

I placed the orange juice in front of Keith and sat down on my stool. His face was still frozen solid, although maybe the corner of his right eye was twitching. It was hard to tell in that soggy pub light.

Silent seconds turned to minutes. Keith's face was still completely vacant. I felt that it was going to fall to me to break the spell.

"Is that her then?"

"Yes," Keith replied, still in his trance.

He closed his eyes and shook his head infinitesimally. When he opened them again, his eyes had come back from whatever faraway place they had been to and focused on me.

"Yes, that's the bitch."

I was taken aback by the bitterness in Keith's voice. It was only much later I found out that Keith had lost his virginity to Nerys.

"Keith, we appear to have made contact - do we need to abort?"

I'd picked up some of the jargon myself.

"No, Shaun," his gaze drifted from me to the group of women at the bar (who were cackling at this point over the word "cocktail"). "We proceed as planned. This changes nothing."

We watched them for about an hour, sipping our drinks in awkward silence. They drank, squawked and from time to time popped out in pairs for a cigarette or to go to the toilet. Every so often, a man would sidle over and attempt to engage one or another of the group in conversation, but he would quickly be rounded on by the entire troupe and embarrassed into a hasty retreat.

I was unnerved by Keith's apparent discomposure.

"What are we going to do next?" I asked.

"There's a night club a couple of doors down the road. It opens at 9, but no one ever goes there until 10 at the earliest. It's free for women until 11," he replied without taking his eyes off our quarry.

"They'll go there between 10 and 11. See how they're scaring the randoms off? That means she's meeting someone later. Otherwise they'd be all over the poor unsuspecting bastards. That means we should go now, so that you can get back here to follow them there when they leave. We've still got at least an hour until then. C'mon."

Keith got up. I hastily downed the dregs of my pint and followed him. The pub - practically deserted when we arrived as the last of the day shift was drifting away - was filling up now. Isolated groups had coalesced into a single mass. The bands of office workers out for payday drinks were dwindling in numbers as they headed home to wives, husbands, cats and kids. In turn, they were being replaced by those who had already been home and were embarking on big nights out of their own. There were single sex groups of older women - like Nerys and her crew - and of younger men, their steroid-enhanced arms bulging like tree trunks, scoop-necked t-shirts exposing colossal swollen but strangely hairless chests. Their massive top-heavy bulks tapered away through waspish waists to tiny, plimsoll-clad feet topped by two inches of naked twig-like ankle. Their appearance combined ferociously aggressive masculinity with feminine delicacy, expressed in their immaculate hair, shaped eyebrows and golden-brown coloration.

Naturally Keith and I were both thoroughly intimidated by them, and we made our way through the crowd doing our best to avoid them. Although the crowd seemed like a single mass, it had a cellular structure with intergroup faultlines running throughout. Backs facing backs, chairs pushed under tables, the glass collector's section of the bar. The trick, for any departing solitary pub goer was to navigate these interstices to the exit.

Keith was dawdling, casting suspicious eyes towards Nerys' group. I could see his problem - he couldn't get out without putting a hand on someone's shoulder so as to deliver the line "excuse me mate". I took control of the situation.

"Excuse me mate."

The groups in front of us compressed slightly, permitting us to squeeze through. Keith followed closely behind me. Once or twice, people in our wake would sniff the air with aghast expressions on their faces, and glances would be cast our way.

"Was that you?"

"I think it's that freak in the coat."

"Smelly bastard."

"Shhhh....not so loud. I'm not getting stuck talking to a nutter."

Keith's stale aroma stood out sharply in the haze of Lynx, fashion designer-branded aftershaves and sour drink.

One last push stood between us and the exit: a tangle of student types, male and female, conspicuous in the bar by a deliberate scruffiness that was in its way no less meticulously constructed than the appearance of anyone else there. I could not see the natural way through. Go around? No. Bodybuilders to the left, hen-do to the right. People facing every which way, no clear logic to their organisation.

I leaned in to the nearest girl.

"Excuse me."

She didn't hear. I put my hand up to her shoulder and cupped it - without touching, but close enough for a microscopic change in local temperature to be registered by each of us.

"Excuse me please."

The girl inched forwards enough for an opening to be apparent. I went in crab-wise. Through my trousers, my penis brushed against her elbow - I felt a surge through my lower spine evaporate at my pelvic floor and melt into my thighs and testicles. Please God, let me get out of here. Don't let me get an erection now. We wriggled further into the group. Keith had his eyes shut. At his approach people were starting to look round and back away.

Eventually we squeezed out onto the street, as if the pub itself had disgorged us. A pair of doormen in black eyed us disdainfully.

"Right Shaun. You go home, and you know what to do next." I did.

"I'll sit in the kebab shop over there. If she goes anywhere other than Rumours before 11, I'll call you. If you don't hear from me, assume we are go."

Keith had regained his composure now we were out of the pub's crush and out of sight of Nerys' gang.

"What if she hasn't gone anywhere before 11?" I asked.

"She will. Trust me. I know how this goes."

I didn't ask how he knew but this was Keith's show and I trusted him. I bid him goodnight and set off home.

"Aha!"

A familiar voice boomed out from behind me.

"Verily, 'tis a merry-andrew wending his way home from the tavern!"

I turned and saw my work colleague, Derek. Neither of his eyes were looking directly at me, but seemed to be swimming back and forth. He was with a group of similarly odd-looking men and was holding a wooden staff.

"Evening Derek," I said.

"We've not seen you out and about on dark nights such as these, young Master Strong. Hast thou been partaking of the fermented beverages?"

"Um, yes. I've just been to the pub with a mate, but I'm off home now."

"Ah! The magisterial grain! My jolly band of loafers and I are headed cityward - to the capital, the capitolium, Londinium..."

"Plowinida," one of Derek's crowd added.

"Not proven Martin. Conjectural. Objection sustained, m'lud! Yes, London-bound are we, on um iron horse. How..... nnnnnnghhhhhhfffff" Derek stifled a gargantuan belch. His nose dripped a little from the effort.

"Come on Derek, or we'll miss the train."

"Excuse me. Jesus, where did that come from? Yes, CAMRA annual convention at Alexandra Palace. Bloody great do. You should tag along. It's ticket only though. Members only. One of the two."

"Derek!"

"Coming! Well Shaun, I bid thee a goodnight! Wait for me comrades! Tovarishchi!"

Derek waddled off in pursuit of his friends, coughing intermittently and leaving me alone again.

It was a walk of twenty-five minutes or so from the station back to my house. As I passed through the town centre and into the suburban streets beyond, the dribs and drabs of people on their way out for the night became less frequent. Boy racers sped up to traffic lights and screeched to a stop, their flared exhausts emitting stuttering bass growls. Late night dog walkers shuffled across the pedestrian crossings, followed by their reluctant companions. I walked down the steps to the canal path. Here nothing moved - or nothing that I could see anyway. The roar of the A road above faded as I headed back towards my house. The path was deserted and I jumped when a flapping sound burst out of a bush behind me. My brain knew it was just a bird, but my body had reacted with the second shot down my spine of the evening before I could tell my central nervous system there was nothing to be frightened of.

Soon, I could see the end of my road - the road I had grown up in, the only home I had ever known. Lights were on in all the other houses except mine, which was dark. I walked up the driveway, unlocked my front door and went in. As usual the house was empty.

18

I got myself ready for bed. I brushed my teeth, took off my shirt, trousers and socks and tried to have a dump. No such luck. I put the TV on and flopped into my bed. You would suppose that the excitement of the situation - a real adventure! - would have kept me awake, right? Wrong. Soon my eyes were dropping, although the thought of that student girl I'd pushed past kept circling back through my mind. Then I was on the slide.

I went left and what felt like seconds later I was on the ceiling. Now I had to go all the way back into town to where I'd just come from. That was a pain in the arse. I glided through my bedroom window and onto the street. Back on the canal path a rat skittered out in front of me and stopped to eat something or other it had found on the floor. Maybe a fried chicken bone? Yes, there was a discarded cardboard carton with coleslaw spilling out of it a few paces ahead. The rat couldn't see me.

To break up the tedium of retracing my exact steps, I floated over the surface of the canal itself and drifted up to the height of the treetops so that the sleeping water was like a glittering grey carpet beneath me. The lights of the A324 receded into the distance ahead and beyond them the black silhouettes of office blocks and the multi-storey car park. I flew along the treeline, over the main road and back into the town. Nothing much had changed in the hour I'd been gone. The pedestrianised streets were empty. Noise and heat pumped out of the bars and restaurants. A pair of police officers in hi-vis waistcoats, thumbs tucked into the lapels of their webbing, strode watchfully along the pavement.

Back on ground level, I turned into the station road and past Shunters. Keith was still sat in the kebab shop opposite looking out of the window. It was well past 11 by now. Along with his phone, he had an orange polystyrene box in front of him. A soggy pitta bread festooned with a few strands of wet iceberg lettuce languished in the bottom of the box. He looked miserable.

I carried on down the road towards the nightclub. A blue neon light flashed above the doorway. "Rumours". The sign illuminated a sagging, grimy banner emblazoned with "For mad-for-it people only" above various disclaimers about underage drinking, drug use and fighting on the premises. Another pair of bouncers stood outside. These two were older, more shop-worn and less well-dressed than the chain pub doormen we had seen earlier. One smoked listlessly, as the other nodded an all-male group of punters in. I joined the back of the crowd and followed them in.

Inside, the club was much like any other second-rate small town night spot across the UK. I'm sure you know the type. Through the door, you go down a flight of dimly-lit steps to a window where a bored-looking woman with totally impractical fingernails takes payment and coats. From here, you pass through a heavy door set with panels of chequered-plate aluminium flooring - not unlike the entrance to the industrial zone of The Crystal Maze. As you push this open, a cloud of steam, dry ice and body heat is blasted outwards by a medulla-shaking, vertigo-inducing thunder of bass noise. Your eyes adjust, and what appeared to be the mouth of hell itself opening up before you turns out to be a half-empty room, with a back-lit bar, banks of built-in seating around the outside and a laminate dancefloor (held together with conspicuous strips of well-trodden electrical tape) in the centre.

The *son-et-lumiere* display of lasers, rotating multi-coloured spotlights and sublimated carbon dioxide was in stark contrast to the languid attitudes of the seated clubbers and the desultory shape-throwing or semi-ironic pissed-up abandon of the small groups of dancers. I'd been to places like this before. Not often, but enough for it to be familiar. If my sense of smell had been available to me in my spectral state, I knew there would be an eye-stinging miasma of bleach emanating from the toilets, no doubt masking something worse.

I located one of Nerys' girlfriends. It appeared that the group had dispersed on entry. Two of them were gyrating on the dancefloor in a manner I can only assume they intended to be erotic. In a loose perimeter around them, werewolf-eyed middle-aged men postured, trying in vain to attract their attention. I scanned the scanty crowd but Nerys was nowhere to be seen. Shit.

All at once, I couldn't breathe or move. A soft, aromatic presence filled my senses for a second - and it was gone as soon as it had appeared. It left the thought of the taste of iron in my mouth. Nerys was standing in front of me, having stepped straight through the space my consciousness was occupying. She was holding hands with a sheepish-looking man, whose lack of tie and two open shirt buttons failed to disguise the way his suit proclaimed that he had come here directly from a very straight-laced workplace. The man appeared reluctant to proceed, so Nerys moved around in front of him, turned her back to him and wound her waist up and down, rubbing her plentiful arse against his suited crotch. Spotting this, Nerys' friends cheered from the dancefloor and trotted over with their hands in the air. They took the man by one hand each. He looked even more embarrassed than before and glanced helplessly around over both shoulders, but there was no escape for him now.

I settled in to observe how events would unfold. The thing about being a watcher is you have to be patient. Dramatic events rarely follow hard and fast upon one another's heels. A seemingly endless series of distractions, blind alleys and pointless delays come between important developments in what turns out afterwards to have been the plot. I'm used to it though - the kind of seductions I am accustomed to are seldom smooth, rarely romantic. Alcopops and bottled beers have to be consumed in quantity to create the mood; toilets frequently frequented; passing acquaintances chatted with; drunken friends propped up.

However, within an hour Nerys and her man were all over each other. That's what I like about middle-aged couples. What they lack in attractiveness over the young, they make up for in getting to the point. In a quietish corner of the nightclub, he was seated with her straddling him. Mercifully, she was wearing trousers. From my vantage point above, I could see his hand was inside her blouse. I wondered how long it would take them to remember that they weren't teenagers and that they probably did have somewhere else they could take this.

Not long. Soon Nerys stood up. The man immediately leaned forwards to conceal the erection straining against his flies. He stood up, sticking his rear end out in a bent over pose, picked up a bottle from the table and held it at an unnatural height in front of his crotch. Nerys laughed. The man laughed too, yanked at the front of his pants and then stood up to his normal height - the boner successfully concealed somewhere or other. He put his arm around her shoulder and they walked to the exit together.

I hope this fucker's married, I thought.

I was not disappointed. Indeed, Peter Smithson turned out to be an excellent investment for us: a steady, reliable source of income who provided us with a gentle learning curve into the blackmail business.

Peter and Nerys took a taxi to the Holiday Inn just as Keith had said they would. Once there, they had a drink in the bar but soon found themselves unable to keep their hands off one another. They headed upstairs. No sooner were they in Peter's room, than they were ripping one another's clothes off and they were doing it.

What made things particularly interesting though was that after the initial flames of passion had cooled down, Peter popped into the bathroom and came back with a small plastic vial. He tapped out a small pile of white powder from it onto the desk and, using a credit card, arranged it into two lines. Cocaine. This was a turn up, I thought.

Anyway, things went from that point where you might expect them to. Coke was snorted, sex was had, more coke, more sex, then sleep. I got Peter's name from the credit card, helpfully left the right way up on the desk. It was a corporate card for some huge company I'd heard of but had no idea about what they did - they sponsored a Premier League football team. That was a good sign. I just had to wait now and find out who Peter Smithson was. I wandered around the hotel corridors, the kitchens, the fire escape, looking into a few of the bedrooms now and then to kill time. Every ten minutes or so (or what felt like ten minutes) I popped back to make sure they were still asleep.

I said I'm patient, but I'd never really had to wait like this before. Once the sex was over, I would usually head home for my solitary gratification. This time though I was excited for different reasons. It was like being a detective and I was impatient to get things moving again. I tried to clap my hands, push glasses off the bedside tables, make hissing sounds, but to no avail. I could only watch them sleep. I felt very alone at that moment.

Eventually Peter stirred. It was about 7am. He got out of bed gently and tiptoed to the bathroom. Having had a quick shower, he collected up the previous night's clothes and stuffed them into a plastic bag. From a suit hanger in the wardrobe he took out another, more or less identical shirt, jacket and pair of trousers. He got dressed quietly, all the time checking Nerys for signs of awakening. He packed the suit hanger, his wash bag (into which he put the half-empty canister of cocaine), the plastic bag and his other belongings into a large holdall. He slipped the credit card back into his wallet, put his wallet in his back pocket, unplugged his phone from its charger and put the phone inside his jacket.

With the exaggerated care of someone who knows full well he's not going to be caught but is enjoying the dramatic possibilities of imagining what might happen if he were to be, Peter padded over to the hotel room door, opened it and left. Nerys grunted as the door clicked shut and rolled over in her sleep. In the corridor, Peter smiled to himself as he hung the "do not disturb" sign on the door handle.

I tailed Peter. Passing the breakfast buffet, he walked straight out into the car park. It was a beautiful cold, sunny morning - the light was virtually arctic in its clarity, and the breeze made him shiver like antiseptic on a graze. He opened the boot of his black Mercedes C-class and lifted up a panel in the carpeted floor. He pushed the holdall into the compartment, closed the lid and slammed the boot shut. Casting a look back at the hotel and smiling as he got into the driver's seat, he drove away.

I realised at that moment I had no way of following him. Panic flared through me. What would Keith say? But wait. I had a name and an employer. The car paused at the entrance to the hotel car park before it turned out left. Now I had a number plate. I drifted into the air and watched the car getting smaller as it headed west. Away from London, I thought, as the car blended into the traffic where I lost sight of it.

19

I woke up. I was back in my bedroom with the same dazzling light streaming through the curtains.

Keith was at my front door half an hour later. I explained the previous night's developments. He was pleased with my efforts.

"You've done a great job Shaun. We have a tremendous opportunity now. We know enough to find this Peter Smithson and work out where to hurt him. Plus, where there's one middle class prick with drugs, there will be others. A tremendous opportunity."

The look of devious satisfaction that had taken over Keith's face soon dissolved though.

"Ah…Shaun. Last night…did you…? I mean, when you were there, did they…? Errrm…you know…"

I asked Keith what he meant.

"You were there, so you must have… while they… did you…? I… ah, never mind. We have a tremendous opportunity here Shaun."

The mantra allowed Keith to regain his composure.

"How can we find him?" I asked.

"These dickheads are all on LinkedIn – it's a kind of directory for twats," Keith replied. "He won't be hard to find, believe me."

He wasn't. After trawling through a number of Peter Smithson profiles, we found one with the same employer. And there he was. A lawyer. So now we had his contact details - email, mobile phone, office address. But we really needed to find out where he lived. Scanning through the endorsements by colleagues and shared links to fatuous blog posts, we learned that people didn't call him Peter - they all referred to him as Pete. Looking at his club memberships, we found they were clustered around Guildford. I was right about him driving away from London.

We were closing in. Keith hopped over to Facebook and searched for "Pete Smithson Guildford". There were a few results to sift through but there he was again. No privacy settings, lots of pictures of himself, his wife and his kids doing family things together. Keith scrolled back through his timeline. After a few minutes, he let out a bleat of triumph.

"Ha! Look at that."

Keith showed me a picture of a trestle table in the middle of a wintry suburban street, with bunting hung from the naked trees at the front of sweeping lawns. Happy, healthy faces bedecked in expensive-looking knitwear smiled out at us.

"February 2012 - Manor Gardens Diamond Jubilee Street Party," Keith sat back, a malevolent goblin in his moment of victory. "Pack your bags Shaun - you and I are going on a little road trip."

It certainly was a little road trip as Guildford is only about 15 miles down the road. I packed an overnight bag and we headed off on foot back to Keith's to borrow his mum's car (a ten-year-old blue Nissan Micra, with a heavy dent in the front passenger's side wing panel which she couldn't afford to get fixed).

We found Manor Gardens: a broad boulevard of spacious properties in generous settings. Cruising along we saw a lot of black Mercedes parked on sweeping driveways.

"Which one is it?"

"I can't tell from here. Maybe that one?"

"Maybe? Maybe Shaun? Maybe he doesn't live here anymore. Maybe he was visiting someone when those pictures were taken back in 2012. Maybe Shaun? Maybe isn't good enough."

"Can we drive up closer?"

"We can't drive up to every house. Look at this place. Someone has probably already called the police on us just from the look of our car. No, wait. I've got an idea."

Keith reached over and opened the glove compartment. Inside was a pile of leaflets.

"My mum does Slimming World and she's supposed to give these out. She won't, but she doesn't want to upset the leader so they've been piling up in here for months. Go and stick one through every letterbox until you find the right car."

I objected that the leaflets were for a Woking-based group and that therefore it was somewhat implausible to be leafleting in one of the nicer parts of Guildford. Keith replied that it didn't matter as no one would read the leaflets until we were long gone, if at all. The point was to have a credible reason for walking up to each house in turn.

"Don't just go to the ones with Mercs outside. You have to do them in order or people will get suspicious," Keith insisted. "Go on."

Reluctantly, I got out of the car with the wad of leaflets in my hand. Keith drove away to park up around the corner so he could come back on foot to do the other side of the street.

But before he got back, I'd found the right car sat outside an open garage door. I went up to the front door to try and get a house number, but all I could find was a name: "The Larches". I pushed a leaflet through the slot, turned on my heels and walked (sprinting headlong in my head) back down the drive.

As I trotted past the garage though, there came the sound of out-of-tune, absent minded singing.

"When I get lonely and na na na had enough, she sends a cumble bumble in from above. We don't need a waddle a WAAAAAAHHHHHH!"

Peter Smithson came striding out of the garage, holding a bicycle pump. On seeing me, he pulled two slender white plugs out of his ears.

"Morning!"

I stopped and held my breath as I awaited some glimmer of

recognition. Could he have seen me on that night I spent with him and Nerys? That split second seemed to last for hours, as I scanned his face and his body language, as I tensed myself to run, as I tried not to look like I was about to run in case no flash of acknowledgement came. Blood sang in my ears.

"New Slimming World group," I muttered holding out a leaflet.

"Thanks buddy. Have a great day!" Peter walked past me, towards his house, resuming: "We've got a thing that's called radar luh-hurve...."

He didn't know who I was. Indeed, he had forgotten me already - thinking instead about how many "k" he would cover that morning on the South Downs and the beauty spots and picturesque hard-earned pints he and his cycle-bore pals would Instagram along the route, not about how his life was about to be kicked firmly in the bollocks.

Keith was standing at the bottom of the driveway.

"The Larches," I said.

"What number is it?"

"It didn't have a number. Just a name."

"Well what number is next door?"

"I don't remember."

"Shaun!"

"He's there. I just spoke to him."

"You made contact?"

"He came out of the garage as I was coming away. He didn't recognise me."

We started to walk back to the car, faster and faster until we turned the corner of Manor Gardens. Then we ran. Back in the car Keith's interrogation continued.

"What did you say to him?"

"I gave him a leaflet."

For some reason, I held the stack of leaflets out to Keith, as if to prove the veracity of my statement.

"Did he say anything to you?"

"He said 'morning.'"

"That was it?"

"He wished me a great day, or something like that. He was singing."

"What was he singing?"

"Ummm... Radar Love."

"Golden Earring...1973...," Keith seemed distracted momentarily as he recalled the song's metadata to mind. Then he was back: "You sure it was him?"

"It was him," I said.

"We're fine," Keith relaxed. "We're fine. Just one more research trip and we are up and running. C'mon. Doo do do do do do duh-doooo. Doo do do do do do duh-doooo. I've been driving all night, my hands wet on the wheel...."

That afternoon we checked into the Guildford Travelodge. I had wanted to go home, but Keith reminded me that - under the rules that governed my astral travel - to have done so would have required me to float at walking pace for several hours back to Guildford, possibly missing the important interactions between Peter Smithson and his family we needed to observe. Keith had thought through the mechanics of my universe far more thoroughly than I ever had.

So that night I went back to the Smithson's and confirmed the following: superficially happy marriage to attractive wife - check; apparently loving relationship with pre-teen daughters - check; evidence of recreational drug use absent from family home - check. It wasn't an eventful evening. I shan't bore you with the details, as I don't know how long we've got left. Suffice to say I came away convinced that Peter Smithson was a heartless bastard. A bastard who could be fucking Nerys in a seedy hotel one night and back here, posing as the beloved paterfamilias the next. Who better than a bastard to blackmail? Especially one who can afford it. Nobody's going to get hurt so long as he pays up. And if they did find out ... well, it's his fault not ours. Better they know, because it will all come out sooner or later.

Over our full English breakfast (included in the price of the room) on Sunday morning, Keith and I plotted our next moves. Well, Keith plotted our next moves. I nodded along mostly. We would send a note to Peter at work, along with photos of Nerys harvested from the abundant source of her Facebook page and extensive descriptions of what we had seen. We would demand only a small sum not to tell his wife and kids about Friday night's antics. For now.

Keith explained that as we didn't have conclusive proof we could show anyone - psychic phenomena being, at best, controversial from an evidential perspective - demands for a lot of money could result in Smithson trying to balls it out and just deny everything. If we only asked for a few hundred quid though, a man like Smithson would probably rather just pay up than deal with the hassle of the whole thing coming to light.

Plus, he would assume - when we asked for that same amount the next time - that we were small-time idiots, who he could take care of another day, Keith explained. To a man like Smithson, buying time at a highly affordable rate would be a price worth paying. But he didn't realise at that time that it would become easier and easier just to put the day he sorted it out off. To us, it was our seed capital, our proof of concept.

I had to admire Keith's perceptiveness in figuring all this out. He had a pretty sound grasp of psychology for someone who shunned almost all social interaction. Everything unfolded exactly as Keith had planned. Smithson paid up.

I was there with him when he got the note. He read it, stared into space for a few seconds, swallowed, read it again, then put the note into his desk drawer. I was right behind him. I could see the hairs on the back of his neck stand up as he read. Five minutes later he took it out and read it again with his hand over his mouth. He leaned back in his chair, looked at the ceiling and exhaled heavily.

I was there with him that evening when he didn't say anything to his wife. It meant another night at the Travelodge - but as Keith said, you've got to speculate to accumulate.

"I'm hooooome!"

"Daddy!" A cannonade of little feet down the stairs.

"My monsters!"

"Hello darling. Good day?"

"Not too bad thanks. Off my shoes please Florence. Just so busy this time of year."

"Anything interesting to report?"

"No, just another typical day." Peter Smithson hugged his wife.

Lying bastard. That moment - that was when I realised I was ok with extortion.

I was there the next morning when he didn't call the police. I was getting a lot of sleep in those days.

We asked him to leave the money under the wooden walkway in the middle of Whitmoor Common. Not overlooked, lots of people passing by at all times of day. Smithson didn't let us down. Indeed, he had thoughtfully put the notes into a little Ikea ziplock bag to keep them nice and dry. To do him justice, he was a model client from day one onwards.

We had our start in the blackmail business.

20

It was easy thanks to our "competitive advantage", as Keith liked to put it. When you're undetectable, when no barrier can keep you out and you've got all the time in the world, it certainly isn't difficult to catch people off their guard.

I will admit that I was a little queasy about it at first, but then I saw how Peter Smithson was betraying his family - a family that loved him and suspected nothing. As Keith rightly pointed out, nobody was forced to pay us - they were choosing their preferred option of two available. And nobody had to do the things we caught them doing that they were so ashamed of.

Did I have qualms? Sort of. I've never liked hurting people or upsetting them. Fear of letting people down is one of the reasons I've always kept my distance from others. I can't bear to disappoint, and so I reasoned it's better not to create any expectations at all.

But it was an easy jump from watching to knowing. And although I had thought it was a huge leap from knowledge to action, Keith's certainty and conviction, his lack of hesitation, made it possible for my actions to remain the same while their character and consequences changed out of all recognition.

We didn't hang around to see the tears, the despair, the stomach ulcers. It's easy. It's frighteningly easy. You could find yourself doing it one day without ever confronting a moment where you consciously decide "yes, this is what I choose now". It's just as much about the choices you don't make as the choices you do. Sometimes, going with the flow takes you beyond a point you can choose to turn back from.

Sometimes it was harrowing. I don't enjoy seeing people suffering. Sure, I always liked to watch fights and accidents and moments of intimate drama, but I was never the cause of it. That was just happening when I happened to be there. It was like watching TV, with a regularly changing cast of characters so you could never get too attached to anyone or too involved in a single storyline. I know that I'm not the most empathetic person in the world, even at the best of times, but being responsible for this distress and having to stick with our clients over time - like people in a soap opera rather than isolated episodes – affected me differently from the way my previous voyeurism had. And not in a good way.

"We're helping them Shaun," Keith would occasionally say.

"For some of them, the money they give us is literally paying towards their atonement. For some, their consciences are soothed by being allowed to feel that they're actually the victims in all this. For others ..."

He paused and looked into the distance, kind of like a rodent Che Guevara, before flicking his eyes back to me.

"Fuck 'em. They deserve it."

Keith was determined from the start that this should be treated like as business, as professionally as possible. Not that we bothered with invoicing, VAT quarters or anything like that - it was a purely cash affair. Nevertheless, Keith's paranoia about surveillance meant that everything was recorded in hand-written ledgers, stowed away under the flooring my dad had put down in the loft ("It's important for that space to be useable," I remember dad saying).

"We're parasites Shaun," Keith explained. "It's nothing to be ashamed of. The System creates whole classes of parasites at the top and the bottom of society. Everyone's getting a meal off someone else. We're just honest with ourselves. We've seen behind the curtain to the cold brick wall at the back of the theatre. We live in a parasite culture, a society of bloodsuckers.

And what, Shaun, is the worst thing a parasite can do?"

I always found Keith's metaphoric excursions hard to follow beyond the literal meaning of what he was saying and the obviously mounting anger or excitement with which he was usually saying it. What was the worst thing a parasite could do? I wasn't sure. Give you malaria?

"Kill the host Shaun. A parasite that takes too much from the host dies along with the host. Well, most of them probably do. There are some kind of wasps I read about... I think...They eat their way out of caterpillars or something... Anyway, we're talking figuratively. A parasite should take only just enough, so that its host stays strong and healthy enough to keep feeding it."

Keith's theory was that we should only extract money from people who could afford it and who would suffer far more from exposure (option one) than from paying us (option two). The "suburban bourgeois pigs" of our local area were to be our prime targets - the poor didn't have enough to give or enough to lose, and the rich ... well, they have a way of coming out on top, don't they? Best not to mess with them. No, it was to be the "strivers", the "squeezed middle", so beloved of the lying politicians (Keith said) - the people in those social strata immediately above our own who were to feather our nest.

If Keith had qualms he never showed it. He threw himself headlong into the details of running an efficient black-mail business. He had spent the days immediately after our holiday borrowing and poring over books from the library's business studies section - from GCSE revision guides through to whatever management theories had been trendy a couple of years ago (library acquisitions being, sadly, always behind fashion). He picked up a lot of jargon at this time and gradu-ally began to envisage himself as some kind of entrepreneurial pioneer. I found it a little bit irritating.

Nevertheless, Keith applied himself diligently and it would be hard to fault the logic behind his projections. "Diversification" was the key to our line of work. A broad client base means that you're never so dependent on any one source of revenue that their financial difficulties disrupt the business. You can lose a few along the way, but while the money keeps rolling in from the others, you've got time to develop and nurture some new leads. "Always be closing, Shaun!" Keith began to love saying.

You've got to identify your audience carefully - to know and understand their needs, desires, fears. You've got to know them better than they know themselves, so you can be sure that you'll always be up the top of the supplier list when they review their budgets and when the bills come in.

Price point is critical. Set it too high, and it hurts when it's time to pay. They'll start looking for other providers, alternative solutions. Set it too low and they won't appreciate your value-proposition. But that's a really fine balance. No matter how well you've modelled your client persona, exactly where the tipping point lies - what's going to be a deal breaker - is different for everyone. Careful red-flagging of risk and strategies for managing it back down are vital.

You can't put all your eggs in one basket either. If you invest all your time in one brothel or one drug ring, say, and the police raid it - well, that's your whole clientele gone overnight, isn't it?

When you put it like that, it's easy to forget that we weren't just trading in widgets. We were ruining people's lives. When a real business comes up against a disastrous lawsuit - because someone's kid has choked on a widget, say - they've got insurance to protect themselves. Hell, the directors can even declare bankruptcy and get clean out of it. What happened with Trevor Long and who he was involved with - shit - even he didn't know what was at stake. Were we responsible? We started that deadly machinery in motion, but still it wasn't me or Keith who killed him, was it? Not literally.

Keith loved it though. He had found his vocation, no doubt about it. Not only did our work give him licence to be judgemental about others' failings, but it also validated his wider view of all humans as falling far short of his exacting standards. He felt that it was us doing the work of justice by punishing our clients. And best of all, it could all be done without any direct confrontation. Power was in his hands for the first time, and he relished that.

We used social networking to grow the business. Peter Smithson's connections lead us onwards to other clients. Keith mined Smithson's social media accounts while I tailed him. We were particularly interested in where Smithson was getting his cocaine from. This turned out to be a secondary school English teacher, a man called Trevor Long who was in the same rugby club. Soon we were blackmailing him as well.

Within a few weeks we had a handful of clients and a steady revenue stream - a nicely differentiated portfolio, comprising adultery, drug use, corporate embezzlement and one man we serendipitously caught pissing through his ex-wife's letterbox. All middle-class wankers who could afford our tithes.

We were pretty naive in those days, and I'm sure we made a lot of mistakes. Certainly, I wasted a lot of nights following people who didn't have any secrets at all worth hiding. At other times we misjudged the situation: our client confessed instantly or they went to the police. Of course, there was never anything to connect Keith or I to any of these allegations. We'd never met them. And Keith's paranoia meant that he never left any loose ends which could give us away. We made a good team.

The point was to make it easy for our clients to carry on living their lives and ignore what was happening. These were weak or lazy people who couldn't confront their wives or their bosses - a few hints about where their kids went to school and most of them would get back into line if there was any hassle. And if they didn't, we could just walk away. There were plenty more of them out there waiting for us to find them.

And we did have standards. Keith drew the line at anything involving people abusing kids. Any time we uncovered anything like that, Keith insisted that we tip off the police and expose the perpetrators. Anonymously of course. So maybe we did do a little bit of good as well.

I don't kid myself though. We did far more harm than good. We made a lot of people unhappier than I suppose they needed to be. And, whatever I wanted my life to be, it has ended in disaster for me and virtually everyone I came into contact with. Now, with hindsight it's easy to say I feel guilty about it and I'll take whatever punishment I've got coming. Not everyone deserved what we brought on them and we never troubled ourselves to discriminate too carefully. I can't blame Keith for it - if I'd never told him about myself, if we'd never met, he'd still be dreaming up shit metal bands and unwatchable TV series. We were two volatile chemicals that caused an explosion when we came together.

Still, I look back of those few months before it all went to shit as some of the happiest times of my life. We were making money - although Keith insisted that we could only spend a small percentage of what we collected in case The System detected changes to our spending patterns. And I felt more whole as a person than I ever had before. What do I mean by that? Well, I suppose I had a purpose. I knew what was expected of me, I knew how to do it and I was good at it. In fact, no one else could have done it quite like I did. The separate compartments of my life had moved into a kind of alignment and that was thanks to Keith. I still had secrets but not so many and not so major. It was as close to feeling like an integrated individual, a properly socialised being, as I ever got.

Of course, it all had to come to an end.

21

We couldn't have known what was going to happen with Trevor Long. It all spiralled out of control so quickly. I tell myself that if we'd just known how much pressure he was under and who he was dealing with we'd have left him alone and none of this would have come about. My rational mind believes that story but my conscience knows better. The heaviest burden a soul ever has to carry is the first death it's responsible for. That's the one that keeps on digging in to you and rubbing, even when everything else you're to blame for is piled up on top of it.

Trevor Long was the dealer who was supplying Peter Smithson and others in his circle with cocaine. His clientele was strictly middle class recreational users - high-functioning, high-status folk who liked to let their hair down in the privacy of their own and one another's homes (sometimes hotel rooms) in ways the law does not entirely approve of. He was discreet, efficient and reliable. His product was always of the highest quality and he evidently took pride in that, although he never touched it himself. Most importantly, as a university-educated professional just like them, Trevor Long didn't frighten or intimidate his clientele like a regular dealer would with their unironic tattoos, scabs and criminal associations. He enabled them to walk on the wild side without having to go anywhere near those of its inhabitants who are there by necessity rather than choice.

Of course they looked down on him, but discretely and

politely. For them, to acknowledge someone who was a good bloke but nonetheless a drug dealer as a proper equal would be asking a bit much.

As for us, we were quite happy not looking any further up the supply chain - "keeping it retail" as Keith put it. We wouldn't have known how to blackmail proper criminals. Reputation means something totally different once you've left the daytime world. We knew where we stood with people like Peter Smithson and Trevor Long.

Trevor was by all accounts a good and conscientious school teacher who genuinely cared about his work. There was no question of him dealing to his pupils. I know. We checked. He was fairly popular with the kids - his nickname ("Longy") betraying no ill-feeling, dirty secrets or unpleasant personal characteristics they could pin on him. It was the kind of nickname you'd give a mate, rather than a teacher.

Anyway, Longy was a good few years younger than me or Keith - maybe in his mid 20s - so he was closer to the kids' generation than ours. He was fit and healthy, playing scrum half at the club where he'd made Peter Smithson's acquaintance. The way I understand it, that's kind of like a quarterback in American football. So he was small, speedy, intelligent and the game often depended on his performance.

At the same time, he was a bit of an intellectual. You know what English teachers are like, right? They understand poetry and see all that stuff in Shakespeare that normal people don't notice. Longy was one of those - he really felt art and literature. I don't. I can look at a painting and I think "that's a good painting", "the person who painted that was good at painting" and "I like that" but it never touches me like it seems to touch some people. I've often wondered what it is that's there that I can't see. I've even been to art galleries at night to stare at the pictures. When you watch a TV programme about art and artists, the presenter gets all emotional and explains what's so good about it and I comprehend the story the picture's telling or what it's supposed to be saying - but I only "get it" to the same

Alan Boyce

extent as when I get a crossword clue: now I know the answer but I'm still none the wiser when I come to the next one. It doesn't make me feel anything.

Longy wasn't like that. He could appreciate whatever it was that was there, or else he could imagine something into being that got him all worked up. He liked all that shit so much he decided to spend his life teaching it to others. "Sensitive" is how my parents would have described him, but sporty at the same time. Best of both worlds, the lucky bastard. He was happily married to Clare, but they didn't have any kids - which is just as well. They did have a dog though, a golden retriever called Colonel Aureliano Buendia. I don't know what that means so I guess it must be a teacher thing. Or a coke dealer thing - it sounds Mexican. Whatever - it's a stupid name for a dog. Dogs should have names like Toby or Gemma.

We always liked it when our clients had dogs. When you've got a dog, nobody questions why you're wandering around abandoned places at unusual times of day. Dog walkers don't need excuses to go out by themselves. Little packages they might be carrying are written off as bits of sausage or cheese, plastic bags as turds for responsible disposal. You come across a dog walker, in the woods, in the dark, by themselves, with a torch, and you don't give them a second glance, do you?

"I'm just off out with the dog," he'd call to his wife as he went off to make another payment to us. She never suspected a thing, poor woman. Not about any of it.

There are loads of woodlands around Woking where dog walkers like Longy could be found wandering all times of day and night. We favoured Horsell Common because of the sand-pits - it looked like a 70s Dr Who set. Nearby rotten trees made perfect dead-letter drops, where plastic bags full of cash could be stuffed deep into hollowed trunks for later recovery. I would be following and watching from the astral plane, and once I was sure that a client had put the money in the tree, that they were out of the woods and that no one else was watching, I would return to my body and let Keith know the coast was clear.

90

22

Unlike most of our clients, I actually liked Trevor Long. He was a nice guy. We weren't all that different really. Similar educations. If things had gone differently, if I'd made better choices along the way, maybe his life could have been my life.

What am I saying?

One morning I was following him and his wife as they walked the dog in the woods.

"We should start thinking about the holiday."

"It's going to be hard getting the time off Trev. Since Mary went on the sick, they need everyone else on the ward."

"I mean during the summer holidays...we're talking a good few months yet."

"Somewhere hot."

"How about Barbados?"

"Trev! We can't afford that! I meant Spain or Greece - somewhere like that."

"What if I told you we could afford it?"

"Don't be daft. I'm a nurse. You're a teacher. Where are we going to get the money for something like that? Don't say the savings. That car is going to start costing us a fortune soon. And then there's the future to think about..."

Longy stopped and took his wife's hand. She turned to look him in the face, with a mixture of suspicion and anticipation.

"We won't touch the savings. The car, I know. And we want to decorate the spare room for...well...for when it happens."

Clare Long sighed and put her other hand on top of Trevor's.

At that moment, a group of teenagers emerged from a side path. They looked at the couple and whispered to one another.

"Morning sir," an athletic-looking girl in a tracksuit called, a gently mocking tone in her voice. Her companions smiled, giving sidelong glances to their teacher and his wife.

"Morning young people!" Longy called back, unselfconsciously. "Out for a healthy hike in the forest? You smoking something you shouldn't be there Tyrone?"

One of the boys - Tyrone presumably - dropped a smouldering scrap to the floor and quickly stepped on it, his eyes swivelling guiltily.

"Where's your dog sir?". The girl deftly changed the subject.

Longy whistled and was answered with a muffled bark, followed by a thunderous trampling of undergrowth. Colonel Aureliano Buendia burst into the clearing, tail wagging frantically, tongue lolling. He ran round and round the teenagers as they stroked and patted him, delirious joy on his face.

"You're a good boy! Aren't you? What's his name again sir?"

"Colonel Aureliano Buendia."

"Colonel...what?"

"Aureliano Buendia. It's from a book."

"He foreign sir?"

"No, he's from Reigate. The book's called 'One Hundred Years of Solitude.'"

"Is it good sir?"

"Yeah, it's a masterpiece. But you need to be getting your heads down with Hamlet. It's not long until your GCSEs now."

"Yes sir."

"Come on Trevor, we should be on our way," said Clare.

"I love your dog Mrs Long."

"Thank you. Come on Trevor."

"Bye sir. See you on Monday."

"Cheers Angie. Tyrone?" Longy pointed to his own eyes and then at the still-downcast eyes of Tyrone. "Just be careful, eh?"

"Sir...." the boy mumbled as the Longs strolled away.

"You're so good with them," said Clare. "They scare me half to death."

"They're good kids really. They're just bored. Nobody expects anything from them and they end up expecting nothing out of life. Nothing beyond getting stoned on a Saturday morning."

"Well, what's wrong with that?" Clare laughed.

Trevor laughed too, but his tone quickly became more serious.

"They've just got so much potential and it's wasted by low expectations and lack of opportunity and self-doubt. That Angie - she's so clever, but she wouldn't dream of letting on to her friends. She'll remember that I mentioned Garcia Marquez."

"She fancies you..."

"Well, I can't help that. I am the best-looking member of staff by a long way."

Trevor took hold of his wife by the waist and pulled her towards him.

"That is true Mr Long."

They kissed.

"Still, look at the competition."

They laughed.

"Clare."

"Trev."

"Don't be angry."

Why would I be?" Imperceptibly, she began to move away from his embrace.

"I want to take you to Barbados. And I've had a bit of good luck."

The atmosphere suddenly chilled.

"Have you been fucking gambling again?"

"Just listen..."

"Don't you ever learn? After everything we went through? You promised. You promised you wouldn't start again. After my parents bailed us out! What are they going to say?"

"Clare, it's different this time..."

"What did you just say? What did you fucking say?"

93

The temperature hit zero.

"Clare please - just listen. Yes, I went into the casino. And yes, I laid a couple of bets. My first stake on roulette - it came in. I won £3,500. Just like that. Then I stopped. I cashed my chips and I walked out. I hated myself for going in. I know I have a problem. But I stopped myself. A year ago, I'd have lost all my winnings and come out with nothing. But I stopped Clare. I stopped and I walked out."

"You lied to me."

"I know, I know and I'm sorry. But it's £3,500 Clare. Don't blame the money. You deserve it Clare. Let's enjoy it."

"I just can't believe you did it Trev. After everything."

Clare was still angry, but a thaw was in the air. Longy sensed it and tried to follow up the advantage.

"Come on Clare-bear. You work so hard. Let's go to Barbados! And sip pina coladas on the beach while the sun goes down…"

"You are unbelievable Trevor Long," said Clare. She set off walking, still holding her husband's hand.

23

While business was booming Keith was keen for us to find out more about the world of the paranormal.

"Don't you ever wonder where it came from Shaun?"

"Well ... sort of."

As I mentioned earlier, I was somewhat sheepish about how little I had bothered to investigate it.

"The thing is, how do you know that this is all you can do? Maybe you could - you know - level up. Develop your powers somehow to be more useful. All these occultists I've read about have grades and progressions. I don't mean that what you can do isn't useful - it's great Shaun, really great. But imagine what we could do if you could ... I don't know ... make your body appear and disappear at will, or read minds, or just go slightly faster ... If you didn't have to walk everywhere, you know? It would be bloody useful. We know you can leave your body behind, in defiance of everything scientists say they know about physics. So why should we just assume that's the only exception to the rules? There could be so much more."

Keith's attention was wandering as he was saying this. He seemed to be addressing these thoughts to himself more than to me.

"And what if it's not just you Shaun? Sure, you might have been born with the gift or whatever you want to call it. But it stands to reason that if one person can do it, others can too. Don't take this the wrong way Shaun, but what's so special about you? What could possibly make you so unique that you can do something nobody else in the whole world can?"

I wasn't offended. Why would I be? He had a point. What was so special about me?

"What if this is something I could do too? If we figured out how you do it ... I could learn how to do it as well."

So we began to attend readings and séances, and Keith began reading books about Tibet, alchemy and theosophy. And we met Schneck - or to give them their full title, the Surrey and North Hampshire Esoteric Circle. Clearly, "Schneck" is a not an accurate abbreviation of the name, but that's what Keith and I called them, because SNHEC looks like it sounds like "Schneck". It was through Schneck that we met Sandra, and through her - after I died for the first time - that I encountered Dr Claudius.

Schneck met in a church hall just outside Woking every other Wednesday evening. Keith had seen a flyer for the group in a chip shop, which claimed that its mission was "to investigate and explore the powers of the human mind". It sounded like a good place to start.

The first time we went to a Schneck meeting, it was raining heavily. Arriving in Keith's mum's Micra outside the hall, we were fairly surprised to see the car park was full. The building was a one-storey breeze block construction, with a corrugated roof that almost certainly contained significant deposits of asbestos. The door was open and we could see along a corridor through another open door into the wan light of the hall itself. A heated argument appeared to be underway between two older men.

"Is this a good idea Keith?" I asked.

In retrospect, the doubts I felt at that moment were probably as close as I ever came to being able to foretell the future. Everything would certainly have turned out better if we'd never gone in.

"We're just here to listen and learn Shaun. Remember, no matter how mental this lot seem, they might have something they don't know the value of."

The corridor was lit by a single fluorescent tube that flickered every few seconds, causing me to twitch. The walls were lined with posters for Scout groups, local history clubs, parish council notices - almost all of them long out of date. Scuffed plastic chairs in acidic orange and green were pushed back against the walls. The doormat was sodden with mud and water, and filthy footprints covered the grey tiled floor that led through to the main hall.

"You go in first Shaun. While they're looking at you, I'll scope the crowd."

I walked into the main hall. No one looked at me. This room was wood panelled for the most part in amber-lacquered pine. Almost certainly, it was a veneer on chipboard. In the middle of the room were a number of trestle tables, topped with various model trains. These seemed to be the crux of the dispute.

"We have this hall from 6.30pm. You have it until 6.30pm. Until! It's your responsibility to be out of here by the time our slot starts. Every week this happens!"

The speaker was a willowy older man in a tweed suit. His hair was white and his skin was almost translucent. As he spoke, he jabbed his forefinger into his thigh, emphasising the first syllable of each word. The gesture was clearly a sublimated proxy for poking the chest of the second man, this one broadly-built wearing a purple hooded anorak. The second man had a look of amused but rapidly dwindling tolerance on his face.

"Our speaker got here late because of the traffic on the A3," he replied patiently. "He brought his locos all the way from Southampton. We've only overrun by five minutes."

"That's not the point!" the first man shouted, turning away, gritting his teeth and clenching his eyes shut all at once. "SNHEC pays for an hour and a half. You finish late every week. You don't even start putting your little trains away until half past. Every week!"

"These are not trains ... " the second man said, in a way that suggested this was a conversation he had had many times before.

"Every week! You are STEALING ten minutes a week from my group and my members."

It was not hard to tell which groups the other people in the hall belonged to. Drifting towards the doorway Keith and I had just come in through were several casually-dressed men in their 50s and 60s, each clutching a little cardboard box. They had the confident, easy manner of people satisfied with what they had achieved in life and unabashed about what anyone might think about their hobby. When not regarding the row with amusement, they were discussing which of the village's two pubs to retire to.

The other group, which was moving deeper into the hall as the other moved outwards, was what you might call "eclectic". There were women and men, both young and old. One enormous woman was draped in multi-coloured kente robes and a white kufi cap, and was carrying a wicker basket, behind whose metal grill the green eyes of a furious-looking black cat blazed out. A younger man with thick glasses and the hood of his coat still up had put down his Morrisons bag-for-life (the one with a bunch of carrots on) and began to move the chairs around the hall. I looked at the hem of his trouser legs. As I suspected would be the case, an inch of sock was visible.

The others occupied various points on this spectrum between dowager witchdoctor and bullied nascent psychopath. There were eight of them, which we were soon to learn was the usual turnout for a Shneck meeting.

"I will be raising a formal complaint with the committee! This has gone on for too long!"

"You do that ... "

The second man was packing away the last remaining models, with a care and attention that told of the love he had for these objects, but which also - coincidentally - meant that his progress was maddeningly slow. He was fully aware of this and had no intention of speeding up. Indeed, the angrier the thin man got, the more cheerful this one became.

"And don't think I haven't noticed where your car is," the

first man stuck out his chin as he followed the other (finally finished) to the doorway.

"I know where you parked! You parked in the bishop's space! That's reserved at all times! I know your car. What if he needs it?"

The second man gave a tired, mocking wave over his shoulder as he left the hall.

"The bishop's parking space!"

The pale man slammed the hall door behind the departing model railway enthusiast. Now he saw us.

"Who are you?"

Keith stepped forward.

"Mr Parsons?"

"Par-SON. Par-SON - it is Par-SON singular, not Par-SONS plural. But yes, I am he," Mr Parson stood back cautiously, his hands in his pockets.

"We spoke on the phone earlier in the week. My name is Keith ... " - there was an infinitesimally short pause - "Smith. And this is Shaun."

"Shaun ... Jones," I added.

"We're interested in your group ... in your ... work. The work," Keith resumed, glaring at me.

"Ah well, welcome! Yes, welcome! Welcome to the Surrey and North Hampshire Esoteric Circle, Mr Smith and Mr Jones." If Mr Parson had found our choice of pseudonyms in any way suspicious he did not show it.

"The work ... yes, the work," he continued. "Sandra! Sandra!"

A woman, perhaps the same age as me, and by far the most normal-looking person in the room, trotted over. She had a pleasant if unremarkable face and was wearing an equally pleasant and unremarkable waterproof jacket. She smiled at Mr Parson and then at Keith and I.

"Sandra, please take these gentlemen into the kitchen and give them tea or coffee and one of our biscuits while the brothers and sisters ready the *mise-en-scene*." With these last words, Mr Parson looked up towards the roof and theatrically spread his open palms alongside his chalky face.

"C'mon lads," Sandra spoke with a West Midlands accent and indicated a door in the side of the hall. The door led into a small kitchen. The other members of the group had stopped what they were doing and watched us walk towards it. The kitchen's roll-up serving hatch was shut, and Sandra closed the door behind us once we were inside.

"Tea or coffee?"

"Errr ... tea please," Keith replied.

"Tea as well," I added.

"Don't mind that business you saw when you first arrived. We have it most weeks. Mr Parson gets ever so cross about late starts. That train lot tease him something awful. It's really not good for him or his energy. I tell him, 'think about your kamarupa Mr Parson' but he gets so worked up. Biscuit?"

Sandra reached into a cupboard and brought down a Tupperware container labelled "Property of SNHEC. Do not remove". She opened it and peered inside.

"We've got digestives and rich tea. Or, I should tell you, Anne usually brings one of her wonderful home-made cakes along for the break. Mmmm ... they're so moist but really light. She's a wonderful baker is Anne - but you mustn't believe a word she tells you. She full of S-H-One-T, if you'll pardon the expression."

Keith declined, saying he would wait for the cake. I had a digestive.

"What you'll find out about the Circle and others like us, is that only a small number have real gifts. And you can tell them apart from the frauds because their auras are righteous. That lot in there, only Mr Parson really knows what's what. He's very wise - you can learn a lot from him lads if you're interested in the spirit. And he's a lovely man with it. I look after his mother. She's eighty-five but is away with the fairies most of the time."

There was a knock on the door. It opened a crack, and the creepy young man stuck his face in. He still had his hood up.

"Bring them in," he said peremptorily, without making eye

contact and withdrawing his head as he did so. You got the sense from him that if he did turn his gaze on you, you'd either be reduced to ashes or a fit of giggles.

"He's a strange one," Sandra said, shaking her head. "Barely says a word to anyone. I could see him as a black magician. His mum's lovely though, and so proud of him. Drinks far too much though, she does, poor woman. Called the boy Ethan. Ethan Oliver. Karma."

We all went back into the hall, where the group members were sat in a semi-circle, facing Mr Parson at a desk along with the non-specifically African-themed woman and her cat basket. Again, all eyes were on us.

"You must excuse us," Mr Parson addressed us from across the room as we headed towards the three remaining seats. "You will understand that there are certain elements of our proceedings which are only for the eyes of the initiated - and so, should you come again, you will have to be confined to the kitchen area during the opening phases of the Circle's convocations. I hope you don't mind, it's just, you know ... "

The others nodded solemnly and appreciatively. No matter how amusing the miniature railwaymen found Mr Parson, his authority was undisputed here.

"Now, we have a special treat in store tonight. Mrs Thomas," he indicated the woman, who nodded and smiled graciously, "will be telling us about animal familiars and their invocation in the traditional religions of West Africa - with the help of her cat, Charlie."

"Charles," Mrs Thomas interjected, in a voice several registers deeper than Mr Parson's.

"I beg your pardon: with the help of Charles. So without further ado - as we are already running very late due to the lack of consideration of other users of these facilities earlier this evening - I will hand you over to our esteemed speaker."

I didn't really follow a great deal of what Mrs Thomas had to say. Using a lot of terms I couldn't understand - such as "neo-pythagorean", "the pleroma", "candomble" and "syncreticism" - she seemed to be telling us that Charles was in fact, not a cat, but the reincarnated soul of an Ashanti shaman, who could talk, fly and bestow valuable gifts of some sort or another. However, he chose not to do so during the meeting, and merely sat staring with terrified malice from the corner of his basket.

The rest of the audience appeared to be taking this perfectly seriously. The serial killer was taking notes. Eventually Mr Parson rose to his feet. I noticed that Sandra had gone.

"I think we'll take a five-minute break now. If we only take five minutes instead of the scheduled ten, Mrs Thomas should be able to get back on schedule following the late start and we will have time for some questions."

"I've finished," Mrs Thomas boomed.

"Err ... well, let's have a five-minute break and then perhaps Mrs Thomas can answer the many questions I'm sure you have about Charles."

His final words were drowned out by the sound of the shutter being rolled up on the kitchen hatch. Sandra was there with a row of mugs and the SNHEC biscuits, now on a plate.

The meeting ended shortly thereafter, as nobody really had any questions to ask Mrs Thomas and Charles persisted in refusing to display any unusual qualities.

"Well, thank you very much to Mrs Thomas for coming and giving us such a ... stimulating account of ... her cat. Thank you also to Anne for her splendid cake."

Anne looked up from her knitting, smiled sweetly and gave a little wave.

"And I'd just like to remind you that there will be no meeting next week, as Mrs Parson is hosting a candle party, which I am unavoidably committed to attend. We will be back in two weeks, however, when our very own Sandra will be giving us a demonstration of some of the more advanced yoga positions and the theory behind them."

As the group broke up, Mr Parson started coming over to us.

"I really want to get out of here," Keith said to me under his breath.

"Gentlemen! I hope you weren't ... errr ... disappointed this evening. As I'm sure you can imagine, the work attracts ... errrm ... particular types of people, some of whom ... ahhh ..."

"No, we enjoyed it enormously, didn't we Shaun?" Keith replied. "I really feel ... um ... a sense of kinship here. I feel that we could really learn a lot from you and your fellow initiates."

"Really? Well, that's wonderful! Wonderful. Now, I do hate to bring this up, but we do ask for £3 from everyone who comes to our sessions to cover the room hire costs and the refreshments."

Soon we were speeding back towards town.

"Shaun, it's a start. Obviously, that cat woman was just insane and the rest of them don't seem much better. But that Parson - even if he doesn't know anything himself, he'll know what to read and he'll know other people. It's social networking, Shaun, like with the business."

24

When it all kicked off, we were collecting a few thousand pounds a week and it was easy. Did we get complacent? No. We weren't taking any more risks than before and we were as careful as we had always been about the big things. But you know how it is when a small business expands too quickly? That special something they had gets lost. That attention to detail that made them successful in the first place gets left behind. That's what happened to us.

Clearly, we couldn't take on more staff, so expansion stretched me and Keith further and further. We had less time to spend really getting to know our clients, figuring out what made them tick and keeping track of what was going on in their lives. By the time we took Longy on, we were going through the motions of a well-rehearsed routine. Success breeds complacency, no matter how careful you are. We had no idea what kind of pressure he was under and when he started to crack up, we didn't see the signs until it was far too late.

It turns out that Longy was not only a drug dealer. He was also a serious problem gambler with considerable debts. He had lied to his wife about the casino visit being a one-off. He was there most lunchtimes losing steadily.

The proceeds of the coke enterprise were largely soaked up keeping whoever he owed money to off his back. We thought he was stashing it all away in savings, not paying down debt. Classic failure to do due diligence, Keith would later lament.

Longy's attitude to money seemed to be "easy come, easy go". The dealing seemed more of a romantic enterprise than a financial one - a way for him to appear Byronic and dangerous in front of the squares, and to preserve his youthful rebellion in the face of the creeping barrage of adulthood's demands. He certainly never gave any sign that money was a worry. Until he did.

We didn't realise how much paying us would hurt him and how much danger it would put him in, because we didn't have the time to manage the account properly. I was asleep trailing people here and there more and more of the time, while Keith was handling the financial side of the business. I mean, nine times out of ten you can get away with a little corner-cutting like that. You can't predict the appearance of somebody like Nigel.

I hadn't seen Longy for a couple of weeks - most clients paid monthly for mutual convenience. That day (a Sunday) he was due to make payment by the sandpits as usual. I was there early taking in the golden afternoon sunlight through the last leaves of autumn. The woods were damp and varicoloured fungus was sprouting from the roots of trees, on stumps and piles of yellow and brown leaves. Crows and pigeons pecked around in the sand, oblivious to my presence. I was hovering maybe fifteen feet in the air looking out for Colonel Aureliano Buendia, as the dog's arrival would herald the imminent appearance of his owner.

I heard a loud "woof" behind and below me and, turning, I saw the Colonel lolloping into the clearing. The birds scattered. Seeing the sand, he bounded straight into it. As soon as his paws made landfall, he stiffened with excitement. He jumped, putting his head down and his front legs out, poised as if someone were about to throw a ball for him. He spun round and round again in a circle in hot pursuit of his flapping tail. He stopped, quivering, and pricked his ears looking to left and right - as though he suspected someone was creeping up on him. Then he started to dig. Slowly at first, then faster and faster. Colonel

Aureliano Buendia's back legs hopped up and down as he dug, like they were impatient for it to be their turn to join in the fun. The result was that the dog slowly described a perfect circle around the pit he was excavating. He stopped suddenly.

"Woof! Woof! Woof!"

Then he started again.

I like dogs and their unselfconscious fun. Imagine feeling that much joy just from digging a hole in some sand and barking a bit. How much easier life would have been as a dog.

While I was pondering this Trevor Long appeared. He looked in a bad way. Usually Longy was pretty well turned-out, but today he was wearing tracksuit bottoms and a big overcoat. And odd shoes. He hadn't shaved in days and his eyes were piss-yellow. He kept scratching his head, and the patch on his scalp where we was doing it was red and starting to go bald. Longy was mumbling to himself and occasionally let out a high-pitched, staccato laugh. When he emerged into the clearing, the dog stopped digging and looked sympathetically at him. Colonel Aureliano Buendia could tell something was wrong. Dogs know, like with epilepsy. He trotted over to Longy and pressed his chin against his thigh, looking up at his owner. Without looking back, Longy took a treat out of his pocket and held it to the dog's mouth. Reassured, Colonel Aureliano Buendia snuffled it up and ran back to the sandpit, whose thrilling pleasures he rediscovered as if they were entirely brand new to him.

Longy walked on to the appointed tree and took a wad of notes out of his coat pocket. This was unusual as we were pretty clear with clients that cash had to be concealed and deposited in a waterproof container, particularly at this time of year. Laughing bitterly to himself, Longy stuffed them one by one into the trunk's hole. I may not have a golden retriever's sixth sense but even I could tell that this was looking like a risky client.

I followed Longy as he shambled through the woods, seemingly oblivious to his surroundings. Colonel Aureliano

Buendia would gallop past every so often, engaged upon unfathomable canine errands at distant points in the forest. At some point, as happened on most of these walks, he came back soaking wet and covered in mud. Under normal circumstances, this would elicit a groan of disappointment from Longy and an unheeded lecture to the filthy pet - whose face always betrayed his immense satisfaction at successfully getting covered in black slime, no matter how apologetic he tried to look. Today though, Longy barely acknowledged the coming and going of the dog.

I shadowed the pair all the way home: past the Muslim cemetery and out of the woods, onto a dreary industrial estate. Skeletal buddleia sprouted from cracked concrete on boarded-up and fenced-off empty lots. Anti-climb paint flaked like sunburn dripping red welts of rust from the grey walls of flat-roofed units, crowned with razor wire. Dirty white air conditioners hummed on the rear walls of the few premises that were open that day. One had a plastic bag caught in its grill, which fluttered spasmodically like a dying bird trapped under the paws of a cat. Security companies' faded signs hung from the walls, threatening would-be intruders with long-gone CCTV, rottweilers and guards.

The very same dead leaves that had been so uplifting in the woods here formed a coagulated scum-froth on the pavement, clogging the drains. Clouds had covered the sun, and the damp grey sky bled into the grey buildings. Longy was walking in the middle of the road. Even irrepressibly cheerful Colonel Aureliano Buendia hung his head as he trudged along at his owner's heels.

Exiting the desolate business park, the man, dog and ghostly stalker found themselves on a broad grass verge bordering an empty access road. On the other side, there was another verge, bounded by a long fence - wooden this time. Over the top of the fence peeped the upper floors of a row of identikit starter houses. The two-tone brickwork gave a Lego vibe to the estate, emphasising its flimsiness and impermanence compared to the weight and solidity of Keith's squat Victorian terrace home.

A hundred yards to the left, there was a gap in the fence and a path leading through. This is where Longy was heading. He weaved between two overlapping steel barriers, fixed in place to prevent motorbikes using the alleyway. I glided through a few paces behind. Colonel Aureliano Buendia stopped to sniff a still-steaming pile of horse shit, but his investigations were left incomplete as Longy walked on, pulling the dog along in his wake.

Exiting the passage, we emerged onto a street of bulk-built semi-detached houses. Gardens identically furnished with immature trees and still-labelled shrubs gave away how new this street was, as did the yellowy-grey sand and cement smear along the road's tarmac. Longy and Colonel Aureliano Buendia turned up the narrow empty driveway to one of the boxy houses.

I had been here before of course but not during the daytime. The darkness highlights the difference between these houses; daylight brings out the similarities. I remember all of this vividly because of what happened next. Like my brain already knew what was coming before I did.

I drifted upwards as Longy let himself in, keeping a whining Colonel Aureliano Buendia out with his foot. Moments later, he emerged holding a tattered towel, with which he proceeded to scrub the mud-caked dog. From above, the houses were even less distinguishable. Only the occasional back garden trampoline, line of washing or shed broke up the uniformity. After a few minutes of surveying the houses, the crumbling industrial estate and the woodlands beyond, I glided back down and passed through Trevor Long's still-open front door.

25

On an Ikea sideboard unopened mail was piled up high alongside several empty wine bottles. Shoes and coats were strewn across the entrance hallway's floor. The doormat was rumpled and folded over, no doubt from high speed canine cornering.

The Ikea theme was continued in the living room - minimal Scandinavian design abutted full English clutter. A *Noda* coffee table was topped with plates bearing the remains of several meals in various stages of decay. The beige carpet was marred by dark muddy footprints leading to Colonel Aureliano Buendia's filthy dog bed. I went on into the kitchen-diner, where Longy was sat on a white *Leifas* chair at a white *Billsta* café table, scratching his bald patch, face lit by the cold glare of his laptop screen. It made him look even more ghastly pale. There was a bottle of whisky on the table and a cupboard door open behind him. The sink was full. The microwave door was open as well. Flies buzzed around the lidless *Knodd* bin and the dog's bowl. A note was attached to the fridge door with a magnet saying "*Lago di Garda*". It said: "I've gone to my mum's. Don't follow me. Don't call me. Just do whatever it is you have to do. Clare".

The laptop was a chunky old thing, that looked at least seven or eight years old. A big metallic label was affixed to the lid, reading "Everard Academy - a good school, raising aspiration in the community". Where the label was peeling away, it had left a gummy white residue. I could tell just by looking that it was still extremely sticky.

I drifted round to look over Longy's shoulder. He was trying to open Word. Nothing was happening. He clicked on the icon again. Then again. There really is no point in hitting a mouse button over and over again, even if it feels like there is. It doesn't help and it often makes things worse. I know. Longy let out a harsh sigh and his face dropped into his hands. Colonel Aureliano Buendia's head appeared around the living room door, his eyes saying "U OK hun?"

After a few seconds, Longy lifted his face back up to the screen. Word still hadn't started up. He pursed his lips and exhaled heavily, reaching for the whisky bottle. Dropping the lid on the floor, Longy took a long swig. The reappearing dog sniffed at the fallen bottle top and - appalled - skulked back into the living room.

Once the program had finally started up, the teacher/dealer began typing what appeared to be a letter.

Dear Sir,

I am so sorry to let you down like this but I have come to the conclusion that I must bring our partnership to an end. I am very grateful for the opportunities you have given to me, and naturally I will pay everything that I owe plus whatever interest and exit charges you think are appropriate.

All I need is a week to get the money together. We have always had a good relationship and I hope you will understand my decision. I owe it to my wife and my parents to get out of this self-destructive cycle.

He paused, thinking what to say next. At that moment, a black window opened at the bottom of the screen. A white vertical cursor flashed in its top left hand corner. I assumed it was one of those background things computers are always doing for themselves, until letters slowly began to appear.

You will pay and youw will not stop. The consequencs will

otherwise be bad

Whoever this was coming from was a very bad typist. There were a lot of corrections required to get even that message across. It continued.

I oen you. You have until tomorrow you CNUT

Mr Long stared at the screen, his face absolutely frozen. He moved his own cursor into the black box and clicked repeatedly, so as to either delete or reply to the unknown source of the threats. But nothing happened.

Slowly and one by one, the letters T, U and N disappeared. They were replaced by a U, an N and finally a T.

Longy leapt back out of his *Leifas*. The whisky bottle tottered on its end, but luckily did not fall over. He blinked. His left hand twitched.

The doorbell rang.

I jumped nearly as much as Longy did. His face was white, like a sweaty ghost. Staring at where the sound had come from, he sat down then stood up again. A silhouette could be seen through the frosted glass of the front door. The shadow raised its right arm and banged out a cheery "shave and a haircut" on the frame.

There was a pause that seemed to last for minutes. Longy stood with his mouth open, goggling at the front door. Eventually he looked at his watch. He blinked, shook his head and wiped his face, as if coming out of a trance.

"Fuck!"

He picked up the booze and stuffed it back into the open cupboard. He lurched into the living room and scooped up the plates, cutlery and other mealtime detritus, whisking it into the kitchen. Closing the kitchen door firmly behind him, Longy went to meet the visitor.

His right hand on the door handle, Mr Long wiped his mouth with his left hand. He opened it.

"Nigel."

Outside the door was a man in his 40s, holding a stack of lever arch files under one arm and with a proper old-fashioned leather satchel slung over his shoulder. Compared to the mess that was Trevor Long, he was immaculately dressed. Deck shoes, red trousers with deep maroon stitching and brass rivets, pink linen shirt under a Barbour jacket. Deep colours glowed out from his clothing that contrasted starkly with the grey/beige decor of the Long house. The man's skin glowed too. It was tanned but still youthful, not leathery. His hands were huge, half as broad again as Longy's. The handshake he delivered jolted the spindly teacher's shoulder. The new arrival smiled like someone who has never been nervous, never felt awkward, never given blending into the background of a scene a second thought. I had never seen anyone who looked so fucking healthy before.

"Trevor! Not early am I?"

The visitor had the vestiges of a Yorkshire accent under his Surrey drawl. He moved slowly as if to look at a watch.

"No! No, no, no. Come in. Please."

The sheer presence that this Nigel was emitting had turned the terrified zombie I had been watching a few minutes ago into an obsequious, fawning subordinate. I could have sworn Longy was even stooping, so as to appear smaller.

Nigel strode into the living room and placed his folders down on the recently-vacated *Noda*. He stroked Colonel Aureliano Buendia's head. Satisfied that everything was in order, the dog trotted out of the room.

"Thought I'd just pop these round for review. Touch base so to speak before the FGB on Wednesday. Want to make sure all key personnel are properly briefed..."

As he spoke, his eyebrows rose very gradually and expectantly. There was a moment's pause before Longy grasped what was expected from him, and resumed the Uriah Heep act.

"Can I get you anything? Sorry. Tea? Coffee? Please, have a seat."

"Tea Trevor, unless you've got a fresh pot of coffee on. Can't bear instant, can you? Milk, no sugar."

Nigel unslung the satchel from his shoulder as Longy scuttled away, repeating "Tea. Milk. No sugar." Slipping through the door into the devastated kitchen, Trevor Long closed it silently behind himself once again.

I followed Longy through the door. He slammed the lid shut on the computer and grabbed the kettle.

"Tea. Milk. No sugar," he intoned under his breath as he filled it under the tap. "Just deal with this for now. Concentrate. Be normal."

As Trevor made the tea, things appeared to have become normal again. But that's just how it looked at that precise moment.

I went back into the living room. The curtains were closed and plastic sheeting had been laid over the floor and the two *Ekenäs* armchairs beside the kitchen door. Nigel had his back to me and was fiddling with something in front of his stomach.

I didn't know what I was looking at.

A moment later, Longy came into the room backwards, pushing the handle down with one bum cheek, a mug of tea in each hand.

"Sorry about that Nigel. The wife's away and... errr...I had forgotten to chuck the old milk away. It's ok, I had some more. Semi skimmed, I hope that's alright."

He noticed the plastic sheeting, and turned around - a puzzled expression on his face.

"What's this Nigel?"

"I own you. And you don't have until tomorrow."

Two muffled gunshots rang out.

Blood, bits of brain and skull, tea - they all went straight through me and spattered the living room wall behind. Trevor Long fell back into the kitchen door and then slumped forwards, dead.

Again, time stopped. I stared at the body. Nothing moved.

"You weren't there a moment ago. Where did you come from?"

I looked up. Nigel was staring straight at me. He was wearing an apron and leather gloves. And he was holding a gun, with an elegant matte black silencer on the end of it.

On the brink of panic, I glanced around the room looking for whoever he could be talking to.

"Yes, you. I can see you," Nigel said.

I need to get out of here. Time to wake up, I thought. But nothing happened. Nothing happened. I decided to run, out via the kitchen and away through the gardens back towards the industrial estate. I ran. I looked back over my shoulder as I headed for the back door. Nigel had started walking after me.

My ear and shoulder exploded in a burst of pain, and I fell hard to the floor, cracking the rear of my skull on the tiles as my head whipped back, sending the *Billsta* and the laptop flying. I had run into the door. The door. My skull. The tiles. I was solid. My body was here with me.

I was here. In the flesh.

"Who are you? Where the fuck were you hiding? Come back!"

Nigel's eerie calm had evaporated and his confusion was quickly turning to anger. He pulled a mobile phone from one pocket with his free hand and speed-dialled a number without taking his eyes off me.

"Get round the back of the house right now. There's somebody else here."

I scrambled to my feet, grasping for the door handle as the killer advanced towards me. I heard the garden gate begin to rattle violently.

Only then did I wake up.

26

My heart was pounding - my real heart, in my real chest. I was staring at the ceiling of my bedroom. I put my hand to my ear. It hurt like hell. I looked at my fingers and there was blood on them. Was it all mine?

I sat up and began to cough. The bruise on the back of my head came to life and began to ache, worse and worse as my chest heaved. There was a gentle but impatient knock at the door.

"You alright in there?"

Keith.

"You've been ages. What's the problem? It's Trevor Long for Christ's sake. How much easier can it get?"

Now my shoulder added its deep burn to the pain ensemble. I staggered out of bed and opened the door. There was Keith, clad in an oversized black t-shirt - this time bearing the legend "Brusilov Offensive" and a monochrome picture of a pine forest with barbed wire entanglements strung between the trees. He looked more irritated than concerned.

"Has he gone?" he asked, as though addressing the question to an exasperating child.

"Keith."

"Shaun."

"Keith ... "

"What? What the fuck is the matter with you?"

"He's dead."

"Who's dead?"

"Trevor Long."

Keith squinted at me, as though what he was hearing could be made sense of by focusing his eyes properly.

"Trevor Long is dead?"

"Some guy called Nigel. Shot him. At his house."

"Shot him?"

"He shot him. With a gun."

"Yeah I assumed you meant 'with a gun' Shaun. Not a fucking harpoon."

"I was right there."

"Well, that's drug dealers for you I suppose," Keith said turning away to walk back down the stairs. "Comes with the territory, as they say. The cash is in the tree as usual though, right?"

I came out of the bedroom and ran down the stairs. Keith was putting his shoes on as I skidded to a halt in front of him.

"This is a problem," he commented absent-mindedly.

"Yes. Yes it is," I panted in reply.

"Where are Peter Smithson and his mates going to get their coke now? How does this play out for us, I wonder? Presumably somebody further upstream will reach out to Longy's customers sooner or later. Although I suppose they don't still have to be using to want everything keeping quiet. Actually Shaun," Keith looked up, becoming more animated. "We could tell them all we know about the killing, make vague threats about tangling them up in it…turn the screws a bit, put the rates up! We'll at least cover what we lose from Longy, and probably be able to make a bit more to boot!"

"I saw him die Keith. I felt it on my face."

"Don't be dramatic. Metaphors are rarely helpful in business, Shaun. You didn't 'feel it' because you were here, in your bedroom the whole time. Maybe it felt like you felt it, but that's just your emotions talking. You have to keep them in check. You've had a shock - I understand. Of course, it's very sad and everything but you can't be sentimental. None of it's real."

116

None of it's real? My forehead felt suddenly cold and damp. Not only was it real, but it was our fault. We had driven Longy to the despair that got him killed. It was our fault. My fault.

"It is real."

"Well, you know what I mean." Keith waved his hand in irritation. "You know why I liked you from the moment we met, Shaun? I could see you were a man who could manage his emotions. We are rational people. Emotions are not for people like us - they're for the herd, who can't think with their brains the way we can. Now, I'm not saying you didn't see Trevor Long die. If you did, I'm sure it was very traumatic for you. Personally, I think you're blowing it out of proportion, but that's probably how most people would react to that experience. You just need to take a deep breath and think carefully about what this means for us and our business."

Having finished his speech Keith turned away and then turned back. He looked closely at me, inspecting me.

"What have you done to your ear? There's blood all over your collar."

Now Keith began to look concerned.

"Keith, he saw me. I was there."

"Who saw you?"

"Nigel. The killer."

"No he didn't. That's impossible. How could he have seen you?"

"I was there. I mean, I was really there. I tried to escape when he saw me, and I ran into the back door."

I wiped my palm across my ear. It was raw and felt gritty.

"You were in there." Keith nodded towards the bedroom, an expression of terror germinating on his face. "How could you have been somewhere else? Physically."

"I don't know. I don't know! Keith, I don't know what happened. This bloke came round, shot Longy and then I was there in the room with him. He looked me straight in the eye and said 'where did you come from?' I thought he was talking to someone else, but when I realised he meant me I tried to

117

wake up. I tried to come back to my body like I always do. But I couldn't. Nothing happened. Nothing! That has never happened before. So I ran. I know I was there in the flesh. I know, because I ran straight into the door. It's our fault Keith!"

Keith had both hands over his mouth now and was staring at the floor, his eyes wide, his pupils fixed on a point some thousand yards underground. No light was reflecting from his pupils at all.

"What are we going to do?" I said.

I was terrified. Ever since my first few forays onto the astral plane - or wherever it was I went - I knew where I stood. I knew what the rules were, how things worked and most importantly how to get back. All that had changed suddenly.

Was it real? I might have written it off as a dream or an hallucination, were it not for my ringing ear, my clanging skull, my screaming shoulder and the blood on my palm. And anyway, I knew it had been real. I could try to fool myself with theories and explanations, but I knew in the base of my spine and in my liquefying bowels that the unthinkable had just happened. It was real. It was my fault.

Keith began speaking.

"OK, first off - it's not my fault. It's not your fault either. Did you pull the trigger? No. Did you get Trevor Long mixed up with criminals? No. All we did was make a bit of money. A perfectly reasonable sum of money. Were we greedy? How were we to have known any of this would happen? It's not our fault. End of. Now, secondly: were you followed?"

I looked up. Keith was breathing slowly and deliberately. His attempts to regain some of his composure appeared to be working.

"Did you see this guy anywhere beforehand? Tell me everything that happened."

I did.

27

An hour later we had a plan of sorts. Keith would drive round to the Longs' street and see what was going on there. I was to stay here at my house with the curtains closed and find out who this Nigel was. We knew he had something to do with the governing body at Longy's school, Everard Academy. That was plenty to get started with on the internet.

Keith took ages. It was dark by the time he got back.

"Well, it looks like you were right Shaun. Police are everywhere, all over that estate. And there's an ambulance parked outside the Long's."

An ambulance? Did that mean he might still be alive?

"And the stupid bastard just stuffed the money into the tree, not even in a bag. Look at it!"

Keith withdrew a wad of soaked £10 notes from his coat pocket and threw them onto the kitchen table. So he had been to get the money as well.

"Peel them apart and pop them on the radiator Shaun."

Out of his rucksack, Keith pulled something that looked like a chunky walkie-talkie. He plonked that on the table as well.

"Been on the police scanner the whole time. They've got a dead body and they don't have a suspect. Forensics are on their way over."

Keith turned a knob on the top of the scanner and muffled voices began to emerge from the static crackle. We huddled around it, listening intently like Londoners during the Blitz.

"So who is he?"

I told Keith what I'd found out.

"Nigel Darwin. He's the deputy chair of governors at Everard. Owns and runs an IT company. Married with one teenage daughter. Nothing to suggest he's a drug trafficker or a murderer."

"There never is."

Every online trace I had found portrayed Nigel Darwin as totally normal. Highly successful, alpha-male, man-of-action type, but normal. Came from a poor background up north. Self-made man and all too happy to tell anyone who would listen about being working class from the comfort of his mansion or his Bentley. There were local news stories about the school featuring his picture. About his company expanding from ring-road units into a tower block in the town centre. About him skydiving, running ultra-marathons and even doing an iron man (whatever that is) - raising thousands of pounds for good causes in the process. Everything screamed "here is a pillar of the community".

Yeah, I thought: just like Peter Smithson. Only far, far worse.

"Have you seen him before?" Keith asked.

"Never. Papers say he lives out Chobham, Virginia Water, way."

"OK. OK, so we have no reason to think we're going to stumble across him anywhere around here. But he's going to be looking for you, if what you say is true Shaun. Luckily you don't leave much of a trace - even when you're not having an out of body experience. Shit! He might think that he hallucinated it all, what with you disappearing at the end there."

He had a point. Nigel had been striding towards me, his gun extended in front of him, when I woke up at my house a few miles away. What had he seen happen next? The police scanner had only said one body, and this was definitely the one I'd been over there in. My ear throbbed as if to prove it. Had I left anything behind?

It's funny but we never even discussed the most obvious

solution to our immediate problem, which was getting out of town. It certainly occurred to me, but I thought of it only to dismiss it straight away. Where else could I go? This was my home and had always been my home. Plus, we were a team and Keith was the one who made the decisions. If he didn't think I needed to leave, I was happy with that. For people like me, reasons are just there to justify doing what we are going to do all along.

"You need to lie low for starters."

That was pretty much how we were living anyway.

"Who can connect me to you Shaun? Think. You need to stay in hiding, but I can still move around. Investigate. Keep watch. Do the shopping."

I couldn't think of anyone who could link Keith and I. He had been coming and going to my house for months, but I wasn't aware that any of the neighbours had acknowledged his presence. Or mine for that matter. We were both beneath most people's notice.

"We need to get rid of everything linking us to Trevor Long. We need to burn the books."

"What about evidence at his house?", I asked.

"Shaun, he never knew who we were. How could he have? Sure, he may have some of the notes, a couple of emails. So what? If he'd worked out who we are don't you think we would know about it by now? And this Darwin? The last place on earth he'll go sniffing around is Long's house. He's on the run too, remember."

Nevertheless, we decided that it would be sensible for me to scout round the house again that night. It was important that I get back on the horse, so to speak, after my surprise materialisation. See what the police had taken. We needed me doing The Thing more than ever if we were going to make it through this period unscathed, Keith said. Most importantly, we needed to track Nigel Darwin and see what he was doing about it - and that was best done from a plane of existence other than this material, knife-, fist- and bullet-vulnerable one.

The Long house was sealed off with tape. Bulky police vans were parked on the driveway and the pavement. Buttery sodium light drained all colours to different shades of grey. I approached the front door and reached out with my hand to the glass where earlier that day I'd caught my first glimpse of Nigel Darwin. It went straight through. I followed my hand into the house.

The hallway had been tidied up. The coats, shoes, letters and wine bottles were all gone. The kitchen too had been cleared and cleaned. The note from Clare was gone from the fridge door. The laptop was missing from the now-righted *Billsta*, but its charger was still plugged into the wall, the cable draped across the tiled floor.

Sheets hung over both doors to the living room. I went in, and the scene was much as it had been when I'd left Nigel there for the first time to follow Longy into the kitchen. A few ornaments and books had been put in plastic bags and left on the *Kivik* sofa. Cases of what I assumed to be forensic equipment sat dormant in the room's corner waiting for morning, when the search for traces of what had happened would begin again.

Had the police cleaned the house? Or was it Nigel? And who had the laptop now? I went to the back door and waved my hand through it, then brought it up to my ear. If that had been bleeding when I woke up... had I...? But there was no sign of blood on the door. No sign of blood anywhere.

It would take me hours to get over to Virginia Water and besides, I wasn't even sure exactly where Darwin lived. I would have to look in on the man I now assumed was hunting me another day. His company's offices were just up the road in Woking though. Evolution IT Solutions, based in Prospect House. I left the crime scene and drifted towards the town centre's periphery where the tower blocks stood.

Oh God. How the hell had this happened? All Keith and I had wanted to do was make a little easy money free-riding on other people's misdemeanours. Nothing really bad, was it? We hadn't even had a chance to spend any of it. Now we were wrapped up with a murderer who had not only seen my face, but who also knew that there was something super-, para- and/or abnormal going on. And we knew he was a man with resources.

The houses on the estate bumped shoulders with one another, resolute in their inward gaze, each imagining itself a proud, isolated fortress in spite of the cars parked outside overlapping the ends of one another's driveways and the hedges encroaching on one another's airspace. It reminded me of the London Underground in rush hour - bodies squeezed together, minds focused on denying it.

The residential overcrowding abruptly gave way to suburban/ light industrial prairie. Bridges and embankments, bollards and traffic islands, resplendent in a rainbow of yellow-grey concrete tones. Patches of dead grass and bramble left to spawn between functional municipal ziggurats. All lit up by sky glow, the re- flection of southern England's night-time activity bouncing back from the permanent layer of colourless flaccid cloud.

Taxis hurtled through me as I walked down the middle of the A324. What did I expect to find at Evolution? Over the central reservation, across the carriageway and through the crash barrier. A screen of leylandii trees hid the A road from the town and muffled its roar. I passed between them.

I had seen Prospect House before. It was a non-descript office building on the edge of Woking's centre, seven or eight stories tall. Red brickwork, a forest of masts and aerials on the roof. A masterpiece of 90s banality, just old enough to not look new anymore, the sort of building that left no impression on a passer-by. Even the name signalled its interchangeability with any of its equally forgettable neighbours.

The lights were on in the reception area, but above that it was dark. I floated upwards and in through a first storey window. I was in a large open-plan room, with lines of desks separated by partitions. LEDs flashed under tables, and the silence was broken only by the never-ending hum of computers doing whatever it is that computers do at night. To my left, a glass wall enclosed a bank of racks housing more flashing lights and bundles of multicoloured cables. Here and in empty commercial premises across the world, the economy's mind was getting its shit in order, before the humans came back in the morning and started interfering again. There's an eerie, frozen quality to office buildings at night: mugs of tea left half-full, women's shoes tucked neatly under desks, scribbled cryptic notes hinting at a universe of missing context. And the machines, still hissing and humming, flashing signals to one another that don't make sense even when the people are there.

I shuddered and floated up to the next floor. More of the same. On the third storey were meeting rooms and offices. The next two floors were empty and silent. The only light was the dull glow of the streetlamps reflected in the windows of the buildings next door, amplified every so often by the searchlight sweep of passing cars with their full beams on. I sank back down to the third floor to take a closer look at the offices. The largest, on a corner facing the panorama of Woking's rooftops, soon revealed itself to belong to Nigel Darwin. On the walls were framed certificates of completion for various feats of sporting endurance and photos of the grinning killer, mud-spattered, one arm around a mate, the other holding aloft a tiny medal. This was him alright. On the desk was another photo, this time of two smiling women - one around my age, the other about eighteen. Both were stunning, transfixing. Looking at them, I almost didn't notice that the only other thing on the desk was a hacksaw.

I stepped through the wall and hovered over the sleeping town. It was raining. The dripping heavens were now a dirty orange-brown above me and the A324 thundered below. It felt like a last moment of freedom and I didn't want it to end.

28

"Wake up!"

I was back home. Keith was nudging me with a hardback book.

"It's a woman."

"Huh?" I was groggy, coming round slowly.

"The body. It's a woman. It's not Trevor Long. It's his wife."

I was wide awake now.

"Look!" Keith held up my laptop to my face. A news story glared out at me: "Woking woman found murdered at home. Police have named the victim as Clare Long, a nurse. The police are keen to speak to her husband, Trevor Long, who has not been seen since the day of his wife's death."

"That's not possible," I said unnecessarily. "She wasn't there when I left. There was a note, saying she'd left him. You were round there - what? - an hour and a half later and the police were already there."

"But where is Long?"

"He was dead, I swear Keith. Half his brains came out."

"So where is he now? And where did his wife come from?"

"She wasn't there..." I replied. "She wasn't there."

"Ok. Ok. Darwin must have put her there" Keith said. "He must have had her already, killed her, taken HIS body and left HER there instead to throw the police off the scent. Or something like that. It's the only thing that makes sense. What we have to ask... is this a good thing for us, or a bad thing?"

I didn't understand.

"Shaun, you have to try to keep up - it's quite important now. We had nothing to do with Clare Long's death, right? And nobody knows Trevor's dead. So for now, nobody is going to be looking for anyone who might have been blackmailing him. And that's a positive.

"Secondly, your disappearing act didn't knock Nigel Darwin off his stride. Even though there was a witness to the murder - a witness who appeared from out of nowhere and then vanished - he didn't panic. Whether he'd already killed Clare or he did it between then and the police turning up, Darwin managed to clean the scene up, swap the bodies over or whatever and get away. So we know we're dealing with one clever, calm bastard. That's a negative. But - and this is the bit that matters Shaun – it shows that you weren't his top priority."

"Either that or he's used to seeing people disappear. Maybe he's schizophrenic. Maybe he knows he hallucinates. Maybe he doesn't believe I was really there."

"Schizos don't get features written about them in Surrey Life, Shaun."

My bloodied ear. When I ran into the back door.

"Keith ... I ... "

"What?"

Keith had sat down on the floor and was intent on the laptop, googling for whatever he could find about the killing.

"Nothing."

Nothing. Best not think about it. I was sure there would be a better time to mention that I had left a big fucking bloodstain at the murder scene which wasn't there later that day. There wasn't.

"This works to our advantage Shaun. Our man Darwin has enough on his plate before he starts worrying about witnesses who are quite likely figments of his imagination. Worst case scenario for him: you're real and you go to the police. The moment he lost sight of you, what's his next best move? Find you before you squeal. But how? Where would he start to look?

We don't leave our footprints all over the internet, and it's not like there have been many stories about you in the local papers over the years.

"Looking at all this from his point of view, why would you not have gone to the police by now? You witnessed a murder. He doesn't know why you were there. The key is to not go to the police, Shaun."

I wasn't sure I followed. Wasn't the rational thing to go to the police?

Keith sighed.

"Shaun... if you want all this..." Keith waved his arms around, indicating the contents of the room. "...all this to end, then yes, the rational thing is to go to the police. Go to the police and explain how you witnessed the murder, and why you happened to be there. What happens if they don't believe you? What happens if they do believe you? Either way, we're out of business. Don't forget - we're criminals too.

"No, the thing to do is to lay low and let this blow over. Every day that passes, you will seem more like a dream to him. Something he saw, but not someone who saw him. Seriously Shaun. We keep our heads down and everything will go back to normal."

It was wishful thinking. Even then I could see that. But I really wanted Keith to be right. I wanted pretending it had never happened to be the right thing to do. The path of least resistance was irresistible, even when it was clearly a slip road onto the hellbound carriageway: no stopping, no reversing, nowhere to turn around.

"Plus," Keith went on, redundantly "We have no idea what went on between those two before now. If the police are going to figure this out, they'll figure it out without you. Why get mixed up in it? We just have to make sure he never finds us, and in a few weeks we can get back to business. We've lost one client, yeah. But he's led us to one bloody big new prospect. A man like that, with plenty to hide... "

Keith was starting to see this as a future opportunity rather than a present crisis.

"The key is to keep Darwin under constant surveillance."

There's always a fucking key, isn't there? In Keith world, there was always one magical thing you have to do to make everything alright; to turn the tables of misfortune around in one sudden move. I've learned to see life as more like a Rubik's Cube than a lock. Every time you think you're getting one part sorted, it turns out you're buggering up the five sides you're not looking at.

"That's the key. Watch him and find out what moves he's making. Firstly, to see if he's looking for you Shaun. Secondly, to find out why he killed the Longs. We probably ought to assume he did both of them. Thirdly, to feel him out as a prospect. Probe his weak spots. Wife and kids. Reputation. All that.

"We have to assume Shaun that the reason you ... err ... manifested yourself yesterday afternoon is the trauma of what you witnessed, right? You've not done it before or since. So there's no reason for you to change your travelling behaviour. Just don't watch anyone else getting murdered."

We both laughed weakly.

"Busy day tomorrow."

29

In fact, the following day was not busy at all. Nor was the next day. Even though Keith was desperate for me to start tracking Nigel Darwin, he was too paranoid to push me hard. And I really didn't want to leave the house, physically or metaphysically. We sat round the police scanner and the laptop, waiting for something to happen.

Inertia is a deeply underestimated force, probably because it's all about stopping things from happening. So when it's at its strongest, nothing happens. We hid for three days before we did anything, rationalising it: we need to see what will happen; most killers are caught within the first few hours; we're safe here if we just keep our heads down; if we were to be caught, it would be best to be caught on home territory. These were just some of the reasons we came up with to avoid admitting that we were too afraid to move. Afraid and lazy. Above all lazy. That path of least resistance again.

All matter is subject to inertia. We just thought we were in a state of rest. Actually we were moving in a straight line.

Nigel Darwin was the last person I wanted to see, ever again. What if it hadn't been the shock that had made me reappear? What if Nigel had a power of his own that cancelled mine out? Maybe he was the Magneto to my Professor X. What would I do if I looked into those eyes again and heard him say "you weren't there a moment ago"?

On the third day:

"You have to go to his house Shaun. You have to go to Virginia Water."

I knew Keith was right.

"We could be sitting here while the net is closing in on us. I've done everything I can."

I wasn't sure precisely what that was. Keith had been as paralysed as I was since he'd finished flushing pages from his notebooks down the toilet.

"Only you can do it Shaun."

Keith was right.

"Can we get a hotel?"

"No. No way. No way are we showing our faces in public anywhere near where he lives."

"But it's such a long way to walk."

I was complaining and looking for excuses, but I knew I was going to do it.

"If I put the back seats down, you can sleep in the car. Chuck some blankets over you, ramp up near to his house."

"I don't like sleeping with anything over my face... "

"Shaun! For fuck's sake! You have to go to his house, unless you want him to come to your house. Do you want to just sit here until he finds us? Don't you want to try and take control of this situation?"

At 3am that night, Keith parked the Micra outside Wentworth golf course. We had lost the excuse of not knowing precisely where Darwin lived a couple of days earlier thanks to Companies House. Directors have to register their home addresses, you see, and they get published on the website. It was a clear, frosty night and even before we got out of the car, we were both shivering.

Keith opened the boot.

"Hop in and make sure you wrap up nice and warm," he said, steam streaming from his mouth and nostrils. "The hot water bottles are under the duvet there somewhere. If it gets too cold, I'll start the engine up for a bit - but remember, I'm the one taking the risks here Shaun. I'm the one sitting in a shitty car in the middle of the night round some of the biggest houses in Surrey listening to a police scanner. With a dead man in the back. I mean a sleeping man ... you know what I mean. The last thing we need is for me to get arrested."

I climbed back into the car, took my shoes off and buried myself in the pile of blankets, cushions and bedspreads we had gathered - making a cocoon that nevertheless kept a clear tunnel open for me to breathe through. I have to breathe proper night air to sleep comfortably. I hate sub-duvet air - it's too hot and it probably doesn't have as much oxygen in as it needs. It was pretty cosy to tell the truth. A bit cramped, but soon I was dozing off.

I found myself outside the car, looking back at myself through the rear windscreen. I walked round to the front. There was Keith, bundled up in a duvet in the driver's seat. He appeared to be writing in one of his notebooks.

The greens of the golf course were white with frost and looked even colder under the occasional lonely floodlight. Clumps of black woodland loomed on either side of the fairway and a sheen of ice was beginning to form on the surface of the water hazards. There was no wind - everything was still. It was like walking through a black and white photograph.

I trudged along the edge of the woods listening out for signs of wildlife, but there was no sound at all. Funny how, even when we don't have to, we tend to stick to paths. Walk through any field or meadow - where you can go any direction you choose - and you'll find yourself drawn towards that worn, well-trodden route that everyone else takes. Like a bit of fluff in a sink circling the plug hole, sooner or later you'll end up going the same way everyone else does.

I knew it was getting even colder but I couldn't feel it. The frost crystals looked burlier, more confident than they had when I'd first set foot on the golf course. In the distance I could see the club house as if through a waterfall, the thickening mist turning straight lines into gentle curves. A fleet of buggies was parked outside, silent, abandoned to the night. I turned my back and glided on away from the lights, feeling profoundly alone.

As I walked, I gazed upwards. The sky was clear and it was almost as if I could really see how far away the stars were, just like that night above the clouds when I fell out of the back of the aeroplane. The moon was huge and shone with a light that was almost unbearable to look at in that deep, still dark.

A fox darted out from a stand of trees and ran in front of me. It stopped, one paw held in the air, looked around and sniffed. Then it ran on, disappearing into another patch of identikit ersatz forest. This evidence of other life broke the spell of solitude I was falling under and reminded me that I was on a mission.

Eventually I reached the other side of the park, which was bounded by thick rhododendrons. I'd memorised the route across to Nigel's house on Google Maps. Ten feet deep into the thicket, I encountered galvanised steel palisade fencing. W-section, seven feet, triple pointed. Frost crystals on the upright stakes twinkled in the filtered moonlight. This was the boundary of Nigel Darwin's domain. I crossed it.

Emerging from more rhododendrons on Nigel's side of the fence, I came out onto a sweeping lawn. Shrouded in thick mist a couple of hundred yards away was the house. Where it was dark the fog looked still, but where security lights cut sharp metallic shafts through it, the mist could be seen as a roiling, swirling - almost living - thing. It looked like the house itself was breathing.

It was huge and hard to take in all at once. Like a medieval cathedral, the house appeared to have had new bits tacked on in the style of the moment as the years went by. A black and white half-timbered Tudor wall would give way to a Disney turret, which in turn abutted a titanic wooden frame filled with glass. As I circled round the house, I saw that a new wing was under construction. A gigantic pit, surrounded by towers of breezeblocks, wheelbarrows full of hardcore, and mud-caked filthy plant. In the pit was a cement mixer, no metal visible on the drum under the crusty layers of sediment. A brown plastic pipe, propped up on a couple of half bricks, bisected the floor of the hole. The earth in one corner of the pit looked unsettled, looser somehow. Had it been dug up here and filled back in? Was this... a grave?

I left the building site and headed back to the vast glass doorway. As I approached, keeping to the darkness, I saw a huddle of human figures, their shadows moving towards me. I froze. Oh God. Have I made another, terrible mistake? I stood rooted to the spot. The figures froze at the same moment. The shadows stopped moving. Nothing moved. I inched closer. The shadows split in two and rotated around the stationary figures. I traced the shadows' angles back and saw two security lights, one filtering through the hanging branches of a willow. The figures were still. As I got closer, I couldn't see faces, but one looked familiar. Something about the way he was standing. Were they... naked? Was that Michaelangelo's David? Fucking statues. Mass-produced, concrete-cast garden centre scale models of the great works of Renaissance sculpture. Christ.

My heart was still fluttering as I came up to the huge sliding doors at the back of the house and peered in. I walked round the house to the front. A gravel driveway snaked up to the Barratt-palladian portico from out of the darkness. In front of the house, a black Range Rover and a silver Porsche squatted, filigrees of ice blossoming across their windscreens. I drifted up, trying to look into the curtained first floor windows. Anything to put off the moment when I had to go inside. The moment I had to see him again.

Oh Shaun. Just do it.

I did.

I threw myself in through an upstairs window. I was in a bedroom. And there he was. In bed asleep, his wife - the older of the two beautiful women from the photograph - beside him. They faced in opposite directions. His mouth was open. Hers was closed. She looked completely peaceful and serene.

Now what?

Search the house.

I went from room to room, looking for anything that pointed to this man being a killer - but I didn't find anything. It was a normal family home. An eff-off massive family home, to be sure, filled with expensive-looking stuff in the middle of a private park in the most expensive part of the county. But a normal family home nonetheless. The house's interior was just as eclectic as its exterior. Scandinavian minimalism - the real thing, not the second-hand Ikea version – cohabited with Edwardian clutter. Chinese styles sat uneasily next to Italianate, Indian, Mesoamericana. There was stuff everywhere. Rich, sumptuous stuff - coffee table books of unmanageable size, ornate cut-glass decanters filled with deep red liquids, potted trees, exercise equipment, bronze horses. I could see how each room and each item, taken by itself, might have been a triumph of design and good taste. But all together, the sensory overload, the sheer "too muchness" of it all was migraine-inducing.

I say it was tasteful. There was one room which stood out for its absolute hideousness. It was decorated in the manner of an Alpine hunting lodge, complete with wall-mounted rifles and a chandelier apparently made out of antlers. What made this room stick in the mind, though, was the taxidermy. A variety of animals, large and small, native and exotic, was scattered around the room, frozen in dramatic poses. A weasel, a red deer, a wolf, a giant tortoise, a heron…the list went on.

Whoever had stuffed these creatures had a bizarre talent for taking something more or less mundane and rendering it terrifying and uncanny. The deer's legs bent as if they had human knees, and a sneer on its papery lips revealed pointed, decidedly non-cervine fangs. The stupidly smiling wolf had a bit of wire sticking out of its backbone and had gone as yellow as a chain smoker's index finger. The weasel was posed leaping into the air, but its black dead eyes seemed to drain all motion and energy out of the scene. One paw was nailed to a tree stump to keep it suspended, mid jump. The display filled me with a profound sense of unease and I was glad to leave it.

I searched the garages (the familiar lines of a classic Jaguar under a plastic dust sheet, a Ducati, a Harley Davidson, a John Deere ride-on lawnmower), the attic (orderly rows of file boxes, hanging rails packed with full length suit carriers, miscellaneous furniture that even the Darwins couldn't find a place for), Nigel's office, hunting for any sign of guns, drugs, bodies or some kind of evidence. Nothing. Back outside the bedroom I stood pondering whether I had made a mistake. Apart from the anomalous hacksaw on his office desk, I had seen nothing weird, nothing sinister at all about this man's existence.

Beep beep. Beep beep.

My heart lurched and my stomach discharged an oily gout of acid.

An alarm.

An alarm clock.

Then it stopped.

I was on the landing. I heard bodies stirring inside the bedroom. Groans. Bodies turning over. Then light shone from the crack under the door.

I was about to poke my face through the door when I thought better of it. Work out your escape route first this time, Shaun. I came back towards the staircase and looked through the wall. The pair of them were sat up in bed. Nigel had kicked the duvet off himself into a pile. He was wearing retro pyjamas - like something from one of the hospital-set Carry On films. He had a pair of glasses perched on the end of his nose, attached to a chain around his neck. The woman, by contrast, was sat neatly. She could have been naked, but for the delicate lace straps across her tiny shoulders. She looked otherworldly, barely constructed from the same material as the gross being beside her. Like a bird, a Catholic madonna or one of those black-haired elves from Lord of the Rings. They were both studying their phones.

Then they were talking.

"How did you sleep love?"

"Lousy, I was awake for hours. I couldn't stop thinking about everything I've got to do today. Sophie will be home from uni tomorrow and I've got the hairdresser's and a training session before I can even start thinking about getting things ready for having everybody over at the weekend."

His wife was Yorkshire too. More so in fact. I've always thought Yorkshire people sounded thick, but this voice was like music.

"I think you slept better than you think you did. I went to the toilet about half two and you were snoring away. I didn't sleep well at all. My brain just wouldn't switch off."

"Oh poor you," Nigel's wife said with a hint of sarcasm, and without looking up from her phone. Her fingernails were painted some shade of pink that looked natural, and evoked a warmth, a heat radiating from somewhere underneath.

"Yeah ... " he continued, now looking at her. "I went to the toilet a few times and you were sound asleep."

"And you kept pulling the duvet off me. That didn't help."

"I've said we can get two separate duvets."

"That's how it starts Nigel. That's the start of the slippery slope towards separate bedrooms. Is that what you want? Just try to be more considerate, will you?"

Nigel sighed resignedly, put his phone down on the bedside table and got up.

Was this really the same man I'd seen on Sunday?

"Put some coffee on if you're going downstairs."

"Mmm-hmmm."

I followed Nigel, but my mind was entirely on his wife. When she glanced at the space I was occupying, the impact of her gaze struck me like the first drop over the top of a rollercoaster. It was as if she was looking right at me, and I knew - I knew - that if she did ever look at me, she would be able to see me in a way that nobody had ever seen me before. None of the girls I'd been infatuated with before - and had eventually come around from - had this inner quality I was seeing. It was a reflection of the quality goods and artefacts her house was filled with. Her eyes were luminous. Her skin glowed. I can't describe her - I'm not an art person. Maybe Trevor Long could have explained what it was. I don't know what beauty is, but I know it when I see it. She was beautiful. I didn't even want to fuck her. Well, I did. But I wanted to do it in a protective, loving, gentle way. I wanted it to be me having breakfast with her. It would have been enough for her just to smile at me.

I know now it was transference, same as it always is. And maybe I knew it then. It had happened to me before and every time it did, I swore that it was for real this time. It never crossed my conscious mind what was happening while it was happening. But that moment - that great "what if?" when all your emotions line up and tell you "we've been talking ... and we've made a decision" that constitutes the love-at-first-sight delusion - well, it feels great. It doesn't have to be real to feel great. Right then, I decided I was in love with Michelle Darwin, the wife of the man who would go on to kill me. Obviously, this was a complication, but the heart wants what it wants doesn't it?

Usually I'm self-aware enough to know when I'm falling in love with my idea of what a person is like, as opposed to the person as such. As Keith always said, to be too conscious is an illness. But what made it different with Michelle? Obviously, she was unattainable but then so was the overwhelming majority of women to me. Clearly, she was beautiful, but that's just a necessary condition not a sufficient one. In the past when I've become fixated on someone, the more time I spent in their company (you know what I mean by now) the sooner the infatuation would wear off. Absence may not make the heart grow fonder, but it does allow it to idealise without the unpleasant intrusions of reality. It wasn't like that with Michelle. The more time I spent around her the more I convinced myself she was like me. And that she would like me.

By 7am, they were downstairs in the cavernous Norman Rockwell kitchen eating breakfast. Nigel was in his dressing gown reading a newspaper while Michelle was wearing a vibrant pink and black lycra gym kit. She looked athletic and voluptuous at the same time, her hair pulled back sharply in a pony tail. It caught the light like the surface of a river in the morning sun. She finished her coffee, took a gilet from a hook on the wall and picked up a pricy-looking holdall.

"So ... I'll be back about two-ish."

"I'm heading to the office later on. Got some meetings. Home about seven, eight."

"Don't forget to drop the Ranger Rover in for its service."

"I won't."

"I know what you're like Nigel. Do I need to text you?"

"I will ... not ... forget," he said, a look of irritated unconcern on his face.

Michelle jog-skipped to the door, blew a kiss in a direction that was unmistakably not towards where Nigel was and left the house. They didn't make eye contact the whole time they were having breakfast. What a woman.

The front door slammed shut. Moments later there came the deep growl of a powerful car engine starting up. Soon, it faded away. Once the sound could no longer be heard Nigel slapped his paper down on the breakfast bar and looked up.

I held my breath. I put my hand through the patio door, just to be sure I could still get away. When I turned back, he was looking my way. He was looking at the space where I was. He was looking straight through it. He couldn't see me.

Nigel puffed his cheeks out as he exhaled deeply and slipped his hands into the pockets of his dressing gown. He wandered down the wide hallway and peered out of the front door. Seeing that Michelle's car was gone, he walked back down towards the kitchen, scuffing his slippered feet on the rug beneath them.

Coming alongside a vast, gilt-framed mirror, he paused and caught sight of his reflection. I was standing in the kitchen as he turned away from me into profile to face the mirror. Nigel Darwin stared at himself in the mirror for five, maybe six seconds.

Then he screamed.

The sound he made was inhuman. It was like the pressure being released from a vast boiler through a tiny hole. It was like a jet engine. It was like the roof being torn off a car. It went on and on. Then it stopped as suddenly as it had begun.

Nigel's eyes were dripping and he was panting like a dog. He wiped his face on his sleeve, composed himself and pulled himself up to his full height - his eyes still fixed upon the reflection.

"This is my world. My world."

He paused, then began to smile.

"This world is mine."

And with that, the spell was broken. Everything went back to normal. He shuffled back along the hallway into the kitchen, right past me. Out of a drawer in the kitchen he took a mobile phone that looked exactly the same as Michelle's. He scanned through its contents, occasionally snorting or rolling his eyes. "Fucking women", he muttered as he tossed the phone back into the drawer, covered it up and pushed it closed. Two hours later, he was driving away in his Range Rover, leaving me standing on his gravelled driveway as the automatic gates swung closed, understanding even less than I had done the night before.

30

When I re-entered my body, I found that it was shaking with cold. Disoriented, I dug my way out from under the blankets. The car's engine was switched off, the windows were steamed up and Keith was nowhere to be seen. Wiping the condensation away from a side window, I saw we were parked outside my house back in Woking.

My joints throbbed. The car stank of sweat and trapped farts. I put my shoes on and pulled a duvet tight around me as I spilled out of the Micra's back door and ran up to my house. The door was locked. I fumbled through my pockets, looking for my keys. My phone was there and my wallet was there, but the keys were not. I banged on the door and waited. The house was silent. I banged again and shouted through the letterbox.

"Keith!"

Silence.

I went back to the car and rummaged through the piled bedding in the back, trying in vain to find the missing keys.

Glancing back at the house, I saw a face peering through the living room curtains. It was Keith. Seeing that I had spotted him, he gestured furiously for me to go round to the back door before slamming the curtains shut theatrically.

"Get inside and keep your head down," hissed Keith as he let me through my own back door and locked it behind me.

"What happened?" I asked.

"What do you mean 'what happened'? I thought you were

going to tell me what happened."

"I mean, how did we get back here?"

"I drove back."

"Why?"

"Shaun, you'd been hours. Hours. And it was freezing. My fingers are barely back to normal now."

Keith held up his hands and flexed his fingers, as if to demonstrate.

"How did you get in here?"

"I took the keys out of your pocket."

The tendons in Keith's neck contracted as he spoke, as if the memory was rekindling a recently extinguished bout of nausea.

"No point in us both getting frostbite, right? I would have woken you up, but I didn't know what you might have been getting into at any given moment, did I?"

"You went through my pockets and left me in the back of the car?"

"For fuck's sake Shaun. Take one for the team, will you? I would have left the engine running and the heater on, but it would have looked weird sat here outside your house. Your neighbours might have thought you were trying to top yourself. And the last thing we need is for anything around here to look out of the ordinary. You'd have done the same if it had been the other way round."

I wasn't sure that I would but ignored the suggestion. This was a revelation of sorts. I knew that I was a heavy sleeper, but I had no idea just how much poking and prodding I could tolerate while my mind was elsewhere. Nor did I know that my body could be moved while I was out of it without me being aware. I'd wasted all that money staying in hotels.

"Plus, I got some food in at last," Keith said, indicating a cluster of plastic bags.

"You went shopping, while I was asleep in the back of the car?"

"Just essentials. Don't be such a knob about it! Jesus ... I was out for ten, fifteen minutes max. We have to eat, don't we? We

Alan Boyce

can't do an online shop when we've got some fucking IT expert who can hack into computers after us, can we? Someone has to keep this show on the road. You do your job and let me do mine. Now, what did you find out?"

I let it go and related the story of the last few hours.

"We can't jump to any conclusions Shaun, but this is all quite promising. He's holding it together and he's getting on with life. Apart from the mad screaming obviously. His missus doesn't seem to suspect anything, which makes him vulnerable to us. Plus, you didn't shit yourself in the back of Mum's car when you saw him. So that's a bonus.

"But we need to keep an eye on him. See what he does when he's on his own - because as you've seen Shaun, what he gets up to by himself is pretty odd. This man is leading a double life, so we have to find out where one life crosses into the other."

And so we began to keep Nigel Darwin under surveillance. At home, at work, spending time with family, friends and acquaintances. While I watched him at home and at Prospect House - places he could be expected to be - Keith followed him on the road. Offence being the best form of defence, we thought that if we knew where he was, we'd have advance warning of any attempts on his part to find out where we were.

That night we went back to the golf course. I still felt lousy from the night before, but we knew that the Darwins would be at home - their daughter was coming home from university - and (although I didn't tell Keith this) I was desperate to see Michelle again.

We parked not long after sunset, this time agreeing that once I was asleep Keith would drive back home and take measures (unspecified) to ensure that I was not left freezing in the car all night again. I soon fell asleep in the back and made my way across the golf course back to the Darwin house. Nobody was home and the Range Rover was missing from the drive. Maybe they weren't back from collecting Sophie? I decided to explore the house - by which I mean "look for photos and other signs of Michelle" - while I waited for them to return.

Her eyes were so bright ... I could see, just from our fleeting encounter that morning that we were kindred spirits. That she would understand all of it when I told her. That she was someone I could make something of my life for.

My reverie was interrupted by a door banging open followed by three raised voices all speaking at once.

"I don't know why you were going so bloody fast Nigel - you know full well there's a speed camera there."

"Well I'm sorry for wanting to spend a few more minutes' quality time with my daughter before her 'other plans' take precedence over seeing ... take those headphones off!"

"Do not raise your voice at us Nigel. You know what I've said about that."

"Mum. MUM! Can I have a lift into Windsor for about 9? And have you got a charger?"

"Welcome home Sophie! 'I've missed you so much Dad' What was college like? 'Oh let me tell you all about it."

"Sarcasm does not help. Why do you think she's like this when you only ever speak to her like that?"

"MUM."

"YES - 9 o'clock. Just put your phone down for a minute and talk to your father, as he's suddenly so keen for a conversation."

"Oh it's all my fault, isn't it..."

I looked down from the top of the staircase at the returning Darwins. That moment encapsulated the three-way relationships I would see unfold over the following days and nights. Michelle and Sophie treated Nigel with distant contempt. Both behaved as though time spent in his presence was a kind of purgatory, to be endured between the real episodes of their lives which were conducted elsewhere.

Michelle and Nigel seemed less like a married couple than a pair of prisoners, shackled to one another and forcibly engaged against their wills on a necessary but unpleasant mission. Nigel took little or no interest in his wife while she was present, poring instead over her iPad and the cloned copy of her phone he kept hidden in a kitchen drawer in the conviction that she was shagging either a builder or someone at her gym. Michelle in turn regarded Nigel with more-or-less naked distaste whenever there were no third parties present.

When entertaining visitors or attending social events, Michelle would do most of the talking for the couple. Nigel would nod along and laugh when prompted, only occasionally breaking away from the groups of couples with other men to engage in generic male banter.

Disappointingly, I never once saw them have sex.

Towards Sophie, Nigel's behaviour swung from sentimentally bewailing how he wanted to be "the best dad in the world" when she was not around, to displaying intensely frustrated resentment at her persistent failure to acknowledge him as such whenever she was. His idea of being a good parent was to buy his daughter things, and then to complain loudly about having to do so and about how unfair Sophie's ingratitude towards him was.

Sophie seemed utterly indifferent to both her parents, spending as little time as possible at home. When she was there, she would be locked in her room, constructing, polishing and adorning her portfolio of carefully-crafted social media profiles. She regarded her father as ridiculous. Her opinion of her mother was slightly better, but she still considered Michelle to be hopelessly lame. My heart broke for Michelle every time she was on the receiving end of Sophie's scorn.

Some of the happiest times of my life were spent hanging around the Darwin house when Nigel was out, because it was then I discovered what it was Michelle and I had in common. When she was alone in the house, Michelle would open up her laptop and watch live webcam feeds of birds' nests - bald eagles in Yellowstone Park, herons in East Anglia, falcons on the top of skyscrapers. It wasn't the birds. It was the watching. The characteristic that defined me, I shared with her. You might call it a hobby or even a quirk, but to me it was a blazing lance through my chest and my ability to concentrate. There could be no doubt, it wasn't the idea of Michelle I was in love with any more.

Nevertheless, neither she nor Sophie seemed aware of Nigel's other life. To me, it seemed as though they sincerely thought of him as a typical specimen of white, Home Counties, middle-aged masculinity: to be tolerated for facilitating their lifestyles, but no more than that.

As an alternative to spending time in the company of his wife and daughter, Nigel preferred to hang around the building site, attempting in vain to win the approval and respect of the various tradesmen employed there.

"Alright lads?" Nigel would shout as he strode over to the slouching gang smoking roll-ups by their van.

The men would nod or grunt in reluctant acknowledgement, stiffening uncomfortably as it became apparent that Nigel was not simply passing by but intended to engage them in conversation, by force if necessary.

The group's leader was a gangling, sunburned giant. Tattoos on his forearms and hands had blurred into nothing more than navy blue smears. The bridge of his nose was practically flat to his cheeks. Along with a beetling, overhanging brow, it gave his face the concave aspect of a congenital syphilitic.

"Alright boss?" he drawled as he sucked on the tiny smouldering stump between his spade-like fingers. He had the deepest voice I'd ever heard, vocal cords ravaged by cheap tobacco and cement dust.

Nigel was a good head shorter than the foreman. He had just come back from a run and was dressed in shorts and a sweat-soaked vest. The contrast between Nigel's pampered, consciously-designed physique and that of the scrawny, knots and ropes form of the builder could not have been sharper. Nigel looked like he had been sculpted out of wax or lard by Tom of Finland. The other looked like he'd been torn off a dead tree.

"Lovely morning for a quick ten kay...personal best, fifty two twenty four..."

"Oh aye...?"

"Two and a half kilometres round the perimeter of the ground. Why bother with the gym when we've got all this here, right?"

"That's right mate…"

"So what's the order of business for today?"

"The what?"

"What are you working on?"

"Pilings need to go in."

"Right, right…of course…"

"Specialist's coming over from Kingston. Reckons he'll get here three-ish."

"Three? Why so late?"

"Dunno boss…I can give him a ring if you want…"

"No, no, it's fine. It's just…what else is he doing? Why can't he get over here at a decent hour? In my line of work, when we agree to take on a customer, it's all about respect. Quality of experience. I want them to say 'Evolution - I want them, not anyone else'. The market wouldn't stand for this…this… disorganisation. You know what I mean? Communication. It's key. It's the most important thing. Three o'clock? Why? It's a fucking joke…"

The foreman shook his head sagely, as if this were simply one of the universe's great ineffable mysteries. A skinny youth on the edge of the group turned his back to Nigel and said something inaudible to his colleagues. They laughed, a harsh, bitter but joyful explosion. The foreman smiled enigmatically like the buddha.

Nigel smiled too, but with no mirth. Tiny movements in his jaw betrayed his grinding teeth. His eyes blazed like cold infernos.

"Well, I'll leave you gentlemen to it. No doubt you've got plenty to be getting on with."

As Nigel stalked away, the foreman called out to him.

"Wife in today?"

Nigel stopped in his tracks and turned his head. His arms hung loosely at his sides, but his fists were clenched and pulsating.

"Sorry?"

"Mrs Darwin. She in today? Me and the lads got some equipment to pick up later. She be in when Tony comes with the pilings?"

"I think so. I'll ask her on my way out. You need anything else?"

"No boss."

"Alright then. We'll catch up later."

The foreman made a sound of disappointed assent, and Nigel turned to walk away. Five steps later, there was another burst of laughter from the group. The foreman was smiling broadly, exposing long wolfish incisors stained yellow and brown. He waved a thumbs-up at Nigel who looked back again at the smirking crew.

So he did have his insecurities after all.

Nigel spent a lot of time at work, but from what I could tell, he didn't do much when he was there. Perhaps he had ascended above and beyond the need to actually involve himself with the business, which was run for him by managers. A day at work for Nigel would involve turning up at Prospect House around 11am, chatting to various colleagues for an hour or so as he would make his way up to his office, checking his emails and reading books on management theory at his desk and sitting largely silently in meetings. Nevertheless, in stark contrast to his home life, Nigel was never treated with anything less than respectful awe by his colleagues. His pronouncements were treated like tablets of stone descended from the heavens. But by 3pm, he was usually on his way out of the office.

It was difficult to really get a sense of who Nigel Darwin was. Being unable to follow him between locations, I had to choose between Nigel at home or Nigel at work - and each seemed to be a different person from one another, let alone from the calm, icy killer I had seen that Sunday afternoon.

It was the same story for Keith. Nigel would usually go to the gym on his way to work and sometimes again on the way home. He lived an apparently routine life, untroubled by cares or passions, undisturbed by traumas or tragedies. If he was a drug trafficker, a hacker or a murderer, it was hard to see when, where or why he was any of those things.

Two weeks later we were no closer to finding any trace of Nigel's secret life. However, I did have a serious chest infection, which prevented me from spending any time sleeping in the back of the car, because Keith had not - as he had insisted he would - remembered to take measures to keep me warm until I woke up each night.

"Are you sure it was him?"

"It was him Keith."

"Don't take this the wrong way ... but are you sure it actually happened?"

"Trevor Long is dead."

"Clare Long is dead. You're the only person saying Trevor Long is dead."

That was true. Surrey Police were conducting a manhunt for the missing teacher, implying that he was the prime suspect insofar as the news wasn't saying anything to the contrary.

"There was the screaming."

"OK, assuming it did all happen like you say it happened. We've been following Darwin now for weeks. His family life is strained. And he is boring. Really boring. Psychopaths (to the best of my knowledge) are not boring, conventional people. And running a drug racket (I would imagine) takes up a reasonable amount of one's time. He's not giving anything away. Maybe he's stopped? Maybe after seeing you he thought better of it all. Because we are just not seeing any signs. Of anything.

"The only way to be certain is to get you in front of him in the flesh and see what he does."

That sounded like a terrible idea.

"But we don't need to be certain, do we? We just need to be careful. We can live with a little uncertainty, can't we? Every day that he doesn't come after us, every day that the police don't find Trevor Long, is another day closer to everyone forgetting all about this. Drug people - they kill each other all the time. Just watch anything on TV, Shaun. It's not a big deal to them. And sure, you're a witness, but you're already in witness protection, aren't you? He has no idea who you are, where you are or if you were even really there."

But the blood.

The blood from my ear on door. The scab had long since crumbled away. But the blood had been wiped clean when I went back to the Long house. Did he have it? Did the police have it? And the laptop was gone too. Could our emails to Longy be traced? Our situation was worse than Keith knew, but even then I couldn't tell him. He was giving me hope that it would blow over and I didn't want to take that away, even when I knew it wouldn't.

"You're probably right Keith."

"Of course I'm right. You'll see I am. We just need not to lose our heads. We've got a business to run after all."

I started coughing and it hurt.

31

It seemed like Keith was right. Things did start to get back to normal. Time passed, my chest got better and money carried on piling up in dead trees across Horsell Common. We kept one eye on Nigel Darwin, who continued to do nothing out of the ordinary, while swivelling the other back to our remaining clients. The Clare Long case faded out of the news. We even started our research again, paying the occasional visit to Schneck meetings. It was like none of it had ever happened.

It was clear that if anybody was going to be able to help us unearth The Thing's secrets, it was Mr Parson. Apparently, his first name was Lionel - although I never heard anyone refer to him as such. By profession, he was an antiquarian book dealer. Yes I know. An antiquarian book dealer who dabbles in the occult. Pretty gothic. As for which was the cause and which the effect, I really couldn't say.

Nevertheless, far from inhabiting an eerie, dark bookshop at the bottom of a gas-lit alleyway - all bullseye glass and the smell of damp - Mr Parson's business operated almost entirely online. This left him optimal free time to pursue his esoteric studies, he explained. It also relieved him of the need to employ staff or to pay rates on any business premises, the local council being on a par with the infernal red-hat *dugpas* of Tibetan *Bon-Po* in his eyes. He would have no truck with either necromancers or Environmental Health Officers.

It was always hard to know how seriously to take Mr Parson.

Projection

I find first impressions very difficult to shake off, and the whole episode of the overrunning model train demonstration and associated dispute over the episcopal parking space gave me the initial sense that he was a fundamentally silly man. Not that there's anything wrong with that of course. Who am I to accuse anyone of wasting their life? No, Mr Parson just seemed like the sort of man who could just as easily have dedicated his life to cataloguing orchids, hoarding late 19th century stamps or any number of other eccentric pursuits that require an encyclopaedic compulsion to accumulate detail.

Keith took a different view. Although he had initially been sceptical, he gradually came to suppose that the ritual we had been excluded from on that first visit bore some greater significance. Although he never said it in as many words, Keith had begun to believe that Mr Parson's erudition had to be underpinned by some sort of practical experience.

Having dismissed the rest of the Schneck as hopeless cases ("lonely, gullible misfits - too weird even for church. They're drawn to one another. I know their type Shaun. I know their type only too well…"), Keith was determined to earn admission to the imagined inner circle of which Mr Parson was a part.

For his part, Mr Parson was delighted to have two new acolytes who appeared to take him seriously, who did not persistently cough, rustle sweet wrappers or knit during his learned addresses and who always paid their £3 dues at the time of the meetings rather than months later. He seemed profoundly relieved when we returned to our first Schneck meeting since the murder and subsequent time off the grid.

"Messrs Smith and Jones! What a pleasure it is to see you again! I feared we had lost you. Our path is not for everyone, as you well know. But the Aten be praised you have returned! That will be £3 each please."

Mr Parson was beaming as he strode towards us as the group broke up in the aftermath of a session entitled "Mystery cults of the Lydians". This had turned out to be a slide show of Anne and her sister's recent holiday in Rhodes.

"I apologise for …errrmmm…that, my dear fellows. Anne is… well, Anne is a friend of my mother's, and …errrrmmmm…"

"Mr Parson," Keith interrupted. "While Shaun and I enjoy these Schneck meetings…"

"SNHEC."

"Um, yes. While we enjoy the SNHEC meetings, I think it must be clear to you by now that Shaun and I are - how shall I put it? - eager and ready for more."

"More?"

"Yes more. Initiation."

Mr Parson gasped sharply. His eyes bulged and he glanced around in an overly conspicuous manner. Only Sandra remained in the hall, stacking the chairs and pushing them to the side of the room.

"You wish to be initiated into the deeper mysteries?"

"Yes please."

"Is this also your sincere desire, Mr Jones?"

I nodded.

A look of innocent delight spread across the old man's pale face. His lips trembled and a damp sheen spread across his forehead.

"Well this is marvellous! Marvellous!"

Tears seemed to be welling up in the corners of his powdery eyes.

"We must begin at once! Tomorrow, I mean. Come round to my house at seven and we can plan out your apprenticeship!"

The next day, Keith and I found ourselves outside Mr Parson's 18th century farm cottage. The wrought-iron gate creaked violently as I opened it. Seconds later, our anticipated mentor's alarmed face popped up in one of the mullioned window panes. Tapping forcefully on the glass, he pantomimed that we should back up and meet him around the corner, and that we should do so quietly.

"What was all that about?" Keith asked, as we stood back in the street, a little way away from the cottage behind a Amazonian-scaled privet hedge. I shook my head.

Presently, a recomposed Mr Parson joined us.

"Gentlemen! My sincere apologies. I was so overcome when we spoke yesterday that it quite slipped my mind that Mrs Parson hosts her... errm... Pilates and Prosecco group at home on a Wednesday evening. The...errm...spectacle would be quite detrimental to our embarking on the Great Work, I fear. Perhaps instead, we could have a preliminary discussion of sorts, at The... um... 'White Horse' hostelry, there?"

Mr Parson indicated the village pub opposite limply.

The White Horse could barely be discerned under a flowing blanket of clematis, ivy and other climbing plants. It was a squat toast-brown brick building of similar vintage to the Parson cottage, with a roof that could just as easily have been thatch as a crazy jumble of tiny, misshapen slates - from ground-level it was hard to tell. Tiny dark windows peeped out from the rampant vegetation like frogs' eyes, bordered by shutters in Farrow and Ball pastel tones. A rose border in full bloom enclosed the beer garden - a scattering of picnic tables, occupied by ruddy faced and trousered country squires smoking cigars and guffawing ostentatiously, and city emigrés in expensive shorts, sandals and polo shirts or floral maxi dresses.

We found an empty table and sat down. Keith and Mr Parson looked expectantly at one another. Silence descended. Looks continued to be exchanged. The silence was becoming awkward.

"Shall I get us some drinks?" I finally said.

"Thank you, thank you my dear boy. I...errr...appear to have left my wallet at home. Dubonnet with a twist, if I may."

"I'll come and help you with the drinks," said Keith rising from his seat.

The bar was empty.

"Let me do the talking Shaun," Keith muttered as the barman pulled our pints. "Don't give anything away until we know what Parson is really all about."

Back at the table, Mr Parson had placed a cardboard folder on the table between us.

"Gentlemen, I have been waiting for this moment. I knew from the moment I set eyes on you that you were different. The SNHEC... I mean, they are enthusiastic...most of them are perfectly decent people...but you understand, they represent the exoteric aspect of our discipline."

"And you represent the esoteric aspect?"

"Precisely, Mr Smith. You have hit it on the head. We organise these sessions to attract the true seekers after holy wisdom - after *hagia sophia* herself. I am the sentinel, charged with separating the wheat from the chaff. The sheep from the goats. Those with real potential from...people like that appalling cat woman you saw."

"And so you are part of another, secret group of acolytes?"

"Yes. Well...errmmm...yes. Sort of. It's just me at the moment. But I knew! I knew as soon as you walked in the door of that church hall. I had a sense...a premonition. Card fifteen of the Major Arcana. Practically there before my very eyes. I knew, Mr Smith, that you and your friend here were different. That for all our apparent differences, we are very alike."

Mr Parson sipped his fortified wine and reverently opened the folder in front of him. With both hands, he presented me with what appeared to be a car sticker. I took it and turned it over. It was a rainbow flag.

"By these signs, you will know them... This shall be our signal - the sevenfold light of Ahura Mazda, representing the seven principles of the soul from *atma* down to the *sthula sharira*. The one light, divided but indivisible. Stick that in your car window, and our brethren will recognise us!"

Keith and I looked at each other.

"That's not what this means, Mr Parson."

"Well, I know it's a heterodox interpretation, syncretic if you must, but for monists like ourselves, what better metaphor for the fundamental unity of the universe is there than light? Besides, synchronicity was clearly at work - I found a pile of these in my son's old bedroom the very night you first appeared at the SNHEC."

"Mr Parson," Keith seemed genuinely agitated. "This symbol...ummm...it means something completely different. It's nothing to do with light."

The old man was becoming indignant. This was clearly not how he had envisaged the first gift bestowed upon his apprentices to be received.

"Oh? And what, may I ask, does it mean?"

"It's...errr...I mean..."

"It's a gay pride flag Mr Parson," I interrupted.

"What?!"

"Gay pride. You know. It's the symbol for the LGBT movement."

"The Lymington Grand Baphomet of Thelema?"

"Ummm...no. Not that. It stands for lesbian, gay, bisexual..."

"What! When did this happen?!"

"Errr...."

"The 60s was it Shaun?" Keith suggested.

"The 60s. Maybe the 70s," I added.

"Is that...well-known?"

"Fairly well-known," Keith mumbled.

"It's only really become mainstream quite recently," I offered, apologetically.

"Good heavens. I had no idea."

The awkward silence returned. Mr Parson studied the glass in his right hand. I glanced sidelong at Keith, who was staring in turn our presumptive mentor.

"This is just like when the Nazis ruined swastikas," he muttered, shaking his head in disbelief. "It should go the other way round, you know? The proper one. Can I have that back please?"

We were all quite keen to move the conservation on to other matters after this uncomfortable misunderstanding.

"So...Mr Parson, Shaun and I are very keen to learn everything you can teach us. We are particularly interested in... astral travel."

"Ah yes. Well, you'll find that is well covered on the reading list in your folder. If you have any trouble getting hold of anything on there, just drop me a line. It's all fairly accessible. The library should be able to get hold of it all for you. A nice solid grounding in the hidden sciences. Work your way through all that, then we can meet up again to go through the next books to study..."

"Shaun and I are more interested in the...ah...practical side of things."

"Practical?"

"Yes. You know. More doing it than reading about it."

"Doing it?"

"Yes. Travelling. Astrally. And that."

"Gentlemen, gentlemen," Mr Parson closed his eyes and spread out his palms condescendingly. "Years - nay, decades, possibly even lifetimes of tireless study must precede what you so casually call 'doing it'. Even for something as mundane as the astral plane, one does not simply open a door and off the linga sharira flies! And even if it was that simple - the perils! The inhabitants of those parts...higher and lower beings, beyond the comprehension of the human mind. No, no, no Mr Smith. You must prepare your mind, your soul. You can't just wander out there into the *pleroma*. Even I would hardly dare..."

"So have you done it then?"

"Studied, yes. For years."

"No, I mean have you travelled to the astral plane?"

"Well ... I...not as such. But there are very few people in the south east who know more about it than I do."

"Do you know anyone who has?"

"Really Mr Smith, I don't tend to associate with THOSE sorts of people...Knowledge, gentlemen, is the true reward. To know, to understand - what does 'going to the astral plane' mean when you compare it to the glory of understanding it? Of course, there are plenty of people who claim to have taken the risks - recklessly, I hasten to add...vulgar sorcerers..."

"Is there anybody we could speak to?"

"Well, there is one chap I came across in the course of my

work. But I really don't think he would be good for you. Oily fellow. Most mediums are....well, let's just say that polite society is forced to tolerate them for their utility. I could invite him to a SNHEC meeting...? But gentlemen, the reading list! Don't be seduced by the left-hand path - the books! The books have everything you need!

"We would very much like to meet...?"

"Dr Claudius, he calls himself - although I doubt very much that is his real name. So be it," Mr Parson threw up his hands. "But this is just to show you the folly of...people like him."

"Yes, we will get on with the reading in the mean-time Mr Parson."

"You will?"

"Yes, of course. Won't we Shaun?"

I agreed.

"And, please, forget that I ever mentioned Lymington."

32

Two days later, Mr Parson phoned Keith to let him know that Dr Claudius would be coming to the next SNHEC meeting the following week.

"I continue to advise against this, gentlemen. As seekers after truth, what have we to learn from a man like this? He is not without talent - far from it - but his gifts are so entangled with his charlatanry that I doubt even he knows where one ends and the other begins. The books, Mr Smith. I implore you, let them be your teachers! If we must bring Dr Claudius to the SNHEC, remember what he is! A corrupted soul, who has squandered what has been given to him for base motivations - who aspires to nothing greater than what this world has to offer!"

"Thank you, we understand. We will be on our guard," said Keith. "We want only to see what snares lie in wait to entrap the unwary and the hasty."

"Oh my dear fellow! You don't know what it means to hear you say that! My greatest fear in taking on apprentices is that the efforts and studies required to advance towards enlightened adepthood tempt you into taking shortcuts..."

Like I said, things had got back to normal, for a little while anyway. We had been making regular trips to the library to borrow the books Mr Parson had recommended to us, and it was pleasant to see my old colleagues again. It helped me to put the murder and its potential aftermath out of my mind.

Keith had cheered right up. After the first flush of paranoia had drained away, he seemed to consider the Nigel Darwin problem adequately dealt with. He became more and more confident pretty much from that first morning when he had to let me back into the house. The storm had passed over our heads and it was in everyone's best interests to just get on with their lives, Keith said. He threw himself back into the business and even revived the Aldous Fuxley persona, much to the dismay of the online metal community.

I wasn't so convinced that everything was alright. Keith, after all, remained unknown to Nigel Darwin. On top of that, Keith had not left a bloody earprint at the scene of a murder. He didn't have quite as much at stake as me. I still had no idea why I had materialised at that terrible moment and how I dematerialised again just before I was shot. I like to know where I stand and up until then I knew where I stood with The Thing. I knew the rules or at least enough of them to play the game.

But still, if Keith was calm, I was prepared to go along with it. That's probably my biggest flaw: I don't trust my own instincts so I follow other people's assessments and decisions. And look where that got me, although having said that the one decision I made all by myself (to tell Keith about The Thing) was the one that started this fatal Indiana Jones giant boulder rolling. I was pissed at the time though, wasn't I? I'm not sure I can really be held fully responsible.

To tell the truth, if Keith hadn't been going on about it, I would happily have jacked the business in about this time. I used to enjoy The Thing for where it led me, peering into people's lives, seeing things that weren't to be seen. I know that I wasted the chances life had given me and I was ashamed of all the spying and the intrusion. The wanking too. The business had given me a purpose, but ... I don't know ... it kind of takes the fun and the possibilities out of astral travel when it ends up as your job. Occasionally, without telling Keith, I'd just go for a wander around town. Look in on old haunts, look up a few old faces. Watching them would take my mind off the situation. The situation that was always there, lurking in the background.

And of course, it all came back up to the surface not long after the Schneck meeting.

Keith and I pulled up outside the village hall to see a vast, jet black Range Rover occupying the bishop's parking space. The engine was still running, and nothing could be seen through its tinted windows. As Keith parked the Micra, the front passenger door of the colossal SUV opened and a tall, slim man in a brown or plum-coloured suit stepped out. He had grey hair down to his shoulders and held an umbrella in one black-gloved hand. Closing the door gently, the man walked towards the hall's entrance, only to be summoned back to the Range Rover by a banging from inside on the window. He turned back, clutching his umbrella in front of him like a talisman as the window slid down. Words were exchanged between the man and whoever was in the driver's seat. The man took another step towards the car with obvious reluctance and ducked his head down to look in through the open window. His body lurched as something within grabbed him and pulled him forward - then he jerked back shakily, as whatever it was released him. Illuminated by the instrument panel in the dark interior of the Range Rover, I could see the white top of a shaven head with black eye sockets shadowed beneath and four gigantic fingers curled over the window frame. The vision receded into the darkness within and the window slid shut once more. The Range Rover pulled away out of the car park leaving the man standing by himself.

The man smoothed down his suit jacket and shook his hair back. He had a handsome, tanned and ageless face - he could have been thirty or he could have been sixty. He strode to the door and disappeared inside.

"That must be Dr Claudius," said Keith.

"I wonder what that business through the window just now was."

"Ah, you know what Uber drivers can be like. Come on, let's go in."

The meeting hall was packed by Schneck standards. There must have been almost twenty people in there before we arrived, more than double the usual attendance. Mr Parson was speaking confidentially to Dr Claudius as we came in. His expression of harassed concern contrasted with the look of indulgent amusement on the other man's face. As we came in Mr Parson spotted Keith and gave a little nod of greeting. The long-haired man looked round and sized us up with glittering blue eyes. His smile widened slightly and I felt myself unable to break his gaze. Fortunately, at that moment Sandra jostled him, passing through with a tray of mugs. As Mr Parson continued to address the visitor, Dr Claudius switched his attention to Sandra, watching her as she retreated into the kitchen.

We took seats at the back as the meeting was brought to order.

"Well…" began Mr Parson, his manifest distaste very obviously souring any attempt to welcome either the guest speaker or the expanded audience. "We shall begin this evening without our usual…err…formalities, there being so many… um…new faces here…"

Keith nudged me and whispered: "Be thinking about how we're going to catch Claudius for a private chat without Parson noticing. We don't want to make the old bugger cry."

"Ladies and gentlemen, allow me to hand you over to Dr Claudius."

A polite ripple of applause breathed through the audience.

"Thank you!" Dr Claudius boomed in a deep, rich voice that might have had a hint of something foreign about it or may not. It may just have been theatrical.

"Thank you indeed, Mr Chairman. Perhaps before I begin I may request a small indulgence? My spiritual helpers are more amenable to the desires of the living under lighting conditions that resemble the gloom of their dwelling places. May I therefore ask that we turn out the lights and proceed…"

He reached into his inside jacket pocket and drew out a long, black candle. The audience inhaled simultaneously.

"By candlelight!"

"Yes. Yes, that would be in order although I must point out

that the emergency lighting will have to remain illuminated. For safety reasons. Fire exits. Should there be an emergency, you understand. Sandra? Sandra, would you mind?"

Sandra got up from her seat and turned out the fluorescent tubes, one by one.

"Kitchen as well, Mr Parson?"

"Kitchen as well, doctor?"

"Erm…yes please. And could someone close that door?"

Finally, the room was dark - except for the eerie green glow cast by the fire exit sign. Dr Claudius' voice broke the silence.

"Spirits - hear me. It is I, Claudius. Hear my voice. I summon you here. I call upon you. I…yes."

With that final word, the candle sprung into life. Dr Claudius was leaning forwards, holding it under his chin so that his long hair hung down around the lonely flame, giving the impression that the weak light it emitted was swirling in a constant dance of rays and shadows.

Mr Parson sneezed loudly, but nobody noticed.

"Pardon me."

The room was rapt. Even I found myself entranced by this performance.

"My name is Dr Claudius and I have travelled to many far-off places."

He was walking amongst the audience now.

"I have seen and learned much. I have bound the inhabitants of other realms who are now sworn to do my bidding. When I focus my energies - my will and my imagination - you will see that I speak the truth."

Dr Claudius held the candle out at arm's length in both hands. The flame crackled and began to grow taller. Slowly, steadily, it became longer, until it reached a height of some eight inches. Then it split into two flames, which leaned away from one another, coming to a halt in a V-shape, each at 45 degrees from the vertical.

The light went out.

"It has begun. They are with us."

Dr Claudius relit the candle. It behaved like a normal candle once again.

"You."

Dr Claudius handed the candle to the person he was standing in front of. As Dr Claudius faded into darkness, the face of creepy Ethan was illuminated.

"There is someone who is very important to you, isn't there? A parent? Yes. It's your...your mother, isn't it? She's worried about you. Worried about what you're doing with your life."

Keith nudged me again.

"Fucking hell. I didn't realise this was what we were in for. We could have seen this at psychic night down Shunters," he whispered.

"But she shouldn't be worried about you Ethan. She is in terrible danger herself. She's been unwell, hasn't she? Tired all the time? Nausea?"

"Yes!" said Ethan nervously.

"Jaundice? She's jaundiced, isn't she? She's not just run down. She's been slurring her speech the last few days hasn't she? More than usual. More than ever before. Ethan, you have to get her to a hospital. Your mother - she drinks, doesn't she Ethan?"

Ethan was sobbing spasmodically now.

"You know what it is, don't you? The spirits are telling me Ethan. It's not too late. You have to save her from herself. Go to her Ethan. Go now."

Dr Claudius took the candle back and we heard a harsh scrape as Ethan launched himself out of his chair. The door swung open and light flooded in from the corridor as Ethan ran out into the night.

Pushing the door shut again, Dr Claudius resumed his wandering through the audience.

"Everyone here knows his mother's an alcoholic," Keith hissed to me. "We should have listened to Parson."

"You."

The candle changed hands again, and Sandra's face emerged from the darkness.

"You are known to the spirits Sandra. They recognise you. They remember you. Do you remember them? From when you were a child?"

Sandra gasped.

"Things moved around your home without explanation, didn't they Sandra? Shoes went missing. Plates were smashed on the floor in the morning. You heard scratching in the walls every night, didn't you?"

Sandra nodded, her eyes wide with a mixture of wonder and fear.

"Your parents and your sister thought you were making it up. Thought you were playing tricks. You never told anyone what you saw, did you? You never told anyone about Old Jeffrey?"

Sandra let out a quiet whimper.

"But he's here now and he says it's all in the past. He wishes you well and he's sorry for frightening you. He's leaving us now, Sandra. I think he's finally at peace."

"Wait...!"

"He's gone Sandra. He was smiling as he faded away. The spirits know all, ladies and gentlemen." Dr Claudius took the candle back from Sandra and began to walk again, this time towards the back of the room where Keith and I were sat. We both shrank down into our seats.

"The spirits know and see all. Nothing can be hidden from them, and there is somebody here tonight who is hiding something. Hiding a terrible secret."

Oh fuck. I tried to sink my head into my jacket collar. Not me. Please not me.

"Somebody here wants to hide the truth, but the truth doesn't want to be hidden. The truth wants to be shouted from the rooftops."

Dr Claudius came closer, until he was stood beside me.

"Somebody here knows a terrible truth but won't face up to it. They want to pretend it never happened and just carry on like before."

Oh God. Dr Claudius whirled round to face back towards

the front of the hall.

"You have been right all along Mr Parson. All your suspicions were correct. Right now, in your home, in your bed, your wife is fucking the fish man."

The audience burst out in laughter. Dr Claudius blew the candle out, switched the lights on and opened the door to the corridor.

"Ladies and gentlemen, it has been a pleasure," he said. And he turned and walked out.

33

"Did you see his face?" Keith smirked as I set two pints down on the table. "I thought he was having a stroke!"

We had retired to the village pub when the Schneck meeting broke up in disorderly fashion. Sandra had got up and followed Dr Claudius out of the hall as soon as the lights had come on. Mr Parson had sat at the front, seemingly paralysed since Dr Claudius' revelation. The casual visitors had pulled their coats on and left in good cheer, while the Schneck regulars had hung around with concern until it became apparent that Mr Parson was not going to say or do anything. Then gradually they too drifted away. Keith and I tried to leave as inconspicuously as possible, attaching ourselves to the departing group of Anne and two of her friends, whom we had not seen before.

"Do you think he'll speak to us again?" I wondered.

"Ha! I doubt he'll ever speak again, full stop!" Keith snapped. "What a clusterfuck. In bed with the fish man though, eh? I wonder if it's true."

"Of course it's true," a familiar woman's voice said. We both looked round and there was Sandra. With her was Dr Claudius.

"May we join you?" he asked.

Keith indicated with his hand that they were welcome to do so.

"How did you do it then?" he asked.

"Do what?" Dr Claudius's accent had changed slightly. The theatrical bombast had been replaced by a harshly nasal, estuarine tone.

"Ethan's mum. Obvious. Everyone knows about her. But what about this poltergeist story? Is Sandra in on it?"

Keith addressed his questions to Dr Claudius, ignoring Sandra herself.

"The spirits, innit?" Dr Claudius shrugged.

"I've never told anyone about Old Jeffrey," Sandra said, a look of the utmost seriousness on her face. "The plates, the shoes and all that. We all saw that. Me whole family. My Dad's a Methodist minister. Didn't want to believe there was anything going on. I'd see him at night, at the end of my bed. An old man with long white hair. He'd talk to me. Said his name was Jeffrey. I never said a word. No one would have believed me."

She turned to gaze at Dr Claudius, who was blowing his nose.

"He knew. How could he have? I never told anyone. I haven't thought about Old Jeffrey for twenty five years or more. One day, it all just stopped."

"What happened?" I asked.

"My Dad got a new job in Kidderminster and we moved house."

Keith snorted.

"You can make fun Keith, but I know you two take this seriously. Mr Parson told me all about your visit," Sandra snapped back.

"Surprised you didn't bump into the fish man," Dr Claudius said, and we all laughed - happy to find common ground at Mr Parson's expense.

We stayed and chatted for half an hour or so, but it was soon very clear that Sandra wanted rid of us. She stared at Dr Claudius continually and derailed all attempts to change the topic of conversation to anything not concerning the mysterious psychic. Naturally, Keith was deeply put out at not being able to pursue his own agenda and eventually declared that we were leaving.

As we got up to leave, Dr Claudius stood and reached out to

shake my hand.

"Let's keep in touch," he said, smiling a lop-sided smile that revealed one large, yellow canine tooth.

I nodded. As he withdrew, I felt a small card tucked into the palm of my hand. It read simply: "Claudius" and a mobile phone number. I put the card into my pocket and nodded again, but Dr Claudius was already engrossed in intimate discussions with Sandra.

"He was interesting," I said as we drove home in silence.

"Hmmm…," Keith replied, his eyes fixed on the road ahead.

34

Everything kicked off not long after that meeting. It was a Friday and I had been checking up on Peter Smithson's monthly payment. We had him coming over to Woking to make the drops now, because ever since I caught that chest infection I wasn't keen on sleeping in the car unless it was absolutely necessary. Everything had gone smoothly: the money had been deposited (Ikea bag as usual) and Smithson had buggered off home. I headed back to my body and sat up in my bedroom. I pulled back the curtains and looked down the street. I sniffed my armpit (by default, the right one - it always smells worse than the left one) and decided to change into a fresh t-shirt. I threw the one I was wearing onto the floor, picked another out of the wardrobe and put it on.

Nowhere could have been more familiar to me than that room. The bedroom I'd had ever since I was a little kid. The furniture and the decor had changed over the preceding decades, but I knew every inch of that room. I had no idea that this was the last time I would ever be there.

Down the stairs I trotted, calling to Keith.

"You're good to go."

No reply.

I put my slippers on at the bottom of the stairs and walked into the living room.

And there he was. Sat in my Dad's old chair. Smiling at me.

"Shaun ... "

It was Nigel Darwin.

"We need to talk."

He was holding something yellow and black in his right hand. A red LED flashed twice on it and there was a whooshing sound. Something pricked me hard in the chest.

And then I was in excruciating pain.

It was like every nerve in my body had exploded at the same time. Like fireworks. Excruciating is the only word for it. All the air seemed to have been sucked out of my lungs and I thought my heart was going to claw its way out of my chest. I was trying to move, but my muscles didn't respond to anything my brain was telling them. My body had gone completely limp.

Time had slowed to a crawl. I could see the wires running from Nigel's hand to my chest. I knew I'd been tasered. I wondered where Keith was. I could feel myself drop to my knees. "I'm going to hit my head on the fireplace when I keel over", I thought - a spectator of what was happening to my body.

I tipped over forwards. I hit my head on the fireplace. And everything went black.

DEATH I

35

You dream when you're asleep. You might not remember any of it once you're awake, but your brain has been dreaming. It can't help it. That's just what brains do when they're left unattended.

But you don't dream when you've been knocked unconscious. One minute you're in this place, there's a thump and then you're somewhere else at some other point in time.

Where I was, was inside a wooden box. What time it was, I had no idea.

The box was human-shaped. My elbows were pressed against my sides, my forearms crossed over my chest. I lifted my right hand and touched the rough surface of the crate, a couple of inches above my face. For the sake of being thorough, I stretched my feet out. Yep. I was boxed in down there too.

All I could see was a tiny pinprick of light. I moved my fingers towards it and found that there was a plastic straw stuck through the ceiling of what was clearly my coffin. So when Nigel Darwin had said "we need to talk", it seemed that he had actually meant "I am going to bury you alive".

Bury you alive.

I started to breath faster. Cold beads of sweat burst out of the pores on my forehead. I felt them run down my temples and into my ears.

Buried alive.

I began to struggle. I tried to kick and I tried to push at

the ceiling, but I was squashed in too tightly to get any sort of power behind my efforts. I banged my head back and forth on the ceiling and the floor. The deadened thump of my blows on the wood let me know that the box was embedded in some kind of absorbent material. Like soil. With that thought, I noticed the dampness of the air, the hiss-hum in my ears, the sense of weight bearing down upon me from above.

I screamed for help.

And the pinprick of light went out. Tiny granules fell onto my face from the spot where it had been.

My hands scrambled frantically for the straw. It had gone. And now the darkness was total. I didn't know if my eyes were open or closed, but from hitting my head, from hyperventilating or maybe from panicking, a pinkish cloud was seeping into my field of vision, starting in the outside corners of me eyes and spreading. I was going cold, but cold from the inside out. When I said it was dark on the golf course, I hadn't known what darkness could really be like.

The light had gone. And that meant I was sealed in. Airtight. Probably. That's what I thought at the time anyway. I tried to slow my breathing down, but I couldn't. I arched my back and stubbed my penis on the roof. I hadn't realised until that moment that I had an erection.

I screamed one more time.

There was no response. Once I stopped screaming, all I could hear was my heart pounding in my chest and my rapidly accelerating breath.

What could I do? Think Shaun.

I can't think. I'm about to suffocate. I'm about to die.

Think. Can I kick the bottom out of the coffin?

You're buried alive. Buried. Underground.

Can I ...

Can I fall asleep, let my spirit out and see where I am?

Do you feel like you can fall asleep? Do you feel calm?

No, I don't. I know I have to stop panicking, but I can't. I'm panicking. Everything is getting faster. I'm crying. My breathing has turned into gasping. I'm letting out a little whimper every time I exhale.

I don't want to die.

Do I?

No, but I think I am going to and there's nothing I can do about it.

My cock is straining against my trousers. It's the only part of me that hasn't given up on getting out.

There was a thud, a groan and then a creaking, splintering sound. Light flooded into my coffin from the right-hand side. I gasped for breath, instinctively moving my left hand to try and conceal my premature antemortem stiffy from whoever was exhuming me.

"Surprise!"

Nigel Darwin flung the lid back and it crashed to the floor.

"Now don't do anything silly. Don't make me taser you again. Or make me hit you with this," he said, tapping my groin-protecting left hand with a cold metal crowbar.

I was not about to do either of those things.

"Get up. Get up Mr Strong. I have brought you back from the dead for a reason."

I sat up. The coffin was a human-shaped packing crate, which had been dropped into an enormous wooden trough, full of damp earth. It looked like one of the flower planters the council installs in the middle of Woking's pedestrianised town centre. Glancing around, I saw that I was in some kind of empty office building. The great open space was broken up only by white-painted pillars and the occasional bundle of cables dangling through holes in the ceiling where tiles were missing. Rows of windows occupied the two longer sides of the room. It was dark outside. Of the others, one was a featureless white wall - the fourth was a featureless white wall with a light wooden door and two fire exit signs pointing towards it.

There was a chest freezer some twenty feet away from the trough I was sitting in. A cable ran from its base up through the ceiling. Nigel Darwin was leaning on the side of my planter. I shuffled backwards to move as far away from him as I could.

"Shaun. Don't be alarmed. I'm not going to hurt you. Unless you make me. You are going to help me - help me to ... ah ha ha ha ... let's say, fulfil my destiny."

He was smiling. It was a kind, sincere smile. His eyes were wide open, his eyebrows raised. His body language was completely relaxed. He was wearing a navy blue tank top over a checked shirt. Only the leather gloves, the crowbar in one hand and the taser in the other belied his friendly demeanour.

There was another person in the room. In the far corner, a figure was slumped on the floor. It was attached by the wrists to a ring on the wall.

The figure rolled over. It was Mr Parson. He seemed to be unconscious.

"Come on, hop out. How'd you like the Edgar Allen Poe there?"

Nigel casually indicated the partially-interred box with a wave of the crowbar.

"Bit of drama, you know? Helps to get the vibe right. Sets the mooood."

He widened his eyes and curled his mouth into an o-shape as he drew out the last word into child's parody of a cow.

"Obviously, you already know Mr Parson over there. Mr Parson has been telling me all about you since we met earlier today. You and I have history, as I'm sure you remember."

The smile was no longer there. The light in the eyes had gone out. I could not read any motive in that face, but it made me afraid.

He turned his back and walked slowly towards the freezer.

"You look different with your clothes on for a start!"

He laughed hard, explosively, and when he turned round that look of a dead shark had gone, replaced by a friendly human face once more.

I hadn't realised that I'd been naked when Nigel saw me, but then I suppose there was no reason to believe that my clothes were capable of astral travel.

At that moment, the room's one door opened and two figures entered. To my dismay, I immediately recognised the one in front as Keith. The one behind was pushing him forward, with a hand on Keith's shoulder the size of bear's paw. He towered over Keith by more than a foot, not only in height but also in breadth. As the man came closer, I saw tiny black eyes, cheekbones like knives and a broad snout-like nose. His skin was white to the point of being luminous and a light mist seemed to swirl around his roughly shaven temples. He was wearing a black polo neck shirt with a leather jacket over the top. He looked as though he had been designed specifically for the task of destroying other human bodies.

"Allow me to introduce my head of information security and chief negotiator!" Nigel declared cheerfully. "This is Yevgeny. Yevgeny Kuss...net... how do you say it?"

"Kuznetsov."

Yevgeny's voice was deeper than any I had ever heard. It sounded like the earth's tectonic plates grinding against one another. He led Keith to a nearby office chair and directed him to sit in it with an extended finger and an exhalation of breath.

"I'm interested to know... " Nigel exhaled heavily, paused, and waved his hands in little circles in the air. "... what happened, I suppose. In your words. Keith's already filled me in on the need-to-know but ... I think ... I think I'd like to hear your perspective, Shaun."

Nigel stood up, put down the crowbar and the taser, folded his arms and raised his eyebrows in anticipation.

"Let's have it. Of all the gin joints in all the world Shaun... How did you and I end up here?"

I looked at Keith. He shrugged.

"Go on Shaun. He knows everything. Just... just answer his questions."

"Yes. Answer the questions. I think you can probably guess which parts I'm particularly keen to hear about. And do get out of the box, otherwise you won't have anywhere to sit. Actually, I'll get you some furniture."

Nigel took a mobile phone from out of his pocket, removed his gloves and started writing a note on it.

"You're going to be here for a while and I don't want you to be uncomfortable. Although you'll have to do without anything tonight I'm afraid. The trouble with this stuff is ... err... ah ha ha... I can't exactly get the office staff to do it for me. Keeping hostages is harder work than I thought. Ah ha ha ha ha! Do you like birds?"

"Umm ... yes," I said, not quite sure what that had to do with the line of questioning I was being subjected to - but not wanting to piss Nigel off.

"Great."

He started typing on his phone again. When he had finished, he looked up and leaned back on his makeshift seat.

"Come on then... I'm a busy man, I'm sure you can tell."

And so I told a second person - this time a killer who had taken me prisoner - all about myself and The Thing.

Naturally I didn't tell him the whole truth. The back story I gave him was the same as the one I'd told Keith. I finished at the point where I woke up after hitting Trevor Long's back door (keeping quiet about the blood). I thought it best to avoid any mention of having watched him and his wife in bed and stalked the two of them and their daughter for several weeks. No way of telling how that would go down.

Nigel listened carefully to the whole tale, signalling for me to pause every so often as he responded to incoming messages on his phone.

At the end he nodded.

"Well. This has been a pleasure. I look forward to working with you Mr Strong. You as well Mr Pardew. I'm going to have to ask you to chain yourself up until the morning. Very sorry about that - everything happened a little bit suddenly today, didn't it Keith? No time to sort out the furnishings. Secure them over there and take the old man downstairs please Yevgeny."

Yevgeny fixed Keith and I in turn with his steel gaze, grunted and indicated with a tilt of his head that we were to get up and take ourselves over to where Mr Parson was attached to the wall, assuming we didn't want to be seriously hurt. This we did without delay.

"Come on, hurry up," Nigel said impatiently. "They might be handcuffs, not manacles. I don't really know the difference, if there is one. That's it. Not too tight? Splendid. I'll be back ... 6 or 7-ish. I'm an early riser, lucky for you. Just put up with it until then. I'll turn the heating up on my way out."

I was now sat on the floor next to Keith, chained to a steel hoop screwed into the wall. Yevgeny hoisted the unconscious Mr Parson up and over his shoulder like a child.

Nigel Darwin scooped up his crowbar and taser and sauntered to the door, jauntily swinging the former like a vaudeville cane as he went, followed by Yevgeny. As the enormous Russian held the door open for him, Nigel turned to address us.

"Gentlemen, I bid you a good night! Oh, and the lights will switch off after about ten minutes if you don't move. Sleep well!"

And with that, he was gone, the fire door closer gently shutting us in.

"I knew this would happen," said Keith, moments after Nigel had left.

"Which bit of this did you know would happen?"

"I mean the general fucked-ness Shaun. I did not, if we're debating semantics, anticipate any of the specific details of... all this."

"Is he going to kill us? What does he want?"

"He wants you Shaun. Isn't it obvious? That 'fulfil my destiny' speech? He's expecting you to teach him how you do it."

"But I don't know how I do it."

"You'd better start applying some thought to the problem then. Because I don't think Nigel Darwin is used to taking no for an answer."

We sat in silence for a few minutes, until I said:

"Where are we?"

"His office building. Prospect House. The top floor. This one

177

and the one below are empty, so don't think that making a noise is going to help."

"How did he get you?"

"Came to the door while you were off in the woods with Peter Smithson. Punched me out cold when I opened it."

I looked closely at Keith's face. I couldn't see any signs of him having been hit.

"There's got to be a way out of this," I said.

Keith didn't reply. He just laid down and curled up into a shape as close to the foetal position as somebody chained to a wall can approximate.

"Go to sleep Shaun. Let's see what tomorrow brings."

After a few minutes the lights went out.

36

I awoke the next day to crashing sounds. Keith was already awake and watching Nigel attempting to keep the fire door open with one foot while dragging a refrigerator into the room. Behind him were some office chairs, a table, two sleeping bags and a bulging cool bag.

"Right you two - help me get this stuff in."

Nigel walked over to us and tossed a set of keys towards us. They bounced off Keith's forehead and into his lap. Keith scrabbled around trying to pick the keys up and unlocked his manacled wrist.

Rubbing the area where the cuffs had been, Keith stood up and brushed himself down looking warily at our grinning captor. Only then did he remember that I was there too and he handed the keys to me.

"No funny business boys," said Nigel as we followed him to the wedged-open door. "You can see I'm armed" - he patted a bulge under his jacket, which we took to mean "gun" - "and I think you both know I'm dangerous. Ha ha ha."

We stepped through the door into a bare concrete loading bay with a pair of broad metal lift doors facing us. A panel said "Schindler". Schindler's lifts.

"This is the service lift, and it's biometrically operated. You know what that means? It means you have to scan your fingerprints to use it. And your fingerprints? No on listy!"

Nigel laughed again in his annoying way. He pressed

his hand against a black glass panel and the doors slid open. Inside was a fully loaded palette, wrapped in cellophane, on a transporter.

"Pull that through there chaps. Then you can make yourselves at home. No need to keep you chained up any more is there? We're all friends here now aren't we?"

Neither Keith nor I had ever used a palette transporter before. We took hold of the handle and pulled. Nothing happened. Nigel stood behind us, his arms folded.

"Well go on then. Give it a good yank."

We tried again and the palette ground against the floor of the lift.

"It won't move," Keith said, confused.

"Of course it won't, you pair of daft bastards! The brake's on. Ha ha ha ha. Kick that pedal down. Ha ha ha. You fucking idiots. I can see I'm going to have my work cut out here making you two useful."

Having taken the brake off, the palette moved smoothly. We got it caught in the doorway, much to Nigel's amusement, because those things are really hard to steer. Eventually we manoeuvred it over to the vicinity of the chest freezer and the planter, which we had implicitly begin to treat as the focal point of the empty room.

"Come on then. Unwrap it. I can't wait to see your little faces! It's like Christmas morning."

Keith and I began to unwind the plastic bandages cocooning the palletised mummy. Static electricity made it stick to our hands and clothes, but eventually we got it all off and saw what Nigel had brought us.

A chemical toilet; an exercise bike; several multi-gallon bottles of mineral water; a portable stove; a 24-pack of Stella Artois; sets of overalls; a plastic crate of books. And another plastic tub, this time full of dead, day-old yellow chicks.

"You'll want to get that freezer on and stick those chicks in it quick. I bet you're wondering what they're for aren't you? Well, Shaun, you said you like birds."

Nigel was practically hopping back and forth with glee.

"I'll be back in a minute. Get your fridge working and arrange your new living quarters to your liking."

Nigel ran back to the lift, closing the fire door behind him.

"Well, at least we know he's not going to kill us," I said.

Keith was strangely quiet as we dragged the fridge alongside the freezer and plugged it in to the dangling wires. It came to life with a quiet hum.

"What does he want?"

"I don't know. We'll have to wait and see," Keith replied, not making eye contact with me.

I walked over to the window and gazed out over Woking. We were prisoners, locked away in a secret seventh-storey dungeon overlooking the town I had spent my whole life in. It was a grey morning, with the first signs of weekday life stirring on the streets below.

My reflections were interrupted by a loud crash behind me. I turned to see Keith standing at the other window, one of the office chairs upside down at his feet.

"Doesn't look like we're getting out of the windows," he said.

At that moment, the fire door opened and Nigel reappeared. On his hand he wore a giant leather gauntlet. Standing on the gauntlet was a colossal brown bird with yellow feet, piercing yellow eyes and a furious expression on its face. The bird stretched out its enormous wings to steady itself as Nigel walked towards us.

"Meet Ragnar. He's a golden eagle. Cost me £6,000. Haven't a clue what to do with him. Here - tie him onto that."

Nigel held out a metal stand.

"You're in charge of him now."

Ragnar screeched, a plaintive squeal that sounded far too high-pitched for such a large bird. Then he lifted his tail and expelled a jet of liquid shit onto the office carpet.

"There's cleaning stuff on the palette there. You get used to the shitting. It doesn't smell to begin with. Only when it's really started to seep in does it start to stink. So you wipe it up quick like. Can't teach the fucker to do anything cos I got him as an adult, didn't I? Turns out you have to be training them from day one, because eagles are thick as pig shit. Killed the fella who sold him to me over that, didn't I Raggy? Fed him back to his fucking owls.

"Still, you might be an idiot," Nigel was talking to the bird now "but you're majestic, aren't you? You're a majestic symbol. A majestic symbol of my great ambitions. Soaring above the herd below. He'll be even better when I've stuffed him - wings outspread, gazing towards the horizon. I'm something of a taxidermist, you know. Bit of a gifted amateur, if I do say so myself."

We placed the bird's stand on the floor in a far corner of the office and walked back towards the freezers.

"Just take good care of him. Feed him and clean up the shit. Let him look out of the window as well."

Ragnar ruffled his feathers and settled his head into his neck. He looked wholeheartedly pissed off.

"Don't forget to put those chicks in the freezer or they'll go off in that box before you know it."

Keith - who looked no less unhappy than the unfortunate eagle - walked over to the palette and picked up the plastic tub. As he approached the freezer, Nigel giggled. "Go on, open it!"

"What's in that freezer?" Keith asked.

I wasn't sure I wanted to know.

"I'm not going to tell you. That would ruin the surprise!"

We both leaned over the freezer as Keith pushed the lid back. A cloud of freezing steam burst forth. As it evaporated to nothing and our eyes cleared, we found ourselves looking into the familiar face of a frozen solid corpse.

"I believe you know Trevor Long."

37

Keith was crouched over with his back facing Nigel and I, dry-heaving convulsively.

"I didn't really know what to do with him, so he's been up here since I shot him. I mean, you can move the freezer out by the lift if it bothers you. Just keep it plugged in because you don't want him defrosting. If you think those chicks stink when they've gone off, you do not want to smell a dead teacher."

Nigel cackled at his own joke.

"Right gents. I shall leave you to get everything how you would like it up here. Have a bite to eat - I got you a McDonalds' breakfast each on the way in. They're in the cool bag there. Ragnar's already eaten so don't worry about him. He'll settle down so long as you don't get too close to him. Yevgeny'll bring the old boy up in a little while to give you a hand. Let you chaps get reacquainted. See you later - I've got a company to run!"

He turned and walked back to the fire door, where he turned back to face us.

"I'm going to make dinner for you tonight and I'll explain everything. You both like Chinese?"

We nodded assent.

"Splendid! Ta ta for now!"

Once the door had closed behind Nigel, I turned to Keith. He was sat on the floor, his legs splayed in front of him like a toddler, a dazed expression on his face.

"Keith, are you alright?"

Under normal circumstances this would elicit a burst of sarcastic rebukes, but Keith simply replied: "I don't think so."

"He's a maniac," I said.

Keith nodded slowly.

"I'm starving. Grab the cool bag Shaun. We've just got to wait and see."

"Shouldn't we at least try the lift?"

"Shaun, he went to the trouble of telling us why we wouldn't be able to use the lift. I doubt he was kidding. There were no stairs out there. The windows are ... I don't know ... reinforced glass or something, and in any case, we're seven floors up. What could we do if we did break a window? We're trapped. I don't see any way out. The floor is solid too."

Keith kicked his heel against the floor and it gave a dull thud.

"Like you said, he's not going to kill us yet. He wants something. It's your power Shaun. What else could it be? Why keep the witness to that," - Keith nodded his head towards the freezer - "alive otherwise?"

"Shall we move him?"

"I don't give a damn Shaun. Dead body here? Dead body fifty feet over there? What difference does it make?"

I'd never seen Keith like this. He seemed to have completely given up after throwing the chair.

"Shaun... "

I looked up, and Keith's face seemed to have come at least partly back to life.

"You have to tell him how it's done. You have to teach him - it's the only way."

"But I don't know how I do it! You know I don't Keith!"

"If you don't know," Keith was angry now "you had better figure it out and tell it to him. We're not getting out of here otherwise, and I for one don't want to end up in the freezer.

"Just fucking apply yourself Shaun. If not for my sake, then for yourself. Look!"

Keith had opened the crate of books.

"Out-of-body experiences. Astral projection. Mediumship. Siberian shamanism. Esoteric Buddhism. Tibet. Carl Jung. The Art of the Deal...? Is that supposed to be in here? It's signed. Crowley. Blavatsky ... It's all here. Oh and look - a Post-It note on top saying 'get on with it.'"

He waved a Book of Thoth at me emphatically.

"You have to work it out or we are both dead."

The timing was uncanny. It was almost as if Keith knew what was in the crate before he looked.

But I didn't say anything. We just sat down to eat our breakfasts in silence. Keith grimaced.

"Oh for God's sake - he's put sugar in my coffee."

Mine had sugar in too. Fortunately, I can take it either way. Some people have very strong opinions on sugar in hot beverages, but not me. I mean, I would have preferred tea, but we were hostages after all.

I walked over to the eagle on its perch. The bird eyeballed me with silent, motionless malevolence. When you see a creature like that in its natural habitat, circling in the sky above mountains and lochs, you can understand why primitive people thought they were nature spirits or messengers of the gods. I've never seen a golden eagle in the wild, obviously, but I've seen them on TV. They really do look majestic, just like Nigel said. Airborne with wings outstretched an eagle looks like it could carry you off in its talons. But with his wings folded in, tied by the ankle to a wooden block with a metal perch screwed into it, Ragnar looked small, sad, scared and terribly alone. It probably didn't mean much to him, but I knew how he felt.

Keith was gazing out of the window.

"I can almost see your house from here. And look - that's where Trevor Long's estate is ... Do you know how to work one of these toilets?"

We got down to work trying to set everything up. More practical people would have needed less time, but as Keith pointed out this was what we had been training for in Northumberland. I presume he was equating this experience to a kind of camping, because I did not feel that this was something we had prepared for at all.

After we had been struggling with the stove for about an hour, the door opened. A dishevelled Mr Parson was led in by Yevgeny. He was protesting vigorously.

"I don't know who you think I am! This is nothing to do with me. Who are you? You can't just grab people off the streets and hold them hostage! This is Britain! This is Surrey! I don't know the people you're looking for...You have to believe me! I've never heard of Shaun Strong or Keith...whatever his name was. You can't do this to me! People will be looking for me!"

As Yevgeny led him over to our makeshift campsite, Mr Parson caught sight of us.

"You! What are you doing here? What is going on? This... man...has brutalised me. Me!"

Yevgeny, chatty as ever, pointed at Keith and I in turn.

"Pardew. Strong."

He shoved Mr Parson towards us so that the old man stumbled to his knees. I went to help him up.

"Oh these animals! Get off me! Who are you? Shaun Jones? Or Shaun Strong?"

"Shaun Strong," I admitted.

"You lied to me! I accepted you as my apprentices and you lied! I took you into my home!"

"You made sure we didn't go anywhere near your home," Keith pointed out with a smirk. "It was Pilates and Prosecco night. Or was the fish man coming over? I can't remember."

The mention of the fish man took the wind out of Mr Parson. He slumped onto one of the chairs and clutched his head in his hands, emitting a groan that summarised a lifetime of woe. Keith took a step back, unsure whether his cruel joke had perhaps been too much for the old man. We glanced at each other nervously.

"I should have known. I should have known! I said to myself - 'Lionel, no good will come of this!' but I trusted in you! I believed in your sincerity, even when you forced me to bring that dreadful man…that villain…into the group. So what is it that you want from me? What new torments do you have in mind? You have me snatched off the street and…violated…by that monster. Is it the books? You want my books, don't you? Of course, that's what it is…."

"We didn't kidnap you," I said. "We're prisoners here too."

"A likely story. People will be looking for me you know!"

"It's true," Keith knelt down beside Mr Parson. "We're here because of him," Keith pointed at me, "and him" this time pointing at the freezer.

Mr Parson sighed: "I don't understand…"

"Shaun here is an astral traveller," Keith began. "He can leave his body at will…"

"It's not entirely 'at will'," I interrupted.

"More or less at will - that ok Shaun?" Keith asked with venomous sarcasm. "May I continue? Thank you so much. I have been helping him to develop and use his gifts. Hence, we came to you looking for guidance. Guidance which to date has amounted to little more than 'read these books' - none of which make any sense or are any help whatsoever."

"That reading list contains the fundamentals! The very foundations of the esoteric system! By its very nature, the corpus is concealed. That's what esoteric means! You can't expect them to be laid out like a…like a Haynes Manual!"

"Anyway," Keith shushed Mr Parson with his raised hands, "by a long and tangled sequence of events which it is not necessary for us to dig into right now, Shaun here witnessed a murder. The victim is in that freezer. Somehow, Shaun was spotted at the scene of the crime by the perpetrator - who is the owner of this building and the employer of the thug who just brought you in here. That man, whose name is Nigel Darwin, told us that he expects us to help him fulfil his destiny. Given that you're here as well - an apparent expert in the occult - it would seem reasonable to infer that Nigel Darwin intends to discover how my friend here does his thing, by whatever means necessary. And that brings you pretty much up to date. That cover everything Shaun?"

I nodded: "That's about it."

"And where am I supposed to fit in to all this?" asked Parson feebly.

"I don't know. But I would imagine you're here as some sort of expert consultant."

"I've been kidnapped!"

"Yes, that too."

"You." Parson pointed at me, his watery eyes looking even more diluted than usual. "Why did you never say anything about this? Why did you allow me to believe in your sincerity?"

I shrugged and mumbled "I don't know", looking away.

"Look. There's no point in recriminating about it now, is there? We're here and we can either do what they want or we can try to escape. Shaun and I have already assessed our chances of breaking out and we're of the view that they are rather slim. I might venture to add, they are hardly enhanced by your addition to the escape committee."

Mr Parson snorted with indignation, but otherwise remained silent.

"So," Keith continued "he's got the skills and you've got the knowledge. I can't believe it's beyond our capabilities to figure out how Shaun does his thing. After all, if Shaun can do it, how hard can it be? No offence Shaun."

It was my turn to shrug now.

"Gentlemen, gentlemen..."

Mr Parson had taken a seat and was resetting his disarranged clothing and hair. He looked up at us and sighed, smiled and spread out his hands in front of him simultaneously in a theatrical manner.

"It can't be done. It is simply impossible."

"If he can do it, other people can do it too."

"It's not possible. Your friend here," Mr Parson indicated me, "must be experiencing lucid dreaming or some other kind of hallucination. Are you a heavy drug user?"

I shook my head.

"Mr Pardew, I have dedicated my life to the study of the occult. I have spent thousands of hours researching the subject of astral travel alone. If it were possible, I would understand it. Do you see? There is simply no question that the phenomenon could exist. I have examined every source from the last three thousand years, my good fellow, and nothing has convinced me of the likely efficacy of any of the methods or rituals described."

"Have you tried the methods and rituals described?"

"You know how I feel about thaumaturgical practice. The point is never to do. The wise man seeks to understand."

"But you don't understand, do you? You don't understand what Shaun does."

"Your friend…," Mr Parson smiled a smile of condescending empathy. I was surprised he didn't pat the back of my hand while he spoke. "Your friend is a confused young man. Perhaps he believes what he has said to you. I cast no aspersions on your honesty Mr Jones. But I fear that a tall tale has got out of hand."

"You have no practical knowledge then?"

"My learning is…ah…purely theoretical."

"There is nothing you can do to help us show that man - that man who kidnapped you, and us, and killed the teacher in that freezer - what he wants to see?"

"There's a teacher in the freezer? Oh my word!"

Keith turned his back on Parson and stared at me. He threw his hands into the air.

"Well, it's up to you now Shaun. He'll be no help. How are you going to get us out of this?"

"Keith, I don't know how I can show him. I would if I could, I promise."

Mr Parson let out a scornful bark.

"I promise I would if I could," I repeated.

38

The three of us said very little after that. It must have been about 10pm before Nigel came back. He was carrying two bulging and steaming carrier bags.

"Boys boys boys! I was going to cook for you, but it's been one hell of a day in the office. I won't bore you with the details - I doubt you'd understand it all. But I promised you a Chinese, and Chinese we shall have!"

He held the bags aloft, like a champion athlete on the winner's podium.

"Here, grandad. Set the table and grab us some cans. Might as well try and be civilised, eh?"

A few minutes later our feast was laid out before us. There was far more than we could have hoped to get through even if Keith and I hadn't only had one meal in the last 36 hours.

"Cheers, gentlemen!" said Nigel, cracking open a beer. "Now I expect you're wondering why I brought you here."

We filled our plates and listened expectantly as Nigel leaned back in his chair.

"Let me tell you a bit about myself. I'm a very successful man. I've made a lot of money. I've worked bloody hard to make it, but now the money makes itself. I own maybe twenty properties that I bought with the profits from Evolution. So I don't have to work any more. I have a beautiful wife, a beautiful daughter and a beautiful home. People know me round here. I'm an important man and I command respect wherever I go.

"I started from nothing, you know. Grew up in Bradford, didn't do too well at school - I was gifted, a smart kid, but school was ... I don't know ... too small for me, somehow. Got into a bit of trouble back then like a lot of lads do. But then I discovered computers, and I knew - I knew right away - that this was my way out. Out of poverty, out of the herd, out of that fucking Yorkshire rain. I started Evolution when I was fifteen. What were you doing when you were fifteen, eh?"

Neither Keith nor I said anything.

"Some people are just born with the drive and the ability to achieve greatness. Some aren't - not their fault, of course, but don't pretend it's not true because it's not 'politically correct' or whatever. We're not all created equal, and once you accept the real consequences of that... well... anything's possible.

"It all came so easy to me, the success. I never doubted Evolution or myself. As the money poured in, every investment decision I made turned out to be right. I could not lose."

Nigel took a swig from his beer and stared long and hard at Keith and I.

"Once I had decided I was going to succeed, nothing could stop me. Nothing. And that's the difference between me and the rest of you. My will. My iron will and resolution. Pass them prawns over Shaun."

I slid the plastic carton along the table, while Nigel went over to the fridge and took out another four cans. He tossed one to me and I caught it. Then he threw one to Keith, still underarm, but twice as fast and directly towards his face. Keith instinctively raised his hands to protect himself and the can glanced off his wrists, upturning his plate and rolling off the table onto the floor. Nigel was grinning, with an expression I was all too familiar with - the expression of a bully, in total control of the situation.

Keith said nothing. He just picked the can up and wiped the food that had spilled onto the table back onto his plate.

"Come on drink up. You finished that one Keith? I'm beyond material success, lads. I'll let you in on a secret. Once anyone passes a certain level of wealth, you undergo a kind of testing experience."

Keith sat up, listening intently - presumably in anticipation of the imminent revelation of one of The System's great mysteries.

"You know Alexander the Great? 'And when Alexander saw the breadth of his domain, he wept, for there were no more worlds to conquer'. You know that line? Hans Gruber says it in Die Hard. What a film. I bet you love Die Hard, don't you Shaun? Well that was me. I'd got everything I wanted. I've got a yacht, you know. Down at Southampton. Cost me a couple of million give or take. How many times do you think I've been on it Shaun?"

I had a mouthful of Singapore noodles. I grunted in a way that was supposed to convey that I had no idea.

"Go on, have a guess."

"How long have you had it?" I ventured.

"Three times," Nigel proclaimed, ignoring my question. "I've been out in it three times ever. Turns out sailing is really fucking boring. Can you believe that though? I spent more money than most people will ever see in their little lives on a boat that I don't really want. And it made me realise: for someone driven like me, for someone with a conquering spirit, when you can just have anything you want, you stop wanting all those things you can have. What I understood - and I think very few men have made this breakthrough in history before me - is that material success, social success... it's all an illusion Shaun. It's all just Monopoly money at the end of the day. It's fine when you're playing the game by the rules, but why are you playing the game in the first place and who do the rules benefit?"

Nigel raised his eyebrows and nodded slowly, as if he expected the profundity of his words to be sparking a powerful revelation within us. I was mostly thinking how full I was, but when I looked at Keith something on his face told me that he was taking this seriously.

The monologue continued.

"A lot of rich men - they never have that moment. That

moment when they see how futile it all is. How more possessions will never make them happy. How the praise of their inferiors will never bring contentment. A great spirit can never be filled up with junk food for the soul. Creation. That's the only thing that can fulfil people like me. Me and Alexander the Great and Alan Rickman. When I understood that, I began to look for satisfaction elsewhere. I could see that creating a world where the rules were mine and the stakes were whatever I wanted them to be was the only way for me to fulfil myself. But that's easier said than done, right? I bet you wouldn't know what to do with real freedom if you had it, would you? Most people wouldn't. And that's because real freedom can't be granted. It has to be taken.

"That's why I got into the whole drug business, with your mate over there. I'm not interested in fighting the system. That's for kids. I've set up my own system where I'm an absolute monarch. Actually, I'll tell you how it started - this is an important story. In fact, you!" Nigel nodded at Keith "You're a writer, aren't you?"

Keith hesitated for a split second and then nodded.

"Write all this down. I'll want a record of all this. You can be my chronicler. Until I get fed up with you. Ah ha ha ha. No, no - I'm just messing with you. Or am I? Ah ha ha ha ha. Got to keep him on his toes, isn't that right Milky?"

Nigel clapped Mr Parson on the shoulder. The old man looked aghast.

"He looks like the Milky Bar Kid, doesn't he Shaun? Milky Bar Kid's dirty uncle. You want to get out in the sun a bit fella. You boffins don't take care of yourselves properly. Bad diet and hunching over dusty books in bad lighting. Anyway…where were we? Oh yeah, you got a pen and paper now Keith? Make sure you get this down - it's an important bit.

"So a couple of years back, I'm at a trade fair in London - IT stuff, you know. I meet this Russian fella. Little beard, funny eyebrows. You can always tell a Russian, can't you? Just something not quite right about their faces. This bloke - Golovkin - he has the palest blue eyes you've ever seen. Not like Milky's. Really striking. Anyway, we get talking as you do and we hit it off. Similar stories, you know? He pulled himself up from nothing under Brezhnev to build an international security business. Now, he lives in Mexico - would I come out and do a bit of consulting?

"Anyway, it takes a few weeks to sort out - my people, his people blah blah blah. A month later, me and a couple of engineers from Evolution are landing in Mexico City. Have you been to Mexico? Beautiful country. Fucking mess though. We're met in the airport by another Russian - cheekbones, bald head, bomber jacket. You met him earlier. Leads us out to what can only be described as a motorcade. Blocking the taxi rank. Four or five black SUVs - great big American bastards. Bigger than anything we have over here. Can't remember what they're called. The Russian lad, Yevgeny, he directs us into the back of the middle one and there's Golovkin. Brown suit, black shirt, bottle of vodka, ice bucket…"

"'Velcom! Velcom!' he goes as we're driving off. Speaks very good English, you know. Just a bit of an accent - speaks better than either of you twats. 'Velcom!' he goes as we're setting off. That's when I notice them. Clipped to the wall - pair of Glock 18s. Fully assembled and accessorised. You know what a Glock 18 is? It's a submachine gun. Special forces use them. My lads see them too and one of them, Johnny, he looks right nervous. Fat kid, he is. Knows network security like the back of his hand though. Golovkin notices and he bursts out laughing. Yevgeny's up in the front and he snaps round, right hand in his bomber jacket. Golovkin laughs again, quieter this time, and he pats Yevgeny on the back of the head. It's like a child's hand up against that melon. Face like a fucking iceberg. Anyway, Yevgeny relaxes and turns back and Golovkin grabs Johnny by the knee and goes 'you like?' Full Borat. He starts laughing again, and I'm laughing too now. Johnny's not laughing. He's shitting himself, but that's only making us both laugh more. Hummers. That's what the cars were. Hummers.

"Golovkin unbuttons his jacket and pulls it open. He's only got two holsters - pair of Sig Sauer P238s. Desert model. In beige. Johnny's sweating like a pig now. His head's pulsating. You can see it. He's scared out of his wits, such as they are."

"I don't blame him," Mr Parson mumbled.

"Most people would be scared, I admit. But I'm not most people, am I? I knew, even then, before I realised what I was truly capable of that I was an exception. I don't fear other men and what they can do. So I take the bottle off the seat next to Golvokin, I open it and take a long swig. It's good vodka as you'd probably expect. And I hand it on to Johnny. We have a moment, me and Golovkin then. He knows and I know he knows. He can see I'm a kindred spirit.

"So we're driving for a couple of hours - talking shop - out of the city into the mountains, towards the sea. Everyone's forgotten about the guns, even Johnny. We're onto Apache, Hadoop, data centres…you wouldn't understand it. We pitch up at this massive ranch. There's horses everywhere. Lads with guns. In cars. On horses. Mexicans, Russians, all sorts. It's Golovkin's *estancia*. That's Mexican for 'estate'. And it's about a mile up a private road to his house. Fucking massive, it is. It's more like a castle than a house. And you know what he's got parked outside? A pair of armoured cars. South African Eland Mark 7s. You know them? Fucking great cannon on the front of the things - 90mm Denel GT2. Turret-mounted grenade launcher as well. Brutal machine. Got these steel plate cow catchers riveted into the front."

Nigel appeared more and more transported with ecstasy as he described Golovkin's *estancia* and its arsenal in luxurious detail.

"I'll get you some pictures Keith. Help you to visualise them when you're describing them. Anyway, for the next few days, the lads are up at Golovkin's offices back in Mexico City, and me and him stay at the mansion. And we get to talking. Deep conversations. And I don't mind saying - because I'll say what's on my mind no matter what, I've got nothing to prove to anyone - I don't mind saying, those conversations changed my life. Gave me a completely new outlook. Well, not completely new. The ideas were all there beforehand, but I just hadn't... crystallised them. Brought them to the surface, so to speak.

"Golovkin's story...he ran a security company somewhere in the middle of Russia. Got into business not long after the Wall came down. So the USSR is collapsing, Yeltsin's pissing the country down the drain. The population's in shock. They've had everything provided for them for so long - jobs, housing, futures. Then it's all gone. And most Russians, they stand still not knowing what to do. But a few of them, like Golovkin, they seize the moment. Entrepreneurs start springing up. And yeah, some of them make it really big - the oligarchs, buying up fertiliser plants and copper mines and all that for nothing. Point is, it's the wild west - the wild east, rather. Everything's thrown into the air, and you can wait and see what lands on your plate, or you can get up and start grabbing what's falling around you. Course, he's not the only one. Long story short, bigger fish... mafia... put him out of business. He loses everything. Police, authorities - they're no help. When they're not powerless to stop the crooks, they're actively working with them or for them. His world's shattered for a second time.

"And so he leaves Russia. Starts all over again, in Mexico. Cos he studied Spanish at university back in the USSR. Did I mention that? Oh well, he did. But he's learned his lessons. He's not going to be defeated again. There's nothing he won't do to get what he wants. Nothing. Iron will that man. And Mexico suits him down to the ground, because wealth and power count for everything there, same as in Russia. The government, the police, the cartels, the church - they're all just separate sources of authority. Not like here, where there's the state and the law and morality and they're all carefully knitted together, to the point that you can't imagine life without them. In Mexico, an agile man can slip between the threads and set up his own sources of authority in the gaps. And that's what Golovkin did. He works for the government, for the corporations, for the gangs. It's all the same to him. And that's when it hit me. It's a choice to live by other people's rules instead of your own. It's not a given.

"I tell him that I want what he's got. And he looks me in the eye and studies me. I don't blink. I meet his gaze. He doesn't intimidate me, even though I know what he is. I can't be intimidated. It's not in my nature. And then he nods. He recognises me. Sees what I have in me. He knows that I've seen beyond the money, the *estancia*, the Hummers and the Elands...to the truth. The truth in the distance on the other side of the mountains. The truth that only the furthest-sighted can see, you know what I mean? The truth that men like us can be completely free."

Nigel's mobile phone started to vibrate loudly in his pocket. Digging it out, he checked the screen and rolled his eyes.

"Will you please excuse me? Duty calls. Do carry on without me."

Answering the phone, with an ebullient "Sweetheart!" Nigel walked away towards the fire exit, conducting the rest of his conversation sotto voce. As the door slammed behind him, Parson swung round to face me.

"You have to get me out of this! I am begging you - I have an elderly mother."

Keith chimed in.

"Mr Parson's right. You have to tell him what he wants to know Shaun. Firstly, so he doesn't kill us and secondly, so we don't have to listen to any more of this Scooby Doo villain monologue. 'I've got a yacht' - what a wanker. If I'd had the breaks he had I could have had a yacht. Giving us his hard luck story ... Funny how everyone's working class when they get to talk about themselves, isn't it Shaun? Thinks we're afraid of him. Arsehole."

Keith picked up a spring roll and bit the end off.

"Still ... He's not wrong about all of it. The freedom we think we have is just an illusion that The System allows us to see so we don't start asking questions. It's true, isn't it? Real freedom is more than just having more stuff, more toys to play with while the grown-ups take care of business. And he's right about Die Hard too. That was a great movie. Yipee-ki-yay motherfucker!"

Keith snorted with laughter, choked momentarily and expelled a piece of beansprout from a nostril.

"What other options do we have? We have to co-operate."

"Yes!" said Parson with sudden enthusiasm. "You have to help him!"

"Maybe we could ambush him. Then use his hand to make the lift work."

"Be realistic Shaun. Look at us. You're a blob - no offence. I'm fast, and quite strong for my size, but that bloke's got more muscle on him than us two combined. This is why we should have stuck at the survival stuff. I told you we'd need it one day. Should have exercised more. Anyway, he's like a triple black belt."

"How do you know?"

"He told me."

"When?"

"Ah ... when he took me prisoner. I was ready to fight him when I saw him at the door. Protecting you more than anything Shaun. Anyway, that's when he said it. Black belt. Krav maga. Judo. All that. Look, all we have to do is work with him. He's reasonable."

"He fed a man to some owls."

"I don't think he was being serious. He probably never did that. Human flesh is ... unpalatable. To owls ...I think…"

"There is a dead body in that freezer though."

Keith propped his chin up on his hand and nodded silently. He sighed.

"Yes. That's true. And there's that giant skinhead kicking about somewhere as well."

"Did he taser you then?"

"What?"

"When he caught you."

"Yeah. Yeah ... tasered me."

Didn't he say he was knocked out with a punch?

Keith continued.

"Look, Shaun. I'm begging you now. Just try to help him. Do what he wants. Maybe we'll get a chance to escape later on, but for now we have to play along."

"Yes! Listen to your friend Shaun!" Mr Parson echoed.

The door opened and Nigel strode back in. He looked very pissed off.

"Never get married boys. And don't have kids."

He sat down at the table with us and took a long gulp from a beer can. He put the tin back down with an emphatic bang.

"They make everything complicated. I have a nineteen-year-old daughter, and I give her the best of everything. Do you understand? The best of everything. She's never wanted for nothing...

"Anyway...families...point is, me and Golovkin, we're in partnership. A few of his lads are out here working at Evolution but helping me run the operation - including big Yevgeny. Golovkin also introduced me to some very interesting lawyers: Lavery, Woodward and Saïd. Maybe you've heard of them? Aleister Woodward is quite a character. You'd like him Shaun. Well, he'd like you, which is not quite the same thing. But anyway, it's not about money and it never has been. It's more...personal development, let's say. I have to run, but tomorrow we are going on a little road trip, we three. We three musketeers ... Got a little job for you Mr Strong. And we can get to know each other on the way there. Try to stay awake tonight - I'm going to need you tired!"

Nigel burst out laughing, got up and wandered back to the fire door.

Mr Parson suddenly leapt to his feet. There were tears in his eyes.

"Please! Please sir - let me go! I won't say anything about any of this! You can trust me. I...I..."

Snot was now running freely from his nose.

"I barely know these men...I have an elderly mother...I have a wife and son...I don't know anything that can help you..."

While Parson was disintegrating into the state of snivelling and whimpering toddler, the office door had opened and the colossal silhouette visible in the opening revealed that Yevgeny had entered. He sidled over quietly and stood in the shadows a few metres away from we diners.

"You don't know anything that can help me?" Nigel repeated, interested in Parson for the first time, as he walked back towards the group. "Is that true?"

"His learning is purely theoretical," Keith drawled sarcastically.

"Theoretical? What does that mean?"

"I...erm...have dedicated my life to the acquisition of wisdom..."

"I don't give a fuck about what you've dedicated your life to. Why is he saying that your knowledge is 'purely theoretical'?"

"I have studied..."

"What? What have you studied?"

"Ah...um...all the major sources of arcana in the Western tradition. A little less from the East, but nevertheless I have achieved..."

"Yes? You've achieved what?"

"I..."

"What have you achieved?"

"What you must understand..."

"Why isn't he answering my question?" Nigel asked the now-much-closer Yevgeny.

Yevgeny shook his head resignedly and closed his eyes.

"Why aren't you answering my question Milky Bar Kid?"

"I really must ask you to desist..."

"Can you astral travel...err...who's a famous albino?"

Keith and I looked at each other. We looked at Yevgeny, who looked back at us, his sphinx-like features giving nothing away. We all looked at the terrified Parson.

"There was that monk in the Da Vinci Code?" Keith volunteered.

"Gary Busey" Yevgeny rumbled.

"He's not an albino!" Nigel and Keith shouted, both speaking at once.

"In movie."

"Gary Busey wasn't in the Da Vinci Code. It was…ah… what's his name?"

"It really doesn't matter now," Nigel said. An ominous calmness had descended over his previous mounting aggression. "Mr Parson - are you able to help me fulfil my destiny?"

"I'm sorry but there is really nothing I can do."

"In that case, I would ask you to make your way over to the freezer."

"The freezer?"

"Yes, that one there."

Mr Parson got up gingerly and walked slowly over to the humming unit.

"Excellent. Thank you for your co-operation. And now if I could ask you to climb inside…"

"Inside the freezer?"

"Yes."

"But…I won't tell anyone what has happened…you have my word."

"Climb into the freezer and close the door behind you."

"Please…I just want to leave…"

The room was silent as Nigel leaped forward onto a chair and sprang over the table. An instant later, sound caught up. Plates smashed as the table tipped over. Within two steps Nigel had Mr Parson by the throat in one hand, his phone still in the other.

"When I tell…"

Nigel drove the phone into Mr Parson's forehead.

"..you to do…"

He did it again.

"…something - you will do…"

He hit him again.

"…it when…"

Again.

"…you are told."

The final blow made a sickening crunch. Nigel threw the limp body of the unconscious old man to the floor. As he hurled the bloody phone at the office window, he emitted a savage animal scream.

Nigel recomposed himself.

"Put him in there. And get that out of here," he snapped at Yevgeny.

Yevgeny grunted.

Nigel turned back to us. His face and clothing were spattered with streaks of bright red blood. His right hand dripped gore as he wiggled his fingers. There was a disturbing light in the eyes of his bloody face. He spoke calmly but with a quaver in his voice which suggested that whatever had just come over him was only barely under control now.

"Mr Strong - I very much hope for both your sakes that you can show me how your magical powers work. Or I will make you regret it. I will make you regret it more than you have ever regretted anything before."

"I really … I don't know how I do it. I can't teach you. I don't know how it works myself."

"That's not what your pal tells me."

I looked at Keith. He was staring back at me, a look of defiance, guilt and calm determination was etched on his face.

"You know you can help him Shaun. Don't try to hide it any more," Keith said slowly, nodding, as my stomach dropped away.

"Listen to your mate Shaun. He might look like a fucking twat but he's got a brain or two in his head. Don't make me extract them one by one. Ah ha ha ha ha ha."

This time, his chuckle was entirely without humour.

39

Nigel left us alone again.

"Why did you tell him that Keith?"

"I'm not apologising."

"But you know I can't... "

Keith stared theatrically into the corners of the room. Security cameras.

"Go along with it..." he murmured, keeping his lips motionless. "Useful is alive. You've seen what happens to people who can't help him..."

Despite Nigel's instruction that I should stay awake and the trauma of dinnertime's possibly fatal beating, I slept like a log that night. The camp beds were comfortable, the sleeping bags were warm and I quickly got used to Prospect House's background hums and glows. Of course, I had been handcuffed to a wall the night before, so anything was an improvement.

I woke to a shrill yelp and the flapping of wings. Ragnar had attempted to take off from his perch and was now slapping repeatedly into the floor as the cord around his ankle pulled tight. As I sat up, the bird stopped struggling and stood stock still, his beak open, panting like a dog. Yevgeny had taken the plastic tub of frozen chicks out and left it on the floor when he removed the freezer that evening. A damp smell of decay oozed out when I opened the box. The chicks looked asleep with their eyes closed like they were having a bad dream, expressions of distaste on their defrosting little faces. I tossed them one by one towards Ragnar, who pretended not to notice. Keith remained curled up on his camp bed, his back towards us.

I walked over to the window and gazed out in the direction of my home. Next door was an office block under demolition. From the ground floor, you'd hardly notice it because of the hoardings put up all around the site. From up here though, we had a perfect view of the derelict building in cross-section, sliced through like a cake. That column of concrete - that would be the staircase. Those rows of pillars on each floor, just like the ones here in our prison. Were those desks? The ruined block was like a ghost ship, mysteriously abandoned with all hands lost. Bent rods of rebar steel dangled from the floors, with titanic lumps of cement hanging off them. From here they looked like white conkers suspended on a shoelace, but some of them must have been the size of a small car. I remember being impressed by the force it must have taken to rip the missing part of the building away, pulling metal and masonry to pieces like paper. A semi-visible cloud of dust hung around the demolition site's ground level like mist on a river's surface at dawn.

Have you ever been a hostage? I expect that the problem most people have with it is the loss of control - of being in someone else's power and at their mercy. Will I be released? Will I be hurt or even killed? When you're left alone, not knowing what your captor has in store for you, your mind will start to race, imagining the worst possible scenarios or working out hopeless plans for breaking out. Some people fall in love with their jailers - what do they call it? Stockhausen Syndrome? No ... that doesn't sound right. Well anyway - you just want something to happen. Anything. And they're the only people who can make things happen.

Perhaps that's what happened to Keith. He became very eager to please Nigel, very quickly. I couldn't tell if he was sucking up or whether that speech about "real freedom" had made an impression on him. The worse Nigel treated him, the more desperate to win his approval Keith became. I had already started to suspect that something strange was going on, but I never saw it all clearly until it was too late.

I didn't mind being held prisoner that much. It was just a bit boring being cooped up in that office, but I had Keith and Ragnar for company, and we had a great view north and south. When you're used to other people making decisions for you, losing control isn't so bad. It was just dull, sitting around waiting for Nigel to come back and move the plot forwards. 'The plot' I call it - I'm talking about our lives, lives that are now over. But I was so used to seeing lives as stories. Even when it was my own life, I was still somewhere outside the story looking in.

"You should be reading those books."

Keith had woken up. I sidled over to the crate and took out a copy of Ouspensky's "In Search of the Miraculous". It was full of stuff like that - systems, cosmographies, meditation techniques. Words. Words words words. Studies, Mr Parson would have said. When the experience comes from within, how can you fit words to it? Words are for sharing meanings and experiences with other people, but what about stuff that can't be shared? I'm alone in my head, and I'm alone with The Thing. I'm just as isolated from the rest of humankind when I'm awake as when I'm asleep. Because you can never really share any experience with another person. They're all alone in their heads too. All you can share is the words.

I flopped down on my bed and started leafing through the book.

God. Mr Parson. I had almost forgotten about him already. I felt bad for him. He was harmless. He didn't deserve what had happened to him. But when does anyone get what they deserve?

"Look Shaun. I believe you when you say you can't describe how it's done. But at some level you know. Just look through the books and maybe something will jog your memory."

Keith scanned the room and picked up an empty beer can. He tossed it towards Ragnar, who screeched and tried in vain to take flight once again, making a horrible racket as he did so. Right before the eagle calmed down again Keith hissed at me: "Or make something up. Just keep him interested until we can figure out a way out of this."

Hours later, Nigel returned.

"It's Pinky and Perky! Ready for an outing? Put the handcuffs back on and out to the lift with you. Like I said, we are going on an outing and I don't want any funny business. You behave yourselves, nothing bad will happen. You muck me around... "

Nigel tapped his trousers' waistband, concealed under his tweed jacket.

Once our hands were bound, Nigel led us to the lift. He pressed his hand to the black glass plate and the doors slid open. We stepped in, the doors closed and we began to descend. They reopened to reveal an underground car park, empty except for the Range Rover I had seen outside Nigel's mansion. He took out his keys, pressed a button and the indicators flashed twice as the doors unlocked.

I couldn't see the exit ramp. I hung back as Nigel and Keith walked towards the car, trying to spot the way out of the garage.

"It's a locked metal gate, Shaun. I know what you're up to. Come on. In front of me now. Open the back door. Right, pull the seat forwards. That's it - hop into the back there. Seven seater. Five plus two. Optional on the Sport."

I squeezed my way into the vehicle's luggage compartment, where two miniature chairs had been flipped up.

"There's not a lot of room back here..." Keith began. He was cut off by Nigel slapping him, hard, around the face.

"Get in. Take notes. And don't speak unless you're spoken to."

40

Keith was still clutching his jaw as we drove out of Woking towards Chobham.

"You have to sit back there, Mr Pardew, because I do not fancy one of you jokers grabbing me round the back of the neck while I'm driving. Didn't I tell you before? You can't outsmart me."

It was really very uncomfortable. The seats were not designed to be occupied by two adults, particularly ones with their hands tied. Getting my seatbelt on had been quite a challenge, and I had to keep shuffling my feet around to fit them in.

"Now, where did we get to last night?"

"Real freedom can't be granted - it has to be taken," Keith blurted out, tailing off into a mumble as he realised with apprehension that he had spoken again without a direct invitation.

"Oh yes. I remember now."

Keith relaxed, realising the moment of danger had passed without incident.

"Material success... it's fine up to a point. But once you reach that point are you satisfied? Isn't it just limited minds, restricted minds that say to themselves 'that's enough for me'? Like I said, I'm not stopping at winning the game. I'm creating my own game with my own rules."

Nigel went on to repeat a lot of what he had said the previous day, including the yacht anecdote in its entirety. This

Alan Boyce

time, when prompted to guess how many times he had been on it, I surmised that giving the right answer would be the wrong answer. I said seven times.

"Wrong! Three times! Just three times, boys. I spent more money on that boat than most people... "

Like I said, the story continued more or less word for word as it had done on our last outing. Eventually Nigel branched off into a new, unexpected direction.

"I've always liked crime dramas on the telly. What's your favourite Keith?"

"Errr ... I don't know. The Bill?"

"That's not a crime drama, that's a soap opera that just happens to be about policemen. No, I mean proper crime. I'll tell you what mine is. Have you seen Dexter? He's a scientist in the Miami police homicide department, but the twist is ... right? ... he's a serial killer."

Keith and I nodded along and made approving sounds. We had both seen this programme and felt comforted to find something we could call common ground with our captor, even if the mention of serial killers was rather ominous.

"Anyway, he only kills villains, but the story's told from his perspective. Usually, you get it from the point of view of the people tracking down the murderer, and you take all their assumptions for granted. But seeing it through Dexter's eyes, I understood: these killers, they're a kind of higher man. I mean, they're always fucking geniuses for a start, but that's not what I'm on about. It's not about breaking the law or breaking the rules for them - they transcend them. You know?

"The structure of the story and the form of telly casts them as the 'baddies', yeah? That's what we expect, that's how it's supposed to go. But Dexter, he plays by a different set of rules to everyone else. So he can do things that no one else can. And it's not about the killing... Well it is. That's his thing. Gets off on it, I reckon, although you don't see that. Writers probably think that'd make him too unsympathetic. Did you see the final episode? What a fucking let-down that was. Whole thing went downhill after the series with John Lithgow in it."

"Oh yeah," Keith murmured. I nodded in silent agreement. He had a point.

"Anyway, it's like, in these things, there's a genius villain and a genius cop on their trail. That's how it goes. And everyone else, they're just chumps - extras. They only see what's there on the surface, not the real game going on underneath, between the main characters who are just... beyond what they can imagine."

We were driving through wooded heathland now, heading towards Ottershaw or maybe Chertsey.

"What did your Grandad do during the war Shaun? Conscientious objector or something like that, eh? White feather brigade? Ha ha ha. Just kidding. You heard of Operation Chariot? The St Nazaire raid? My Dad's Dad - he was one of the commandos. You know the story?"

Neither of us said anything.

"What the fuck are they teaching in schools these days? The Greatest Raid of All, they called it. He was on one of the motor boats when the Campbelltown rammed the dock gates. He stabbed three Germans before he was captured the next day couple of miles up the river after it all went tits up. Loved telling that story, he did. Really made you feel like you were there, the way he told it. Him and his mates, all crammed onto these little ships, setting off from Cornwall into the Atlantic. Cramped together on deck in the howling wind, until they eventually see land and then all the shit hits the fan at once. Bombs, guns, no one knows what the fuck is happening. My Grandad, he falls out of his boat, drops his rifle and has to swim to the shore. Then he's creeping along the river bank back towards the battle, knife between his teeth. Sees the sky light up, followed by what he thought was an earthquake. Like the force was coming right out of the ground, you know? Campbelltown was packed full of explosives and it blew up - ruined the docks for the rest of the war, killed hundreds of Nazi bastards.

"They didn't have radios back then so my Grandad, he gets back near the town, sees our boats heading off, dust cloud, rubble, everything on fire. They knew the score, them commandos. Knew what they were getting themselves in to when they set off. He knows he's on his own until he can find his unit or what's left of it - and then get out of France somehow."

We turned off the road into a layby half a mile or so outside Chertsey and came to a halt. Nigel turned round to face us.

"So, Grandad - he hunkers down for the night in a farmyard. Got his dagger in hand in case he's taken by surprise. German patrol comes round first thing next morning. Grandad would never tell us how it all went down, but he spent the rest of the war in Stalag 133."

"Where was that?" Keith asked, apparently transfixed.

"Ohh ... ahhh ... now you're asking ... Somewhere in Brittany. He said it was alright. Food wasn't too bad. Met back up with a few of his pals, pieced the story together a bit. Yeah, he was a hard old bastard was my Grandad. Not like young folk nowadays. The lads my Sophie hangs around with ... "

Nigel laughed bitterly.

"Well, you could hardly imagine it. Worried about messing their hair up or breaking a nail. Point is, lads: World War Two. That was probably the last time men could really be men, you know? Running around, fighting hand to hand, kill or be killed, man versus man. A cause you could believe in ... What a time to be alive, eh? That's my point. Real freedom! Do what you like. Do whatever it takes. Get a medal at the end of it."

"Since then, it's all missiles, computers, no room for a man and his hands to make a difference. Techno-war. Our creations have displaced us, you know? Like in Terminator. The robots won't need us sooner or later, and then what?"

A wistful expression drifted across Nigel's face. Nobody spoke. I looked over at Keith who was staring out of the window, still rubbing his cheek. Nigel recomposed himself.

"On the subject of computers ... we're here now. Shaun, I require your assistance. Mr Pardew tells me you can fall asleep more or less at will. That right?"

"Well, it's not always that easy ... "

"Good! So, you see those buildings over there? There's a business called SmrtHole based in the nearest one. Just some boring little tech start-up, nothing you'd be interested in. But they're on my radar."

"Smurt Hole?" Keith asked.

"Well, it's supposed to be 'smart' but in tech you leave out the vowels. So 'smrt' - s, m, r, t."

"That's the Serbian word for death," Keith smiling faintly now.

"Is it really?" Nigel momentarily appeared fascinated by something someone else had said. "Serbian word for death, eh? Death Hole ... very ironic."

"As in '*Ujedinjenje ili smrt*' - 'Unification or death', the group better known as the Black Hand, which organised the killing of Archduke Franz Ferdinand in Sarajevo in 1914. In Cyrillic, it looks like C, M, P, T ... "

"Yeah, alright whatever. Good to know though. 'Smrt'. I'll remember that. You might end up being useful after all Mr Pardew! Anyway, these kids used to work for me and I'm always ... ahhh ... interested in what my former protégés are up to, you might say. They have a meeting with some investors this afternoon and you, Mr Strong, are going to tell me what happens."

"I don't know if I'll understand it. I don't know much about business or computers," I warned.

"Do not panic Shaun. Priority one: they're going to demo some software. You tell me everything it does. Priority two: do the money men come out of the meeting looking happy or unhappy? You get me that info and I'll take care of the rest."

"Right - you," Nigel addressed Keith. "Jump out and put the seats down so our mutual friend has a bit of room to spread out."

Keith attempted to do as he was told, hampered greatly by having his hands bound together. Eventually, he was outside the car, staring at the array of handles, knobs and buttons on the side of the Range Rover's rear seats. He pulled one handle and tried to lift the seat up to no avail. He tested another - this time the seat slid backwards, trapping my knee.

"I can't see how to do it."

"For fuck's sake! I can see why you live with your mother, you useless pillock. No common sense - that's the trouble with people like you and Milky Bar Kid. All chock full of grand ideas and theories, but you can't put a car seat down, any more than you could garrotte a Waffen SS guard."

He pronounced it "vaffen", not "waffen".

"It's that one! Pull it. No, pull it! Careful! This car costs more than your bloody house! That one! No, THAT ONE!"

Nigel stormed out of the driver's seat and stamped round to the rear passenger side door. He shoved Keith out of the way and yanked on one of the handles, while trying to lift the seat. Still nothing happened.

"What have you done to it? For God's sake, I only had this serviced last month. You clumsy idiot!"

"Maybe if you try…" Keith leaned in and pointed with both index fingers at once.

"Just leave it! Don't touch it! You - climb out and we'll see if we can't get it down flat on that side."

I crawled over the seat and slid face first out of the door onto the floor at Nigel and Keith's feet. As I sat up, Nigel stepped forward and pushed the flipped-forward seat back into position. He pulled a lever on the side and in one fluid movement, the seat popped up and the back collapsed down flat.

"Huh…I forgot you have to put it back in position," Nigel mumbled, sauntering round to the other back door and repeating the operation with that seat.

"Right, back in. Off to beddy-byes Shaun. Do you need a pill to help you get off? Here." Nigel opened the glove compartment and took out a brown plastic bottle with a child-proof lid on, which he tossed over his shoulder towards us. "They're the wife's. Help yourself."

The situation was not particularly relaxing, and so I decided to take Nigel up on his offer. I picked up the bottle, but with my hands tied together I kept fumbling it. Eventually, we got it open, with me holding the container and Keith undoing the lid.

"Don't come back until the finance people have left. It's vital that I know what they say on the way out. Don't let me down Shaun."

I was asleep in minutes, looking down on my sleeping form from the Range Rover's ceiling. Keith nudged me.

"He's gone."

"Good."

"Can I sit in the front now?"

"No."

41

I set off towards SmrtHole, drifting through the thick bushes that shielded the business park and across the car park towards what looked like a main entrance. There, I found a board showing a plan of the park and indicating the SmrtHole were based round the far side.

As I floated round the series of low brick buildings, I noticed how new and pristine everything looked out here. The verges were immaculately tidy. The stone benches were smooth and lichen-free. There were more bicycles parked outside than cars.

Eventually, I found my way to SmrtHole's offices - where I encountered three twenty-somethings - two men and a woman - in the midst of an argument.

"It's just a tie Gabriel. Please put it on," the woman sounded exasperated. All three were wearing business suits that they were obviously uncomfortable in. Tattoos peeped out from the woman's frilled white blouse cuffs as she exhorted her colleague to put on the tie he was holding. Her blue hair was pulled back in a severe ponytail.

"Don't you think it's strange?" The man referred to as Gabriel replied. "The way that we signal our respectability to the rest of the world is with this?"

He waved the tie with a contemptuous sneer on his face. With his other hand, he pulled at his full red beard.

"A noose. You put a noose around your neck to prove it. To prove your submission. I'll show you what I think of their ties."

Gabriel slipped it over his head and pulled it tight above his ears like a bandana.

"I'll wear it like this. I'm not putting it round my neck."

"Geoffrey, you talk to him!" The woman walked angrily out of the room. At the doorway, one of her high heels gave way and she went over on her ankle and staggered heavily into the frame. The two men - now deep in discussion - did not notice. The man called Geoffrey looked a lot more normal than his colleagues, with a bowl cut hairdo and a pasty complexion that suggested a life spent mostly indoors under monitor light. He was a head shorter than the burly hipster Gabriel.

"These people are very conservative Gabe. Think about the money. This is what we've been working for."

"It's not about the money G," Gabriel whined, scratching compulsively at the shaven back of his head. "This is not us! This is him. This is what we left Evolution to get away from, isn't it?"

"The lawyers say that we just have to do this one time. Just one meeting with them and they can take care of everything until payday. All we have to do is make a good impression. They know it's a great bit of software. They can see the potential. It's just about making sure they trust us now."

"I just don't see why we have to pretend to be people we're not…"

"Gabe, don't think about the money. Don't even think about doing it for Jaz."

Geoffrey waved in the direction of the departed woman.

"Think about the look on Darwin's face. His stupid, fat, smug arsehole of a face. When we're millionaires. Come on. Isn't it worth putting a tie on for an hour - just one little hour - for that? To piss him off that badly?"

Gabe snorted.

"Well, if you put it like that…"

He popped his collar up and pulled the tie down from around his head.

"It's only a tie I suppose."

"Good...good..." Geoffrey patted Gabe on the shoulder. "Now, we're going to have to talk about the sandals as well."

Two hours later, the meeting was over. In spite of the pre-show theatrics and nerves, Geoffrey, Jaz and Gabriel had performed impeccably. Gabe, in particular, had made an excellent impression on the Dhaliwal brothers and their legal team. It turned out that he had spent part of his gap year not far from the brothers' ancestral village in Punjab. And that his father was the county council portfolio holder for planning and development.

The Dhaliwal brothers - they were referred to exclusively and interchangeably as "Mr Dhaliwal" - could not have looked much less like brothers. One was tall, slim, handsome and wore an immaculate Saville Row suit. The other one looked like Super Mario antagonist Wario and was dressed in lurid tweeds that looked fit to burst at any moment.

I couldn't really follow what happened in the meeting. At the beginning, everyone was wary. Geoffrey, Jaz and Gabe seemed very anxious and the Dhaliwals seemed a little bored. Most of the running was made by the sets of lawyers who had come along. Gradually though everybody warmed up and when the meeting ended, they were laughing and joking like old friends and the lawyers were mostly quiet.

After the brothers and their lawyers left, the SmrtHole team's lawyer - a smooth-looking public school type around my age - shook hands with each of the three. He clapped Geoffrey on the shoulder.

"Well done. Well done. You've just taken a big step along the road to riches, my friends."

As he was leaving the room, he turned back, pointed, winked and said: "You're going to make a lot of money."

Geoffrey, Jaz and Gabe were left alone in their conference room, breathing deeply and smiling sheepishly at one another.

Finally, Gabe spoke.

"Let's get these fucking shoes off."

42

Back at the Range Rover I explained what had happened. Even without mention of Geoffrey's remarks about his "stupid, fat, smug arsehole of a face", Nigel was not pleased with the news. We drove back to Prospect House in silence, Keith and I jammed into the miniature back seats once again.

We stopped in the underground garage. Nigel was staring out of the windscreen, gripping the steering wheel. The car was still running, but Nigel's ever-deeper exhalations were all that could be heard.

Nothing moved. We sat motionless in silence. I tried to catch Keith's eye, but his gaze was fixed on Nigel. I found myself holding my breath.

Then, all at once, Nigel switched the engine off, undid his seatbelt, flung the door open and drew out a long metal rod from under the passenger seat - all in one seemingly simultaneous action. He leapt out.

As he swung the metal rod back - now held in both hands - over his right shoulder, time stood still again, as if the air was being sucked in before an explosion. In that frozen moment, Nigel's stupid, fat, smug arsehole of a face was overtaken by a look of such demonic fury that I felt my heart contract in my chest.

Nigel screamed and smashed the rod into the windscreen of the Range Rover. It was the same inhuman, mechanical screech I had heard at his home that morning. The glass shattered.

Nigel continued to beat the windscreen as his lungs emptied. The monstrous sound he was emitting gradually subsided into a human voice once more.

He hurled the rod onto the floor. The clang it made was louder than the smashing glass had been. The metallic sound seemed to bring everybody round. Nigel looked up and breathed in deeply. Keith and I sat up in our seats.

"Back in the lift chaps. Thank you for your help today Shaun. Disappointing news, but now we know, don't we? Now we know."

With that he went silent again. Nobody spoke in the elevator up to the seventh floor. As we walked back into our office prison, Nigel started speaking again - as much to himself as to us.

"Those kids…those ungrateful…bastards. After everything I did for them. The opportunities I gave them. It just shows you, doesn't it? The joke will be on them soon though."

He chuckled nastily and looked up at Keith and I.

"People. They always let you down in the end, gentlemen. Give the bird something to eat. He looks hungry."

And with that, he slammed the office door shut.

"What was all that about?" I asked.

"The SmrtHole people - they used to work for him," Keith replied. "He reckons they stole some idea of his. Smashing the windscreen was a surprise. He seemed very calm and composed when he explained the situation to me. It sounds like these people have made a great success of their business. They're about to cash in and Nigel can't stand it."

"Do you think they really did steal his idea?"

"Does it matter?"

"What's he going to do?"

"Your guess is as good as mine Shaun. I doubt it will be good though."

Keith began to stroke his chin patch thoughtfully as he went to fetch Ragnar a chick from the now stinking tub.

The eagle stared hatefully at us, then turned his back. Keith edged towards him, dangling the dead bird by the toe between his thumb and forefinger.

"Come on Ragnar. Dinner time."

Keith waggled the chick as he slid closer. Ragnar paid no attention, hunched sullenly on his perch.

"Come on birdie…"

Ragnar closed his eyes.

"Fuck you then," Keith tossed the chick at the back of the eagle's head. And all hell broke loose, once again.

Ragnar began shrieking and attempted to take flight, only to be pulled - time and time again - to the floor by the tether around his ankle. The giant bird flopped heavily against the floor, once, twice, three times…

And so the day ended in much the same way as it had begun.

43

The next morning, we found out exactly what Nigel had done about SmrtHole. He came in early with our breakfast, smirking.

"Morning boys. Did you hear what happened out Chertsey way last night? Terrible affair - fire at a business park. And to think, we were just near there yesterday. Three dead they're saying on the news. Very sad. Very sad indeed."

Nigel walked over to where Keith and I were sitting and tossed some packs of sandwiches onto the table.

"Tuck in. Yeah…it was a company called SmrtHole. Some of them used to work here. Authorities are saying it was some kind of drug binge gone wrong. Cooking up crack or something, I heard. Getting more and more fucked up, until… oops…something catches fire. And you know what coke-heads are like, I'm sure. Not exactly a great help in high pressure scenarios.

"Yes, what a terrible shame. I hear they were doing really well too."

Keith opened a pack of sandwiches. A fart smell drifted out.

"Did you start the fire?" he asked.

Nigel adopted an exaggerated expression of shock.

"I did no such thing! How could you think that Mr Pardew? No, I did not start the fire. I made that little shit Geoffrey do it. I made him set his friends on fire. The only people who could stand to be around him. And then I made him overdose.

Which, I add in my defence, he was quite happy to do by that time. Snivelling shit. 'Don't kill me! Why are you doing this?' You know what I told him? 'Why not?'"

"Ming the Merciless," Keith whispered.

"Ming the fucking Merciless. Well spotted Keith. Dino De Laurentis, 1980. Cinematic masterpiece. And that soundtrack! Duh-duh-duh-duh-duh…."

Keith joined in.

"Duh-duh-duh-duh FLASH! Aa-aaaaaaaaa!"

They both collapsed in laughter. Nigel held out his palm and Keith high-fived him.

"Yeah, terrible tragedy. Still, that's what happens when you mix drugs and bad karma. They stole from me Shaun. I did everything for them and they repay me by leaving to set up their own company. Ingratitude. It's the one thing I can't stand. Steal from me. Then get it all going with daddy's money. No one ever gave me anything! I built all of this! From nothing! Nothing!"

Nigel's cheerful demeanour had evaporated and he was furiously angry again. But I wasn't listening to him. I was thinking about that high-five.

I asked Keith about it later.

"What's the big deal? We're stuck here with a psychopath. I'm just trying to get on his good side. Don't forget, I'm the one who's dispensable here. I'm not the one who's got something he wants, and you'd better start thinking about how you're going to show him. He won't wait forever. If we're going to get out of here, you need to work out how to teach other people to do it."

"If I knew, I swear, I would… It's not that I don't want to. I just don't know how…", I protested.

"It's not me you have to convince Shaun. It's him. That man who took us hostage and locked us up here. Who just killed three people because he was jealous. Don't worry about what I think. Worry about what he thinks. Look…why don't you explain how it works for you to me again?"

I did.

"So it's something to do with falling asleep? Something that happens as you're falling asleep.... OK, that's somewhere to start. We can rule out everything in the literature that doesn't start from falling asleep. Come on Shaun, grab a crate. At least we'll be doing something rather than just sitting here waiting for him to go mental again and kill us."

We pored over the books all day and well into the night. Nigel didn't come back at all, meaning we only had another pack of sandwiches to share between us for the whole day. But neither of us noticed the hunger. We had a purpose of sorts and that kept us going.

We tried out a few of the rituals and practices described, but nothing seemed to make a difference. For starters, Keith couldn't fall asleep like I could.

"Every time I start to doze off, I notice it and I wake up! How do you manage it? Are you narcoleptic or something? This is bullshit! It doesn't make any sense that this is something nobody but you can do. It's totally irrational! What's so special about you?!

"You know what happens to me when I go to sleep? I dream. Usually I dream about getting beaten up at school. Pretty straightforward, that. Don't need a psychology degree to see where that's coming from. What about this then? Two nights ago, you know what I dreamed about? I was at an aquarium, and this huge fish kept swimming round in a circle and sloshing water over the top of the tank onto me. I banged on the glass to try and get its attention, but it just swam on without me getting a proper glimpse of it. Other people said it was a barracuda, but it looked more like a goliath grouper. You know, one of those massive lumpy fish. Kind of red and green and brown.

"Anyway, I kept hammering on the glass with each circuit until finally, the fish noticed and slowly it turned towards me. It had the face of Glenn Hoddle."

Unfortunately, I had a mouthful of water at this precise moment. The punchline of Keith's dream made me convulse with laughter, spitting the water out of my mouth and nose. The sensation was like having the mucous membranes in my lower nasal cavity sandpapered.

"What does that mean Shaun? Why would I dream about a former England manager's face on a giant fish? I'm not even interested in football. I only know who Glenn Hoddle is because of all that mad shit he said about disabled people on Richard and Judy.

"I'll tell you what it means. It means nothing at all Shaun. It's nonsense. There's no significance to dreams beyond what goes on inside your head."

"I never said there was…" I pointed out.

"All this," Keith waved angrily at the pile of books. "It's all just bollocks! It's all just 'oh, it takes years of practice and blah blah blah' but none of it explains what's happening. What do they want? Faith?"

I took a piece of kitchen roll from the table and began to wipe up the water I had dribbled over myself. We had been held hostage for five days now and in spite of everything that had happened, Nigel had not mentioned anything about teaching him how to do The Thing to me - apart from that vague reference to "fulfilling his destiny" right after he had let me out of the crate, if that counts. It was Keith who kept going on about it. So far, Nigel had only got me to spy on people. Whom he had subsequently murdered.

Things continued for the next couple of weeks in this vein. Every day or two, Nigel would take us out in the Range Rover, park up somewhere or other and tell me to go and sit in on a meeting or read pages of a notebook over someone's shoulder or memorise a door security code. He seemed to be planning something relating to the Royal Surrey Hospital out the other side of Guildford, but Keith and I couldn't work out what it was and (with our cell being monitored by CCTV) thought it best not to talk about it too much. I had been regularly using Michelle's tranquilisers to help me get off to sleep for espionage missions, and I was starting to use them back at the office for normal sleeping.

Each time we went out, Nigel would regale us with either the yacht story or the St Nazaire raid story or his theory about Dexter while he elaborated on his personal philosophy.

"You know what my motto in business and in life is?" Nigel asked us one sunny morning as we drove out of Woking. Presumably the question was rhetorical, as he didn't wait for an answer. "Woe to the vanquished. You know who the vanquished are? Everyone who submits. Everyone who knows their place. Everyone who takes what they're given and says 'thank you'. When I look at the people who work for me - and I include you boys in that, even though I'm not paying you, ah ha ha ha! - when I look at them, I think 'you can only eat because I allow it'. Wage labour is the main clause in the treaty under which the defeated are permitted to exist. Nice line, eh? I got it from a book. Golovkin showed me it.

"You may think, why would a businessman like me - someone who lives by his instincts and gets what he wants through determination - be reading books that say stuff like that? Well, it's like I said before. What do you do when you've got everything you want? When you can have anything you want? Did I tell you about my yacht?"

Nigel repeated the story of how he had bought a yacht and then not used it.

"Law and morality. Who creates them Shaun? The winners, that's who. Here's another nice quote for you. 'Prisons are built with stones of law - brothels with bricks of religion'. You know who said that?"

"Blake," Keith said.

"William Blake," Nigel went on, apparently not having heard Keith's reply. "'The Proverbs of Hell'. I may not look it, but I'm a deep thinker. Spiritual victory…it requires the overthrow of what went before. The transvaluation of all values. That's Neetch that is."

I glanced at Keith. I'd worked in libraries long enough to know that anyone over 19 years of age who mentions Friedrich Nietzsche is an immediate red flag. The glance was purely instinctive, a habit from my previous life. It reminded me with a little jolt that we were still in deep trouble, even if we had fallen into something of a perverse domestic routine with our captor.

Keith, however, was nodding.

Nigel continued.

"The ancient Greeks, you know - their word for 'good' has the same meaning as 'noble'. And 'bad' means 'common'. Did you know that? To be good for the Greeks was to be happy, strong and healthy."

"'The purpose of all culture is to breed a tame and civilised animal out of the beast of prey man'," Keith murmured.

"Exactly!" Nigel shouted, delighted. "Who said that then?"

"Nietzsche. Genealogy of Morals," Keith replied quietly.

"Keith knows what I'm on about. Who was Jesus anyway? Didn't work. Lived on handouts. No kids, hung around with a bunch of men. A scrounger and probably a queer. Not that there's anything wrong with queers but still. You know what my lawyer's business card says on it? 'Do what thou wilt shall be the whole of the law'! He's a character..."

Nigel turned in to a small car park at the edge of a pine tree plantation. He turned round to face us.

"You think I'm a fascist, don't you? You think I want to enslave the masses? Wrong. You couldn't be more wrong. I'm not a racist. My daughter - she has a couple of black friends. People do these days, don't they? They've been over to our house. I'm fine with that. I don't hate anyone for things they can't do anything about. But my real contempt...my scorn... my...my....yeah, contempt is for the blindly submissive and the victimised...spaniels that roll onto their backs when you kick them. I'm not interested in them. They're beneath my notice. This is about me - just me. I'm creating a new world in the midst of this ruined and fucked-up one. You know what they call a being that creates a world? A god. But a new kind of god - one that doesn't depend on the worship of the failures and the weak. What kind of a god needs praise? A neurotic, inse-cure god! A god that sits staring at Facebook, anxiously waiting for someone to mention him in their prayers? No, I'll be one that generates my own energy. That is my challenge, gentlemen. Living independent godhood."

I didn't really know what to say to that. It was a new level of crazy, even by Nigel's standards.

"We can help you," blurted Keith. "Shaun…knows things. He has powers. Let us help you."

"Oh, we'll get to that. Don't you worry Mr Pardew. I have big plans for our friend here."

"Let me help. I can help. I want to help."

"What do you think you can do to help me?"

"I got him for you, didn't I?"

I felt stomach acid rising up my oesophagus. Yes. Keith was pointing at me.

"I brought you two together! I've given you the means to fulfil your destiny! Just…let me serve you. Let me contribute to your glorious task!"

The car was silent. I realised both of them were now looking at me. Keith had an expression of defensive defiance mixed with wary terror on his face. Nigel's eyes were wide, and he grinned broadly. He cocked his head towards Keith and pointed at me.

"He didn't know, did he?"

The Range Rover rocked back and forth as Nigel guffawed with uncontrolled laughter.

Now, I know that I've dropped hints while I've been telling you this story that I suspected Keith was up to something. But that's all ex post facto rationalisation by me, the narrator. As you've probably already realised, I'm not the most reliable narrator either. Up until that moment, it had never crossed my mind that Keith had sold me out. My only friend.

They talk about a 'sinking feeling' sometimes, don't they? Well, that is exactly what I was feeling right then. Like I was sinking through the car seats, through the chassis, through the asphalt, the hardcore, and tumbling down, deeper and deeper, towards the earth's core. The one thing I had thought I could count on - that one cord securing me to the surface had snapped.

Eventually, Nigel's laughter calmed down. His face was bright red as he wiped tears from the corners of his eyes.

"That's hilarious. You two… Anyway, back to work. Shaun, I know you've had a shock, so take a couple of extra pills if you think you need them. You can sort this out between you later. I need you on good form. I have a special job for you today."

44

The special job in question was to keep an eye on Nigel's wife, Michelle, at their family home. Building works were continuing and Nigel was determined to find out if she was getting up to anything with the builders while he was out.

My head was spinning. Keith had betrayed me. This was all happening because Keith had colluded with Nigel. I couldn't believe it. Or could I? There had been signs. But friends aren't supposed to sell each other out, are they?

But you know what? That wasn't the real reason my head was spinning. I was going to see Michelle. In spite of the appalling revelation I had just been subjected to, I felt a frisson of excitement and gratitude when Nigel explained what I had to do. Oh well - my best friend has betrayed me into the hands of a murderous lunatic, but I'll get to see HER again. She might even be... That sense of anticipation and pre-emptive shame I had come to know so well, which I had almost forgotten about in the last two weeks washed over me once again. My fingertips were tingling and I felt my bowels were ready to burst.

I know it doesn't sound normal. Clearly discovering that Keith had set me up was a much more important life event than getting to see Michelle, a woman I had never met and essentially knew nothing about. I could see that even then, but - what can I say? - I thought I was in love. I'm also excellent at compartmentalising my feelings and resigning myself to my situation. Tuck that sense of dread and overwhelming horror away for now Shaun. It'll only stop you enjoying what happens next. There'll be time to worry and fret later. Right then, there was no suffering I wasn't happy to endure, no misery I wouldn't have embraced for a chance to live out my pathetic fantasy. Of course it wasn't love. But the anaesthesia that was my life up until then had made it very difficult to tell what - when I occasionally did feel something - it was I was feeling.

"I want to know everything she does, everyone she speaks to - and if there is anything going on, you find out which one of those fuckers it is and come back right here. I don't want you perving over her. Got it?"

"Yeah," I replied.

"Good. Take as long as you need. Mr Pardew and I have things to do in your absence, don't we?" Nigel chuckled and shook his head. "I can't believe you didn't know. That's so funny. Now go on and take your medicine."

I popped a couple of sleeping pills as Keith climbed out of the back and put the seats down. The Halcion took hold quickly, quicker than I had expected. More like an anaesthetic than a tranquiliser. Were these the same kind as I usually took? I glanced at the bottle as I slipped away - Midazolam...?

I felt very strange as I glided along Nigel's road towards his driveway, the Range Rover speeding off in the opposite direction. It was like a state of dissociative drunkenness. I had all the perceptual signs of being wasted - everything seemed to be spinning slowly and I found myself veering off to the left as I moved along. And yet my mind was completely clear. I had none of the fuzzy-headedness that accompanies those physical symptoms. Indeed, it seemed as though I was watching myself heading towards Nigel Darwin's mansion from somewhere else entirely.

The silver Porsche was on the drive, along with two dirty white transit vans and a half-full skip. Here we go then, I thought, as I levitated to survey the whole scene from upon high. Since I had last been here, the pit had been filled with concrete and levelled to a smooth screed with bits of ironwork poking through. It reminded me of the demolition site next door to Prospect House. There was no sign of life outside except for a bounding yellow dog, tearing around the lawn and in and out of the thick bushes that bordered the estate.

That dog looked strangely familiar.

"Woof! Woof! Woof!"

Fucking hell. It was Colonel Aureliano Buendia. What was he doing here?

Distracted by the surprise presence of the late Longs' family pet at the home of their killer, I found myself sinking and soon I was heading down the Darwins' chimney stack. I found myself in the fireplace, looking at the woman of my dreams, standing by an open patio door.

"Toby!"

"Woof!"

"Come on in boy!"

"Woof! Woof!"

"Toby! Come on."

Colonel Aureliano Buendia lolloped into the room, wagging his tail with carefree abandon and jumped up to land his huge shaggy paws on Michelle's shoulders.

"Good boy Toby! You like your new garden, don't you?"

I couldn't help but admire how Michelle had renamed the ridiculously-monickered animal with an authentic dog's name. We had the same sensibilities, I could tell.

"No Toby! No! Put it away! Dirty boy!"

Colonel Aureliano Buendia's bright red lipstick had popped out and he was shuffling his back legs in an effort to manoeuvre into a more auspicious position for putting it to use.

"Dirty! Dirty! Out!"

Oh God.

The dog sprinted back outside barking cheerfully, cock retracting. If only I could forget her like that, I thought sadly. Michelle slid the door shut and padded out of the garden room, barefoot. I collected myself and followed her into the kitchen. She made herself a coffee and sat down at the breakfast bar, swinging her legs back and forth. Michelle took a sip of coffee, checked her phone and gazed around the room. She caught her own eye in the giant hall mirror - the one Nigel had screamed into - and stared distractedly at herself.

Michelle's phone rang.

"Hiya. Yeah. No. Tonight? In the West End? Yeah. No, I don't know who he is either but it'll be a good show if it's on there. And…ha ha ha. Yes, absolutely - cocktails after. Up to you love. He won't give a shit if I come home or not. He can walk his own fucking dog, can't he? Five? What is it now? Two? Alright, I'll pick you up at yours. Ok, bye bye. Bye bye."

Michelle ended the call and smiled as she put the phone down on the breakfast bar. That smile broke my heart. Well, kind of. It was like I could feel the plaque all around my heart beginning to crack from the inside - like it was moving for the first time in years. Lightning arced down my spine, spiralling round and round my coccyx and diffusing outwards through my balls. Not romantic I know, but that's what it felt like.

Clutching her mug in both hands, Michelle walked out of the kitchen and into the hall. As she passed the taxidermy room, seeing that the door was open, she snorted, rolled her eyes and closed it. "Jesus," she hissed under her breath, checking her phone once again as she continued along the corridor.

And that was how things went for an hour or more. Michelle would amble about the house in her dressing gown, stopping every so often to reply to a text. She never spent more than two or three minutes in any of the rooms she passed through, until she came to a halt in the master bedroom. The place where I had seen her for the very first time.

She stood looking out of the window, leaning on the sill. The view overlooked the building site, where a number of workmen - including the lupine foreman - were loitering, having returned from wherever they had been when I was floating above the estate. She stared at them for what seemed like a few minutes, until one of their number noticed that they were being watched. He nudged his mate and pointed up at the window. The group of men now all looked up. Michelle gave them a small wave, and they all burst into coarse laughter. I hated them.

Michelle lay down on the bed and I lay beside her, counting the tiny hairs on her cheek and ear.

Maybe it was thirty seconds later, maybe it was thirty minutes - but the peace of that perfect moment was brutally broken by a banging, thumping and scuffling sound bursting out downstairs.

"Michelle!"

It was Nigel.

Distant thunder came closer and closer. The door burst open and Colonel Aureliano Buendia/Toby ran in, navigated two tight circles and ran out again, destined for who knows where.

"Michelle! Why is the dog shut out?"

Michelle sighed deeply and got up from the bed. Pulling her gown tight around her shoulders, she set off slowly towards the top of the stairs, dodging nimbly as the thickset retriever barged past her and barrelled down the staircase like a slobbering avalanche.

"MICHELLE!"

"I'm here! What's the matter?"

Standing at the bottom of the stairs was Nigel.

"The dog was shut out. He was scratching at the front door. What were you doing up there? You can't just forget about him like that."

"I hadn't forgotten about him."

"You banged on about wanting a dog for so long, Michelle. I get you a dog and you just leave him in the garden."

"Two things Nigel," Michelle's face was twisted into a sneer. "Firstly, it was Sophie who wanted a dog, not me. I barely have time to myself as it is and now I'm expected to look after this thing after she fucks off back to uni. Secondly, it was supposed to be a puppy - something for us all to choose together and for us all to take care of, like normal families do. But no, Nigel has to go and 'sort it all out', doesn't he? Swoops in, bringing a fully-grown dog home from God knows where and then disappears back to Woking again."

"You definitely said you wanted a dog."

"No I didn't."

"Yes you did! I distinctly remember it - we were in Paris…"

"Paris! That was eleven years ago! Eleven years ago, Nigel! I agreed to the puppy idea, which you pushed and pushed Sophie on until she gave in. She doesn't even live here any more! She's not a little girl!"

"She'll always be my little girl."

"Maybe so, but she's off at Durham for three quarters of the year, isn't she? So who's going to walk him when she's not here? Who's going to stop him digging up the lawn, or humping your stuffed monstrosities in the hall of horrors, eh? Me, Nigel. Me. As usual."

"So what were you doing upstairs?"

"Nothing. Just having a lie down."

"Busy day, is it? Got episodes of Corrie to catch up on? Instructing the cleaner taking it out of you?"

"You know what, Nigel? Let's just not have this argument and tell everyone we did. I can't be bothered. You win. Congratulations. I'll add it onto your total on the scoreboard. Anyway, I'm off out. I might not be back tonight."

"You don't say! Where is it this time?"

"West End with Tina. She's got tickets to see 'You Make Me Feel Like Dancing - The Leo Sayer Story'. We'll probably stop at a hotel."

"Leo Sayer, eh? Never knew you were a fan."

Michelle shook her head in resignation.

"I'm not. But if it gets me away from here, I'll give it a shot."

With that she walked back to the bedroom and slammed the door.

Smiling humourlessly, Nigel waited until the sound of his wife had receded into silence and then called out: "Follow me Shaun. I know you're here and you're not going to want to miss this. And don't think of going and spying on her instead, you dirty bastard."

No point pretending. I did as I was told and followed Nigel out to one of the garages. Keith was there, standing between two dust-sheet covered cars. Nigel spoke.

"Now then Mr Strong. Are you with us? One knock for yes, two knocks for no. Ah ha ha ha. No, assuming you are here - and there will be penalties if I find out you are not - we have a few things to go through."

Keith had hopped up onto a workbench and was sat with his hands tucked under his buttocks, kicking his legs back and forth. He had a faint smile on his face, but his eyes looked haunted. What he'd done came to the forefront of my mind again and I was engulfed by nausea all over again.

"Up until now, Shaun, I've not really asked too much of you. You've helped me out a few times, and I'm grateful for that. But come on Shaun. How much louder do I need to drop the hints? Louder than the sound of bones in the old boy's face shattering? I feel like you're taking the piss out of me. Is that what you're doing? I don't think you're a piss-taker, but how am I supposed to take it? Your mate's been telling you to get on with it. You should listen to him. It may surprise you to hear it today of all days, but he's got your best interests at heart."

"Shaun, you need to show him how to do it," said Keith. "One way or another, you have to teach him. I warned you. I told you again and again."

"You most certainly did Mr Pardew! But you're determined to keep it all to yourself, aren't you Mr Strong? Your little secret isn't for sharing, is it? Your friend here tells me you don't know how you do it, but I simply find that implausible. I do not accept that as an excuse. So, allow me to apply some alternative motivation. You see this?"

Nigel held up a package, wrapped in a cloth. Teasingly, he unveiled it to reveal a laptop.

"Not just any laptop. Do you know whose laptop this used to be? Mr Pardew, would you care to enlighten our friend?"

"It's Trevor Long's laptop."

"The late, lamented Trevor Long's laptop. Quite right. Covered, may I add, in your fingerprints. It may surprise you to discover that you've been handling this object this very morning, while you've been distracted by my wife. So it's quite covered in your fingerprints and your blood. Blood which can also be found under the nails of our refrigerated friend. Blood left by Trevor Long's killer at the scene of the crime, you may recall, in the shape of…"

An earprint. Oh fuck.

Nigel went on.

"A laptop, moreover, which contains emails between you and Mr and Mrs Long - all properly time and date-stamped I hasten to add - in which you were threatening them. Making serious, credible threats upon their lives, all on account of your pathetic, tragic, dark obsession with Trevor's wife. It's a fairly damning piece of evidence, this laptop. And if that's not enough, there's the corpse hidden in a certain freezer at your home, Mr Strong."

At my home? My head was spinning.

"Yes, the police would certainly be very interested to find this laptop, having hit a brick wall with their investigation and everything Why, it would lead them straight to the murderer! But the police need never see the laptop Shaun. I'll destroy it myself for you. All I ask is one little thing in return and that is that you just share your gift with me. You've got two days. I expect to be on the astral plane before Thursday lunchtime, or you will be off to the big house for a long, long time."

Everything went white. I came to, soaked in sweat, hyperventilating, my heart hurt with every beat. I was in the back of the Range Rover. My hands were bound together. I sat up and fainted again, the world wheeling around me. Gradually, my heart rate dropped and I pulled myself up. The Range Rover was on the Darwin's driveway. Michelle's Porsche was gone and so was the builders' van. Apart from the cable tie around my wrists, I was loose. I tried and failed to reach the switch on the seat in front of me to flip it forward, so I began to crawl over it instead. As I was shuffling my groin over a leather headrest, the chair back gave way, rolled forward and I slid face first into the footwell, biting my lower lip as I landed. I spat hot iron-flavoured blood onto the mat as I slithered the rest of my body down to where I had landed and hauled myself back up onto the seat. I tried the rear door. Child locked. So I began to pull myself between the front seats, taking care this time not to snag anything on the gearstick.

I got my bum into the passenger seat and swung my legs over the driver's seat. The leather interiors were ideally suited to this type of sliding. Soon, I was sitting upright. Now what?

Escape of course.

Nobody knew I was here and not in the garage. All I would have to do would be to run down the drive and out of the gate. Twenty seconds. That's all I'd need. And then I'd be free.

I opened the car door. The alarm went off.

45

The piercing howl of the alarm smothered all other sounds. I jumped out of the Range Rover onto the gravel drive, losing my footing and stumbling to the floor as I landed, not realising how drowsy I still was from the new sleeping pills. Looking over my shoulder as I climbed unsteadily back to my feet, I saw the garage door swing open and from the darkness within, two figures sprung. Nigel saw me first and sprinted towards me, Keith a few paces behind him. Nigel was shouting something I could not make out over the electronic shrieking.

I ran towards the gate, which I could see was closed. With Nigel and Keith just a few metres behind me, I knew I wouldn't have time to climb it before they pulled me back down. I had to lose them in the grounds and buy the time needed to climb a fence to escape. Changing direction at the last moment, I darted into the rhododendrons that bordered the gates. I put my head down, my hands in front of my face, and hurled myself through the undergrowth so as to be sure of getting out of sight of the path. Thorns and twigs tore at my skin and clothes as I dived into a small depression, deep enough to be invisible in if I pressed myself to the ground.

The alarm's scream soon halted and silence prevailed. I could hear myself breathing and my heart beating, blood pounding in my ears. I could hear slow footsteps on the gravel.

"Shaun! Don't be an idiot! Come out! You're just wasting your own time!" Nigel was shouting. But the sound was receding. He had gone past me and was heading off towards the gardens at the rear of the house. I inched myself noiselessly through the mud towards where I thought the fence must be.

What was the boundary of the estate built of? Was it a fence? Or was it a wall? A hedge? I wracked my brain, trying to remember what I'd seen as we drove in just a few hours earlier. What time is it? Nigel had said lunchtime. Michelle had said it was two. It's afternoon. That means the sun will be in the west. I think. So…if that's west…which way does the house face? No idea. OK, start again. It'll be lighter nearer to the garden, so I should head away from the light. Right? Just head to where it's darker. Go deeper, and eventually I'll come to the edge. That's right isn't it?

I slithered deeper into the tame forest's interior darkness, inching forward by tiny degrees so as to remain silent. Through leaf litter and over exposed roots I hauled myself. Ants were crawling on the back of my neck, making no such attempts to go unnoticed about their business. Dust from the powder-dry soil tickled my nostrils and coagulated on my mucus membranes. My shoelaces snagged on a branch, and when I turned back to disentangle it, I found myself staring into the eyes of Colonel Aureliano Buendia.

The dog was twenty feet away, just beyond the dip where I had hidden myself. His gaze was calm, but his features radiated alertness. The immediate future flashed before my eyes - the dog would bark; Nigel and Keith would come crashing into the undergrowth and see me; I would run; they would run; I'd trip before they would. And that would be it.

But that didn't happen. Colonel Aureliano Buendia held my gaze for what seemed like whole minutes, his whole body poised and quivering, his tail motionless. Then the spell broke. The labrador cocked his head, swallowed and relaxed into a posture of amiable stupidity. Wagging his tail, he ran off. Did he…recognise me? Seconds after he had disappeared from my field of vision, but by now at some distance, Colonel Aureliano Buendia began barking hysterically with a high-pitched yipping.

Was he leading them away from me?

"Over there!" I heard Nigel shout. "Toby! Where are you boy? Toby! Show us where he is! Toby! Where is he?"

There was a pause.

"Oh my God! What have you rolled in you filthy bastard!? It's all over your fucking head! And your collar! Jesus Christ!"

"What is it?" Keith's voice now.

"The dog's found a pile of fox shit…"

I seized the opportunity Colonel Aureliano Buendia's diversion had afforded me and climbed to my feet. I ran away from the voices, hoping to lose them completely while the shit-caked dog had their attention. Oblivious to making a noise now I ran, lifting my feet and knees comically high to avoid stumbling on vines and deadfall. I ran blindly, not caring where I was going so long as the voices were behind me.

Somehow, I found myself back on the driveway. And the gate was open. Wildly, I looked around but there was no sign of Nigel or Keith. This was my chance. It looked like my luck had changed. I sprinted towards the open gate, not knowing where in the world beyond to head for or what I was going to do when I got there, but I put my head down and ran as fast as I could.

And that's when the car hit me.

46

I don't know how long I was unconscious for. I came round flat on my back, looking up into the faces of Nigel Darwin, Keith Pardew and an attractive young woman who looked a lot like Michelle, only younger and with broader features. It was Nigel's daughter Sophie.

"Who is he? Why was he running out of the gates?"

"Just a colleague. Training exercise. He looks alright to me. He look alright to you Keith? He's just winded, aren't you Shaun?"

"We have to call an ambulance! Look, his head's bleeding."

"There's no need love. Here Keith, help me get him up on his feet."

The two men knelt down and tucked their heads under my shoulders. They hauled me into a standing position, Nigel conspicuously doing the bulk of the lifting.

"I'm calling an ambulance," Sophie was rummaging in her handbag for a phone now.

"Sophie! Please! I will take my friend here to hospital myself. Your insurance is quite expensive enough already young lady without…getting involved in all this. Don't you worry about Shaun. Me and Keith will take him down to A&E at Chertsey right now. You're alright, aren't you Shaun?"

For some reason, I grunted assent. That's the trouble with being a yes man. Even when your life's at stake, you just want to please people.

Nigel had peeled away to forestall Sophie's phone call, transferring my full weight onto Keith's scrawny frame. He staggered forward to catch me, and as he did so breathed into my ear: "Historical Jesus explains everything."

"He's fine. He's a tough lad is our Shaun. Don't worry about the car Soph - I'll get it fixed and valeted for you. Best we don't mention this to your mum, eh?" said Nigel, taking one of my arms over his shoulder. They were half-leading, half-dragging me towards the Range Rover now.

"I'll give you a ring and let you know what the doctor says where we're all done. Don't worry yourself about it. It's just a training exercise. Work thing," Nigel pushing me into the back seat now, with Keith following behind.

"Call Yevgeny - get him to come and pick the car up. Take one of the others if you need to go out again," he called, climbing into the driver's seat.

"And don't let the dog into the house whatever you do!"

With that we were gone, leaving Sophie standing on the gravel drive, drops of my blood staining the pebbles red at her feet.

"There was no need for that Shaun," Nigel said shaking his head. "You disappoint me. I am making you a perfectly reasonable offer. Perhaps you don't think I'm serious? I'll show you who's fucking serious."

We drove back to Prospect House in silence. I tried to make eye contact with Keith, but he was staring out of the window, determined not to look at me.

As we were approaching the building, Nigel made a phone call.

"Come down to the garage. Bring your tool kit. Yeah. *Spasibo.*"

Yevgeny was waiting in the car park. He was squatting by the door to the service lift and stood up to his full height as we came to a halt. In his hand was a long sinuous pole. As he walked towards us, it made a metallic scraping noise on the floor.

241

"What's that you've got?" Nigel asked. "Fucking hell. Careful with that axe Yevgeny!"

Keith sniggered.

"What the fuck are you laughing at?"

"Aaaaaaaaaarrgggh!" Keith pantomimed a scream at low volume. "'Careful with that…' It's a song…"

"For Christ's sake…" Nigel turned his attention back to the Russian. "I want you to persuade him, not chop him up!"

"You say tool kit Mr Darwin. I presume you were speaking of disposal," Yevgeny said, his black glittering eyes fixed on me.

Suddenly, the side of my head where I'd hit the drive felt cold. I looked down and my shirt was covered in blood. I passed out.

47

When I came to this time, it was dark. And I was back in the Range Rover driving through the night. I was alone in the back and Yevgeny was driving. I tried to sit up and found that a dressing had been applied to my injured forehead.

"I'm taking you to the Royal Surrey," the driver said. The voice was like the call of an enraged water buffalo. "You have a pretty bad headwound there. In Chechnya, I see men die from this, I tell Mr Darwin."

"Were you in the army?" I asked.

"Mmmmm… sort of… back in Russia, I was a hydraulic engineer. We go in after worst of the fighting - try to restore some of the infrastructure. Water systems for me. See some very bad shit out there. England is much nicer. Better than Mexico. Too fucking hot there. You been to Llanberis in Wales? Dinorwig hydroelectric plant? They call it 'Electric Mountain'. Wonderful place. Well known in my corps."

I replied that I had not and we lapsed into silence once more.

"How you get mixed up in all this?" Yevgeny eventually spoke. "Your friend, I understand. You not so much. You really have magical powers? Mr Darwin, he talk so much shit I never know if he is joking or serious. He is a very strange person."

"What did you do to Mr Parson?" I murmured.

"The old man?" Yevgeny sighed. "Better you don't know. Unpleasant business. He a friend of yours?"

"Sort of."

"You have my condolences. There was very little suffering. You been to Scotland?"

"I hired a car at Edinburgh airport once."

"I have never been to Scotland. Whisky - of course, why not? But mostly Falkirk Wheel. Hydraulic lift for canal boats. It is a dream of mine to visit."

"I've seen it on TV, but I've never been there. Do you know the Anderton Boat Lift in Cheshire?"

"I have not heard of it."

"It's near to Northwich. It's over a hundred years old and it does the same sort of thing as the Falkirk Wheel. It's not as impressive to look at, but it's historical. It shifts boats from a river to a canal. Or the other way round."

"Where is …Northwich?"

"South of Manchester somewhere. I'm not really sure - I've lived my whole life here around Woking. I don't know much about the rest of the country. I think I went there with my Mum and Dad when I was a teenager. It wasn't working when we saw it, but they've restored it since then."

"This is very interesting. The canals of Great Britain are a fascination for me and other men of my specialisation. When I first learn about the *Belomorkanal* in school…that was when I knew I wanted to be an engineer. It is strange how our lives turn out, is it not Shaun? In Russia, there is a saying: 'Where you are born is where you are useful'. But here I am and so are you. Perhaps one day you will show me this Anderton Boat Lift, eh? Ha ha ha! And together we will ride the Falkirk Wheel and burrow into the Electric Mountain!"

My vision was still blurry. I looked out of the steamed-up windows. We were speeding through woodland along a single lane road. All of a sudden, Yevgeny's head whipped round and he began to brake.

"You see that?"

"What?"

"At the side of road."

We had come to a halt now on a grass verge. I looked back to where he was pointing. There was a dark shape lying at the edge of the tarmac about twenty feet behind us.

"That?"

"Yeah. What is?

I rubbed the condensation off the window and squinted. On closer inspection, it looked grey and white.

"A dead badger maybe?"

"Hmmm."

With that ambiguous sound, Yevgeny opened the door. Over his shoulder, he said: "You stay there. I fuck you up if you move."

I watched him stride over towards the heap at the roadside. He poked at it with his boot and flipped it over. Then he bent down, picked it up in both arms and came back to the car. Holding it up in the doorway for me to see, Yevgeny asked: "This a badger?"

It was. I nodded.

"Hmmm. Mr Darwin always looking for badger. He likes to stuff dead animals."

"I've seen."

"Hmmm. He tell me 'you find badger in good condition, you bring it back'. Stuffing animals…to me, this is ridiculous. And he is terrible at it. He cannot be satisfied with these… abominations. But I say ok, no problem. This one looks pretty good - no smashed bones, very little blood. Maybe he won't fuck it up completely. Here. You take it."

Yevgeny held the badger carcass out to me. Not quite knowing what to do next, I took it from him. It was heavier than it looked. And still warm.

"Put it down there in footwell. Do not touch it too much or you will get ticks off it, maybe other parasites. We get your head checked out, next I take badger back to Mr Darwin. Then, you tell Mr Darwin what he want to know or I pull all your teeth out."

I was in no position to argue, so I deposited the creature where Yevgeny told me to. He got back into the car and we drove away.

"Yes, I enjoy life here in England. Quiet. Not much to do. Mexico, Russia…very violent. Here, not so much. Mr Darwin, no one expect him to be gangster. Business pretty smooth. Little call for serious harm. Most trouble comes from Mr Darwin himself. *Psikh*. Crazy bastard. But not all the time…I am learning a lot about computers. Data science, very interesting. Maybe one day I go back to Russia, but I prefer to stay here for now. Not too hot, not too cold. But where you are born is where you are useful. I miss my home."

Yevgeny continued in this vein, talking as much to himself as to me. As far as I could see, I had just under 48 hours to live. Part of me had not quite believed Nigel's threats. I certainly hadn't believed that he'd fed anyone to owls. But that afternoon's events combined with the strange calmness of Yevgeny - a man whose capacity for fatal violence was so unambiguous - had changed my mind. Nigel's violence was explosive and unpredictable, but Yevgeny's workmanlike demeanour radiated the simple, efficient inevitability of death. I knew even then that there was no way I could talk this man into letting me go. He was just doing a job that he was completely indifferent to.

"What is the English word for this animal stuffing?"

"Taxidermy."

"Taxi. Dermy." Yevgeny rolled the word around his mouth like a sip of red wine. "It is quite unpleasant. Taxidermy. Good practice for this line of work though. Need a strong stomach. Animal anatomy, human anatomy. Not so very different. Scale. Proportion. Sometimes a tail. How's your head? Warm enough? You want I turn the heated seats on?"

Was there a way out? At the hospital perhaps? Could I get away from my captor there? Maybe there would be police at the Royal Surrey and I could let them know that I was being held prisoner. Were my chances better with Yevgeny than with Nigel? Or worse? My head was still swimming. I was in no fit state to break away from him. Other people would have to be my salvation. There would be plenty in A&E. Other people, who could rescue me.

"You want the radio on? Some music perhaps? Why not? We have Strauss, Wagner…"

"I really just want to go to sleep."

If I went to sleep and left my body, could I play dead? That might get me away from him, if the doctors thought I had to be operated on. They'd take me into the operating theatre and he'd have to wait outside. I'd be standing nearby, ready to leap back into my body and tell them the truth - about Nigel, about Trevor Long and about me and Keith. About everything. They'd have CCTV there. If Yevgeny tried to drag me out, our faces would be all over it. I'd shout out his name and who he worked for. Then people would come looking for me. If he couldn't get me away, he'd have to kill me to keep me quiet. The question was, would Yevgeny really kill me in a crowded hospital?

No.

The question was: did that dead badger just move?

I didn't have time to check. The Range Rover was instantly a flailing mass of fur, claws and teeth. The badger - suddenly very much alive - launched itself from the floor at the back of Yevgeny's head. Blood exploded from his neck dousing the leather interior. The Russian grabbed at the animal and as he did so, pulled the steering wheel sharply to the left. The car swerved hard. I felt it skid. Then it began to roll.

"*Grebanyy suka*! *Barsuk*!" he bellowed as we both hit the ceiling. The windscreen shattered and the badger landed in my lap, ten kilos of enraged muscle. I felt it coil in on itself like a spring, then it leapt at the gaping hole in the glass, winding me as it did so. The car was still rolling, and I was being tossed around like a doll.

Finally it stopped. We were upside down in a ditch. The badger was gone. Yevgeny's bleeding head hung loosely, swinging back and forth between his outstretched arms. I had half slipped out of my seatbelt, which was wrapped around my shoulders, my legs now straddling the front passenger seat's headrest. I was alive. Was he?

All I wanted to do at that moment was sleep. My head was throbbing and my fingers were cold and tingling. As much as I wanted to just lie down though, I knew this was my chance. If Yevgeny was dead or even if he was just unconscious, there was an opportunity to escape. I unclipped my seatbelt and fell in a heap onto the car's ceiling. Righting myself, I tried to open the door. Miraculously, it opened and I crawled out onto mud and grass. I scrambled out of the ditch and sat myself at the edge, looking down across the smashed chassis.

The night was silent except for the hissing of the wrecked vehicle and the ringing in my ears. A full moon hung heavy in the sky, casting a spectral blue light over the pine trees that bordered the road on both sides. All I wanted to do was sleep, but unsteadily I got to my feet. As I did, I realised that my left leg hurt badly. I tried to take a couple of steps, but a freezing wave of nausea rose up through my body. I stumbled down onto my knees.

A groan rose from the car. Yevgeny wasn't dead after all. I looked up the long, straight road and then down it and realised I had no idea where we were. I knew I could only limp slowly on my damaged leg, so if Yevgeny was about to get out of the car he would be bound to spot me hobbling away. The only way I could lose him would be to go into the woods.

"Mr Strong! Where are you?"

As I staggered away from the ditch, through a dense barrier of ferns and into the trees, I heard him calling.

"Are you ok? Can you help please?"

His voice faded as I made my way deeper into the pines. All vibrations became deadened as if I was in a submarine. I tried to adjust my eyes to the overwhelming darkness, lurching forward to avoid putting my weight onto my left knee, holding my arms out in front to make use of any passing tree for support. I probed the forest floor with my bad leg, searching for dead branches or pot holes that would send me flying. The ground seemed clear except for a sound-devouring bed of pine needles and the trees were evenly spaced - it must be a plantation rather than a natural forest.

"Mr Strong! Help me please!"

Yevgeny's voice came through the pines as nothing more than a hiss, like the sound of a scratchy old record. For the second time that day, I navigated blindly by moving as far from its source as possible. Going back to help him never even crossed my mind. I was a frightened animal with nothing on my mind beyond survival.

But was the voice closer than it had been before? Or was that just the weird effect of the pine woods, smothering all echoes and bending the normal laws of acoustics? I could feel my knee swelling up as I walked. Was it broken? I switched my attention to my aching head and the stinging sensation I was beginning to notice from the wounded area. Not much better. Just try to concentrate on not falling over.

As I groped my way forward from tree to tree, I began to reflect on everything that had happened up to that moment. The blackness was all-encompassing, just like the packing crate Nigel had entombed me in. Without vision or hearing, pain welled up to fill the gap in my sensory field. In the absence of light, my mind's eye began to unleash itself. Exhaustion and pain made it hard for me to convince myself that the coalescing images now emerging from the darkness were not real. I saw the statues in Nigel's garden, but rather than Michelangelo's David, the only one I could identify was a woman - Michelle Darwin. Her eyes were blank, her expression unreadable. Two of the other statues began to move and transform, legs shortening, bodies elongating. Hunching over, they lost their bipedal form and dropped to fall fours. One became a dog, the other a badger. The dog was Colonel Aureliano Buendia. The badger was...well, the badger from the car accident, I presume. I never got a good look at its face. The two animals stared at me before running in opposite directions and evaporating like smoke rings. The trees that formed the background of the tableau now appeared to be made from smooth white marble.

I could hear footsteps, but was that an hallucination too? I pushed myself forward, towards the statue. The sound of my own steps were quieter than those following me. As I came within arm's length of Michelle, the image dissolved and reformed. Now a short distance in front of me was an open chest freezer standing up on its end. Or was I floating above it? I could no longer tell where the ground was.

"Mr Strong!"

The voice was much closer now, but it was Keith's voice.

"I take you to the hospital!"

It was Mr Parson's voice.

"Shaun! Where are you?"

Nigel's voice. So close I could hear it breathing.

A light flicked on, and the marble forest vanished. I was lying on my back panting hard, staring up into the indigo night sky. Yevgeny was standing over me, holding a torch and wearing a strange set of goggles over the top of his head. I tried to focus my eyes on him as he pulled the goggles back off his face.

The light went out. Seconds later, it was replaced by the green glow of a phone screen. I heard the rapid tones of a speed dial.

"Doesn't look good. We are not far from the hospital - you want I should...?

A tiny, crackly version of Nigel's voice hissed forth into the silent woods.

"No. Too much hassle, you turning up there on foot, covered in blood with him over your shoulder. Not what we need. I'm afraid it sounds like our Mr Strong has missed his chance. Bad luck, but was it really working out for us? Probably not. Do what needs to be done please."

"Hmmm..." Yevgeny replied.

The green light went out and darkness returned.

The torch snapped back on. Yevgeny was sighting a gun along its beam at my head.

"Shaun, *moy drug* - I am sorry."

He shot me. And for the first time, I died.

INTERVAL

48

Now, I'm sure that at this point you have a lot of questions, most of them concerning the question of what dying is like and what it's like to be dead. And I'm going to put my hands up and admit that I can't really be a lot of help to you. Each of the three times I died, it was totally different. Perhaps that was a reflection of the dramatically different circumstances of my various demises. What I'm experiencing now in this tunnel or whatever it is with Nigel Darwin's terrified remnants struggling to cling on to me is nothing like it was when Yevgeny shot me in those woods.

For what it's worth, I'll tell you how that was now. Looks like we've still got time.

I remember seeing the muzzle flash, a light within a light of the torch beam, but I didn't hear anything. In retrospect, that'll be because I was dead before the sound reached my ears. Probably.

Everything went black and silent, like when you turn off the television. But gradually, I became aware of time passing. And in becoming aware of time passing, I became aware that I was - in some sense - still here. And who was this "I" character? Ah now...it's on the tip of my tongue. It'll come to me in a moment. Let's figure out where I am. These are trees, I think. Tall, thin trees with red bark wrapped around the trunk. There's a pale light filtering through the trees - not bright enough to cast shadows but enough to see by. There are ferns in the light

251

patches. And nettles. The last thing I remember… it was night, wasn't it? I remember a flash of light and then…nothing…

A flash of light, and my leg hurt. My leg and my head. They don't hurt now though. There was a voice too. A deep voice, deep like an underwater volcano. I'm alone in a forest. Have I been here before? Yes, I was here when it was night - but I only saw it in flashes. Flashes from a torch and flashes from a gun. What was it that the voice had said.

"Shaun, *moy drug*…I am sorry."

Shaun. That's my name. Shaun Strong. It's coming back to me. I was in a car crash, then I was chased into these woods and shot. I was shot. Where was I shot? I move my hands to feel my face, and that's when it hits me. I'm not there. There's nothing there. No hands to touch with, no face to check for bullet holes, just "I". Just Shaun Strong.

Fuck.

No hang on. This feels familiar. I think I've been here before, and I don't mean in the woods this time. I've been outside my body before, haven't I? I'm starting to remember. Something about falling asleep. Sleeping and leaving my body behind. Yes, it's coming back to me. It didn't feel exactly like this though. That felt more…specific? This feels vague. General. As if my attention is spreading out over a wider and wider area, making it hard to focus on details. But all I've got to do is wake up, right?

That's a lot of rhetorical questions, isn't it?

I try to wake up, but nothing happens. I'm still there in the woods. The pale light is getting a little brighter, but it's a washed-out, sad light. Like an energy saving bulb starting up. Nothing like the morning sun I'm used to. I can't tell where the sun is. The light seems to be coming from the whole of the sky equally. And still no shadows. Wake up Shaun, wake up. I was in a car crash. I must be in hospital. Maybe I'm under anaesthetic right now, and that's why I can't wake up and why everything feels so strange. I was shot. Maybe I'm in a coma and that's why I can't wake up.

It didn't occur to me that I was dead. How could it? "I am dead" is a paradoxical thought. If you have it, it can't be true. I was quite clearly still here in some form. Plus, I was struggling to keep my mind on one thing. I felt very distracted. You know how when you're tired, your eyes just fall out of focus and you get this feeling of vertigo? That's what it was like, but with my whole sense of self. I kept drifting away and it was taking more and more effort to keep holding myself together. If you fall asleep in your sleep, where do you go?

I'm dissolving at the edges and my attention is drifting out to eroding boundaries. I shake my head metaphorically and I coagulate again. But maybe there's just a little less of me than before. A few particles have been shaken loose and drifted away. Concentrate. Concentrate on waking up. On moving. Yes, I start to move. I'm out of the woods and on a road. I was in a car crash, but there's no car here now. The light is the same as under the forest canopy. It's no brighter. We were going to a hospital, but I can't remember which way we were going. I look up the road, then I look down the road. I can't make up my mind.

OK look, what starts happening now is a bit strange. What's particularly odd is that it felt totally natural at the time. Of course, now I can see that it was not normal at all - and it must have been some symptom of my ghostly state and the traumatic circumstances of my ending up in it. The edges of my field of perception were disintegrating again, but something new was forming there. I tried to ignore it, to focus on making up my mind which way along the road in the forest I needed to go, but I couldn't help myself. I wanted to see what was coming into being in the corner of my eye. It was something. Not nothing. My attention teetered back and forth on the brink - the road, the new picture, the road, a room. It was a room. I'd been here before as well, but it looked different now. There had been furniture before. The room was empty and dull. There had been a man here before. A man and a dog.

And then I was in the room completely. The road had gone and I was in an empty house. I walked through an interior door and I was in a kitchen, again stripped bare of everything portable. I surveyed the scene - oven, sink, cupboards, back door. The back door. A bloody earprint flashed through my mind.

I still didn't realise that anything unusual was happening. Looking back, it felt like one of those dreams people have where impossible things are happening, and the thought that they're impossible does occur to you, but you give your senses the benefit of the doubt and think "well, if it's happening, it must make sense". Even when you're switching bodies or seeing a tortoise that you just know and just accept is actually your mother. And a tiny part of your brain knows that there's something warped in the logic of the experience, but it's easier to go along with it than to start thinking properly, which would mean you wake up…

That's what it was like. Sort of. One minute I was at the side of a road in the middle of a pine wood, then next I was at the site of a murder I had witnessed.

I began to explore the house. The carpets had been taken up and the wallpaper stripped. Looking out of the living room window, I saw a "for sale" sign staked at the edge of the front lawn. There was a full skip on the drive. I went up the stairs and on the landing I had a minor realisation. I had not been here before. The forest, the road, the living room, the kitchen - these were all places where things had happened to me. Important things.

But I had never been upstairs in this house. I looked down at the dusty, bare floorboards. The doors to all the rooms were closed and there were no windows, but the light was the same as before and as it had been everywhere else: tired, dim, monochrome.

If I'd never been here before then what I was experiencing couldn't just be a series of memories – a montage of my best bits before I was directed off stage to polite applause.

Had I thought it was? I'm not sure. Once I realised it couldn't be, I recognised that that idea must have been one of the explanatory hypotheses my unconscious had knocked up to put what I was experiencing into context. There must be other possible explanations, but I'm fucked if I can tell what they are. If this isn't a memory, what is it?

I went through a door and found myself in what had once been a master bedroom. Built-in wardrobe doors gaped open like broken jaws. An empty light fitting dangled from the ceiling like a noose. I looked out of the window each way down the street. Life was taking place to the left and the right. People were walking along the pavement, mowing lawns and washing cars. Children hurtled to and fro on bicycles and microscooters. But all was still in and around this house. Passers-by gave it a wide berth, unconsciously repelled as if by a negative magnetic field. The children stayed away. Even cats and birds turned back on approach. I looked down into the skip. A double mattress lay on top, concealing whatever else was being discarded. It reminded me of a tomb stone.

Again, a lightbulb switched on in my mind. That's an awful lot of pretty overt symbolism, isn't is Shaun? This is a cursed place, a house of the dead - I get it. Does it really look like a grave? Or am I imposing a meaning onto what is in fact just a mattress in a skip? Are people and creatures really avoiding the house or is it a coincidence? No one has any business coming here. So why am I here? And why am I here now? Are those people on the street real or are they projections emanating from me? Why am I doubting that they're real now when I never doubted that other people existed before?

Look at him over there. There's a man, in shorts and a vest. He's bald. Completely bald. The top of his head is reflecting, even in this flat light. Folds of skin are bunched up where his neck joins his head. His neck is thick. Thicker than the width of his head above the ears. His vest is soaking wet down the centre of his back. There are beads of sweat on the exposed flesh around his armpits. His trainers are bright green and his legs appear hairless. His shorts are black and shiny. The vest is black too and it says "McGuigan's Gym" on it in faded lettering. He's turning around now and I see he's holding a water bottle. A strange looking thing, oval-shaped with a hole in the centre. He's breathing hard, panting. I can see steam coming off him. Or is that a metaphor? He's put his hands on his hips (a gout of water spurts out of the bottle's nozzle) and tilted his head back.

Now he's taken hold of his left ankle and is pulling the bottom of half of his leg up against his buttocks. He's swapped the bottle to his other hand, and now he's doing the same action with the other leg. He coughs and spits something into the gutter. Then he runs off.

Why the hell would I make all that up? In dreams, details are smudged into an impressionistic whole - but I could see the sweat running out of that bloke's armpits. There's no psychological reason for that. There's no hidden layer of meaning in that. His dripping pits seem like a pretty conclusive argument for what I am seeing being some sort of objective reality. Because why would I make that up?

So if this is the everyday world and not some didactic virtual reality simulator, where does that leave me? Where do I fit into this world? I was in a car crash. The man has run around a corner now and I can't see him, but he's still there - he's just behind those houses. I was running through a pine forest. That is just a mattress in a skip. It doesn't look like anything else. I've never been upstairs in this house, but I have been downstairs. Somebody died here and I was here when it happened. He had that dog. Trevor Long. His name was Trevor Long. I saw the earprint again.

The name. The earprint. It all came back to me at once. And as it did, I felt a terrible cold envelop me because I remembered that I had died.

And yet, here I was. Not in heaven; not in hell; but in an empty house on an estate in Woking. Presumably, this situation had significant implications for most major religions. Before I could properly digest the theological impact of what was happening, the edges of my vision began to dissolve and re-arrange again. I wanted to see where I was going next and as the picture reformed, I recognised it immediately. The seventh floor of Prospect House emerged out of the mists and I was back in my former prison. There was the crate of books and the two camp beds. There was the freezer - just one now. There was Ragnar the golden eagle, tethered to his perch, his wings half-spread, his beak wide open. There was the chemical toilet.

It occurred to me, that if I was now dead, couldn't I leave all this behind? The game was played and I lost - that much was clear. Why not leave Nigel and Keith to it? You could do anything, Shaun. Go anywhere. Just walk through that wall, through that door, and never look back. So why don't you?

"Historical Jesus explains everything."

I remembered why.

49

I stuck around for revenge or at least for answers. When I got them - and I suppose I did get them both, in a way - I'd be the first to admit they were not entirely satisfactory. Maybe not worth the hassle in the light of everything that happened from this point onwards. But still, revenge and answers gave me enough purpose to resist the disintegrating forces that I was discovering exert themselves on the newly dead.

We were talking about what it's like to be dead. Well, on this occasion it was all about the disintegration and the phasing in and out of places. How can I describe it? Whatever "I" was at that time, it was soluble in whatever medium I was occupying. Like a sugar lump dropped in warm water, it was seeping into me, dissolving my outer edges. And, as my outer layers peeled away, it flowed deeper towards the core of my being. What was "I"? The best way I can put it is that I was a centre of attention - if you'll pardon the pun. So, I felt myself evaporating as a darkening and a closing in of my peripheral vision and hearing. The bits of me that were detaching weren't ceasing to exist though. They were dispersing and joining with the fabric of that reality, moving from consciousness not to unconsciousness but some state that transcended both.

I told you it was hard to explain.

So there was that, and then there was the fading out from one place to reappear or refocus in another. First the forest on the road to the hospital, then Trevor Long's house and then the office. And it went on like that for a while, with me starting to drift away, pulling myself back from the edge and finding that I was somewhere else. Woking Library. The sand dunes overlooking the causeway between Lindisfarne and the mainland. Keith's house. Manor Gardens in Guildford where Peter Smithson lived. All places where I had taken another irrevocable step along the path to this purgatory and none of them places I wanted to see again. Never my house. Never Nigel's house, where Michelle might be.

I could explore them as if I was really there. Just like at Longy's house where I went up the stairs, I did not seem constrained in any of these scenes by what I actually remembered of them. Nor did I seem to be outside of time in any way. People came and went, the sun and the moon rose and set, things happened…all oblivious to my presence, such as it was.

Sooner or later though, I would begin to get distracted and the focus that was holding me together would weaken. Like when you're reading in bed and your eyes close, and you're still thinking, but you're not aware that you're not thinking about the book in front of you anymore, but about something else that's been generated inside your own unconscious mind. That's what I mean by "pulling myself back from the edge": that jolt of recognition that there's a discontinuity you hadn't noticed before. That jolt that brought me back around would be what started the ineluctable transition from one vista to the next.

My memories came back gradually, each scene and the thought processes I went through triggering a few more recollections. In retrospect I realise that I was like a leaking bucket - whatever was poured in at the top was offset by what was dripping out of the bottom. As I remembered more, I became narrower and more single-minded. Little by little, without realising it, I was becoming unable to think about anything at all other than those cryptic words Keith had whispered to me: "Historical Jesus explains everything."

I knew it meant something, but what it was would not come back to me. I was turning into what Mr Parson would have called a hungry ghost. That's what not having a body to go back to does to an ex-person.

Still, taking all things into consideration my new state was not that different from how I'd lived my life up to that point. I soon remembered The Thing I Did but, apart from the fadeouts I was struggling to see much to tell that from this.

How did I feel? I don't know. How do I ever feel? I felt less, I suppose. Even less. But again, I didn't notice my emotions and attachments draining down while it was happening. It was only when I finally got a new body (well, new to me anyway) that all that stuff came flooding back to me - but I'm getting ahead of things. We'll get to that bit soon.

I knew that I had to find Keith and Nigel if I was going to understand the secret of Historical Jesus, but I was trapped cycling back and forth through the same handful of locations, unable to control where I was heading next or what would trigger the move. Fortunately, the seventh floor of Prospect House was one of the places I was apparently haunting and it looked like Keith was now living there full-time. There was a dome-shaped orange and brown tent pitched in the middle of the floor, a TV and other accoutrements suggesting that, if this was still a prison, it was a lower category institution than it had been when I was held there. It would presumably be just a matter of time before I materialised there at the same time as Keith.

The question was, how much time did I have?

50

It might have been hours later or it might have been weeks, but eventually I found myself coalescing in the middle of an animated discussion between the two men I was most keen to see. When I realised where I was, I felt the scattering particles of my attention lurch back to the centre, giving me a disconcerting sense of just how little of me there had been left there beforehand.

We were back on the seventh floor of Prospect House, at the camping table where Nigel had explained his "philosophy" to us before brutalising the unfortunate Mr Parson. Seated at the table were Nigel, topless, and another man. Keith was standing six feet away, ironing a shirt. He had a black eye.

Nigel had the barrel chest of a weight lifter, but in a seated position his middle-aged paunch slopped unmistakably over the top of his trousers - hiding his belt buckle completely from view. On his left wrist was a heavy watch, at least an inch and a half across its face, with exposed gleaming golden workings and supplementary dials. His right hand was closed in a fist, resting on the table as he tapped the second and third fingers of his left hand across its knuckles.

The other man appeared childlike compared to Nigel. He wore a light grey woollen suit with absolutely no visible stitching. His sandy brown hair was cropped close to his skull and he had a neat little goatee beard and tidy moustache. Gold-framed octagonal glasses perched on his elegant nose, a golden chain dangling lugubriously from them around his neck. The man peered over his spectacles at Nigel as he wrote notes on a yellow pad in front of him.

"You really must send me a bill Aleister. You're starting to make me feel like a charity case - which, as you well know, is not necessary." Nigel's voice had a tone to it I had not heard before. He sounded nervous and expectant underneath his typical bluster.

The man lowered his eyes and continued to write as he spoke.

"Not at all, Nigel. I understand completely. One moment, if you would…" He finalised his notes with a flourish, put his pen down emphatically and sat up to look Nigel directly in the face. With a long-fingered hand, he slowly pushed the golden spectacles back up the bridge of his nose. This done, he began to smile - an expression that conveyed both complete sincerity and utter detachment.

"There. All done. Now…our bill? Yes. Of course. Rest assured Nigel, payment will be collected when it comes due. My own personal interest in your case is entirely beside the point here - after all, I have my partners to answer to. We have very firm guidelines about taking on pro bono work at LWS…"

Both men chuckled at this.

"But seriously Nigel, don't trouble yourself about the bill for now. I know you're good for it."

"I don't want you to skimp on anything!" Nigel seemed reassured. He had sat back in his chair and crossed his hands behind his head. "Whatever this costs, I'll pay it. Money is no object."

"I know it isn't."

"I don't want you to be out of pocket because things have become more complicated."

"We won't be."

"You finished with that ironing, knobhead?" Nigel now addressed Keith, who propped the iron up on its end and sullenly handed the white shirt over. Bearing in mind Keith's habitual slovenliness, I thought he had done rather a good job.

Nigel continued to talk as he buttoned the shirt up. The man - whom I had realised was the lawyer Aleister Woodward - picked up his pen and resumed taking notes. Keith hovered at Nigel's shoulder, unsure whether to take a seat or go back to the ironing board. There was a frightened, wary look in his bruised eye which had not been there before.

"So…the Longs. My Russian associate has transported the remains and hidden them at the place we talked about."

"Remind me…?"

"Shaun Strong's house."

"Ah yes."

"Under the floorboards. That was Mr Pardew here's idea."

"Spell that for me please…"

"P. A. R. D. E. W." mumbled Keith.

"Thank you. Both of them?"

"No, the police have the woman," Nigel continued. "But everything is suitably…ah…arranged so as match the story on the laptop. Prints on the weapon. Everything cleaned down. All set to tip the police off."

"I see. Don't do that just yet please. What about this other fellow? Parsons, was it?"

"Well, that was just unfortunate really. Collateral damage, you might say."

"Doesn't matter to me. I'm not here to judge you Nigel. We just need to be sure that everything is accounted for."

At this point, Keith butted in.

"Let me do it. Please. I want to help. I can help."

Nigel burst out laughing.

"You? Ha ha ha." He stood up and clapped his shovel of a hand onto Keith's bony shoulder.

"I appreciate the thought Keith, but I think we should perhaps leave this one to Mr Kuss…Kuz…nov…"

"Kuznetsov."

"That's the one. For someone like you…well, you'd be fighting against your nature. You weren't made for this. Not your fault, of course. Some of us are born to be strong, and the rest… but even so, you should take better care of yourself Keith. When was the last time you ate a vegetable? No… you stick to writing stuff down."

"But…I can help you…"

It was now Woodward's turn to interrupt.

"Nigel, is this going to take long? I do have other clients to visit while I'm down here in Woking."

"No, sorry…" Nigel sat down again. "Thank you Keith. I will have a think about it. Aleister, please carry on."

"Thank you." The lawyer spoke slowly and the upward intonation on the second syllable of his utterance conveyed his irritation firmly before he continued.

"So Shaun Strong…?"

"Disposed of. Went on a little fishing trip at the weekend out in the Solent. I've got this yacht down at Southampton. Cost me a couple of million, give or take…"

"Yes. I know all about the yacht. You have told me about it before."

"Ah. Right. Ok. Well. Let's just say Mr Strong is now dispersed over several nautical miles of open water and throughout the digestive tracts of a wide variety of sea creatures."

"Ah ha. Well, I think that covers everything. Once you've tidied up the Parsons business and the authorities locate Mr Long, I think we can take care of everything else. Nigel, it was a pleasure. Mr Pardew, pleased to meet you. I can see myself out thank you gentlemen."

With that, Woodward rose from his seat. He gathered up his papers and carefully returned them to a brown leather briefcase - whose battered shabby appearance was completely at odds with that of its owner. Taking small, deliberate steps, the lawyer walked to the office door and out of the room.

I followed him into the lobby outside the lift. Little finger outstretched, Woodward ostentatiously removed his spectacles and allowed them to hang from their gold chain. He pressed the lift call button and, with the same hand, reached into his jacket pocket. He drew out a Dictaphone and pressed "stop" on it. He had recorded the conversation. So who was Woodward working for?

I leaned in closer, and as I did Woodward sniffed the air and looked around sharply. The hairs on the backs of his hands were standing up. I edged away. The lawyer's eyes darted from left to right and his tongue flicked out of his mouth like a snake's. He turned around slowly and stepped backwards into the lift.

51

I went back into the office. Keith and Nigel were now seated opposite one another at the table. Nigel was chuckling.

"I warned him. You can't say I didn't warn him, can you Keith? Literally told him we'd fitted him up nicely, didn't I?"

"Yes. You did."

"But the stupid twat had to go and get himself run over. By my daughter of all people. Scared the shit out of her, I can tell you. She's never been a confident driver at the best of times. It set her right back you know. Lost her nerve. And then there was... well, whatever the fuck happened on the way to the hospital. I've heard of that before though. Badgers go catatonic when they're in shock. Vicious animals, especially when they're cornered.

"Anyway, it's a shame obviously, but all's well that ends well, eh? I was getting sick of having to store those bodies and laying the blame on Shaun ties up all the loose ends nicely. It was fun while it lasted, wasn't it Keith? Ah ha ha ha. No, I could see he was never cut out for this. Soft, he was. Nice lad but he'd have cracked sooner or later.

"Right. I've got a brunch with Sophie. Whatever the fuck a brunch is. Kids can't even eat normal meals these days..." Nigel began to walk towards the fire exit, talking as much to himself as anyone else. As he approached the door, he turned back to address Keith.

"I'll tell you what. You want to prove yourself to me?"

"Yes!"

"If you can do this for me, I'll believe you've got the stomach and the balls for the job. You think you're up to it?"

"Yes! Of course. I'll do whatever you want. Just give me a chance!"

"Alright then." Nigel took his phone from his pocket and typed in a number.

"It's me. Yeah. Bring the freezer back up here. Seventh. And bring your toolbox. Yes. THAT toolbox. I've got a little job for our mutual friend."

He hung up.

"Keith, it's a crying shame what happened to the old Milky Bar Kid. I really hadn't set out to cause him any harm. I wanted his assistance! But when you told me that he was no use to us... well, you understand, don't you?"

"Yes. I understand."

"So, seeing as we're both kind of at fault for what happened to him, I'll give you a chance. Yevgeny's going to bring him back up here and if you can...ah...how shall we say? ... break him down into manageable chunks that we can safely get rid of, I might be able to find a few other jobs for you."

Keith had set his jaw and was nodding slowly. His eyes were fierce now. Nigel reached out and cupped Keith's face between his thick hands. He slapped him gently around the right cheek, causing Keith to twitch but without taking his eyes off his new master.

"We might be able to make something of you yet lad," Nigel grinned before he turned and left.

At that moment, I felt a fadeout beginning. My peripheral vision darkened and new shapes began to move in it. Not now, I thought and fought to concentrate. The blur receded a little. This was my best chance to find some answers, although I had no idea how I planned on communicating with Keith.

He got up and walked over to a desk, which was piled with books and papers. Sitting down, Keith turned his face up to the ceiling, holding the pen a few inches above the blank paper.

Putting the pen down, he opened a drawer underneath the desk and took out a handful of paperwork, which he put down on the already crowded worktop. Reaching into the back of the drawer Keith pulled out a pencil, but I wasn't looking at him by that time. I was looking at the pile he had taken out of the drawer. On top was a small spiral-bound pad, with the words "Historical Jesus" written on the front of it.

The answers I was looking for were there, right in front of me. I reached out for the book, and remembered that lacking a physical existence, I had no way of interacting with the fatal object. Curls of something like dark smoke were dancing in the corners of my eyes again. I shifted my awareness - under the desk, between the pages of the book, above, behind - but it was no use. I couldn't get it to open.

I turned my attention to the person in the room who could. Keith was still staring at the ceiling. I imagined waving my hands in his face, slapping him, kicking his chair but my flailing phantom limbs made no impression. I shouted and screamed. I ran back and forth, but I could not make my presence felt. The book lay there - its cover may have only been cheap cardboard, but to me it was a mountain of impenetrable rock, a thousand miles thick.

I was trapped behind the etheric barrier with no way of communicating with those on the other side. What could I do? Probably nothing. Did it matter? Probably not. What would I do if I did manage to look inside the book? Would it "explain everything"? If it did, what good would explanations do now that I was dead?

I'm dead. I'm dead. Dead. What good does anything do now? I'm so tired of this, running around, solving tasks like some kind of video game character. I'm tired of this. So tired. So very tired. I'm so tired. I feel like I could fall asleep right now. Fall asleep and sleep forever…

Ragnar began to screech. The sound shocked me back into wakefulness, dispelling the languor that had come over me and the darkness that was filling my vision. Was the bird looking at me?

"Shut up Ragnar!" Keith yelled, tearing off a sheet, screwing it into a ball and throwing it at the unfortunate eagle. As we had seen numerous times before, Ragnar responded by attempting to take flight, only to be pulled to the ground by the leather jesses tied around his ankles, before repeating the manoeuvre - with just as little success on subsequent attempts as on the first.

"Calm down! Calm down Ragnar! I'm sorry," Keith had jumped to his feet and was walking gingerly over to Ragnar's perch. As he came closer, the eagle redoubled his efforts to escape, until exhausted, he gave up and stood panting, his wings dropped loosely onto the floor.

"There, there. I'm sorry. I didn't mean to frighten you."

The bird's rate of breathing increased as Keith approached and his staring eyes grew wider. Keith dropped slowly to his hands and knees and crawled towards Ragnar.

"Come here birdy. Don't be afraid."

Keith sat down, turning side on to the grounded eagle. Avoiding eye contact, he carried on making soothing noises. Ragnar seemed to relax slightly. I moved towards the scene entranced, hovering above the desk and the notepad. Man and bird seemed to be holding their respective breaths.

After a few minutes, Ragnar seemed to settle down - picking his wings up and fussily settling them back into place. Thirty seconds later, he swivelled his head towards Keith, who was still averting his gaze. Ragnar began to preen his chest feathers.

Keith rolled onto his side towards the bird and held out his hand.

"Come on now. Come on Ragnar. There's a good .... AAAAAARRRGGGGHHHHH!!! FUCKING...Jesus! My fucking finger! You bastard eagle!"

Keith's cry caused Ragnar to renew his futile efforts to take flight. It scared the shit out of me too. So much so that the pile of papers, topped with the "Historical Jesus" notebook, exploded off the desk into the air.

Keith clutched his bleeding finger in his other hand and

stared with alarm back at the desk. Even Ragnar had stopped his aimless flapping and was looking with an expression of intense irritation over to where I was.

The book had fallen open.

I swooped down to see what it said. The page read:

People I will never forgive: 1. Dad - For ignoring Mum. For calling me fat and lazy every day of my life. For making me this way. 2. Nerys Shirley - For the way she laughed when I told her that I loved her after she took my virginity. For the way that nothing embarrasses her.

Was that it? How did that "explain everything"? Disappointment enveloped me like a cold bath.

"Shaun?"

Keith was standing above me now, looking round apprehensively.

"Is that you Shaun?"

He looked down and saw the open book. Such colour as there was in Keith's face drained away, darkening the bruises around his left eye to an even deeper hue. He scooped up the papers and the book and ran over to his camp bed. Stuffing them all underneath the bed, Keith began ripping paper and occasionally looking below to see what he was accomplishing. After thirty seconds or so, he seemed satisfied and stuck his head under the bed. He reached in and seemed to be moving papers around. Finally, after another thirty seconds, he came out and rose to his feet. His bitten finger was dripping blood and he tucked his hand under his armpit.

"It's all there," Keith murmured without moving his lips as he returned to the table. "Be quick. I can't leave it there for long."

I glided under the camp bed. It was dark, but there was enough light to read by. The Historical Jesus book sat on the far left of a pile of papers. Pages that had been hastily torn from its interior were arranged alongside it, covered in Keith's tiny handwriting. The mix of blue ink, black ink and pencil with extensive crossings out and smudges, suggested that it had been written over several sittings.

It was Keith's confession:

If you are reading this Shaun, at least one of us is probably already dead. That sounds ridiculous, but this whole situation is ridiculous, isn't it? Anyway, if you are still out there, you deserve some answers. You were a good friend and you didn't deserve any of this.

I suppose I should tell you what happened. They caught me one day after I had been tailing Nigel for a couple of weeks. Yevgeny cornered me in a car park outside Nigel's gym. He bundled me into the boot and the next thing I knew I was in the middle of the woods in front of an open grave. Nigel was there and said I had one minute to convince him not to kill me.

I told him everything about us and about you. I am sorry Shaun. You would have done the same thing I think.

Would I? I stopped to ponder this, but then remembered that Keith had told me I needed to be quick. Yevgeny was supposed to be bringing the freezer and his tool box up.

Nigel believed all of it from the beginning. He never asked for any proof or acted as though our story was unusual in any way. I know I'm pretty convincing when I need to be, but even I was surprised at how casually he took it all in. He said I could live if I brought you to him and you would show him how to do your thing. I had to do it Shaun. I have to live. You understand? It wasn't personal. I really did like you Shaun - we made a good team. But the world needs me and my ideas. I have great things to do - I just need a lucky break so I can get started.

The second page was smeared with blood from the bitten finger. The handwriting was larger and more untidy, but was still recognisably Keith's.

Nigel's company does IT support for the whole of Surrey Police. That's how he knows what's going on before they do. Evolution provided the laptops to Trevor Long's school. Whenever they are on, he can see everything. He's going to frame you for murdering the Longs, and probably Parson and me as well. I am trying to find out as much as I can and write it down in here. Maybe there is something you can do.

The handwriting changed again, back to its original neatness.

Shaun, what Nigel is attempting is something without precedent in human history. I know that he comes across as an absolute wanker, but when you really think about it, there is something very deep in what he says. Not having to hear about the yacht or the St Nazaire raid again is one of the consolations I am taking from my likely imminent death, but the rest of it is making more and more sense to me. You know I am a thinker. I know that The System needs to be destroyed, but I had always wondered what should come after that. I knew it in one sense, but I was never able to put my finger on it until Nigel spelled out his view of the world. People will only recognise me for what I am - they will only do me justice - if I remake the world so that it really does revolve around me. That's what he's doing Shaun. He's trying to make his own reality in which he can have everything he wants. I can see now what my mission needs to be. He's John the Baptist to my Jesus. Nigel will fail, but he's shown me the way. It's not about me though Shaun - you know that. It's for the greater good.

The text became spidery and crooked now. It was written in pencil and was barely legible, especially under such poor lighting.

Shaun I am going to work with Nigel not against him I hope you understand the more time I spend with him the more my eyes are opened I can't do this by myself yet I have to work with him not against him.

If you are reading this get away as far as you can there are worse things than death get away and never look back I hate myself you were my only real friend and I am sorry.

The text ended, with the words "Yours sincerely, Keith Pardew."

I looked up and I was back in the woods at the crash site. The papers, the camp bed, the book - all gone. There was just an empty road, a mass of dripping ferns and the wet silent pines beyond.

52

It was dark. Not night-time dark, but dark like an eclipse. Something felt different this time. Something urgent.

The woods were even darker and so I began to walk along the road. I knew it was the direction I had been travelling in at the time of the accident. As I walked, I felt that there was something behind me, something vast, impersonal and inexorable, but when I turned to look for it there was nothing but the road and the trees on either side. I continued along the grass verge and soon I began to see (did I see it? Or did I feel it?) a glow somewhere in front of me. The symbolism of it all was not lost on me, but I kept on walking: after all, the choices I had were carry on towards the light, veer off into the darkness or allow whatever was following me to catch up. Under the circumstances, the light seemed like the least bad option.

Had Keith's confession given me the answers I wanted? I certainly felt different, as though a burden had been lifted from me. But at the same time, I was strangely dissatisfied. Was that it? What had I missed? If it was the search for answers that had been holding me together did this new picture and this new sensation mean I'd found them? Was this it for me?

The light was becoming brighter as I progressed towards it, but the foreboding presence behind me felt heavier as it approached. The ferns and trees at the side of the road were becoming fainter and harder to distinguish as the unseen sun continued to set and a thick mist rose up from the earth.

It wasn't what Keith had said that had relieved my need to know, I was coming to realise. It was the fact that he had felt the need to say it, even if he suspected he was talking to himself. What that proved was the point. It proved that Keith really did care for me and that was the proof that I needed even though I hadn't understood my need for it. Yes, his betrayal had led to my imprisonment and death, but he felt bad about it. He felt genuinely bad about it. At that moment of realisation, my lifelong migraine of the soul eased off and I felt a deep well of contentment open up within me. It was a real moment of insight: up until that moment, I had absorbed a lot of information but wisdom had been conspicuous by its prolonged absence.

I saw - I literally saw it - that for men like me, Keith and even Nigel, the lag between our levels of emotional development and our intellects makes ideas deadly. Like little boys with fireworks, we're so excited to play with them the thought never occurs to us that they might go off in our hands. Being an outsider doesn't make you special.

The road curved around to the right and the unknown light source now silhouetted the tall pines and cast long shadows along the concrete. Something was moving behind me. Darkness was shining there with the same intensity as the light in front, but negated into its opposite. I was afraid to look back at what might be projecting that radiant black and picked up my pace to a trot. If I don't think about it, maybe it won't be there after all.

Keith had been a true friend in spite of everything. It had been a fucked-up friendship for sure, but that tiny act of contrition in his final words, that crack in his cynical carapace, had shown it was real. I had mattered to Keith, like he'd mattered to me. And in that moment, I swore that I would do anything within my power to rescue Keith and let him see that he was forgiven.

However, I was lost in a pitch-dark forest, being stalked by an invisible (possibly imaginary) beast, lacking any means of exerting influence on the physical plane and - most importantly of all - dead. All these factors significantly inhibited my capacity for fulfilling that vow.

As I came around the bend I finally saw where the illumination was coming from. It was the hospital I had been heading to when Yevgeny crashed the Range Rover. It squatted in a field of light, a low, sullen fortress of brown brick, aluminium vents and exhausted double glazing. An angular blue-grey concrete fire escape clung anomalously to one side of the building, like a gigantic remora suckered onto an oblivious shark. Scaffolding hid the far end of the hospital from view. Light was streaming from all the windows, forming sharp beams in the reflecting mist. The lines of focused luminescence all appeared to be converging, coming from a single source somewhere within the hospital building.

I knew that was where I was heading, even though I had no idea what I would find at the centre. Similarly, I knew that there was something coming for me, behind me in the thickening darkness. If it got to me before I got to the light…

Running now, I crossed the hospital grounds and the car park. At my heels, gloom turned to murk and into pitch black. I threw myself through a fire door and was relieved to find that it did not impede me - I was still, thankfully, intangible. I sprinted along the grey corridor. Ceiling lights went out as I passed, and I heard the tinkling sound of bulbs shattering as my pursuer traced my steps. The glow was intensifying as I neared the source. I could feel it coming through the walls. I followed it, running along corridors, through walls, through wards and courtyards. Reflexively I glanced over my shoulder and saw nothing - a null heart, into which everything was tumbling as if over a precipice.

The dazzle was unbearable as I burst into the room where the source lay on an operating table. It was like staring at the sun or an atomic explosion, but I could just make out a human shape on the table, surrounded by other figures, whose presence could only be made out as faint shadows, marginally altering the refractive index of the light's brilliance.

And now I don't know what to do.

I hesitated and the darkness caught up with me, absorbing everything else in the room except the blazing figure. Then I began to move towards the recumbent form, but I wasn't in control of the movement. I was being pulled towards it and even though I didn't want to go towards the dark, I tried to pull myself back from the light. I couldn't. Its force was overwhelming. I was dragged towards the body, into the body, and as I entered light became dark and dark became light. Then there was silence.

"Time of death…"

"Wait! Look! The ECG…"

"That's not possible. She's been flatlining for over a minute."

"Look!"

"BP's rising. Vitals are stabilising."

"What the hell is going on?"

"Mr Campbell? Oh my God. Her eyes. Her eyes are open!"

"Anaesthetist!"

LIFE 2

53

Everything hurt. Time had passed but I couldn't tell how much. My head hurt. My back hurt. My hands and feet hurt. But most of all my chest hurt. My chest hurt like my heart and lungs were on fire. Breathing was hard work and each breath felt like half the oxygen I was pulling in was leaking out of some unseen puncture. I coughed, and the flames in my chest roared into life. As they died down a pounding behind my eyes welled up and made me afraid they were going to pop out. My throat felt like it was full of dust.

I opened my eyes. I was lying on my back looking upwards at off-white ceiling tiles. A smoke detector in the lower left quadrant of my field of vision winked alternately red and green. Everything however was very blurred, and it was slowly rotating from right to left as my eyes drifted involuntarily to one side. Each time I reset them to vertical again, they began to sag rightward within moments.

"Mrs Sterckx?"

I could hear voices.

"Mrs Sterckx, can you hear me?"

They were getting louder and somewhat clearer.

"Mrs Sterckx - my name is Mr Campbell and I'm the surgeon who operated on you. I'm here with your son and your granddaughter. You gave us all quite a scare back there. But the human body and the human spirit are remarkably resilient, are they not? You're going to have to take it easy for quite some time now, rest, get your strength back and so on, but back in theatre everything went ... well, it all ended as well as we could have hoped for. I see no reason why, if we're careful, you shouldn't make a full recovery. You may be..."

"Ninety-seven," another voice murmured.

"You may be ninety-seven Mrs Sterckx, ...good heavens are you really? Well. Ninety-seven...but I...ah...think you've got plenty...erm... of good years ahead of you. Now, I'll be back in the morning - if you'll excuse me, I have other patients to attend to. I'll leave you in the capable hands of..."

"Agnieszka."

"I'll leave you with Agnieszka. Fluids only please nurse."

"Yes Mr Campbell."

And I heard the click click click of hard-soled shoes walking away across an inflexible floor.

A third voice now, a man's.

"Mother? Mother, can you hear me?"

The voice was behind me. For some reason, I found it irritating. The ceiling tiles made me think I was back in Prospect House. An electronic pipping sound I had not noticed previously began to speed up.

"What does that mean? Is that bad?" the male voice said, sounding more frustrated than alarmed.

A round, heavily made-up female face loomed into my field of vision. It had blonde hair with prominent dark roots, loosely tied back, and it wore an expression of gentle but firm concern.

"Mrs Sterckx, try to relax," the Agnieszka-voice spoke from the face. It was deep and rich and warm, and accented with the tones of somewhere in eastern Europe I couldn't place. The pipping slowed back down as I realised that I was not back in Nigel's office prison. I was in a hospital. I tried to turn my head in the direction the male voice had come from, but as I did the pain in my neck amplified to an unbearable level and the ceiling began to spin. I closed my eyes again.

"Just lie still. We're here." Agnieszka said.

"Is she awake?" Another female voice asked. This one was

shrill and metallic, and the sound grated in my ears. It made me feel stressed to hear it. "She was awake a moment ago, wasn't she?"

I didn't want to talk to these people, whoever they were. Not only were they annoying me, but they had mistaken me for someone else. A woman for starters. Apparently a ninety-seven year-old woman, that one of them thought was his mother.

Probably a dream, I thought as I exhaled deeply and fell unconscious.

When I came around, it was darker than before but the room was illuminated by various pieces of flashing machinery and dull, flat fluorescent lighting from the corridor outside an open door. The corridor light flickered occasionally. I was in a bed with white sheets over my body and on top of the sheets were two arms that did not look like my arms. They were as thin as sticks, mottled with wrinkled skin hanging loosely over prominent bones. The hands looked oversized for the arms, with bulging joints pulling the skin tight across the knuckles. Wondering where my arms were and whose these could be, I lifted my right arm - and the alien arm rose shakily. I tried with the left arm and - yep - that one moved too. I brought my hands to my face, and what I felt was not - as you have probably already guessed - what I was expecting to feel. I cried out in horror and surprise and the sound I heard was high pitched, rough, cracked hissing, which rapidly subsided into agonising coughs.

Before I could collect myself, Agnieszka was back, checking the machinery, adjusting my covers and rubbing the strange hand simultaneously.

"What happened?" I croaked.

"Everything is fine now, love. You're in hospital recovering from a very serious operation. You had a heart attack two weeks ago. Do you remember? You've been asleep since the doctors brought you back and carried out an emergency triple bypass. You woke up for the first time since…erm…for the first time yesterday. None of us thought you were going to make it, but you've put up one hell of a fight."

"No!" I rasped. "What happened to ME? Whose hands are these? Whose face is this? They're not mine!"

Agnieszka halted. The air of unflappable professionalism she displayed in carrying out her normal duties dissolved for a moment and she looked at me startled.

"Mrs Sterckx? Are you alright?"

"Who's Mrs Sterckx?" I shouted, my raised voice coming out as no more than a dusty wheeze. "Get me a mirror! Please! This is not my face! I don't know this face!"

Agnieszka looked frightened now.

"I will go and get the ward sister…"

"No! Please! Don't leave me! Just…tell me who I am. I don't know. I can't remember…"

But Agnieszka had gone. And when she came back with the ward sister, they gave me "just a little something to help me relax". And then I too was gone.

I came round in a different bed, in a different ward.

An exceptionally tall man stood ramrod-straight in front of me. He had a small bristly moustache and was dressed in an immaculately tailored suit. Beside him was a young black woman, with intricately beaded hair that looked not dissimilar to a seat cover of the type beloved of taxi drivers. She was dressed in blue hospital scrubs and had bright orange plastic clogs on her feet.

"Aha!" The man spoke as I opened my eyes. "Our wonder patient continues to surprise!"

His voice was as martial as his appearance. I recognised it as the voice I had heard when I first came to. Mr Campbell, I think they called him.

"I have to say, my dear lady, that your recovery is nothing short of miraculous. When you first came in here, I don't mind telling you, my heart sank. At your age, rates of survival from a cardiac event of that sort are…well…there's very little even someone like I can do. And yet here you are! The nurses tell me you are fighting back and making truly astonishing progress.

I think we should have you out of here and back home in no time!"

"Ah well, Mr Campbell…" the woman interrupted.

"Oh yes. Do forgive me. Not my place, is it?" Mr Campbell said, with gritted teeth. "Well, all the best madam - I will leave you in the more than capable hands of Dr…erm..Dr…ah yes… Dr Atugba."

And with that, he turned on his heels and stalked out.

Dr Atugba was looking at me and smiling patiently.

"Hello. My name is Dr Atugba and I understand that the last time you spoke to anyone you were a little bit confused. Is that right?"

I looked at my hands. They were still the same hands. They were not my hands.

"How are you feeling now?" the doctor asked kindly.

"Better," I croaked.

"I'm going to ask you some questions now. Is that alright?"

"Yes."

"How many fingers am I holding up?"

"Three."

"Good. And do you know where you are?"

"Hospital."

"Good. Can you tell me who the prime minister is?"

I wracked my brain.

"That woman. The awkward one."

Dr Atugba smiled a little more broadly.

"Good. Now. Can you tell me what your name is?"

Shaun Strong. That's my name. Isn't it?

I was about to say so, but then I remembered: Shaun Strong is dead. And Shaun Strong is a wanted killer. So I said nothing.

"Can you remember what your name is for me?"

I looked up at Dr Atugba and lied: "Mrs Sterckx."

"Good. Now, do you remember why you're here in hospital?"

"I had a heart attack. Two weeks ago."

"It's three weeks ago now Mrs Sterckx. You've been sedated for a few more days since you came around the first time. Even

Mr Campbell was starting to get worried. Physically, you have been getting better and better but you just wouldn't wake up. Kept on talking in your sleep though. None of us could make any sense of it."

"Doctor - please can I have a mirror?" I asked.

"A mirror? Of course you can Mrs Sterckx. Why, there's one just here on the cabinet."

She passed it to me, and I looked into the face of a total stranger. A stranger with thin wisps of white hair, deeply lined cheeks with prominent liver spots. My crinkled lips and puffed eye sockets gave me the air of a chimpanzee. Although I could see clearly, my left eye was permanently out of sync with the right one. I opened my mouth and my teeth were crooked and yellow.

"Do you remember your first name Mrs Sterckx?"

"Edith," I said without thinking and without taking my eyes from the face of the stranger in the mirror.

54

Later that day I had visitors. Again, I recognised their voices from before.

"Hello Mother," he said coldly as the woman switched the television on.

He was a heavy-set man wearing grey flannel jogging bottoms with prominent oil spots on them and a corduroy jacket.

"Do you remember me now? It's David. Your son. And Marie. My daughter. Your granddaughter."

His daughter - my granddaughter - was a spindly woman with lank, greasy hair and thick glasses. She looked roughly the same age as her father and was wearing a highly flammable-looking fleece jacket with pictures of various breeds of dog embroidered on it. Every so often she would emit a weak, damp cough, followed by a rasping sniff.

I lay silent, unsure what I was supposed to or likely to say next. Fortunately, David seemed unconcerned. He turned the chair by my bedside to face the television and sat down, tugging at the crotch of his trousers repeatedly as he did so.

"Put the news on," he said to Marie.

"Where's the remote control?"

"I don't know. Where's the remote control Mother?"

I shrugged.

"Go and find a nurse Marie."

"Have you got a call button on there Nan?"

"Nurse!" David shouted.

"Leaves the nurses alone," I said. "Look, the buttons are on the set."

"Nurse!" Marie shouted.

A tired-looking Indian woman popped her head around the door.

"How do you change the channel?" David asked, not taking his eyes from the daytime soap that was showing.

"The buttons are on the set," the nurse replied, walking off.

"Put the news on Marie."

Sucking back a noseful of mucus into her lungs, Marie got up and walked to the television. Peering at it through her jam-jar glasses as if it were a newly discovered artefact of an alien technology, she asked: "Are these the buttons here?"

"Yes," I croaked.

"Try them," my son said.

Marie prodded the first one on the left. Nothing happened.

"Is that it?"

"It hasn't changed. Put on ITV."

"Which one is that?"

"I don't know, do I? Try the next one."

After what felt like a lot more back and forth in this vein, the news was found and they both settled back into their seats to watch it.

Not knowing quite where this sentiment had come from, I murmured: "You'll have had a wasted journey. As you can plainly see, I'm not dead yet."

"Mmmmm…." said David, not having listened.

"Nan, can I have your car while you're in hospital?" Marie asked. Her eyes too were fixed on the TV as she spoke.

But I had stopped listening and was giving my entire attention to the news report.

"The hunt for the Woking man believed to be responsible for the murder of a husband and wife earlier this year has been expanded into a nationwide search. The decomposed body of Trevor Long was found underneath the floor of the home of

Shaun Strong, a 33-year-old former librarian. Chief Inspector Bob Yarrow of Surrey Police gave this statement."

A red-faced man in a cheap suit appeared on screen surrounded by microphones and cameras. The pock-marked flab of his neck spilled over his collar like the filling of a cheap sausage roll. He looked nauseous and spoke in a robotic voice. "Following an anonymous report on the 15th, officers were deployed to a residence in the St Johns area. After a search of the empty property, they discovered..."

He sighed.

"They discovered human remains, revealed by forensic analysis and identifying documentation to be Trevor Long, a teacher. We are looking for the homeowner, a Mr Shaun Strong." The policeman held up a photograph of me in my graduation gown and mortarboard, grinning gawkily, and presented it to the cameras.

"We are urging anyone with information about Mr Strong and his whereabouts to come forward. Members of the public are urged to observe extreme caution, as we have reason to believe this individual to be highly dangerous."

Chief Inspector Yarrow began to cough violently and the report cut back to the studio.

"Scum like that. Want castrating." David spat.

"And hanging," Marie chimed in.

"Hanging's too good for them."

"I meant castrating, and then hanging."

"Still too good for them."

Their voices sounded as if they were a hundred miles away. My mind was racing.

"I'd like to go to sleep now. I'm very tired," I said tentatively.

"What now? After we've come all this way to see you?"

"We really need to talk to you Nan."

"You see," David began uncomfortably, "the heart attack and everything... it gave us all a terrible scare, didn't it Marie? And...erm... well, should anything happen to you..."

"God forbid not," Marie interjected.

"Of course. Of course, God forbid...but if it did...ah, you know...arrangements would...um...need to be made, regarding...errr...the estate."

I had a strong sense that this was a frequent, unresolved topic of conversation amongst the Sterckx's.

"Now I know that you've said you want to leave everything to the Cats Protection, because," David's lips drew back bitterly as he spoke, "we know how much you love cats. Marie and I respect that decision, if that's what you really want to do. But..."

He sighed, and looked significantly at his daughter, who by this time was gazing vacantly at the TV.

"Marie...?"

"Huh? Oh. Erm. Nan...Dad's new book's coming along really well and I really think this will be it, you know Nan? It's just the research. It's very time consuming, isn't it Dad?"

"Very time consuming, yes."

"And, well, at best it's going to take a couple more years."

"Could be more than that."

"Yeah, it could be more than that. And, well, on Dad's incapacity benefit and the royalties from the Kindle sales...it's really hard. I mean, the money you give us really helps, but... erm...you know, there are some publishers interested - real ones - and, well, you know how important it is to Dad. Think how proud Grandad would have been..."

"What are you asking for?" I snapped, more impatiently than I had intended.

"Um, err...I...we...that is...we just ask that you think about the cats and how much difference that money would make to cats and how much difference it would make to your granddaughter and I. You know she can't work because of her nerves and obviously I'm...I...well, writing's a vocation, isn't it? I just think...there's always going to be stray cats."

"That's right Dad. Look at abroad. There's always cats around. Poor things."

"I just mean, cats are going to keep breeding and there'll never be enough people want to own them. Sure, you can help some cats. But cats are a problem that will always be with us. You can't solve it. But with my book...I've got a real chance here. A real chance to change how the world understands Peter Davison's tenure as the Fifth Doctor."

"It's so important to him Nan."

"And when it's a bestseller - and I've spoken a several agents who used that word Mother: 'bestseller' - if it's still what you want, I'll make a donation to the cats. I just think...because I've got a daughter, your granddaughter, to support as well..."

"Dad wants you to change the will."

"We want you to change the will," David rapidly corrected Marie. "Lots of people leave money to the cats. They'll be alright, Mother. They're very popular. Everyone likes cats."

"I don't like cats."

"No, Marie doesn't. But a lot of people do and the Cats Protection will never want for anything, will it? Because old people who like cats... well..."

"They die every day, don't they Dad?"

A glacial silence descended. Even I felt bad for Marie momentarily and I was the old person they were anticipating the death of.

"Anyway. Think about it. You don't have to decide now. And we've brought you a care package," David composed himself and continued. "Marie?"

"Oh yeah." Marie began to fish around under her chair, her eyes still fixed on the screen, and brought out a Nisa plastic bag.

"We've got you some fags, because I know they probably don't give you them in here, do they? And a pack of digestives."

"And Dad ordered you a bottle of that yellow drink off the internet."

"Yep, a lovely bottle of *Elixir d'Anvers*. It hasn't come yet, but I'll bring it in as soon as it does... now, shall we take you outside so you can have a nice cigarette or two?"

I had begun to feel a strange sensation somewhere between my lungs and my hypothalamus. It was a feeling of keen anticipation, a desire for an ache. I could see my fingers shaking even more than usual. The back of my throat throbbed as my eyes remained fixed on the packet of cigarettes David had taken out.

"Yes…let's go outside," I mumbled.

"Lovely," said David, smiling unpleasantly. "We've already brought a chair for you, haven't we Marie?"

"What?"

"The wheelchair."

"What wheelchair?"

But I wasn't listening. I was already sitting up in bed and had twisted round so that my feet were hanging over the side. I slid down onto the floor and I felt the pull of gravity bearing my body down for the first time in three weeks. I was painfully aware of the soles of my feet as I stepped into my slippers.

David and Marie gawped at me in blank surprise.

"Come on then," I said, walking away.

David scuttled after me, taking my arm.

"Are you feeling alright Mother? They said you'd been mostly unconscious since the operation. Are you sure you should be walking?

"Are you sure I should be smoking?" I retorted, which shut him up until we were outside the hospital.

55

My relations left shortly after taking me back inside. Words were exchanged about the irresponsibility of giving cigarettes to a postoperative nonagenarian, which David took with surprisingly good grace. I was soon left to my own devices until such time as a doctor deigned to look in on me (or more accurately, to look in on my charts and test results) and murmur vague platitudes about the signs being encouraging.

Being left to my own devices amounted to watching TV or looking out of the window, as I had been fortunate enough to be stowed in a corner berth with a view over the flat roofs of hospital buildings, the perspective of which drew the eye naturally to the focal point of the incinerator chimney. By day, this was a largely static panorama of listless grey - enlivened only by the odd itinerant seagull which would settle somewhere in the picture briefly before flying away again. By night, however, the featureless view enabled the pane to appear as a mirror, giving me the time to study my new physical lodgings at leisure.

The initial shock now over, I examined the face of Edith Sterckx. Had she been beautiful once? This face had gone past the point of resemblance to any former self. Unless Mrs Sterckx had looked like Yoda when she was young, I could see nothing from which to excavate her. She was tiny and wrinkled, with sprouts of white hair poking out of her chin. Her lips slithered back and forth, as if independently powered and struggling to keep something contained within her mouth. Her eyes were bloodshot and weary, but they sparkled in the hospital twilight. In spite of everything else, this person was undeniably alive.

But who was she? Who was this person? I knew she was Edith Sterckx - 97-year-old heart patient and miraculous survivor, mother of David, grandmother of Marie, committed smoker. And what else?

That was it. It's just a body - just a legal identity; an outward identity. I'm still 100% Shaun Strong, despite being 100% Edith to the rest of the world outside my own head. Shaun separated from his own body was one thing. I was used to that whenever I travelled. I was me when I was away, and I was unchanged when I returned. I felt no different inside a body or out. But the persistence of my identity in a new body? That's a big deal, isn't it? That says something pretty important about the nature of reality. If there's an essence of me that is separate from the cells that made up the body also known as Shaun Strong (now dissolving slowly in the English Channel), then haven't I just proved the existence of…what? The soul?

Don't be ridiculous young man. Pull yourself together.

Who said that?

You did.

I did.

That wasn't me.

It was me. It was the voice inside - speaking from the source of dreams, inspirations and fantasies. Some fantasy this is. It's coming from me, but not the daytime me. Not the me under the control of my ego. It's unfamiliar but I recognise it.

I looked back at Edith's face in the reflection. Ninety-seven. She's nearly three times my age. What the hell must she have seen and done? Jesus - I've had at least one baby! I reached down and felt my stomach through my nightgown. I've never been "inside" a woman before… and I've never seen such an old one. My hand crept up towards my breasts. Maybe just a quick look…

Really? That's your first response to this situation? To start peeking? To start treating this body as another object?

Is this my guilt speaking? Is this shame? Those are familiar choruses to my inner ear, but this...

You know what it is.

I know what it is.

Forget what. Start thinking about why.

Why?

Why you're here. What you've got to do.

I scanned back through my memory. Keith. I was here to rescue Keith. But as I considered Keith, an alternative, simultaneous train of thought became louder and louder, until it took up my concentration in full. This inner voice - it's so strong and so clear. It's telling me what to do and I'm ready to obey it. It's decisive in a way I never have been. I've only ever felt this...what? This directed in dreams. This is the worst dream ever. It's boring and it hurts and I can't wake up.

I closed my eyes, hoping that new hallucinations would come. But they didn't.

You know it's not a dream. Pull yourself together - stop fannying about and start planning how you're going to save Keith and change the will.

The will? I don't understand.

You do.

Deep inside I did, but the knowledge that was welling up in the depths of my mind was not yet ready to surface. I was starting to understand that I had changed, but I was not prepared to admit that the self I identified with was anyone other than Shaun Strong. But I knew where, or rather who, these thoughts were coming from.

I suppose it makes sense really. Mind and matter aren't separate. How could they be? They're entangled at every level, not just the quantum level. Spooky action at a distance is going on all the time. It's selective blindness to claim otherwise. Nothing is really separate from everything else. No man is an island. Or woman. An island, I mean. Some men are women. I'm one of them. I'm Edith Sterckx. I'm Shaun Strong. *E pluribus unum.*

Now you get it. So stop mucking about and start thinking.

I am thinking.

Thinking about what you're going to do about this. You know what has happened. Daydreaming like this, trying to put it into words - it's just another kind of masturbation.

Can we not talk about masturbation?

We have to save your friend and change my will.

What happened in the woods? At the hospital?

Does it matter? And why the sudden interest in understanding? You never cared before.

This is different.

How is it different?

...Errr...

It's not important. What's different is that now you have a purpose. And we have me. You have a backbone.

One last question: why me?

Why not you? Because we were there.

Why did you summon me to the hospital? Why were you encased in flames?

Listen. We have things to do. Let's get them done and maybe, while we're doing them, "why" will become apparent. How many problems have you ever solved sitting in your armchair thinking them through? You learn by doing. We'll work out "why" sooner or later. Or maybe we won't. Maybe some other things will reveal themselves as needing to be done while we're doing these things - and then we'll have a new purpose. The alternative, of course, is to sit here and do nothing. To sit here and wait to die. Which is a shit option.

So just get on with it. It's life - make the most of it while we have it. Do what needs to be done.

56

The hospital staff were amazed at the speed and extent of my recovery. In fact, within a week of regaining full consciousness I was out of bed and walking around the ward with a vigour that is unusual in healthy nonagenarians. Even Mr Campbell the surgeon was interested. He was keen to crack me open again to see how he had managed to restore me to better health than I had been in prior to my admission.

I kept my mouth shut. I didn't tell them that this was no longer just Edith Sterckx, but a blend of two people - one of whom was in the prime of life (sort of) and another with an iron will and a sense of purpose.

As you might expect, this did lead to a few behavioural quirks. I displayed an unhealthy degree of interest in the manhunt that was being reported in the news, annoying the other patients and the staff with endless requests for updates. I was still unable to answer any questions about myself beyond the basics. I was regularly caught trying to sneak out of the ward to smoke and had to be repeatedly escorted out of the male toilets.

One morning from behind the curtain I heard David in conversation with Dr Atugba.

"I'm really not sure she's ready Mr Sterckx. Yes, the physical recovery has been…unprecedented. But I am very concerned that your mother is a lot less stable than she appears. Her mind is sharp, but she's clearly covering up gaping holes in her long-term memory. Of course, it's up to you, but I would strongly advise against discharging her at this time."

"Marie and I want to take her home."

"That could be good for her," Dr Atugba admitted.

"Being around her own possessions and in more familiar surroundings may help to stimulate the recovery of memories."

"I...wait...her home? I was talking about our home."

"Don't you live in a block of flats Mr Sterckx?"

"Well, yes."

"And how many bedrooms does your flat have?"

"Look, doctor...I can see what you're driving at here, but it's really not practical for me to move out to Oxshott with her. I need to be in town for the libraries and Marie has to sign on every other week. There are hardly any buses..."

"Mr Sterckx, I realise that you have Lasting Power of Attorney that allows you to make decisions on your mother's behalf, but I am not prepared to release her into your care if she is not going back to her own home. I'll contest it. I'll refer the matter to Social Services..."

"Whoa! Hold on! There's no need for that!" David sounded panicked. "Of course we can look after mum in her own home. I wasn't saying it was impossible - just that it would be... inconvenient. But I think you're right doctor. She needs to be in her own surroundings, doesn't she? And Marie and I will take good care of her. If we can't manage...well, you know that my mother is wealthy, right? Once she's home and able to transfer all remaining legal responsibilities over to me, I'll be able to sort out the best private care. Money will be no object. But only if we can't manage."

"And she will have to stop smoking."

"She's been smoking for eighty years or more."

"There are services available to help people quit."

"I...alright, alright...we'll try to get her to stop... Now, what do we have to do to get her out of here? When can we take her away?"

It took a few days, but eventually I found myself with David and Marie in a taxi, driving away from Guildford and into rural Surrey. The driver had a terrible cold and whenever he was not making one-sided small talk, he would cough violently.

"Oxshott eh? Nice place. Very nice. I came out here a couple of weeks back with the wife and kids… Lovely to get out into the countryside. Nothing better, is there? English countryside on a summer's day. It ain't the same abroad, is it? There's something about an English summer. I reckon it's the leaves. Something in the leaves and the sunlight. Makes it special. You don't get that abroad. You don't see so many trees anywhere else, do you?"

The driver began hacking. His face reddened as oxygen failed to make it to his phlegm-clogged lungs, until he made a growling noise and emitted a harsh croaking sniff from the back of his throat. Normal breathing resumed and he continued.

"I just can't get rid of this cold. Tried everything, I have. Wife says it's hayfever, but I don't think that's it. Never had it before. I'm just run down. Guess when I last had a day off?"

Nobody replied.

"Ten days ago. Twelve hour shifts every day. Takes it out of you."

I tuned the driver out with remarkable ease. We passed under a Victorian brick railway bridge. Painted in stark white letters above the arch were the letters "HRIST". What was this a reference to? Christ? So what happened to the C? Or maybe it wasn't Christ. Maybe it was meant to say "Hristo". Perhaps somebody out here was paying tribute to the former Bulgarian international striker, Hristo Stoichkov.

Who? That was one of yours, not mine.

They're ours now. Stop trying to separate things. We're the same person now, so just get used to it.

I'm trying. I just didn't have you pegged as a football fan.

There's a lot you don't know about me, young man.

An ice cream van tore past and swerved in front of us. It had a hand-painted version of Mickey Mouse holding up a Lollipop Man's stop sign on the back. It appeared to have been produced by someone who had only had Mickey Mouse described to them without ever seeing him.

"He won't sell much going at that speed," the driver said. "Eh? Eh? That was Morecambe and Wise, that was. Classic."

He sniffed loudly again and cleared his throat.

"Sorry about the cold. I just can't shake it. Wife says it's hayfever, but…"

"Just here on the right," David interrupted.

We pulled off the road between a pair of ancient wooden gateposts and parked on a patch of rough ground surrounded by overgrown grass and hedges. A decaying cottage was just about visible through the proliferating foliage which seemed intent on reclaiming this particular corner of the country for the vegetable kingdom. Did I recognise it? I scanned the garden, but nothing clicked.

"Alright - here we are then. Let me give you a hand with those bags…"

The taxi driver exploded with another coughing fit. David nevertheless allowed him to transport all of the baggage - at least some of which was his own - in from the car, in spite of the driver's gasps and honks.

We stood in front of my front door as the taxi pulled away. David picked through a huge bundle of keys searching for the right one. Eventually he identified one that turned, but when he pushed on the door there was no movement.

"You have a go Marie."

"Do you have a back door key? Nan, do you have any keys?"

"You have to lift it as you push," I said unexpectedly.

David gave the key another turn, pulling upwards on the corroded brass knob with his other hand as he did so. The door swung open with a dry creak. It was a hot afternoon in the garden, chilled and moistened slightly by the chaos of respirating plant life that surrounded us. The sun, where it could reach through the sprawling vegetation, was warm and spread a dappled light where it fell. The taxi driver had been right about English summer afternoons. But that thought was soon swept entirely from my mind. As the door opened a colder, cloying atmosphere spilled out. I breathed in and my hippocampus started as if awakened from a deep sleep. The smell. The temperature. The light. A jolt of uncoordinated recognition. I looked at the dark and cluttered hallway. The photographs and prints on the wall. The staircase and its worn red carpet. The pot at the bottom of the stairs, holding umbrellas and walking sticks. Each object I looked at was strange to me, but taken together as a single whole I recognised it all. I was home at last.

57

The first few days at home were spent in a state of near-constant vertigo. Mrs Sterckx's home was crammed with objects, most of which said nothing at all to me. But every so often I would come across one that sent my brain into freefall. Usually it was the look of a thing, but sometimes it would be the feel of its surface, its smell, its weight in my hand - even the sound of my foot on a groaning floorboard as I entered a room could trigger a flood of remembrance. At first, it would be confused and shapeless - less a memory as such and more of an awareness that here there is a memory still to be extracted. As I studied the object again, fragments would gradually reveal themselves. A snatch of conversation, an expression on an unknown face, how I felt at a certain moment long ago.

A sepia photograph of a tall bespectacled young man in military uniform left me cold, but something surged up from my depths and burst its banks when I picked up the frame. I felt dizzy as I turned the picture over and my eyes were drawn to a brass clasp securing the back plate to the frame. The smooth movement, in and out of the hook; the resistance of the pin when turned in the wrong direction; the delicious ache of pushing the hook between fingernail and nail bed that I felt tingling in the base of my spine. I was a child again. This frame had been with me all my life. I looked at the photograph again. Handwritten in the bottom left corner were the words "Lucas Sterckx, 1947". I stared at his face again, but nothing sprang to life as it had done when I had seen and felt the clasp.

"That's Grandad, Nan. Do you recognise him?" Marie asked.

"Yes," I whispered.

Marie was wearing another hideous cardigan, this depicting one wolf standing on a rocky outcrop howling at the moon as another loomed towards the viewer with an ambiguous expression on its face. Its unnatural fibres would bristle electrostatically whenever another object came too close. Her greasy hair hung in untidy strands over her shoulders. Despite the refracting effect of her thick glasses - giving the impression that her eyes were looking in opposite directions - Marie's expression was one of genuine concern and kindness.

"What do you remember about him Marie?"

"Oh, God, well…not much Nan. He died when I was about ten years old."

"Tell me what you do remember."

We sat down in the kitchen, the picture stood between us like a third party to the conversation.

"He was Belgian, obviously. That's where the name comes from. I remember going over there on the ferry at the end of every summer with you both when I was little. I think he had been a diplomat or something like that before he retired. Any country you mentioned, he'd been there and he knew all there was to know about it. He was very tall and thin, and he had that old-fashioned hair - like in the picture - even when he was young. He always wore a tie, and you could tell that he could be fearsome when he wanted to be. But he was always kind and gentle when I was around. Anything he held, he handled with such care and attention - almost with love."

That sent a shock flash of identification up my neck. Yes. I remembered soft, long-fingered hands, slowly and deliberately wiping, cleaning and oiling some mechanical device I could not yet picture. But the hands and their quality of concentrated, unrushed care. That I remembered.

"You met him during the war Nan. I think you were in Belgium or maybe France. Dad knows the story better than I do."

"It was France," a voice came from the doorway behind us. It was David. "You met in France."

He walked away. When it became clear he was not coming back, I turned to Marie again.

"What else do you remember about him?"

"Aw Nan, it was such a long time ago… I remember coming here. Grandad pruning the fruit trees, you cooking in the kitchen with apples you'd grown yourselves. He'd call me 'little *schatje*.'"

Again, that my senses reeled as that word - specifically the '-je' suffix at the end of it - exposed previously concealed pathways and unlocked previously bolted doors in my mind. That was how Lucas spoke. His immaculate, 1940s BBC English would every so often give way to scraps of earthy Flemish - the clipped, cool diplomat letting the cheeky peasant boy within out for a moment's fresh air. The eyes in the picture now locked on to mine and I knew him. My Lucas. My dear, long-departed husband Lucas.

"Don't cry Nan. Here, look. I think they're under here. Yeah. Look - these were the records you and Grandad were always listening to. Let's put one on."

Marie pulled out an LP whose sleeve featured the head and shoulders of a tanned, thick-lipped man in shirtsleeves resting his chin on his hand. His brow was furrowed in an expression of something like surprised boredom. She put the record onto the player and carefully placed the needle onto the spinning black disc. It gave a dusty thunk and then began to crackle. That sound soon gave way to the sound of tinny applause, with distant cheers and shouts in the background. In turn, the applause subsided and a quavering minor chord surged, played on what sounded like an accordion.

Dans le porte d'Amsterdam
Y a des marins qui chantant

The voice was rich and full, but hoarse and ragged. I was transported. Paris. Olympia 1964. Lucas and I had been there, in that cheering crowd that gloomy October. Jacques Brel had commanded the stage completely, flinging his arms around, sweating and spitting in the harsh limelight as he relayed that ageless tale of filthy sailors and their forever out-of-reach dreams. We had been transfixed and it had been our song ever since.

As the song ended in a rapturous crescendo of voice, instruments and wild applause (giving way to the far less powerful and captivating "*Les Timides*") I remembered how Lucas and I had met. It was autumn 1943. We had been introduced by my friend and comrade, an Indian lady Noor Inayat Khan - better known as Nora. I had just been deployed to occupied France, as a covert wireless operator. Nora had been the first woman that the Special Operations Executive had sent out in that role. I was in the second wave of recruits, for whom Nora had opened the door.

A tiny aircraft had flown three of us across the Channel at low altitude and landed in a clearing in the Ardennes forest. Nora met us and led us to a cabin a mile or so away where we were to stay and await further instructions. In the days that followed, we became fast friends and we would remain so until Nora's life was cut brutally short. She was betrayed later that year, imprisoned by the Nazis and executed in 1944 at Dachau. But it was in that cabin I met the love of my life, a tall, thin agent of the Belgian resistance and government-in-exile - one Lucas Sterckx.

The floodgates of memory now gave way and immersed me in Edith's life story. Marriage in 1946. Life in Brussels as Lucas and his wartime comrades helped to get the Belgian state back on its feet after six years of occupation. Years of travel and adventure, of culture and of love. Then David was born and Lucas was always away on diplomatic missions. Edith rode horses and painted. After a few years, they moved to the coast - to Ostend - as if Britain was calling Edith Sterckx (née

Entwistle) home once more. While Lucas was abroad Edith and young David began to spend more time in London, but they always came back together for joyful reunions in their seafront villa on the dunes to the east of Ostend.

David had grown up a sullen and bitter boy, overshadowed by his parents' achievements and effortless dash. "Failure to launch" was not a phrase in those days, but it applied to David perfectly. His literary pretensions were undermined not only by a lack of ability, but also by a lack of application (effort being entirely beneath him) and he drifted lazily from one disappointment - never his fault, of course - to the next. By the time that Lucas died of cancer in 1988 - brought on by decades of cigarette smoking without so much as a filter between his lung linings and the noxious chemicals - David was a defeated old man, with a watery-eyed ten-year-old daughter by a woman who had died in childbirth to serve as his longstanding excuse for never getting further than he had.

That's who we now were.

The Thing had vanished along with my – that is, Shaun's - body. But now when I dreamed I was transported to Edith's past life. Each night revealed more about this remarkable woman, who was now me. I shan't bore you with too many details. Edith's past, after all, is not strictly relevant to this story. Only the (short) future that followed the recovery of her memories is. Suffice to say she had been right about providing me with a backbone. I found myself unwilling to suffer fools gladly to David and Marie's dismay. I found levels of determination that had been entirely lacking in Shaun. I wondered why I had been so easily led by Keith - led into crime and led by someone who could so clearly not tell what he was getting either of us into.

What on earth did you see in him?

It wasn't that. It was what he saw in me.

I'll tell you what he saw in you. A fool who'd do what he was told.

But...he's my only friend.

With friends like that, who needs enemies? Fat lot of good

your friend did you. Still, you've got to rescue him. That's what we agreed. I'll help you do that if you help me with the little problem of my will.

You know David will be gone the second you've changed it and Marie will go with him, don't you?

I know.

So why do it?

It's not fair, what I did to him. I was angry when I left everything to the cats. It's not his fault he's the way he is. Not entirely anyway. He doesn't deserve the money and the house, but nor does he deserve to be left with nothing. He's my only son, after all.

I understood.

58

"Mum ... MUM!"

David was shouting up the cottage's stairs. I was looking for my glasses, which I had found I could see a lot better with.

"Mum, I need you to take me to Guildford! I've got an appointment at 11 o'clock. It's very important and I can't miss it!"

I looked down the staircase at David. From this angle, he looked like an overgrown child - clad in shorts, sandals and an outsized Michael Bolton 1990 UK tour t-shirt. The luxuriant quality of Michael's flowing mane as depicted on the shirt had not been effaced at all by twenty years of wear, staining and boil washes, and stood in stark (one might even say embarrassing) contrast to the lank, oily clumps that hung from my son's pasty scalp. The singer's nose and chin were stretched and distorted by David's protuberant belly and where the print showed Michael's skin, it was cracked and beginning to peel from too many trips through the tumble dryer. Nevertheless, even subjected to all these indignities, Michael Bolton circa 1990 was a far better-looking man than David.

David's expression was one of petulant resentment - a man in his sixties reduced to asking his mother for a lift, but determined to regard this as an insult perpetrated against him by me. His expression brightened chillingly as I began a careful descent of the stairs, then sagged back to its habitual pout when I got safely to the bottom.

At this point I realised driving a car was numbered among those memories of Edith's I had not yet been able to recover. As Shaun I had never bothered and now I wished I had. Perhaps it was because my mum and dad had died in a car accident? God. All of a sudden, I felt a twinge of empathy for David. How would we cope without our parents to lay blame at the feet of? What else is able to serve as the root cause behind every one of our failures? Who else is there to wipe away our responsibilities, once they've stopped wiping away our tears?

This insight was of little use to me in the moment, however. David expected me to be able to drive the car that was stranded on the driveway of the cottage with dandelions and nettles now growing into the wheel arches.

"I have a meeting with somebody who has come over from the US and I can't be late. Come on - we're cutting it fine as it is."

"Nan!" Marie was calling from the living room. "Nan - there's an update on those murders in Woking on the TV. The police are appealing for anyone with information about that man they're looking for. They're saying he used to work in the library there. Now they're interviewing some man with a beard and cross eyes who used to work with him..."

"Marie, do you mind? Mum needs to get ready to drive me to Guildford."

Marie appeared in the doorway.

"Can I come?"

"No. You need to stay here."

"Why can't I come? I like it in Guildford."

David held up his hands and pursed his lips in exasperation.

"It's a very important meeting! I can't be doing with you tagging along, getting in the way!"

Marie looked crestfallen. I sensed that this was a scene which had played out in slightly different forms many, many times before.

"Come on, we need to go now," David bustled over to me and took me by the arm, attempting to lead me towards the front door. I snatched the car keys and my handbag as we passed the dresser in the hallway. In my brief time as a woman, I had come to appreciate the immense value of handbags.

David positioned me outside the driver's door of the car and walked around to the passenger side. I stood looking at him.

"What? Is it already unlocked?"

"David, I need to tell you something."

"Can you perhaps tell me it while we're on the way? Seriously, I can't be late for this meeting…"

"David, I don't know how to drive."

David put his forearms on the roof of the car and sank his face between them. Five seconds passed and then he lifted his head up again, inhaling deeply as he did so.

"Mum. You do know how to drive. You have a driving licence. I checked."

"I can't remember how to do it…"

"Why are you only saying this now?" David snapped, interrupting me. "Why now of all the days we could have had this stupid discussion?"

"This is the first time it's come up…"

"I have to be at this appointment at 11. Do you understand that? It's vital that I am there. Why do you always try to sabotage me like this? Do you know how much trouble it has caused me, living out here in the sticks? Do you know what I had to give up to come and look after you? And now, you can't just take me into Guildford when the entire cast of Stargate SG-1 are doing a PA at the town hall? You are such a selfish old woman! Marie! MARIE!"

Marie appeared in the doorway again.

"Get your shoes on. You're driving."

"But I've only got a provisional licence…"

"Well it's a good job we have a fully qualified expert here to supervise you, isn't it?"

After 45 minutes of completely uneventful, calm, competent driving, we arrived outside Guildford town hall. David scrambled out and ran away from the car without a word, slamming the door behind him.

"What shall we do now?" asked Marie. "Dad will be in there for a couple of hours at least."

"What would you like to do Marie?"

"Well, it would be nice to go and get a cake and some coffee…" she said.

A few minutes later we settled into uncomfortable metal-framed chairs in a café going by the name of "Cakey Boo Boo Num Nums" in the Tunsgate Quarter. Everything in Cakey Boo Boo Num Nums was pink, powder blue or lavender - including the chairs and the staff uniforms. A burly and extensively-tattooed young man with a waxed moustache and a haircut that last found popular acclaim amongst the members of the Hitler-Jugend came over to take our order. He spoke with a strong Spanish accent.

"Good morning laydeez. What can I get you?"

Marie sat in silence staring at the menu. I looked at her and back to the young man, who beamed at me in a way that suggested his mind was somewhere else entirely.

"A small Americano please. And those cakes over there look lovely - what are they?"

"Ees a coffee caaaayke. A cheesecaaaayke. A lemon caaaayke…", he drawled.

"What would you recommend?" I asked, attempting to sound coquettish.

"The lemon caaayke -ees bery nice. All home-made, fresh thees morning."

"I'll have a piece of that then."

"But the cheesecaaaayke - ees also bery nice. I have a piece yesterday…ees…", he made a gesture indicating satisfaction.

"Why don't you have a piece of the cheesecake then Marie, and we can share?" I suggested.

Marie grunted assent, without making eye contact with either me or the waiter.

"And to dreenk for you meess? Perhaps a whitewine for such a beautiful morneeng…?", he cooed gently, enunciating "white wine" as a single word.

"Latte," Marie replied sharply without looking up.

Once the waiter had brought our order over, he retired to a stool behind the counter where he picked up a paperback book, put his feet up on another stool and began to read. The book's cover featured a black and white rocket with a pair of female legs.

"Why do you still live with David?" I asked.

Marie looked at me as if I had asked her why trees grow up instead of down, or why fish live in the water.

"He needs me, Nan."

"But what about you? What do you need?"

"I want Dad to get his book published and become a famous writer..."

"And then what?"

"And then...and then I'll probably be his secretary, sorting out speaking tours, negotiating with agents...stuff like that."

"Is that what will make you happy Marie?"

Again, she looked at me as though my question was lacking in basic logical structure.

"What about you Nan? You seem better than you have been for years. Do you think you'll be able to move back with us to Woking?"

"Oh I don't know about that dear. I do have a few little jobs I need to get done though. Perhaps when we've finished in here we could just pop to a couple of shops."

"Yes Nan. We just need to not go too far, so that we can pick Dad up when he rings."

It was heartbreaking to see how completely David had brainwashed his daughter into serving his every need. Marie seemed to have no will or desires of her own. The Edith part of me had an idea of how we could start to undo that.

The waiter had reappeared to take away our empty plates.

"Was everytheeng alright for you?"

"Yes, lovely," I replied. "Where do you come from?"

"I am from Colombia. I am stoddying here in the UK."

"This is my granddaughter, Marie."

"Hello Marie. I am Sergio."

Marie said nothing, but looked hideously embarrassed.

"Well Sergio, it was nice to meet you. Good luck with your studies!" I said, as we got up to leave. Not looking where I was going, I collided with another person entering the café and dropped my handbag, spilling its contents over the floor.

"Oh I'm so sorry! Please - don't…let me get that," the voice was familiar and sent a shudder along my spinal column.

I looked up and there she was. Flanked by her daughter, it was Michelle Darwin. She knelt and began picking up the contents of my bag. Sophie sauntered off towards the counter, where she was eagerly welcomed by a fully alert and present Sergio. Marie was loitering outside the café door, not quite acknowledging what was happening.

How long had it been since I had seen Michelle the day I died for the first time? Weeks? I couldn't remember. I tried to kneel down to help her, but my geriatric knees resisted their instructions. Michelle saw what I was trying to do.

"You just stay there my love."

My heart fluttered at those words.

"There we go, I think I've got everything now. Is this yours?"

In her perfectly-manicured, petite hand Michelle Darwin held out a flyer which had fallen out of the café window sill when we bumped into one another. It read "Surrey and North Hampshire Esoteric Circle - Open Night". My heart jerked again.

"Yes it is. Thank you so much. You are so kind and…so beautiful…" I murmured, quite unaware of what I was saying.

"Aww! Thank you - what a lovely thing to say! Did you hear that Sophie? This lady said I'm beautiful."

Sophie was now deep in conversation with Sergio and did not respond.

Michelle passed me the handbag and gave my hand a little squeeze.

"Nan…" Marie grumbled from the pavement.

"Have a wonderful day love!" Michelle called as I walked

out.

My head was spinning. She had touched me! And she had called me "love"! Twice!

I've never heard anything so absurd. The Edith-voice bubbled up from my unconscious. She helped an old woman pick up the contents of her bag and was polite - the last thing that proves is that she has any feelings for Shaun Strong.

I knew. But I didn't care. It was as close as I had or would ever get. And it was enough. For now.

Marie and I walked away from Cakey Boo Boo Num Nums in silence. Gazing blankly into the passing shop windows, Marie walked apparently aimlessly in the absence of any orders from a higher power.

"Right," I said. "In here."

We went into a stationery shop, which also sold books, video games, chocolate bars and - oddly - camping equipment.

"Help me find one of those DIY will kits," I said.

Marie came to life, just as Sergio had done at the sight of Sophie.

"Oh, are you going to change the will then? I think the legal stuff is over there at the back…"

She trotted off and returned moments later with a pack of paperwork, reading "Essential Last Will and Testament" on the cover along with a picture of a simpering elderly couple and a younger couple, who were presumably supposed to be their soon-to-be-somewhat-richer offspring.

"Dad will be so relieved. The whole business with the cats has been a terrible stress for him. He's hardly been able to put pen to paper since you two had that falling out three years ago."

"I'll bet he will be. Yes Marie, I am going to change my will - but I have one condition…"

59

The entrance to the offices of Lavery, Woodward and Saïd was situated at the end of an unclean alleyway somewhere in London's glamorous West End, partially hidden behind a skip filled with smashed panels of plasterboard and scrags of damp cavity wall insulation. On top sat a three-wheeled, fire-damaged pram. The door had been graffitied with bright pink paint that had run. The tag was one circle, with a semi-circle balanced above it.

David had been extremely unhappy about my insistence that the will was sorted out by Aleister Woodward, and perhaps more so that it meant he was obliged to make a trip into London with me. Nevertheless, he agreed - seeing no better way of getting his inheritance arranged with less effort. This did not prevent him from complaining endlessly – about the delayed train, about the very poor quality of train-catered sausage rolls, about the price of Tube tickets and more. By the time we had reached the alleyway, my amusement at his discomfort was giving way to reservations about the kind of a place we had found ourselves in.

To approach the door, we had to pass by a maimed pigeon that was slowly dying. David pressed a buzzer and a sepulchral voice hissed back at us from the speaker.

"Yes?"

"David and Edith Sterckx. We have an appointment to see Mr Woodward."

"Come in."

The lock clicked and the door swung slightly ajar. It led into a poorly-lit corridor with a staircase at the end.

"First floor. Door on the left," the voice added as we stepped in.

"Why on earth are we here?" David whispered. The whining tone of his voice was now tinged with fear. "There are plenty of perfectly good lawyers back in Surrey."

"It has to be this one," I replied. "He's very good."

"It's a will! It's not the OJ Simpson case! And how good can he be if his offices are in a place like this?"

"You know what London prices are like."

We climbed the stairs in silence. The air was oppressive and the building seemed to hum silently. The staircase opened onto a landing. A single unshaded bulb hung from the ceiling, leaving the far end of the corridor shrouded in total blackness. A dark wood door faced us. A brass plate on it read "Lavery, Woodward and Saïd".

David reached out to knock but the door gave way at his touch. He pushed it open and we went in. The black painted floorboards gave way to beige carpet. Antiseptic fluorescent lighting wiped clean the sickly glow of the hallway's lone incandescent bulb.

"Hello there!"

A warm and friendly voice greeted us. It came from a young woman, dressed in a grey business suit, her black hair pulled tightly back in a pony tail. She had green eyes and striking red lips and stood up as we entered the room.

"Mr and Mrs Sterckx. Welcome to Lavery, Woodward and Saïd. Mr Woodward is just with another client at the moment, so can I get you a drink while you wait? Tea? Coffee?"

The woman disappeared through a side door, leaving us sitting on grey Scandinavian-style sofas. There was a well-lit fish tank in the corner of the room but I could not see any fish in it. A low coffee table separated David and I, bearing a fan of publications - not quite books, not quite magazines – with names such as "Substance" and "Number". I picked up a copy of "Number" and leafed through it. The paper was so thick it almost qualified as cardboard, but the pages were covered in nothing but badly-aligned text in a font that hurt my eyes. Occasionally, a page would feature a black and white photograph of a lanky teenager of indeterminate gender wearing three-quarter length trousers engaged in a banal activity - such as looking in a jacket pocket or drying its face with a towel. I put "Number" carefully back on the pile.

David had worn a suit and tie for the twin occasion of a visit to London and an audience with a professional. The suit had gone shiny at the shoulders and knees and had mud (or worse) stains around the ankles. His tie was a dark green with a repeating pattern of Rudolph the Red-Nosed Reindeers on it. He had lacquered his hair into a kind of comb-over, but clumps were starting to separate and come loose from the main body.

The receptionist returned with our drinks.

"There you are. By the way, I do apologise for you having to use the rear entrance. The partners are having a bit of a refurb and - well - it's causing a bit of inconvenience for everyone. And does the entryphone still make me sound like a vampire?"

She laughed over-enthusiastically at this, a kind of whooping rasping yelp that shocked David into sitting up straight.

"I think there's a dead beetle in the speaker that makes it rattle like that!"

She laughed uproariously again.

The phone on the receptionist's desk began to ring.

"Excuse me please. Good morning Lavery, Woodward and Saïd - Lillith speaking, how may I help?"

Lillith scribbled notes on a yellow pad as she listened to the caller.

"I see. And is he expecting your call? I see. I'll try and put you through now."

She pushed some buttons on the phone's base unit.

"Aleister, I have a Mr Bormann on the phone for you - he says...please don't use that voice Mr Woodward. Thank you.

Yes, they're here now. OK, what time? Alright, I'll tell Mr Bormann you're with a client and will have to call him back. Oh, also, what would you like for your lunch today? Aha. OK, I'll send them in."

Lillith put the phone down and smiled broadly at us.

"Mr Woodward is ready to see you now."

She directed us towards a white door on the far side of the room. The office beyond the door took us straight back to the atmospherics of the hallway. The temperature was markedly lower than in the waiting room and it seemed that wisps of mist coiled faintly around the skirting boards. The lighting was dull and claustrophobic, and heavy mahogany shelves and bookcases served to exaggerate the darkness of the environment. Rows of black leather-bound volumes in quarto size occupied almost all of one wall. There were no letters on the books' spines, only gold-embossed symbols of lines and circles. A set of shelves was home to a number of glass jars of different sizes. Cloudy liquids within suspended organic shapes of indeterminate form. A complete skeleton of a human being, only eighteen inches tall, crouched alongside the jars as if ready to pounce on viewers. A stuffed crocodile, blackened with age, squatted balefully on top of a chest of drawers. Its amber eyes glittered and gave the impression of following you around the room. Behind a large rosewood desk, peering over his golden spectacles, sat Aleister Woodward. As he rose to greet us, his eye sockets were cast into shadow by the low-level lighting (whose source was strangely hard to identify) and his face appeared for a moment to be that of a bare, grinning skull.

"Mr Sterckx. Mrs Sterckx. Welcome. It's a pleasure to meet you."

His handshake was cold and damp, like a frog's skin. As he was about to release my hand, his eyes darted to mine and he reasserted his grip.

"Have we met? You…seem … rather familiar?"

His icy blue eyes remained fixed on my face as he continued to speak.

"I do apologise for the state of the premises. Everything is a little up in the air after we had a…ah…a small fire a few weeks ago. I do hope the back way in was not too unpleasant."

"There's a skip in the way of your door and someone's painted graffiti all over it," David replied quickly - identifying an opportunity to gain the upper hand by keeping the apologies coming.

"Oh that's back again is it?" Woodward said absent-mindedly as he took his seat again behind the gigantic desk. "Please, have a seat. Now, I understand that we are here to talk about a last will and testament?"

As David explained the situation, Woodward nodded and took notes. Every so often, his eyes would flick upwards. Whenever I looked at him, his gaze would drop back to his notes. David had been talking for a few minutes, when Woodward - staring directly at me now - opened a drawer in his desk and took out a Dictaphone, which he placed deliberately between us. I looked back at him, and this time he did not drop his gaze for several seconds. It was the same device I had seen him holding in Prospect House, when he had recorded his conversation with Nigel about the Long murders.

When David had finished, Woodward continued writing notes until the silence became uncomfortable. The crocodile still seemed to be looking at me.

"Well, Mr and Mrs Sterckx - I am of course happy to act on your behalf, although your financial situation and your stated wishes are hardly complex enough to justify the fees. I very rarely do this sort of work any more, although of course I do have a lot of experience in the area."

Woodward furrowed his brow and smiled.

"Are you sure we've never met before Mrs Sterckx? There's something at the back of my mind telling me that I know who you are…"

"I really don't think so Mr Woodward," I replied uneasily. "You were recommended to me by a friend of my late husband, Lucas."

"Lucas Sterckx… hmmm… the name doesn't ring a bell, but perhaps we met socially at some point in the past. I'm sure that's what it is. Maybe it's the name I recognise."

At that moment, David doubled over and gave vent to a pained grunt. Woodward sat back in his chair and steepled his fingers.

"Are you quite alright Mr Sterckx?" he asked cheerily.
David stood up shakily. He clutched his stomach. Sweat had broken out across his forehead.

"Could I possibly use the facilities? I've come over…" David grimaced as he spoke.

"Of course! Of course!" Woodward picked up his telephone. "Ms Saïd, could you show Mr Sterckx to the bathroom? Ha ha ha. No, that's right. We don't want him getting lost in here."

Lillith opened the door and said: "This way please Mr Sterckx". David staggered towards the waiting room and she closed the door behind him, after exchanging a significant glance with Woodward.

Once David had gone, I took out the DIY will kit from my handbag and handed it to Woodward.

"This is the real will," I said. "David is not to know."

Woodward pushed his glasses back up his nose and scanned through the documents.

"This leaves everything to a Miss Marie Sterckx?"

"His daughter."

"I see," Woodward chuckled unpleasantly. "Families, indeed…well, I can take care of all this for you Mrs Sterckx. Just let me file this away and when Mr Sterckx returns we can… ah…finish with the dummy papers."

Woodward stood up and took the Dictaphone from the desk. He walked over to the cabinet with the crocodile on top, opened a drawer and put the recorder inside. He pushed the drawer only half shut and turned to me.

"I'll be back in no less than five minutes Mrs Sterckx."

Woodward left through a second door which I had not noticed before, partially concealed to the right of the colossal bookcase.

I leaped to my feet as soon as he was gone and went over to the cabinet. The open drawer was full of miniature cassettes, alphabetically sorted by surnames written on the spines and ordered by date. I scanned the tapes for "Darwin" and found seven bearing that name. When had it been? I had completely lost track of time. I decided to take all of them. One by one, I extracted the tapes from their boxes and dropped them into my handbag before returning the cases to their original places in the drawer.

Within seconds of returning to my seat, Woodward came back through the side door.

"Well, that is all taken care of Mrs Sterckx. I'm sure your son will be back any moment now..."

And then the other door opened, and Lillith led a pale and shaky David back into the office.

"I'm so sorry. Dodgy sausage roll. Did I miss anything?"

We concluded our business with the false papers. Smiling, Woodward shook both our hands and the unpleasant sensation I had felt before when touching him returned.

"It was a pleasure to meet you. Safe journey home - and Mrs Sterckx?" he paused dramatically, "I'm sure we will see you again soon."

60

On the train home from Waterloo, I took the Schneck flyer from my handbag and read it again.

Surrey and North Hampshire Esoteric Circle. Open Night - all welcome. Experience Dr Claudius, renowned medium and clairvoyant. For private readings call this number.

I thought about Dr Claudius as I watched suburban south west London give way to suburban north east Surrey. The fish man trick was one thing, but how had he known about Old Jeffrey? Sandra was adamant that she had never told anyone about her teenage haunting. Was it possible that Dr Claudius really did have psychic powers? If so, could he shed some light on my situation? I leaned back in my seat and was pondering this when David interrupted my chain of thought.

"You know Mum, now that's all dealt with we really need to talk about your care needs. As you know, it was only ever meant to be …err… a temporary thing, me coming out to live with you in Oxshott. I have a lot of things I need to be doing in Woking. And it's a lot of work looking after you."

"Is it?" I asked.

"Yes. I'm not sure Marie and I can give you the sort of attention you need in your condition - getting in and out of the bath, going up and down the stairs…"

"I do all those things just fine by myself."

"I know that's how it seems Mum, but one day - and we just don't know when that might be - you won't be able to. And if you're all alone out there in the countryside, I dread to think what might happen."

I had been expecting this conversation, but not today. Not quite so soon after the changing of the will. David was going to try and have me put away in a care home, so that he could go back to having as little as possible to do with his elderly and infirm mother as possible.

"Also," he went on, "it's not fair on Marie. She has her hands full working for me, without all the burdens you're putting on her…"

This continued until we got into a taxi at Guildford station. David was silent for the rest of the journey.

That evening, when David and Marie were engrossed in a repeat of 'Location Location Location', I slipped upstairs and called the number on the Schneck flyer. The phone was answered by a familiar West Midlands voice.

"Surrey and North Hampshire Esoteric Circle - Sandra speaking."

"Hello. My name is Edith Sterckx"

"Hello Edith love - what can I do for you?"

"Well, I was hoping to speak to Dr Claudius about my late husband. You see, I have been feeling his presence very nearby recently and I'm sure he has something important to say to me…"

"I understand completely. I'm sure Dr Claudius will be able to help you my dear. Would you like a book a private reading?"

"Yes please. I was hoping we'd be able to talk after the Open Night. I'm ninety-seven you see and it's difficult for me to get out and about."

"Don't you worry about that Edith my love. I've got Dr Claudius' diary right here and he's got space that evening. I'll book you in for a chat with him then. I'll look out for you at the meeting and make sure you're alright. Now, ah…can I take payment from you now my love? Just to secure the slot… We have a lot of trouble with cancellations, you know..."

By the day of the Schneck Open Night, I had figured out how I was going to sneak away from the cottage without being detected. I arranged for a taxi to collect me from the Oxshott post office, and once dinner had been finished with and the TV was on there was little chance of David or Marie noticing my absence for quite some time.

"Just popping to the loo," I called to no response. Once in the hallway, I put on my coat, picked up my handbag and house keys and slipped out of the front door. Closing it silently, I walked out onto the road and towards the village.

The taxi arrived a couple of minutes after I had reached the post office.

"Mrs Sterckx? ACHHOOOOO!"

It was the same taxi driver as had brought us back from the hospital. I sat in the back.

"Lovely evening isn't it? Can't beat them can you? English summer evenings. That evening sunlight...hold on...I thought I was going to sneeze then. Been sneezing for weeks now. Wife says it's hayfever, but I don't think it can be. I've never had it before. I'm just run down, that's what I reckon."

I kept quiet and the driver's conversation quickly dried up. We proceeded to the village hall in silence, punctuated only by his explosive sneezes.

The hall where the Schneck met had not changed since I had last been there. The very same posters adorned the corridor's walls, now a little yellower and even more out of date. What was different was the number of people drifting into the main room. When Keith and I had been going, it was unusual for there to be more than ten people at a Schneck session. Hardly surprising - new visitors rarely bothered going a second time. Today though, there must have been upwards of fifty people bustling around, chatting and drinking out of plastic cups.

The left-hand side of the hall was lined with a row of trestle tables. On the tables were a whole host of pamphlets and DVDs featuring the face of Dr Claudius. In addition, there were magnetic wristbands, bottles of coloured liquids, Native American dream catchers, crystals on strings, crystals in boxes, crystals embedded in the eye sockets of pewter dragons, joss sticks, tobacco tins with marijuana leaves printed on them, fruit boxes packed with second-hand Dan Brown and James Patterson paperbacks, a plastic tub full of toy cars and multifarious other assorted jumble. I spotted Sandra standing behind the Dr Claudius-branded tat. I waved to try and catch her eye, forgetting that she had never seen me before. She waved back nonetheless.

"Are you Sandra?"

"Yes love I am. You must be Edith?"

I confirmed this and we began to chat. It turned out that Sandra and Dr Claudius were now engaged to be married. Sandra proudly showed me her ring.

"We met here actually. He knew things about me…saw right into my soul, he did. From that moment on, we were inseparable."

"Didn't another man run this before?"

Sandra looked grim and moved in closer to speak confidentially.

"You mean Mr Parson? Well. Nobody's seen him for weeks. Not since the night Claudius and I met. Claudius played a pretty mean trick on Mr Parson and he just didn't come back. I look after his mother, you know? At Fair Haven in Godalming. Lost her marbles completely. I've tried to ask her where he might have gone but you just get this random babble about anything and everything that's ever happened to her. I don't think she grasps that he's disappeared because - between you and me - he hardly ever went to visit her. Poor woman. She's lovely is Joan. But like I say, completely potty. Can I get you a glass of wine Edith?"

She returned moments later with two disposable plastic beakers. The white wine within smelled strange, but it tasted alright when I took a sip.

"Aye…it was very odd, Mr Parson vanishing like that.

I suppose it's possible that he achieved transcendental illumination, but I'm sure he'd have sent us a message or something from the other side to let us know not to worry. But there I go… he's a grown man. I'm sure he's alright. Oh but look! We're about to get started. Come and sit with me Edith…"

Ethan, the carrot bag-wielding asocial, banged a book on one of the trestle tables until quiet descended. In a high-pitched voice he proclaimed: "Ladies and gentlemen! Please take your seats - Dr Claudius is here and is ready to begin!"

The crowd shuffled towards the chairs that had been arranged in rows facing the front of the hall. Once everybody had sat down, Ethan turned off the lights. A deep voice called out:

"My name is Dr Claudius and I have travelled to many far-off places."

Things proceeded from that point in an almost identical way to the session Keith and I had attended. Dr Claudius wandered around the darkened room, candle in hand, making vague and leading statements until such time as an audience member claimed to recognise who he was talking about. What was different this time was that once his revelations had reduced somebody to tears or a state of breathless excitement, Dr Claudius would instruct the affected party to speak to one of his assistants afterwards to make an appointment for a private reading - there being various additional things the spirits wished to impart that could not be spoken in such a public setting.

After the demonstration, Sandra was busy making bookings and taking payments from the recently bereaved. I decided to speak to Dr Claudius myself without an introduction. I had an appointment (paid for) after all but I felt strangely confident and light-headed. Perhaps the Edith part of me was finally getting hold of the controls from Shaun.

As I attempted to make my way through the crowd to get to him, a huge man dressed all in black pushed his way past me and everyone else, making a straight line for Dr Claudius. The back of his recently-scarred hairless head looked familiar.

I moved into the wake he was creating in the sea of people and followed. When Dr Claudius saw the man's face, his confident and supercilious expression changed to one of dire apprehension.

"You answer calls when you are phoned. Not woman."

It was the tombstone voice of Yevgeny Kuznetsov, dialling up the Russian accent for (entirely unnecessary) extra intimidation.

"Yevgeny!" Dr Claudius said, spreading his arms wide in an attempt to seem relaxed and welcoming. "What a pleasure it is to see you here! I trust everything is well with our…uh… mutual friend?"

"You answer own calls. Not her."

"Look, Yevgeny… sometimes Sandra has to take calls for me, when I'm…uh…otherwise occupied. Can we discuss this somewhere else perhaps?"

"Nothing to discuss. He send you this."

Yevgeny withdrew something from inside his leather jacket's breast pocket. His gargantuan hand covered it completely when he laid it down on the table Dr Claudius was leaning nervously against. Only when he took it away did I see that it was a mobile phone.

"You keep this with you. When it rings, you answer. Nobody else. Or…"

Yevgeny stared at Dr Claudius significantly. Dr Claudius swallowed and pinpricks of sweat appeared on his forehead.

"I understand. Thank you."

With that, Yevgeny grunted, turned around and barged his way back through the crowd and out of the hall. Ethan sidled up alongside Dr Claudius and whispered into his ear.

"Really?" Dr Claudius said. The surprise in his voice had dismissed all the traces of fear that had previously been there. The two men walked off together purposefully, leaving the mobile phone on the table.

Why did I snatch it? I don't know what came over me. But I did snatch it, and once I got out of the village hall, I ran.

61

Perhaps there was something in that wine I drank, but I don't remember many details from the next few hours or why I made some of the decisions I did. The presence of Yevgeny sent me into a panic. If he was here, then Dr Claudius was somehow in league with Nigel Darwin. What would he want with a self-proclaimed psychic? Unless…I was stricken with paranoia. Was he somehow still after me?

Not knowing where I was heading, I set off from the village hall across the playing fields behind it. The grass was well-kept and tidy, disfigured only by cast away Styrofoam fast food cartons and fluorescent energy drink bottles. Beyond the football pitches was open farmland. I tried to run, but even with my 33-year-old spirit, my 97-year-old body was unable to manage more than a few loping steps at a time before I reverted to walking.

Gasping for breath and leaning on a telegraph pole, I looked back at the village hall. Nobody was following me, but if I could see them, they could still see me. I set off across the farmland, wading through long stalks of some sort of grain. The sun was hanging low in the sky, turning the light to a rich golden red. I pushed on through the crops, clambering over drainage ditches and looking for a way back to the road. In the distance I could see a stand of trees, so I headed for that.

Nigel couldn't possibly know that I had returned from the dead, could he? How could he know? It was impossible. But then wasn't all of this impossible? Why should I assume that supernatural factors only work in my favour? And if he knows I'm alive and if he knew I'm Edith, then maybe he's following me. Or maybe he knows where I'm heading - even though I don't - and he'll be waiting there. Maybe he's reading my mind right now. Think yourself somewhere else.

The trees were fenced off with a low string of barbed wire, but a hundred yards to the left I could see it had been flattened at a point where the posts had been knocked over. I crossed it into the woods.

Were David and Marie in on it? Had they been biding their time before turning me over? Was that a figure I saw darting behind a tree? Or was it just my imagination? My hands and feet were covered in mud from climbing through ditches and both of my shoes had come loose. I crouched down to tie my laces and it was then the age of my spine and my bones really hit me. What the hell was I doing? Nobody was chasing me. I pulled myself upright with the help of some low branches and looked around. Where the fuck had I run to? I couldn't even remember which way I had come, my mind had been racing so fast with imagined conspiracies. If there had been anything in the wine, it was wearing off now.

I carried on walking through the woods, hoping that a straight line would eventually lead me to somewhere recognisable. I couldn't phone for help because I didn't know where I was to be rescued from. Crows cawed angrily overhead and looking up at the canopy, I saw power lines. Changing my mind, I decided to follow the power lines, even though it meant turning away from my previous path. At least the foliage was cut back under the cables and I could see a little further ahead. I walked beneath a pylon, its grey metal skeleton towering above me like an alien invader. I felt one, then two, then several drops of rain on my face. I pulled my jacket up around my shoulders and walked faster. The power lines began to buzz in the drizzle.

I could hear the roar of car engines ahead of me so I kept on walking. My wrists and ankles were aching badly now as the drizzle turned to full-on rain. The trees on either side of the power lines were thinning away and a tall embankment of earth rose up before them. Young trees, their trunks surrounded with plastic sheaths had been planted up its slope and plastic netting peeped through the thin grass, holding the soil in place. The electric cables passed through a gap in the rampart and I could see a road in front of me. A very busy road. As I approached it through the gap, the presence of a hard shoulder and central reservation revealed to me that it was not just any road - it was the M25.

Clearly, I was not as lucid as I thought I was at that point because I decided to thwart my pursuers by crossing it. If a witch can't cross a running stream, my mind conjectured, then surely an astral hunter can't cross a multi-lane highway.

The howl of cars passing me at 90 miles per hour was unbearable as I stood at the edge of the hard shoulder waiting for a break in the traffic that would let me reach the middle of the carriageway. The shockwave of displaced air hitting me as cars passed made me flinch, thinking each time that I'd been hit. Passengers gawped at me as they beheld an old lady about to step into the traffic.

After a few minutes of waiting, I saw my opportunity. I made it across the outside lane with no difficulty, but I stumbled and twisted my ankle as I crossed the middle lane. It was harder to walk now, but I still had time. I had only one more lane to cross.

But then I spotted it. A Porsche had pulled out from behind the bus that was sitting rather selfishly in the middle lane and was speeding up to overtake it. I turned my head as the driver flashed the car's headlights. I carried on walking, but my eyes were frozen on the approaching lamps. A horn sounded. I reached out for the crash barrier. The Porsche was almost upon me. Then it was gone. My skirt flapped violently in its slipstream.

I edged along the central reservation's crash barrier, clinging on to it the whole time as if to let go would see me plummet from a great height. Eventually, I found a gap for emergency vehicles to turn round in. Limping badly now, I hobbled to a patch of grass where an upturned milk crate stood among the shredded remains of a blown-out tire and some faded traffic cones. I sat down on the crate and contemplated my next move. No road signs were visible in either direction, so I could still not tell where I was or in which way I was heading. I decided to carry on across the anticlockwise carriageway, through the gap in the embankments on the far side and to follow the power lines until I came to any kind of human habitation.

But when I tried to get up, my legs would not obey me. My knees had turned to jelly and I couldn't stand. I waited ten, fifteen, twenty minutes. Perhaps it will pass - but it didn't. The sun had finally set by the time two police cars arrived, flashing their lights and sounding their sirens, to take me away.

62

"I need to speak to Chief Inspector Yarrow," I shouted at the backs of the policemen's heads in front of me. "Please - I have important information about the Clare and Trevor Long murders."

The officer in the passenger seat turned to face me. He had a thick ginger beard and a Welsh accent.

"You want to speak to Bob Yarrow now do you? Well Mrs Sterckx, I'm not sure there's much we can do about that is there Rich?"

"Not much," the driver said, without taking his eyes off the road.

"You see, Chief Inspector Yarrow's a very busy man. Got a lot on his plate, you know. I think it's best we get you home to bed and then if you still think you need to speak to someone about all that nasty business, we can send someone out to see you..."

"I know who the killer is. And I can prove it - I have recordings. They killed Shaun Strong too and set things up to make it look like he did it. You're after the wrong man. Plus, the people who did it - they've hacked your computers! They know anything that goes through the official channels and gets logged online. I have to speak to Chief Inspector Yarrow now!"

This seemed to make an impression. The policemen looked at each other. Ginger Beard said to his colleague: "What do you think? Can't hurt can it?"

"He's down at Dorking nick. Saw him there a couple of hours ago nursing a hangover. Never goes anywhere when he's in that state. Might cheer him up, eh? Like you say, can't hurt."

Ginger Beard turned back to me.

"Alright Mrs Sterckx. We'll take you to Bob, but don't you be wasting his time. His wife's left him again and he's not been taking it well. What with that and his manhunt going nowhere."

We soon pulled off the motorway and headed towards Dorking. Ginger Beard and Rich led me to an interview room and told me to wait while they went to find Chief Inspector Yarrow, who - a desk sergeant had told them upon enquiring - had most recently been sighted coming back into the police station carrying a doner kebab and a plastic bag full of cans.

The interview room was grey. The chair and table were grey, the bare walls were light grey and the floor and ceiling were dark grey. The coffee I had been given in a plastic cup was greyish too. I heard a clatter from the corridor outside. The handle of the door jerked left and right, but the door itself didn't move. Then it burst open and a dishevelled man I recognised from the TV was standing in the doorway. It was Detective Chief Inspector Bob Yarrow.

He wore a checked brown jacket and corduroy trousers - the left leg of which was stuck in the back of his sock. His white shirt had come loose from his trousers on one side and his tie dangled a solid six inches below his collar. Several days' stubble - or possibly dirt - clung to his cheeks and neck. He opened his eyes wider and looked around with a surprised expression, as if struggling to keep his balance due to loss of blood pressure.

Spotting me seated at the table, Chief Inspector Yarrow shook his head, cleared his throat and walked purposefully to stand opposite me. The air movement carried a waft of stale beer, cigarettes and body odour towards me.

"Now then young lady," he said with forced cheer. "You're here about…? Is it about a bicycle?"

"It's about the Clare and Trevor Long murders."

Chief Inspector Yarrow's face fell.

"Oh. That." He slumped into the chair opposite me.

"Bane of my fucking life, that is. Oh! Pardon me. Sorry about the swearing madam. I'm under a lot of pressure at the moment. I haven't been to bed for 48 hours now…"

I attempted to take control of the situation.

"Chief Inspector, I've seen you on television appealing for information about the murders of Clare and Trevor Long. Well, I know who did it and I have recordings that prove it. They prove that Shaun Strong, the man you're looking for, was murdered by them as well!"

"Ah ha," Yarrow replied peering through his eyebrows in a way that was clearly intended to convey scepticism but which more obviously betrayed his extreme fatigue. "Do you have these recordings with you?"

"No. They're at my house."

"I see," he sighed, leaning back in his chair and putting his hands behind his head. "Are you going to drink that? Mind if I do? Go on then. Who was it?"

"It was a businessman called Nigel Darwin."

Chief Inspector Yarrow spluttered and began to choke on the mouthful of tepid coffee he had just sipped. He gripped the edge of the table as he hacked and rasped, his eyes watering and turning bright red. Eventually, the coughing fit subsided and Yarrow wiped his eyes with the fat end of his tie.

"Nigel Darwin? *The* Nigel Darwin? The computer bloke? The millionaire philanthropist and local charity fundraising hero computer bloke? You're having a laugh Mrs Sterckx! Which one of those two put you up to this? Was it that ginger twat…?"

"I'm being serious. I can prove it!"

"Have you been drinking Mrs Sterckx?"

"Have you?"

Yarrow huffed indignantly.

"Now look madam. I am not officially at work today. For your information, due to…um…some minor misunderstandings at home I've been sleeping here at the police station. So yes, I have had one or two drinks. Purely for purposes of relaxation as many people in stressful jobs do. But I assure you, any problems I may or may not have with substance abuse and a troubled home life in no way..."

He began to retch once more.

"In no way," he resumed, "get in the way of my dogged pursuit of the truth and the justice. Rest assured Mrs Sterckx, I will find the perpetrator of these foul deeds – who I confidently believe to be the weird loner under whose house we found the late Mr Long, in spite of your baseless and unfounded accusations against Nigel Darwin, a great friend to the Surrey Constabulary.

"Now, you will have to forgive me if - insofar as you were discovered trapped on the central reservation of the M25 not knowing where you were going and brought here - I proceed to treat your allegations with less than the utmost seriousness. I suspect you are a crazy person at best and possibly a deliberate wind-up merchant. If I was not on my day off and therefore not technically on police time myself, I would caution you for wasting police time. Consider yourself lucky I have literally nothing else to be doing at this precise moment."

A piece of kebab meat fell out of Yarrow's sleeve onto the table. We both looked at it. He picked it up and popped it into his mouth, staring at me challengingly.

"Now, if you will excuse me - your relatives will be here to take you home any minute now. Good evening."

And with that, he left.

David and Marie soon arrived with the sneezing taxi driver. We rode home in near total silence. The driver even attempted to muffle his outbursts and resisted any temptation to praise the beauty of English summer nights.

The next day, talk quickly returned to the matter of my long-term care.

"Particularly after what happened yesterday, Marie and I think...it would be best if you went to live somewhere... errmm...where they can take care of you properly," David mumbled.

"Somewhere you can't be wandering off from like that," Marie chipped in. "We were so worried Nan. We didn't even notice you'd gone until half nine. Anything could have happened to you."

I had started to think that going into a home was probably the best way to continue in my quest to rescue Keith. Or was that just my Shaun tendency reasserting itself now that Edith's purpose in this life was complete? At the very least it would get me out from under David and Marie's noses. But was I just taking the line of least resistance? Adapting myself to what other people wanted to happen rather than thinking about what I really wanted? I wasn't sure I could tell any more.

"We can find somewhere really nice for you," said David. "As money is no object."

"And we'll come and visit you, won't we Dad?"

"Ah...yes. We'll visit whenever we can. Obviously, I have a lot of work to do..."

In the end, I agreed. But only on the condition that I could go into a facility down in Godalming called Fair Haven, where I had already made the acquaintance of one of the nurses.

63

Fair Haven was a purpose-built, red brick care home on the outskirts of Godalming. It faced onto one of the main roads leading into the town. Behind lay its ample car park and well-tended gardens, where residents wandered under more or less close supervision. I had a small single room on the first floor overlooking the car park (generally regarded to be the better of the two sides), with a spacious ensuite bathroom and the bare minimum of furniture. My days were spent mostly here, in the day room, in the dining room or in transit between these locations. As somebody who was physically fit and mentally alert, I was left alone by staff for the most part. It was understood that I had admitted myself and I was given a fair degree of freedom to entertain myself.

As expected, I saw less and less of David and Marie as the weeks went by, which was no bad thing. Now that David had control of my money and property, he was no longer particularly interested in me. I expect that he was anticipating my demise at any moment, at which point the funding for his groundbreaking work of revisionist Dr Who historiography would be secured. Ironically, this was almost certainly the best guarantee that it would never be written at all. As ever, Marie went along with whatever her father did.

Life in Fair Haven suited me quite well. My needs were taken care of and all important decisions were made for me. Had I been only Shaun, I might well have relaxed into institutionalised geriatric life permanently - but Edith was still there, urging me on to complete the second half of the mission. I had brought very little with me from Oxshott, but I made sure that I kept hold of Dr Claudius' phone and Aleister Woodward's Dictaphone tapes. Whenever I felt myself becoming too comfortable having my meals made for me, watching Midsomer Murders in the afternoons and going to bed at 8pm, I would stare at these objects as a kind of meditation. I would come away with a degree more focus and an Edith-inspired determination to act. Direct action being a bit too much even with Edith steeling me, I decided that the best way to begin was to befriend the two people at Fair Haven with a connection to this whole series of events: Sandra, and her charge Joan Parson, Mr Parson's mother.

Joan was a tiny sweet old lady who was always smiling and who had been living at Fair Haven for several years. She was widely believed to be suffering from dementia, as her conversation - while superficially logical - made virtually no sense to anyone. Nevertheless the happiness she exuded led most observers to the conclusion that, while she may not have been all there, wherever it was that she was was somewhere quite nice.

One day when we were chatting in the day room, I brought up the subject of our children. Joan told me that her son Lionel sold magic books on the internet.

"Having said that, he's a bit down on his luck at the moment I don't mind telling you dear. I said to Margaret - Margaret Painter, you know? Hearing aids, husband ran away with a woman from the garden centre, lives in Worplesdon, beautiful house, son's a homosexual...not, not a homosexual, a vicar...I said to Margaret, what's happening with my Lionel, it's like what happened with Ivor Norton back when he worked at the crem. Do you know Ivor? I used to work with his wife Jean. We went to school together, in fact. Lovely woman - always struggled with her weight, the poor dear. I was there when they met, as it happens. We were at a dance in one of the village halls. Ah now, which one was it? It couldn't have been Worplesdon because that burned down in…now…it must have been 1966, was it? I remember, beautiful flowers they had on. Chrysanthemums. Never cared too much for chrysanths, but oh, they looked lovely. I don't think flowers are quite the same these days, do you dear? They grow them in glass houses, you know? On the continent. Miles and miles of flowers, all indoors…."

After some more digressions, Joan returned to what it was that had happened with her Lionel.

"Yes. So, I was saying what happened to Lionel was just like what happened to Ivor at the crem. Our Lionel - he was a beautiful little boy. Golden hair, he had. It really was golden, not blond. Some people say 'golden', don't they, when they really just mean blond? But Lionel…oh! He was such a happy child until he went away to secondary school, and then within a few months he changed. Never had his nose out of a book after that, did Lionel. Always reading. He'd read anything and everything that boy. I said to my John, his dad, I said: 'John, that lad is brighter than you and me put together', I said. He could have done anything. Kathleen Bishop - her son Dennis, he's a dentist. Got two lovely children, a boy and a girl. Oh hang on. No, it's two girls. I'm thinking of Kathleen Morley. She's the one with one grandson and one granddaughter. Kathleen Bishop, her Dennis has the two girls. Now, why was I…? Oh yes. Dennis is a dentist, practices out in Camberley. He comes to see Kathleen twice a week, and he brings the girls every other visit. My point is, Dennis did very poorly at school, but he applied himself, Edith. He knew what he wanted to do and he worked towards that, and now he has a Porsche and three hygienists working for him. Lionel…"

Joan sighed deeply.

"Lionel never stopped reading. He never stopped, Edith. He'd read anything. Anything and everything. I'd find him reading my recipe books. Oh, that reminds me, I must ask Lena to get some more of those special biscuits. The ones with the cream and the jam. They're gluten-free, you know? I don't know what gluten is. We didn't have it in my day. Yes, Lionel's trouble was that he took what he read more seriously than what was going on around him. And that's not good for a young man, is it dear? They need to be outside burning off all that...all that...energy they have, meeting girls, not cooped up at home. I wouldn't have minded so much if he'd been interested in practical things. He could have been a lawyer - they read a lot, don't they? Their offices are always packed with bookshelves. Well, not that I've ever had much call to deal with lawyers, of course, but you always see them on TV, don't you? Lawyers and policemen. I'll tell you who's taller in real life than you think..."

Gradually, the point came back into view.

"So...now...oh, it must have been twenty years ago, John - that's my late husband - John, he says to Lionel, he says that you should set up a group, try to meet some people who are interested in all that hocus pocus nonsense. That's not what John said to Lionel, of course. John never had time for any of that, but he always respected Lionel's interests. He was a wonderful man, Edith. I can't believe he's been gone these twenty-five years... No, that can't be right. It must have been thirty years ago Lionel set up his club then, not twenty. I do remember it was the year that Princess Diana came to Surbiton and we all got the train up to try and catch a glimpse of Lady Di, and Jenny Hitchin swore blind she wasn't going to go - she didn't have time for all those Royals and all that - but when we got there, we did laugh, because who do you think was right up the front with a Union Jack bowler hat on? Jenny Hitchin, that's who! Cheering away like it was VE Day, she was. She was beautiful though, wasn't she? Lady Di? Such a shame. Such a shame it was, she turned out to be mad and all. I feel sorry for her boys, the bald one and...and...the ginger one."

Joan's monologue was now drifting further away from the business of what had happened to her son and so I attempted to nudge her back on course.

"You were saying about what happened to Lionel."

"Yes. Yes, I said to Margaret, it's just like what happened to Ivor Norton at the crem when he worked there..."

Unwilling to allow the mysterious fate of Ivor Norton to distract Joan once more, I asked her directly when Lionel had last come to visit her.

"Well. Like I said, he's going through a bit of a bad patch and he's not coping with it very well. He wouldn't say anything to me – wouldn't want to worry me - but I think Julia may have left him. I always thought there was something a bit off about her. Very low hairline for a woman. Of course, it was an open secret that she was having it away here and there, but I was always grateful to her I suppose for putting up with Lionel's funny ways. I mean, my John was no angel, but we were both glad when Lionel finally got out of the house and out from under our feet. We turned the spare room back into a guest bedroom - before that it had been full of all Lionel's books. Boxes of them. Some of them very old, dirty and smelly. I said to Margaret - do you know Margaret Painter? - I said, 'Margaret', I said: 'he sells those books on the internet but you can buy books now, on little computers! Over the internet!' It's funny what goes around and comes around, isn't it dear? They call them 'e-books'. Don't mention e-books to Lionel. There's only one thing he hates more than e-books and that's that fucking cunt Claudius."

I was startled out of my increasing drowsiness by Joan's shocking bad language.

"That Sandra. The Brummie. She's one of them, you know. Aren't you Sandra? You're properly into all that fucking shit, aren't you? She's only living with that lanky shitbag now, Edith!"

Sandra trotted over, a look of extreme embarrassment on her face.

"Oh Joan. You're really not to get excited. What did we say last time you started effing and jeffing? Your friends don't like it, do they? We weren't going to do it any more, were we? It's not good for you to get all worked up, and it upsets the others. See you've upset Edith. What will she think of you, hearing all that cursing coming out of your mouth?"

Turning to me: "She's usually so calm and happy, but a few things send her into this sort of a state. Don't think badly of her, please Mrs Sterckx."

Turning back to Joan: "Now Joan, I want you to say sorry to the others for using the swear words again."

"Fuck off."

"Alright, you get it out of your system then. But after I want you to say you're sorry. Look - Mr Armstrong's distraught."

"Fuck him."

"I know you don't mean that, Joan. You and Mr Armstrong get on ever so well since that misunderstanding last Christmas got sorted out. You played dominoes with him and the other gents last Wednesday, didn't you?"

I decided to take control of the situation.

"Joan. It's time. Midsomer Murders."

Joan turned her head towards me and her face assumed its sweet, calm expression once more.

"Midsomer Murders? Ooh lovely. Is it one with Bergerac in it?"

"No Joan, I think we're onto the episodes with the other man in now."

"Oh well. Never mind. It's always a good yarn, isn't it Sandra?"

We got ourselves settled into the good armchairs near the front, well away from the draught that blew continually through the patio doors. Sandra left to attend to other residents once the programme began and Joan had calmed down. I was excited (what would Inspector Barnaby the Younger be confronted with today?) but I pushed myself to stay on topic. When the first lot of adverts came on, I asked Joan what the nature of the problem between her son and Dr Claudius was.

"Oh! Do you know him dear?"

I admitted that I had seen him at the Schneck Open Night.

"Well that used to be my Lionel's group, until that awful man came down from London and without so much as a 'by your leave'... that's a funny saying isn't it? 'By your leave'. Very old fashioned. You can't really imagine anyone young saying that, can you? David Niven perhaps. Oh, he had a lovely voice did David Niven. So smooth and rich. 'By your leave', he'd say. Hee hee hee! 'By your leave'... where was I? Oh yes, without so much as a 'by your leave' took the whole thing over! Humiliated my Lionel in front of everyone. I mean, it was an open secret about his wife, but to say it in front of everyone like that? It's not on, is it Edith?"

Joan gestured at the television set.

"Has it started yet?"

"Yes Joan. We're on the first adverts."

"Are we? I can't remember any of what happened. I'm sure it'll come back to me when it starts again. Yes, so after that, Lionel went very strange. Not that he wasn't strange before, you understand. I can say that - I'm his mother, you know. I'd say to him 'you'll always be my little golden-haired boy Lionel, no matter how old and important you get'. Oh, he was a beautiful child Edith. I wish you could have seen him. Went even more strange, saying he'd had a curse put on him. Thought there were shadowy figures following him around. Shadowy figures indeed! Fancy that! I said to him, 'Lionel' I said, 'if there are they'll be from the Revenue'. Bless him, he's a bright lad but figures have never been his strong point. He's had a few run-ins about his taxes over the years. When he was at school, he was very musical - always tootling away on his clarinet, and if not, he'd be singing. I'll tell you who else is a lovely singer as well as David Niven - that Rihanna. No. Who am I thinking of? With the hair and the... no, hold on. I was right the first time. Rihanna. I love the pop music. John was never keen, but I've always kept up to date with the pop music. It's not easy to stay 'with it' in a place like this though, is it! Hee hee - that's why I took a set of keys from the office. Don't tell anyone about them, will you? It's just nice to know they're there - I like to know that I can go for a walk at midnight if I want to, like I used to with my John. Now, when we were courting...oh look, it's back on."

This was an interesting development. So too was the appearance in part two of a sullen old gamekeeper who never spoke and kept himself to himself in his little cottage at the edge of Colonel Sir Jeremy Bartlett's estate on the outskirts of Midsomer Chettham (transparently, a red herring character - far too obvious to be the actual murderer, but nonetheless important to watch as he was clearly going to play a key part in the plot unfolding). If Joan had a set of Fair Haven's keys, then some kind of a breakout was a distinct possibility. I held that thought and turned it over in my mind as we watched the rest of the episode. As predicted, it was not the gamekeeper, but we all let out a little gasp of surprise when Inspector Barnaby discovered that the killer was none other than Colonel Sir Jeremy Bartlett himself, who had dispatched his victims by means of an antique maypole dedicated by his ancestors for generations to the Great God Pan.

However, it was not necessary to break out - yet. I had the tapes directly implicating Nigel in the murder of the Longs and of myself. Even though Chief Inspector Yarrow had scoffed at my claims when I made them down at Dorking police station, he would not be able to ignore these incriminating recordings. The tapes may not be admissible as evidence (watching daytime TV for long stretches of time was giving me a better understanding of the procedures of criminal law than I had ever really had before) but they would put the police onto the right track.

I posted them directly to Yarrow so that he would hear them before they were logged on any police computer system that Nigel might have access to. I waited a week before any kind of response came. It was a typed letter, which read:

Dear Mrs Sterckx,

How pleasant to hear from you again after our last encounter when you accused me of being drunk when I was not drunk at all. Thank you for the 'decisive evidence' against Mr Darwin that you kindly sent to me. However, I am somewhat at a loss to see exactly what blank cassettes prove about anything.

I understand that the Long case has a high profile and has received a lot of media coverage. You are not the first person to come forward with their own claims about what happened.

Yours is not the most ridiculous - one person has insisted that Russian gangsters are involved - but it's not far off.

I would request that you leave matters to the professionals (i.e. us) and that you desist from future attempts to communicate with me. Whatever the nature of your vendetta against Mr Darwin is, I suggest that it is best taken up with him or left alone completely. This sort of distraction wastes police time and resources and – if I may be permitted to enter a personal note – hampers my recovery.

Yours sincerely,
Chief Inspector Robert Yarrow

Were the tapes blank? I realised that I had never listened to them. I had just taken them from Woodward's drawer and hidden them away at my house. The names and the dates corresponded to the meeting I had witnessed, hadn't they? I was sure they had. Why would a blank tape be labelled like that?

But more importantly, what was I going to do now? I had played my trump card and somehow I'd lost the hand. Part of me wanted to give up – to forget about Keith and Nigel and live out my remaining years as an unnaturally healthy ninety-seven-year-old woman. But I had been changing since I had been Edith as well as Shaun. The merger was becoming permanent and where I began and the other ended was becoming harder to tell each day. For the first time, I knew - as Shaun this time - that I would have to take the harder, more dangerous path and that I was not going to avoid the risks this time.

As I was making my mind up, there was a knock on my bedroom door.

"It's only me, Edith love!"

The door opened a crack and Joan poked her head in. Her forehead was creased into a frown - an unfamiliar expression for her ever-cheerfully distracted face.

"I'm sorry to bother you Edith. Have you seen my glasses?"

"You're wearing them Joan."

"Am I?"

Joan patted her face and confirmed that she was indeed wearing her glasses.

"Oh that is a relief. I've been wondering where they were. Edith...?"

"Yes?"

"Can I talk to you about something?"

"Of course."

"It's my Lionel. I'm starting to worry about him. I know he's very busy and that he's had all that unpleasantness lately, but he hasn't called or been to visit for weeks now. And he's not answering his phone. He usually calls me back within a few days, but it's been...oooh... how long has it been now? Is it still May? Or is it July? Now, I remember we watched that film in May... that was before your time... but I distinctly remember that the big chestnut tree out the front window was in full blossom, and that only happens around May time. Oh, I do love the sight of a horse chestnut in bloom, don't you? Those wonderful pink and white flowers, stretching up like candles. So beautiful. Of course, Lionel always loved horse chestnuts because of the conkers! He was mad about conkers when he was little - 'Mummy, can I go and collect conkers down in the dell?' Of course, that would have been in autumn, not May. You know what they say about conkers and spiders? It's not true at all! My John used to put the broken bits of Lionel's conkers or the little ones too small or funny-shaped to put on a string...he'd collect them all up and place them around the window frames, the doorways, the cat flap. Keep the spiders away, he'd say. They can't stand conkers. Made no difference! Year after year - once it started turning chill, all the spiders want to come indoors, don't they? The cat would eat a few of them, the dirty beast, but no matter how many conkers John put out - well - if anything I'd say there were more spiders. I said to Margaret, I said, 'John and his conkers - house is overrun with spiders!' You know what she said? She said, 'Joan - I swear by vinegar. Rub vinegar on your window sills. Works like a charm.' White vinegar, she said, not the brown stuff. Always reminds me of the chippie in Mayford, that brown vinegar. It used to be our special Saturday treat when John and I were courting... But anyway, I didn't come to ask you about that. I...now what did I come for? Did I leave my glasses here yesterday?"

Of course, I knew exactly what had happened to her Lionel. Nigel Darwin had kidnapped him, beaten him unconscious in front of Keith and I and then - if he was still alive at that point - instructed Yevgeny to clear up the mess. If Mr Parson (I still thought of him by this title, even though I was now several decades his senior and a friend of his mother's) had not been seen since he was snatched off the street, he was surely dead and unlikely to ever be found.

Joan sat down beside me with a sigh.

"It's just so lonely here without him. When my John passed away, Lionel was my rock, you know? And now he's on his own. What if something's happened to him Edith? Now that woman's gone... he doesn't speak to his son... Who's looking out for him? I'm so worried, it's giving me the vapours. Do you think I should call the police?"

Joan reached over and took my left hand in both of hers. I looked up at her tear-flecked face.

"You're a good friend Edith. I'm so glad I found you. I don't know what I'd do without you. I just wish I knew what was going on with Lionel."

Was it wrong to tell her? It was wrong to tell her. I knew it was wrong as I was doing it. Telling her wasn't going to make anything better for Joan. I should have said that Lionel had been in yesterday and that she'd just forgotten about it - she would usually have believed it! I was rationalising as I explained what had happened and how I had been involved: if that was me, I'd want to know the truth; she's desperate to know and I'm the only person who can tell her; she deserves to know - justice demands that she knows; I was shaken up by the letter from Yarrow that was still in my right hand and I wasn't thinking straight.

All lies. I did it for me. I wanted to unburden myself, to reveal my secrets. Just like Keith, I wanted an accomplice and I used my vulnerable friend, telling myself I was doing it for her. Did I consciously select Joan for this role? Joan, who nobody listens to. Joan, whom everyone would assume was imagining things if she called bullshit on my own outlandish tale. Joan, whose Alzheimer's disease and present emotional state left her ripe for exploitation? Am I that much of a user? Was the idea there incubating in the back of my mind before I was aware of it and was I subconsciously on the lookout for…what? A new friend? Somebody to play Shaun to my Keith?

Well.

Who knows?

The point is, I did it. I told Joan what had happened to her son, how I knew about it and how I had ended up as care home resident Edith Sterckx, having previously been unemployed librarian Shaun Strong. Naturally, I omitted some of the more sordid episodes - the blackmail, the voyeurism, all that sort of stuff. To her credit Joan took it all in with admirable stoicism. As my explanation progressed and (let's face it) became more implausible, she became calmer and her face grew grave. She nodded slowly as I detailed The Thing, my trips to the Schneck with Keith, the Long murders, the scenes at Prospect House and everything that followed. Her grip on my left hand tightened gradually until, when I told her about the blank tapes and Yarrow's letter, she finally released it.

"Well Edith. It's up to us then, isn't it? No one else is going to do it - you said it yourself. I can't say I like the sound of this Nigel Darwin fellow one bit. Honour demands that we extract bloody revenge from that piece of fucking shit, doesn't it dear?"

I nodded. Tears were running down my face now.

"Oh there there now…don't cry," Joan put her hand to my cheek. "We'll have a wonderful time. When we've got that cunt tied to a chair begging for mercy, we'll tell him who we are and what he did to us. And then we'll finish him off good and proper - electrodes on his bollocks, chop his fingers off one by one and stuff them up his arsehole…the whole lot. Just like on the telly. It'll be quite a caper, won't it? Hmmm…capers are funny little things, aren't they? Very vinegary. Too vinegary in fact. I can't say I care for them myself. There are so many vegetables these days that we never had when I was a youngster, aren't there? Or are they a fruit? You know, I really couldn't say…"

64

The other person I needed to cultivate at Fair Haven was Sandra. This was easily done as she was my assigned carer on the days she worked (Tuesdays, Thursdays, Sundays). She was surprised to see me when she first came into my bedroom.

"Well I never! Mrs Sterckx! Do you remember me? We met at the open evening!"

I decided to play it dumb - always better to be underestimated.

"Open evening?" I said, my voice frail and confused.

"You were going to have a chat with Dr Claudius, but... errm... well, you did a vanishing act on us. Do you remember Dr Claudius, my fiancée?"

Sandra held up her left hand and wiggled her stout fingers, staring significantly at the fourth one where sat a slender silver ring with a tiny embedded gemstone.

"Oh yes!" I declared. "Dr Claudius! Yes, I remember now. Congratulations!"

"Thank you. Thank you. Yeah, it was a spur of the moment thing. We were at Nando's and he just came out of the blue with it! Gave me the ring, asked me to marry him! I said yes!"

"What a lovely story," I said, forcing myself to sustain an appropriate level of enthusiasm.

"Oh, I know Mrs Sterckx."

"Please, call me Edith."

"Oh, but what happened to you Edith? How did you end up coming to live with us here?"

I mumbled a generic explanation - family no longer able to take care of me, didn't feel safe alone in my cottage etc - before turning the conversation back to Dr Claudius.

"I tell you Edith, I've never met anyone like him. Did you know he used to be on TV? He was in Holby City!"

"Is that Casualty?" I asked.

"Oh no, it's a different thing love. You should hear him telling stories... he's so funny! Cracks me up every time! I say: 'Claudius!', I say. 'Claudius! Stop it! You'll make me wet myself!', I say. He's got such a wonderful way of talking and he's had all sorts of adventures. He used to live in Amsterdam you know, and he knocked about with these two fellas: a big lad from Denmark with holes in his earlobes and a metal bar in his nose. You know what they called him? Nine Inch Nils. Ah ha ha ha ha! Oh, actually Edith that's probably not funny to you. It's a music thing...

"Anyway, the other bloke was African. From Ethiopia, no less. Loved cheese. Always had a block of it in his pocket, and he'd nibble away at it. Claudius does this brilliant impression of him. Nibbling his cheese. They gave him the nickname 'Cheddar'. Cheddar Mengistu, that was him. It makes me laugh just thinking about the scrapes those three got into!"

"Is Claudius a nickname too, or is that his real name?" I asked.

"Ah well, that's a story in itself Edith love. Yes and no is the best answer I can give you. It's his middle name, you see. No one calls him by his real first name - he hates it. He's called Gervase. And his surname's Kenny. He hates that too, so he just goes by Claudius now - ever since he got out."

"Out?"

"He did a few months inside. Nothing serious. A misunderstanding more than anything. That's why he moved to Holland. A few disgruntled former associates he'd rather not run into back home in London were keen to speak to him, if you get my meaning. But he's put all that behind him now Edith. He's helping people - people who've lost people. He's bringing comfort to them, because…"

Sandra looked earnestly at me and took my hands in hers.

"He really does have a gift, you know. I don't know how he does it or where it comes from, but there's a mystical side to him… he knows things. Sees things. He told me things about my childhood that I've never mentioned to anyone. That I barely even remembered myself. Don't get me wrong - I know he's no angel. But…I don't know…he makes me feel…well, you know."

Sandra busied herself tucking fresh sheets in under my mattress.

"It's like he's two different people sometimes," she said when she had finished. "The part of him that comes out when he's communing with the spirits…it's…ah…oh, would you listen to me? Going on and on! You'll have to tell me if I'm boring you Edith - banging on about myself and about him. It's just odd, isn't it? How special gifts seem to be given to the most unusual people. I suppose that's just the way the universe works…"

I agreed.

"Sandra?"

"Yes love?"

"I never did get to speak to Dr Claudius about my Lucas…"

Sandra looked up, as she shook my pillow into a new pillowcase.

"Well, you're in luck there! Among my many other functions, I just so happen to be Dr Claudius' personal assistant! Ever since he moved in with me, I've been taking care of his diary and bookings and driving him to appointments. He doesn't drive. Can you believe that? Him, a grown man. Oh yeah, I was full-time here until just last month, but I had to cut my hours down to fit in all the work we're doing together now. I sometimes wonder how he'd manage it all without me."

Sandra expelled a brief bark of laughter, which sounded more alarmed than amused.

"No but…you know, he's helping people. He's a good man, Edith."

"Just needs the love of a good woman to straighten him out?" I suggested.

Sandra smiled and winked at me.

"I can see you're a sharp one, Edith Sterckx. I'll have to keep my eye on you!"

65

Joan and I had worked out a sort of plan for wreaking our vengeance, which was simultaneously entirely lacking in detail whilst being totally dependent on an awful lot of unpredictable events going our way. However, neither of us felt that we had anything to lose and so we tried to compensate for the plan's poor odds of success with our absolute commitment to carry it out regardless.

Using the stolen phone that Yevgeny had given to Dr Claudius, we would send a message to Nigel Darwin, saying that we (Dr Claudius) had urgent information about Shaun Strong which could only be imparted in person and asking Nigel to set a date, time and location. We would then delete that message and await Nigel's response.

Next, I would give the phone back to Dr Claudius when I went for my private reading, saying that I'd picked it up by mistake. Joan and I would then make our way to the meeting location, where we would be able to exact our revenge.

"But how will we get there?" Joan asked. "I expect they'll choose somewhere deserted and out of the way, so the bus is probably no good. Which is a shame, because we both get free travel. Oh, now I say that. I can't remember when I last saw my bus pass...I definitely had it last April because Lionel took me down to Eastbourne for my birthday. Or was it Eastbourne? You know, I'm not sure now I come to think of it."

I had a car, but I couldn't drive it and it was now in David and Marie's possession. Joan had a driving licence but no car.

"No use getting a taxi. It would be ever so dear and how would we get back? No, I think there's only one thing for it."

Joan reached into the depths of her handbag. She beckoned me closer as she glanced around to ensure that no members of staff were watching. In her knotty fingers she held a ring of car keys.

"Spares. From some of the nurses' cars," she whispered. "They lose them sometimes."

Transport taken care of, we still faced the trickier issue of how we would despatch Nigel. He was highly unlikely to turn up without his Russian bodyguard and, even without Yevgeny, would have little difficulty in physically overpowering two elderly ladies. We had no access to firearms or explosives or any other useful means for killing at a distance.

"What about your friend? The scruffy boy who shafted you?"

"Keith?" I asked, shocked.

Could we involve Keith? He had wanted to help me when he showed me the 'Historical Jesus' notes. But would we be able to contact him? And if we did, could we be sure that Nigel wouldn't discover it? And even if we did and Nigel didn't find out, could we trust Keith? In spite of everything, he had seemed spellbound by Nigel and his theories. He might decide to save his own skin by sacrificing ours once again.

Despite having brought the matter of Keith up, Joan was quick to take a firm stance against it.

"Once a Judas, always a Judas. My John used to say that. He fell out with his brother, Terry. He lent Terry a drill - he loved that drill. My John treated all his tools with such love and care. He bought it not long after we got married. Beautiful wooden case with all the bits in, wrapped in oiled cloth. Well. Terry... he left it out in the yard overnight, didn't he? And what do you think happened? It rained. It rained all night. Never worked properly again. Now Terry insists he did no such thing, but it was plain for anyone to see. Says it was like that when John brought it round. I'll tell you Edith, my John was furious. This was in 1974. They never spoke again. Fifteen years. Terry died in 1989 and we didn't go to his funeral. Because, 'once a Judas, always a Judas', my John said. His own brother! But he was right Edith - that was just a drill. This piece of shit got you killed. No hold on. Was it a drill? It's so long ago now…"

We decided against bringing Keith. In the matter of weaponry, we decided to kill two birds with one stone. It would mean foregoing the pleasure of feeding Nigel his own fingers or clipping a battery to his testicles, but we concluded that running him over with the car we'd need to borrow to get to the meet-up gave us the best chance of killing him before he or Yevgeny had a chance to kill us.

That was our plan. Remarkably it worked. Sort of.

66

I'm going to have to ask you pull hard on the ropes and hoist in any slack that might have appeared in your suspension of disbelief at this stage, because there are even more improbable coincidences in what follows than in what I've told you already.

I know - but bear with me. Some of them turn out to not be coincidences at all.

The rest? Maybe they were, maybe they weren't. It's what happened anyway. Most peoples' lives don't seem plausible when you hold them under the microscope, do they?

I had made an appointment for a private session with Dr Claudius through Sandra. Half an hour before he was due to arrive at Fair Haven, I sent a text from the stolen phone to the one number that was saved in it. The message read:

Have URGENT news on SS. Need to explain face to face asap somewhere we can come and go unseen by ANYONE. Am in Godalming ATM - just tell me when and where and I'll be there.

"That's it away Joan," I said. "No turning back now."

"Lovely."

"So now you need to go and do what we talked about…"

"What did we talk about dear?"

"You were going to go and make sure the doors are open? Find a car?"

"Was I?"

"You've got the keys in your bag."

"Yes, I've got my keys."

"No Joan, the keys for…" I felt a tightening across my chest as it struck me that Joan may have forgotten everything and that we would miss our chance. "The keys! For…you know… the plan…"

"Oh yes. I've got those keys. Don't you worry about that."

Joan sighed and smiled.

"So we're doing that today are we?"

"Yes!"

"I thought it was next week."

"No!"

Joan took out a small diary decorated with flowers from her handbag and inspected its contents.

"You're quite right. I was in a muddle. What am I like? Right, well, I'd best be off then. Wish me luck!"

I was not reassured that Joan was going to fulfil her side of the plan, but what choice did I have? The wheels were in motion. Joan limped out of my room, closing the door behind her. I deleted the message from the phone and put it into my handbag.

Handbags are great, by the way. Did I already say that? Men should give them a try more often. I missed some aspects of being a man - pissing standing up for example - but the practicality of having a handbag full of useful things more than made up for the losses.

I made my way to the day room, where I was due to meet with Sandra and Dr Claudius. I took a seat far away from the big TV and near to the hallway door. This not only meant that I would have a much shorter distance to walk when I made my getaway (an important consideration at my age), but it also meant that I would not attract suspicion for wearing a coat - it was notoriously draughty near to the door and correspondingly unpopular with the residents.

I was starting to doze, when a gust of chilled air let us know somebody had entered the day room. It was him, chatting to one of the male orderlies - a huge Jamaican man by the name of Jerry. Dr Claudius had hold of Jerry by the elbow and was deep in the middle of a monologue.

"No, I'm not musical myself but...well...I was briefly in the music business back in the 90s. I was living in the Netherlands back then. A little bit of ...ummm...trouble at home meant it was best I...err ... kept a low profile, shall we say? Well, you'll never guess what happened. I was in Amsterdam one weekend at a nightclub. I know, I know - I don't look the sort, do I Jerry? But I didn't always look like this. We're talking twenty, twenty-five years ago now. I was a bit of a looker, if you know what I mean? I'll bet you do, eh Jerry? Heh heh heh. Well, nothing special but I always had plenty of female attention. Never had any cause to complain, you know? Anyway, I got talking to this couple, Anita and Ray. Lovely couple - locals. Turns out, they were just getting started with their own group - you might have heard of them: 2Unlimited?"

"Ohhhh...." Jerry nodded in recognition.

"Yeah, you know 'em. 'No no, no no no no, no no no no, no no...'"

"There's no limits", echoed Jerry.

"No no. No no." Dr Claudius shook his head, with mild exasperation in his voice that suggested this was an error he had been forced to correct before. "It's 'No Limit'. That was the single. The one everyone knows. It was the album that track was released on that was called 'No Limits'. With an exclamation mark. Yeah, 2Unlimited - I was their manager for four years."

"You weren't!"

"I swear! God's honest truth. I was 2Unlimited's manager. Oh, happy days. Well, until Ray - that's the bloke - he fired me. I was...ah...you know... me and Anita? I've forgiven though, Jerry. I've forgiven Ray, because it wasn't really about that. It was just the pretext in the end. He was embittered you see, because...ahhh...I shouldn't be telling you this...but...it was me who did the 'techno techno techno techno' line. Improvised it in the studio one afternoon. Just like that. Phil and Jean-Paul, the producers, they loved it. Ray was livid. Never spoke to me again after that. My mate Cheddar: he said 'Ray won't "techno" shit like that'. Techno! Meaning 'take no'...his accent...ahhh... Cheddar. He was hilarious that bloke...always had a piece of cheese...

"Anyway...here is my saviour: the one, the only Miss Sandra Duffy! Jerry, my good friend, I will see you next week - remember, Discreet Fox, 2.30, Cheltenham. But do not tell anyone where you heard this from and do not put any money down before the weigh-in. Do we have an understanding?"

Dr Claudius winked and tapped the side of his nose ostentatiously. Jerry walked away laughing and shaking his head.

The alleged psychic was dressed very differently from the style he had affected previously. Whereas before he had looked like a seedy Hogwarts professor, today he looked like a second-rate 1980's TV magician, in a black shirt and silver tie, a leather jacket, saggy blue jeans and black trainers - the kind you buy at garden centres. His long hair was tucked behind his ears, and he had a big red spot on his chin.

As the pensioners noticed him one by one, he waved and put his fingers to his lips. He winked and pointed to Sandra, who was on her hands and knees looking for something Mr Armstrong had apparently dropped and then kicked under his armchair. Dr Claudius put his hands out on front of him and tiptoed towards Sandra in an exaggerated, pantomime fashion, causing the residents to chuckle. Even I found myself smiling at his mock-stealthy approach, but I was becoming more nervous about the lack of a reply from Nigel. If I didn't hear anything before the reading was over...

Sandra stood up, triumphantly brandishing the pencil stub that Mr Armstrong had lost. Dr Claudius was right behind her now and she shrieked as he grabbed her around the waist to the delight of the day room audience. He spun Sandra round by the shoulder, swept her into a dance hold and whirled her round the floor in an ungainly waltz.

"Mmmm-da da daaaah da daaah da da DAH DAH!", he yodelled mellifluously, as the pensioners began to clap in time to the couple's dance. As they closed in on the exit where I was sitting, Dr Claudius brought the dance to its climax, twirling Sandra around under his raised arm before they came to a triumphant halt. The audience applauded.

"Len Goodman?" he boomed in the voice I was familiar with from the Schneck presentations.

"SevEEEERRRN!" the old folk shouted back. I joined in.

I was close enough to hear their private conversation when the laughter and immediate post-incident commentary and analysis had subsided.

"Jesus Claudius! You scared the shit out of me."

"Sorry babe," his accent had reverted to quickfire Essex. "Couldn't help it. This lot love it. It's good for business, innit? Gotta make sure they all know who I am. Branding. All about awareness. Still, do this lot remember anything?"

"Of course they do. And they do look forward to seeing you love. You brighten up their days."

"All that Strictly bollocks reminds me of a story. Did I ever tell you I sold a dog to Bruno Tonioli? Before he was properly famous. It was a staffie with a hare lip. Called it Judy…"

Seeing that Sandra was not dissolving into uncontrollable laughter, which was by her own admission her usual reaction to such anecdotes, Dr Claudius quickly changed the subject.

"So which nutter are we talking to today?"

"Claudius!" Sandra hissed. "She's right behind you!"

Dr Claudius turned around and scanned the room. I kept my eyes down, pretending not to have heard anything. Dr Claudius indicated me with a questioning tilt of his head. Sandra raised her eyebrows in affirmative response.

"Edith?" Dr Claudius asked in a soothing voice as he dropped to one knee to address me at my level.

"Yes…" I murmured.

He reached for my hands and held them in his own. The

fingers were long and pale and his touch was clammy. Most of his fingernails had been chewed down, and most were flanked by painful looking hangnails. On his left index finger, there was a chunky ring of gunmetal grey stamped with some kind of Nordic runes. On the little finger was a plain silver band. His right hand ring finger bore a thick circlet of gold, with a deep red gem embedded in a basket setting. The gold on the claws had begun to wear away, revealing a greenish copper beneath.

"May I sit down?" Dr Claudius asked, now in the gentle tones of a late-night BBC continuity announcer.

I nodded and signalled towards the chair beside me. Claudius pulled it around so that we were facing one another.

"Now Edith, I never make a date with anyone who has stood me up before... "

A note of friendly mockery and flirtation now accompanied the other elements in Dr Claudius' voice.

"...but I couldn't help myself when Sandra told me just how pretty you are!"

I giggled and drew my hands away from his in the prescribed manner, playing my part in the act.

"Now," the teasing superceded by sympathetic seriousness, "I understand that you lost your husband some years ago, is that right Edith?"

"Before we start," I interrupted, "I have something to give to you."

"Oh don't worry about that now. You can sort all that out with Sandra afterwards."

"I don't mean money. I mean this."

I took the phone out of my bag.

Dr Claudius' lips tightened and his eyes widened as he stared at it. A vein in the side of his head pulsed and his face became paler.

"I accidentally picked it up at that open evening you put on. I had a bit of a funny turn, you know?"

"Funny turn..." Dr Claudius echoed, his eyes fixed on the phone and his mind visibly elsewhere.

"I'm ever so sorry. I forgot all about it until this morning. I've charged it up for you…"

I held the phone out to him. Dr Claudius tore his eyes away from it to look at me, dazed. A bead of sweat had appeared on his left temple. He smiled a weak, humourless smile and slowly reached to take the phone from me. His right leg had begun to bounce up and down on the spot.

"It's on," I said.

"Thank you…" he replied, taking the phone.

Immediately, Dr Claudius checked the call log and the message inbox. His shoulders and torso relaxed as he found that they were both empty. As the tension in Dr Claudius' body drained away, I felt it building up in my own. The tightness I had experienced when I feared that Joan had forgotten our plan was back, this time with a more insistent intensity.

"I was wondering where I'd put that," he said, confidence coming back into his voice with each word. "Now, where were we? I think we were about to talk about your late husband. Is that right Edith? Do you mind if I take your hand again?"

He reached out an open palm to me. His fingers were trembling.

At that moment, the phone on the table between us bleeped. Dr Claudius half-leaped out of his seat and let out a little shriek.

We both leaned forward. The message read:

Turn right quart mile after St Johns Wonersh towards Shamley Gren. Derelict farm barn, 90 mins. Donot disapoint me

Dr Claudius' mouth fell open. His left thumb and forefinger began stroking the red stone on his right hand in a compulsive manner, as if acting independently from the conscious mind they were formally answerable to. He closed his mouth, but it fell open again. Then he swept the phone off the table and into the inside pocket of his leather jacket.

"Edith…I am afraid that we are going to have to do this

another time. You see…my…uh…mother is very ill. And I need to go and see her right away…ah…that was a message from her…I have to go. Very sorry…"

He stood up and walked at high speed over to where Sandra was attending once again to some unidentified need of Mr Armstrong. This time, Dr Claudius ignored the waves, nods and friendly words of the pensioners he passed by. He shook Sandra by the shoulder and she stood up to speak to him. I was too far away to hear their words this time, but it was clear that they were having an argument and that Dr Claudius was pleading with Sandra for something.

I took this as my cue to leave. Experiencing a little dizziness as I stood up, I hobbled towards the hallway exit as inconspicuously as I could. If Sandra was going to give Claudius a lift to the meeting place, I needed to be sat in whatever car Joan had managed to borrow, ready to follow them as soon as they got to the car park. Otherwise, we would almost certainly lose them and risk missing the meeting.

I shambled my way along the corridor towards the dining room, where Joan was due to have unlocked the French doors. A nurse I didn't recognise was a short way ahead of me, talking on her mobile phone.

"I know…well, that's what I said… Really? That's awful… No…"

I stood still, not knowing whether to try and creep past unnoticed or to walk confidently by, as if I had legitimate urgent business in the empty dining room.

The nurse looked up and spotted me. She moved the phone closer to her mouth and walked past me, speaking more quietly.

"Mmmm….I know….what did she expect? No, that will happen…yeah…without UVB light they can't process calcium…that's right. Metabolic bone disease - that's what it is when…right, their shells grow all funny…"

The nurse disappeared into the day room. My fingertips were tingling and cold, but my path to the dining room was now clear. I staggered onwards and pushed the heavy fire door open. The lunchtime settings had been cleared away, but work had not yet begun on dinner arrangements. The tables were bare and the chairs were stacked against the walls, pending a hoovering. There was nobody around. I walked over to the French doors that opened onto Fair Haven's rear patio area. My heart was pounding in my chest once again. I was praying that the door would be open.

It was. The handle rotated and the door swung gently open, admitting damp, leafy air in to cool the overheated atmosphere. I breathed it in deeply as I stepped outside, and the stimulation activated the physical need for a cigarette in me, building up from a tickling in the depths of my lungs. I fumbled in my handbag for a pack and my lighter. Nimbly - the muscle memory of a lifelong smoker being something not even arthritis or possession by the soul of another can efface - I extracted a cigarette and lit it up. The first drag made my head swim, and when the nicotine hit my bloodstream I could feel warmth (or at least, lukewarmth) beginning to radiate outward through my limbs.

I glanced back inside the dining room. Still empty. I pushed the door shut and set off for the car park.

I struggled to see the car that was tooting its horn at me as I rounded the side of Fair Haven overlooking the parking area. Edith was quite short-sighted, and her prescription had been due for review. I could see a red car backing out of a parking space at excessive speed. A blue car was moving slowly along a parallel aisle. The red car moved off, its tyres screeching on the concrete as the driver pulled it out of reverse. As the horn sounded again, I could now place it as coming from the blue car. I walked down the steps at the front of the building towards it and gradually Joan came into focus behind the steering wheel, waving frantically.

I climbed into the car and looked up at Fair Haven. So far, nobody had noticed that anything was happening or that anyone was missing.

"That's them in the red car," Joan said. The car was at the

mouth of the car park, indicating right to turn into the heavy early evening traffic. "Came running out, they both did - Sandra and…err…what's his name? The wanker. Anyway, you've made good time. All set?"

"Whose car is this?" I asked. The dashboard was dominated by a palm cross blue-tacked above the air conditioning vents and a plastic laminated card hanging from the rear-view mirror, bearing the image of a coy, supportive-looking Jesus pulling his shirt open to reveal an exploding Sacred Heart.

"I'm not sure to be honest. It's the only one I have a key for that's a manual. I've never driven an automatic…I remember, I said to my John…oh! I almost forgot. Shall I say it or do you want to?"

"Say what?"

"Follow that car!"

67

It was not a particularly high-speed pursuit. We managed to get out into the gridlocked traffic seven or eight vehicles behind Sandra and Dr Claudius.

"Where are we going?" Joan asked.

"Wonersh," I replied.

"Where's that?"

"I don't know."

"And where are we now?"

"Godalming," I said hesitantly. I was regretting never having learned to drive and having spent my whole life in and around Woking - not for the first time. "Is there a sat nav?"

"Oh, I don't know love. I would have thought so." Joan began to fuss with the dials and buttons in the centre of the dashboard, paying no attention to the growing gap in the traffic ahead of us.

"I'll figure it out Joan. You just keep your eyes on the road."

"You're the boss Edith!" Joan laughed.

I gradually figured out how to work it and entered St John's in Wonersh as our destination.

"MAKE A LEGAL U-TURN," the car demanded.

"Oh, it sounds just like Mr Gregory from down the road. That must have been...fifty years ago now? Mr Gregory! I haven't thought about him for years. Horrible man. Kept pigeons. Shouted at all the children. Said they were frightening his birds when they played in the street. He made my Lionel cry more than once. I said to John, I said, 'you should square him

364

up next time. It's not right, frightening children like that.' But John just laughed it off. Said Mr Gregory was from a different generation, who thought children should be seen and not heard. And besides, a bit of a scare wouldn't do our Lionel any harm. He was right, I suppose. Lionel always was a little soft. Sensitive, they'd say now, wouldn't they Edith dear?"

"MAKE A LEGAL U-TURN," the car repeated.

"Oh shut up! I can't make a u-turn! Can't you see? The traffic's just as bad on that side of the road as it is over here!"

We were still creeping forwards at a very slow rate.

"ROUTE RECALCULATING. AFTER THREE HUNDRED YARDS, TURN LEFT."

"I really don't like his tone Edith. It cuts right through you, doesn't it?"

I could see up ahead that Sandra was indicating to turn left at the upcoming traffic lights. The lights turned green, and the red car disappeared around the corner. The light changed back to red with one car left in front of us.

"NOW TURN LEFT."

"I can't turn left now, you stupid fucking machine! The lights have changed!"

"Don't worry Joan - we'll soon catch them up in the traffic again," I said, attempting to mediate between driver and sat nav.

"Well...he just sounds very judgmental..."

As we rounded the corner, I discovered to my dismay that changing gear was something that required Joan's full concentration and the use of both hands.

"Would you like a mint dear?"

"Joan! Look out!"

A cyclist shouted and gestured angrily at us, his bicycle on the ground at his feet.

"He wants to be more careful..." Joan murmured. "Anyway... oh yes. Sweets. Have a look in my bag, would you Edith?"

I rummaged through the assorted keys, bus tickets, batteries, notebooks, expired vouchers and other debris in Joan's handbag. Eventually, I found a bag of mints. I put one in my mouth and handed the bag to Joan.

"Just pop one in for me."

"Pardon?"

"Pop one in."

"What do you mean?"

"A mint! Pop one into my mouth. I need to keep my eyes on the road now we're moving properly."

I fed Joan a mint and returned the packet to her handbag. The tension in my chest was back and it was more than just tightness this time. It was beginning to ache.

The traffic had indeed begun to break up and was flowing more freely now.

"Now, can you see that silver car Edith?"

"We're following a red car Joan. Look, it's just up there."

"Of course it is. Silver indeed! Brain like a sieve, my John always used to say. Now that man had a photographic memory. Never saw him write anything down. You ask him anything - where he was on a certain date, when something happened... he'd remember it like that. Go on, think of a question."

"A question?"

"Yes, anything at all."

"Errr....who was King of England in...1392?"

"Oh yes. John could have told you that. Incredible memory, that man."

"Who was it?"

"No idea. Brain like a sieve, me. I tried tying knots on a piece of string to help my memory. It didn't help me. I lost the string. I wonder why you don't see blue string any more. It used to be everywhere, didn't it? Blue string. Now, who was it who ate blue string? Oh...Lionel used to love that programme...what was it? Lived on the moon. In holes."

"The Clangers?"

"Hmmm...I'm not sure. You'd have to ask Lionel. Does that say fourth gear?"

"Yes, it does."

"Here, just hold this for a moment."

Joan indicated that I should take the steering wheel while she manoeuvred the gearstick.

The engine wheezed like it had inhaled a bee as we rounded a corner, changing up into fourth at thirty miles per hour.

"Ooh, it didn't like that, did it? Can you see how to move the seat forwards? It's a bit of a stretch for me, getting to the pedals. I remember now, this is Jerry's car. He's ever so tall, isn't he? Lovely man. Good heavens, is that how much petrol costs these days?"

I was feeling an irresistible urge to pick at my fingernails' cuticles. Reaching into my coat's inner pocket, I pulled out a packet of cigarettes. I looked at Joan.

"Do you mind if I smoke?"

"You go on, love. Don't mind me! I never smoked myself - well, only in my twenties and hardly at all after Lionel went away to boarding school. But people are so holier-than-thou about it nowadays aren't they? Apparently, you can't smoke in pubs any more! In pubs! The world's gone mad Edith, it really has. I'll tell you who would have been a wonderful prime minister. Elton John. No, who am I thinking of? David Steel. That's him. He seemed like a lovely man. Scottish, wasn't he? Very sensible. He wouldn't have got carried away if people around him were saying 'ooh, ban smoking'. He would have said, 'let's have a wee think aboot this. The noo.'

"Have you been to Scotland Edith? John and I were going to go up to Edinburgh one year, but John's lumbago was playing him up like nobody's business ever since he dug out that fish pond. They don't call it lumbago any more, do they? It's lower back pain this and sciatica that. He worked so hard on that pond. First week, a heron flew in and ate all the fish up. Never bothered after that."

Closing my eyes, I drew hard on the cigarette, hoping it would exert the calming effect it had exerted on me earlier. The smoke scorched my windpipe and lungs as I inhaled. Instead of making me want to cough it stopped me wanting to cough.

We were out in the countryside now, passing on the occasional gated driveway. There was no other traffic around.

"Yes, that bad back - it changed my John. Every morning, he'd wake up in pain and he'd be in a foul mood from the off. I'm sure that was part of why things between him and Lionel became so strained in the years before he died. He was always just so irritable. The doctor said, he said, 'there's really nothing we can do, at your age, Mr Parson - all we can do is manage the pain'. Well, my John wasn't having any of that. In his family, you only took pills if you were at death's door. His father had had a bad back and his father before him and neither of them had taken anything for it, other than more hard work Edith. I said to him, 'John,' I said, 'there's nothing wrong with taking something for the pain now and again'. And he said, 'I'm fine'. That's all he'd say. 'I'm fine'. I knew he wasn't and he knew I knew, but that's what men from those days were like, weren't they Edith? Was your husband like that? Being foreign and all?"

"AFTER THREE HUNDRED YARDS, TURN RIGHT," the car commanded, adding by way of extra context: "TOWARDS SHALFORD."

"It's always three hundred yards with this one, isn't it? I don't know about you, but I can't tell how far three hundred yards is. Is that the turn off there?"

"I don't think so. Look, the map says it's the third right - so not this one or the next one, but the one after that."

"Oh, is that a map?"

I lit a second cigarette.

"ENTER THE ROUNDABOUT, TAKING THE SECOND EXIT."

"I think it would be better if we went round it rather than entering it, don't you Edith? I don't think Mr Gregory will notice if we're quick."

"Joan! Stop!" I yelled. The red car was stationary right in front of us at the roundabout.

Joan braked hard, but it was too late. We ran into the back of Sandra and Dr Claudius. It was a minor collision, just dented bumpers. The air bags didn't even go off, but our cover was decisively blown. Sandra was getting out of the car now and walking towards us.

"ROUTE RECALCULATING."

"Oh shut the fuck up," Joan swore, switching the engine off. "Getting right on my nerves…"

"What the hell's the matter with you? Did you not see my brake lights? Aren't…Joan? Edith? What on earth are you doing out here?

"Hello dear," Joan replied as she opened the window. "Fancy bumping into you here. No pun intended. Edith and I are just out for a little drive, aren't we Edith?"

"Yes," I said. "A little drive."

"Whose car is this? Is this Jerry's car?"

"Oh no, Sandra dear. This is my son's car. He let us borrow it for our little outing."

Sandra looked pointedly at the palm cross and the dangling Christ and raised her eyebrows.

"Really…?"

"That's mine," I butted in. "I…errr… never travel without… ummm…Jesus."

"Praise the Lord!" Joan added helpfully.

"We need to get you two back to Fair Haven right away! Hop out now ladies. I'll get this car off the road, and we'll take you back home."

"Sandra!" Dr Claudius was out of the car now. He looked frightened and pointed frantically at his watch. "I've got to be there in fifteen minutes!"

"But Claudius, it's two of the old girls from work."

"Bring them with us! I'm sure I won't be long. You can all just wait in the car and then as soon as I'm done, we'll go back together. Please Sandra. I can't be late. I…I may have got in a little too deep over my head this time. I don't know what he wants, but I do know he's not a man to keep waiting!"

"I thought you said he was a concerned citizen who just wanted to help the police and the families?"

"Yeah…I did say that. But it was…it was only to protect you

Sandra. He's…ah…I think…you mustn't say anything, but I think he's with the security services. I think there's more to this than meets the eye. I have a strong feeling. In fact, it's what I suspected all along. That's what interested me in the case when he approached me. It's not just a simple murder. There are…. um…national security implications and I'm the only person who he can turn to. But I really can't let him down, so let's get these two into the car and get back on our way!"

Soon, Joan and I were in the back seat of Sandra's car. Jerry's car had been pushed into a layby and abandoned. Sandra had tacitly agreed not to ask any more questions until, firstly, this mysterious meeting was over and, secondly, until we were safely back at Fair Haven. Joan was not speaking. This was unusual enough in itself. Instead, she was boring a hole in the back of Dr Claudius' chair with her gaze - a gaze that she clearly hoped would soon complete its passage through the headrest and begin drilling into his skull. Fortunately, Joan was seated behind Dr Claudius, so he could not see her attempts at psychic trepanation.

"Who did you play in Holby City?" I asked, attempting to break the uncomfortable silence that had descended. Dr Claudius turned in his seat to face me.

"Oh, so Sandra told you about that did she? Yeah, I was a series regular a few years back. Well Edith, it was a very interesting part. In my first episode, my role was central to the whole plot. You could say that the story revolved around me."

"You had a lot of lines then?"

"Ah no, not as such. No. No lines. But I was in shot a lot of the time."

"Were you a patient?"

"Errm, sort of. I mean, every episode has patients, doesn't it? Do you watch Holby Edith?"

"I watch Casualty," I lied.

"Oh…oh I see. Well, Casualty's good too. The money's better, so I was told anyway."

"Did you play a dead body?"

"Yes. Which is always a wonderful challenge for any actor."

"So you were a corpse, but you were in two episodes?"

"No. No, I was only a corpse in that first one. I was an orderly in the second episode. Made a great impression, got asked back. You know what TV's like…"

"You weren't a series regular then?"

"Well…I…not in the strict sense of the term…"

"But you said you were. Just a couple of minutes ago."

Dr Claudius frowned and stared at the windscreen, as if sincerely scanning back through what he had said to confirm or refute my statement.

"I did, didn't I? I wonder why I said that. I get carried away with myself sometimes Edith. Sandra knows, don't you my love?"

Sandra remained silent.

Dr Claudius giggled and looked up sheepishly at me.

"Half the time, I don't know what I'm saying. It's just verbal diarrhoea, as my old Mum used to say. I get myself into all sorts of trouble with it. You wouldn't believe half the situations my mouth's dragged me into. But you know what?"

He winked lavisciously.

"It's got me out of a few scrapes as well. Oh! That up there is St John's Catholic Seminary, so we're looking for a right turn in a quarter of a mile. How far's that?

"Four hundred and fifty yards," said Joan. "You twat."

"Joan!" Sandra snapped, finally speaking for the first time since we had got into her car.

"That must be it…turn up there," Dr Claudius ignored the insult and pointed to a dirt track surrounded by trees. There were weeds growing in the middle of the presumed road.

"Now, we're looking for a derelict barn on a farm. Or a farm with a barn. He's not the best typist…"

We slowed to a crawl as we joined the track. Flattened grasses on both sides of the lane indicated that a vehicle wider than Sandra's had recently passed this way. Nevertheless, it was impossible to avoid deep ruts and potholes in the baked mud, and the car pitched and rolled like an Irish Sea ferry on a stormy crossing. Low evening sunlight broke through the foliage in blinding flashes, disorienting us all even more. Oily nausea brought me out in a cold sweat.

"Are you sure this is the right road?" Sandra asked.

"It's got to be," Claudius replied. "This is where he said to come. Look! Up there - that's a derelict barn if I ever saw one. And there's a Range Rover parked outside it."

The looming presence of Nigel Darwin's black Range Rover squatted menacingly at the centre of a triangle of ruinous farm buildings. The closest of these was a ramshackle house. Its roof was collapsing at one end and metal plates had been fitted over the ground floor windows. The faded legend "everything of value has been removed" had been stamped across the metalwork.

Fifty yards beyond the house on the other side of a cracked concrete yard now sprouting with man-sized weeds and child-sized trees was an even more tumbledown barn. In its open mouth stood the remains of a tractor that appeared to be decomposing and sinking into the earth itself. One of the wheels had fallen off, and its bodywork and exposed engine had all blended into a continuum of rust colour and texture.

The third building was not a building at all, but two shipping containers stacked one on top of the other. An aluminium staircase led up the side to a door in the top container. The door was open and it swung back and forth, slack-jawed in the breeze.

Other pieces of debris were decaying in the yard: a plastic water tank that had melted in on one side; a pile of hardcore that had turned to cement; a filthy spool of blue rope; the upturned hull of a rowing boat, its ribs caved in. They contrasted conspicuously with the gleaming black SUV parked sulkily among them.

"Right," said Dr Claudius. "I'll just pop over to the barn there and take care of my business, then we can be on our way. Don't worry ladies, we should have you home in time for Pointless!"

"Oh, you do like Pointless, don't you Joan?" Sandra chimed in. "That Alexander and Richard - such nice polite boys. So tall."

Joan emitted a scornful noise that was partway between a grunt and a hiss as Dr Claudius climbed out of the passenger seat. He checked himself in the wing mirror and straightened his tie. Then fingering his collar thoughtfully, he took the tie off and stuffed it into his jacket pocket, before setting off across the farmyard. He glanced from side to side as he went, as though expecting somebody to jump out on him, but eventually Dr Claudius disappeared from view into the dark mouth of the barn.

Once he had vanished, Sandra turned round to look at us, a furious expression on her face.

"You two put yourselves in a lot of danger! Don't think I believe that yarn about that being your son's car for a second Joan Parson. Number one - I know your Lionel - and number two - I see Jerry come to work in that car every day! I don't know what you two are up to and I don't want to know. Joan, I know you're angry about Claudius and Lionel and I'm sorry, but it's not his fault and it's not my fault. You can't stand him, fine. I get it. You never miss a chance to have a go. But you Edith? I had hoped that you'd be a calming influence on her, although I suppose I should have known better after what happened before you came to us. Why were you following us?"

Neither of us replied.

"Come on! Why did you follow us?"

"I thought you said you didn't want to know?" Joan answered, with spite.

"Oh for God's sake! I'm not going to cover for you, you know? If anyone asks me what happened, I'll tell them everything."

"Everything?" I enquired. "Including Claudius' national security connections?"

"He's helping people!" Sandra yelled. "He has a real gift and he's not so far up his own arse that he won't share it with anyone. Not like your precious Lionel!"

Joan sat motionless for what felt like several minutes but was probably no more than a few seconds, and then broke down in silent tears.

But before the argument could proceed any further, we all fell silent and turned our heads to the front passenger side window. Somebody was knocking on the glass and it wasn't Dr Claudius.

68

A huge raw hand, decorated with dark blue scrawls of tattoo ink, was tapping on the window. From the back seat, all I could see was the hand emerging from the sleeve of a black leather jacket and the top of black cargo pants. Now a face appeared alongside the hand. It was as broad as Joan's chest, with tiny sparkling eyes peering out from under a heavy blond brow ridge. The face's skin was cratered and scarred, like a sand-blasted concrete wall, and the top of its shaven head showed patches of healed skin over what looked like fresh burns. It was a face I knew all too well, because it was the last face Shaun Strong ever saw.

Yevgeny Kuznetsov drew himself back up to his full height and stepped away from the car. As he gestured with his titanic thumb towards the barn, I could see that he was holding a baseball bat in the other hand.

"Please. This way."

"Fucking hell! He's taller than Richard Osman!" Joan exclaimed.

Yevgeny tapped the bonnet of Sandra's car with bat and directed us to the barn again, this time with a finger like a baby's arm.

Sandra got out first, holding her hands in the air. First she helped me out of the back and then she helped Joan, babbling the whole time.

"Please...we don't...we haven't...I'm just a nurse...they're in their nineties…nobody saw anything…you can't…please…just let us…where's Claudius? What have you done to Claudius?"

"Your friend - he's in there. He is fine. Nothing to worry. But you go over there now."

"Yes…yes…thank you…of course…but…you won't hurt us will you?"

Yevgeny pulled a non-committal face and shrugged.

"Maybe. We'll see. Why not? This way now please."

We walked in front of Yevgeny, clinging on to one another, as much for physical support as moral support. Sandra was still muttering hysterically. Joan was rummaging in her handbag. Sauntering behind, his bat slung casually over his shoulder like a black-clad Cerne Abbas giant, Yevgeny stopped dead.

"You. *Babushka*. Put down the bag."

"I'm just…" Joan replied without looking up as she continued to search the bag interior.

"You stop now. This is a warning," Yevgeny poked Sandra in the back with the end of the bat. She jumped like a scalded cat. "You tell her. Or harm will befall you."

Sobbing in terror, Sandra grabbed hold of Joan's bag as if to rip it out of her hands.

"Here they are! I knew I'd find them in the end. Would you like a mint Mr Osman?" Joan drew out the packet of sweets and held it out to Yevgeny. The Russian looked dubiously at them, then reached out and took one. He popped it into his mouth and grinned.

"Thank you mother. But you both give bags to nurse woman now. No more funny business, understand?"

"Understand!" Joan replied, smiling back in turn.

Throughout this exchange I had remained silent. My chest felt constricted, as though blood was struggling to reach my body's extremities, and my fingers and toes were tingling with pins and needles. My breathing was shallow and fast and as much as I tried to slow it down, I could not.

We walked past the rotting tractor and saw that there were tendrils of vegetation sprouting from its burned-out engine block and daisies growing in the mud still caking its tyres. A single poppy held its head up from inside the shattered cab. As we stepped into the barn, gloom descended.

In spite of shafts of thin light trickling in through the damaged roof, at ground level the darkness was thick and viscous. It took time for my eyes to adjust to it. Before they could, I heard the sound of a pair of hands clapping slowly.

"Very good! Very good indeed!" A familiar voice. I felt nauseous again on hearing it. "He tells me he has urgent news about Shaun Strong and he brings me...what? The Golden Girls? What's the craic young man? Got an explanation for this?"

It was Nigel. I couldn't see him yet, other than as a patch of extra-dark blackness moving through the shadow. I could smell him though. I could smell that combination of heavy aftershave, used cooking oil, electrostatic carpet and sweat. It took me back to Prospect House in an instant. My bowels began to loosen as my stomach rose. It was really him.

"I can explain!" Dr Claudius sounded close by, but I couldn't see him.

"Well go on then. No time like the present, is there doctor?"

"OK...so I had to get a lift out here with Sandra because of the short notice. I don't have a car of my own, you see..."

"Short notice? You told me it was urgent. You told me that you had to speak to me, in person, right away!"

"I told you...? I'm sorry Mr Darwin, I really don't know what you mean."

There was a brief sound of something whooshing through the air followed by a thud and a groan.

"Turn the fucking lights on Keith," Nigel said with impatience.

Fluorescent tubes began to flicker, revealing the scene inside the barn first as flashing stills.

There was Dr Claudius, kneeling on the floor, clutching his stomach, his mouth agape, strands of hair tumbling from his scalp to touch the dusty floor.

There was Yevgeny behind him, bat held aloft as if ready to receive a pitch. His eyes were narrowed, his face otherwise expressionless.

There was Nigel. His smart, bootcut jeans, loafers and crisp white shirt contrasted glaringly with the commando webbing that was strapped around his waist and shoulders. He'd put on a few pounds since I'd last seen him. He was looking straight at me and smiling.

And there, towards the back of the barn, was another, bizarre figure. A scrawny, pale man clad only in an adult-sized nappy and a plastic Viking helmet. I recognised Keith immediately, even before he turned away from the electrical panel to face us. He had grown a straggling pale blond beard and his eyes were empty and haunted.

As the lights came on fully, animating the scene, a rapid, almost hysterical sound burst from outside the barn.

"Wooo-woo-woo-woo-wooooooooh!"

In charged a golden retriever, tongue hanging out of its mouth. It completed two circuits around Dr Claudius and Yevgeny, before tearing towards Keith, who flinched back in alarm at the dog's approach, raising his filthy hands towards his face and one knee to protect his bruised midriff. Sensing no opportunities for fun here, the dog ran back towards the barn entrance where a pile of broken masonry lay on the floor. Dropping to a flat position, the dog flopped one paw over a loose half-brick and manoeuvred its snout in underneath to chew it. Thus happily preoccupied, the dog raised its eyebrows and scanned the room. I thought for a moment that I saw a flash of recognition in the look that Toby (formerly Colonel Aureliano Buendia) gave me, but he quickly completed his inspection and returned to the compelling business of wearing his teeth down to stumps.

Nigel strode slowly over to where Dr Claudius was kneeling. Snatching a handful of hair from the back of Claudius' head, Nigel pulled the psychic's face up into line with his own. Sandra, Joan and I were frozen to the spot. It had not occurred to any of us that running away right now was a possibility.

"I'll ask you again and I trust that this time you will furnish me with a more satisfactory answer. What is the urgent news concerning Shaun Strong that you have to tell me, which has necessitated our meeting here today at such apparent inconvenience to yourself?"

Dr Claudius gasped and gritted his teeth as Nigel pulled on his hair.

"Please! Please!"

Nigel shrugged, stuck his bottom lip out and released his grip. Dr Claudius slumped forward in relief and began to push himself up onto his feet.

"Well, it's like this..." Dr Claudius' eyes darted left and right, up and down as he spoke. "There's...ah...ok, ok. Erm... you know the street he lived in? Where the body was found? Well...um...the house is empty now, right? Yeah, well: the neighbours...they've been seeing movements in there. Lights coming on and off. Shapes behind the curtains. Noises at night, like...like screams? And sawing. Yeah a loud, slow sawing sound. I had a nose around there myself...heard about it from one of Parson's lot. The creepy kid with the alcoholic mum... Ethan! That's him. Yeah, he told me about it - said he delivers meals on wheels or something to some old German codger lives down there...

"Yeah so, I took a look around - outside only for obvious reasons; police have still got it taped off, digging up the garden or something. Well let me tell you: the energy field at that place? Off the chart. Off the chart, I'm telling you! He's there alright. The other two, his victims - they could be there as well. That's... that's what I needed to tell you. Yeah. That...that is it."

While Dr Claudius was speaking, Nigel's face had sunk into the blank stare of a deep-sea predator that I had first witnessed back at Prospect House when Keith and I were first taken hostage. He looked like a stone carving of a bloodthirsty tribal god. When Claudius had finished, life returned to his glazed eyes and he smiled a resigned smile.

"Gervase...can I call you Gervase? Gervase, are you familiar with the practice of Neuro Linguistic Programming? NLP?"

"Um...no?"

"And is there anything of particular interest...anything of fascination up there in the rafters of my barn and to your left?"

Dr Claudius turned in the indicated direction, peering up into the stratum of residual gloom between the illuminated floor and the leaky roof for whatever Nigel might have been talking about.

"Er...no?"

"It may surprise you, then, to discover that while your aptitude for lying may be good enough for fooling your usual crowd of dipshits, it falls far short of what you need to get the better of me. Did you see him, Yevgeny? His eyes! Up and to the left - textbook constructed visual! You don't fool me, pal. You're lying and if there's one thing I can't abide, it's a liar."

Dr Claudius had his hands up and was backing away from Nigel.

"Now, just a minute. Listen..."

A vast hand closed around his arm. Dr Claudius recoiled forward, but was held fast. He thrashed his free arm, his legs and his body around in an attempt to dislodge the Russian colossus' grip, but the more frantically he writhed, the stiller Yevgeny became. Eventually, Dr Claudius stopped squirming, exhausted.

"Please..."

Nigel closed his eyes and shook his head.

"Yevgeny."

In one fluid move, a noose was slipped over Dr Claudius' head and pulled tight. Dr Claudius clutched at the rope around his neck as Yevgeny rolled him around so that they were back to back. Beside me, Sandra was in silent tears. Joan was making clicking noises at Colonel Aureliano Buendia, who swivelled an eye towards her but would otherwise not be disturbed from chewing his brick.

Yevgeny flexed his shoulders and adjusted his hold on the

rope, getting his hands as far up towards the knot as possible. Then he leaned over forwards until he was bent double and Dr Claudius was hoisted into the air, kicking frantically now, his fingers clawing at the rope. He began to make an eerie squealing noise like a damaged balloon.

Eventually, the flailing subsided into a twitching and the squeal became a hoarse squelch. I couldn't look, so I looked at Nigel. Keith had come up to stand beside him, his eyes fixed firmly on the ground, his finger dabbing at the bald patch on the left of his chin. Nigel was looking at me again.

"Not safe to hang someone from this roof," he said. "Structure's condemned - too many pigeons take off at once and it could come crashing down, never mind him. Have we met before? There's something familiar about you. Keith - what do you think?"

Keith flinched again at the mention of his name, then turned his gaze on me.

"No idea," he murmured before dropping his eyes to the floor again.

"It'll come to me," Nigel said. "I never forget a face."

Yevgeny dropped Dr Claudius to the floor like a sack. The sound of his carcass hitting the ground broke the spell that Sandra had been under, and she rushed over to him, falling to her knees and screaming hysterically.

"Right," Nigel clapped his hands together and took a step towards Joan and I. "What are we going to do with you three then? You think we can trust them to keep quiet about that unpleasant business Keith? Nice old ladies like these two? What's your name love?"

"Joan," Joan replied.

"Lovely to meet you Joan. Sorry about the unpleasantness."

"Oh that's alright dear. I was going to kill him myself when I got the chance."

"And you," Nigel pointed at me. "What's your name?"

"Edith."

"I don't think so."

"I'm sorry?"

"I said, I don't think so. That's not your name."

I frowned, confused.

"That is my name."

"That's not your name."

"It is!"

"Don't lie to me Shaun. If there's one thing I can't abide, it's a liar."

69

My head was swimming and I was struggling for breath. My field of vision had narrowed to a slot, and everything I could see looked far, very far away. Yevgeny was helping me to sit down on an upturned wheelbarrow. Nigel stood in front of me with his arms folded.

"Got you there, didn't I? The look on your face! You should have seen yourself. Thought you were going to have a stroke! No doubt you'll be wanting to know how I knew it was you? Well, don't you worry about that. All in good time Shaun, all in good time. There will be a thorough debrief back at the office very shortly. If you will excuse me, my colleagues and I have a small matter to attend to before we set off. Boys?"

Nigel walked off towards a dark corner of the barn, Keith scampering behind him. As he was merging with the shadows, Nigel flicked on a torch which cast a watery cone of light in front of him.

"It's down here somewhere isn't it Yevgeny? Did you say behind the oil drums? Aha! I see it... hang on... is that...? Oh for fuck's sake! Keith! Keith, get over here! The dog's done a shit in the grave. Fish it out!"

"Have you got a bag?" Keith mumbled.

"No I haven't got a bag! Just fucking get it! With your hand! You dirty sacrilegious dog bastard Toby!"

Colonel Aureliano Buendia responded with a cheerful yip, delighted to hear his new name shouted.

The three men quickly buried Dr Claudius in the corner of the barn. Nigel instructed that Yevgeny take Sandra and Joan back to Prospect House in Sandra's car, and ordered Keith and I into the Range Rover.

"Normal back seats this time lads. Can't use the back row any more because of the dog. Bane of my life that bloody animal is. Toby! Toby! Where's he got to now?"

Nigel stomped off, looking for the golden retriever - who had slunk away unnoticed at some moment between the turd retrieval and the hasty interment of the late Gervase Claudius Kenny.

In the back seat of the Range Rover, Keith and I faced one another.

"Shaun? Is it you?" Keith asked.

I nodded.

Keith took off his helmet and ran his fingers through his dirty hair.

"What...I mean, I don't know where to start. What happened?"

I tried to explain. Keith looked more overwhelmed and confused with each new episode.

"Can you still do The Thing?"

"No."

Keith's bemusement turned to a look of devastation.

"Well that's it then. We're both properly fucked this time. He was convinced you were still out there and that once we'd found you, he'd be able to squeeze the secret out of you one way or another. But if you can't even do it any more..."

"Don't worry Keith," I said. "We'll get out of this, one way or another."

But what that way might be, I had no idea. The plan I had hatched with Joan had backfired completely and somehow Nigel knew who I was. The likelihood of a good end to all this seemed extremely slim.

"You know I really am sorry Shaun. About everything. You were a good friend."

"We still are friends."

Our conversation was abruptly brought to an end as Nigel opened the rear door and lowered the tailgate. Colonel Aureliano Buendia bounded into the boot and curled up into a compact ball on a tartan rug.

As we trundled out of the farmyard and onto the overgrown lane, Nigel began to speak.

"Well, well, well. The gang's all here, eh? I will admit Mr Strong, I was sceptical when I heard that you had returned to walk among us as an old woman, but I clocked you the second I saw you. It's not faces I remember - it's the look in a person's eyes. You can't hide it Shaun: it's useless to try. You've got the same look now as you did before. Like a hunted animal, waiting to be jumped on. Wanting it. Like it would be some kind of relief for you to be torn apart. Prey. You can't hide what you are in your heart Shaun. Not your fault, of course. We all are what we are. That's how I knew I'd find you again. I knew that if you had come back you wouldn't do the sensible thing and get as far away from here as possible - start a new life. As far as that's possible at your age of course - ah ha ha ha ha ha!"

The Range Rover was traversing the ruts and pot holes of the lane with little more than a gentle rolling motion making itself felt.

"No, I knew you'd be back. You bit-part players can't help being drawn back towards a protagonist like me. I get it. Gives you a kind of purpose you could never achieve by yourself - am I right? Of course I am. Your man Keith here? He understands all that now, don't you Keith? Hey, put your helmet back on. I've told you before. Ask me why he's dressed like that Shaun."

Keith put the Viking helmet back on his head and slumped in his seat, looking out of the window.

"My biographer slash jester here used to have ideas above his station. Thought he was a bit special, a bit cleverer than everyone else. Even cleverer than me, I dare say. Isn't that right Keith?"

Keith didn't respond.

"He's a smart lad, I'll give him that. He was quick to pick up my philosophy and I don't think many people could get their heads round it. It's not a gift that I'd vouchsafe to just anyone. But Keith fatally misunderstood one part of it. The most important part. And what was that Keith?"

"It's only for you. Not for anyone else," Keith mumbled without looking round.

"That's it! It only applies to me. Total freedom, you see, can't be shared. There can be only one, as The Kurgan famously said in…what film? Anyone?"

"Highlander." Keith replied flatly.

"Highlander indeed! Frequently misquoted as 'there can only be one' in spite of Freddie Mercury making the correct word order unambiguously clear in 'A Kind of Magic'… Yes, what is sauce for this goose is not for any other ganders. Keith got the wrong end of the stick. He's all 'we should' this and 'we can' that. Needed to be taught a lesson. Brought down a peg or two. Shown where he really fits in around here. So, we took away his clothes, didn't we Keith? Had him running around the place bare-arsed all the time. Very sobering. Gives you a kind of perspective it's hard to get otherwise - always at a disadvantage, always self-conscious and uncomfortable. Bit like you Shaun! Ah ha ha ha. He doesn't need that kind of a lesson, does he Keith? Ah ha ha ha!

"Anyway, in the end the sight of his shrivelled-up cock every time I came to the top floor was making me sick. So now he wears the nappy. To remind him of his place in the world. The helmet's just for a laugh. Cracks me up when he's wearing it."

We were driving through the outskirts of Guildford now. The sun was a flaming orange ball above the horizon.

"So, what's life like as a woman then Shaun? No! I've got another question. What's it like being dead? I tell you, I gave Yevgeny some stick when I heard you were alive. 'Call yourself a killer?' I said. 'Can't even get rid of an injured librarian!' He takes it in his stride does Yevgeny, but I could see it was winding him up. Takes a lot of pride in his killing. Hates loose ends. Now that one - he has the right attitude. Just does what he's told, gets on with it, doesn't think too hard or play games or anything like that. He just does his job and when I don't need him, he fucks off home and does whatever it is he does for fun. God alone knows what that might be, but when I do need him, there he is, no complaints. No illusions, no airs and graces. The highest praise I can give a man Shaun is to call him reliable. And Yevgeny is one hundred and ten per cent reliable.

"But what were we saying? Oh yeah. Highlander. Classic. A true individualist doesn't pretend to be an egalitarian. Nobody is my equal. I'm not interested in other people and what they get up to, but if I could give one rule to the rest of the world it would be this: look after number one. Simple as that. My freedom ends where your rights begin. Do you get me? The mistake people make - the mistake Keith made - when they hear my philosophy, is to think that I'm telling them something that's right for them as well as me. I can't accept a limit to my freedom. You'd have to be an idiot in this life to behave as though you were anything other than the dead centre of the universe. God's dead, so it's every man for himself.

"You know what started me off down this road? Keith, get your notebook - this is important. When I was a lad, I had a lizard for a pet. And I had to feed it these crickets or grasshoppers - whatever the fuck they were. Live food, anyway. You can't feed them dead ones for some reason. Anyway, I started off squeamish. I know it's hard to believe now, looking at me, but I had...what...I don't know what you'd call it... compassion? ... for these fucking insects. I didn't want to see them die. Who would? But me lizard - Gary, that was his name - he loved them. Locusts. That's what they were. And the daft fucker wouldn't eat anything else, so it was either feed him the locusts or watch him die.

"So I fed him - reluctantly at first, but gradually I came to think of the locusts not as living things, but just as food. Same as Gary did in fact."

We were turning onto the A3 now. Nigel had stopped

speaking, which I took to be a cue for me to urge him to continue.

"And so…that taught you…?"

"Disregard for life. How to treat living things as means to an end."

"Really?"

"No! Don't be so fucking soft! You think this is about my traumatic childhood? Mummy didn't love me enough? Daddy interfered with me? Fuck off! That's what your kind can never grasp Shaun. You and all them want to find reasons why people like me aren't responsible. Why we're all victims of something that happened to us. Not me. I chose to do all this. You want to eliminate free will. You want people to be algorithms. Well I'm not an algorithm. I'm a fucking virus. Ah ha ha ha. A virus! I do what I want and I want what I want. How many people can say that? You want to be able to explain everyone - to point to something in the past and say 'ah, that's why'. But you can't do that with me.

"No, the real reason - and I don't think I've ever told anyone this before, so make sure you're getting this down word for word Captain Underpants. Captain Underpants, eh Shaun! Ah ha ha ha ha! The real reason goes back to when I first became a parent. You don't have kids, do you Shaun? So you won't really understand what I'm telling you, but…well fuck it…you two have got nothing to lose now."

What did that mean? I tried the door handle, but it was child-locked.

"When my Sophie was born, I knew that I loved her from the moment I set eyes on her. You know what I mean? I knew I was in it for life. No matter what, that girl would be the most important thing to me. Was I the best Dad? I tried Shaun. I did my best, but it's hard. It's difficult, you know? Kids are… kids are relentless. Especially girls. It's tough being a parent. It's fucking hard work when you've got a business to run and whatnot. I tried to make time, I really did. Deep in my heart, she was always the most important thing…but I don't know…

on any given day, there always seemed to be something more pressing. She got close to her mum at my expense. And that's when it started I suppose.

"I'd imagine that she was being bullied at school or hassled on her way home. I'd imagine her getting hit by a car. Or attacked by a group of boys...mugged and...mugged and raped. And I knew I had to protect her. And I was angry. I was angry with the thoughts, because I knew they were coming from me and I was angry with myself because I was working myself up imagining this, and imagining what I'd do - or rather, what I wouldn't do - to protect her. And I began to wonder, 'why do you keep thinking about these things?' I'd get angry with myself then I'd get angry with her because the way I felt about her was making me think about all this horrible shit. I'd wonder: am I imagining this because I want to stop it happening or because I want it to happen? So I test my resolve to do the things I imagine myself doing. You know what I mean? No, probably not...

"But I'll tell you this. That's a fucking moment boys. That was it. That was when I knew that everything began with control of myself. Control yourself, control the world. Write that down Keith, that's a good one. You let your emotions or your imagination run riot, you're fucked. You bend those things to your will? That, my friends, is the trick."

We drove in silence for a few minutes passing through the villages that make up Woking's outer orbit. Eventually, Nigel quietly repeated: "It's tough being a parent" before lapsing into silence again until we reached Prospect House.

70

As we drove into the underground garage, Yevgeny was standing at the barrier waving. Nigel stopped and wound his window down.

"What's up?"

"The lift. It is out of order. We have to go in through main entrance, so I wait down here - keep everyone in car."

"Oh for Christ's sake!" Nigel snapped. "I told them to get that fixed three days ago. Am I the only person who gets anything done around here? Jesus!"

"Also…" Yevgeny sounded tentative, and pointed with a thick thumb to a grey Jaguar parked in the corner. On seeing it, Nigel calmed down immediately and adopted a business-like air.

"I see. Well, please assist our guests in making their way to the stairs. Keith, pull that blanket out from under the dog and wrap it round yourself. Can't have you walking the streets of Woking dressed like that. The helmet can stay in the car, just this once."

Colonel Aureliano Buendia growled menacingly as Keith tugged on his rug, but he finally surrendered. As Keith pulled it over the back seats, a pungent canine aroma swept through the Range Rover, propelling ahead of it a small cloud of yellow hairs.

Nigel parked the Range Rover and we all got out. Yevgeny released the dog and clipped him onto his lead. Colonel Aureliano Buendia was staring at me with sad eyes, as if he knew this was goodbye.. He was staring at me with sad eyes, as if he knew this was goodbye.

We walked around the side of Prospect House and into the white marble-tiled lobby. Seated on the grey felt armchairs reserved for waiting visitors of importance were Michelle and Sophie Darwin. Doubt, panic and rapid thought danced across Nigel's flushed features when he spotted them. He hesitated, considering turning back, but it was too late. Michelle had looked up and locked eyes with him. Nigel appeared to shrink into himself for a second. Then he puffed out his chest, held his head up and walked to meet the two women who were now coming out of the building to confront him. Michelle looked furious. Sophie looked contemptuous.

"Is there anything you want to tell me about that dog you brought home?" Michelle snapped.

"Dog...?" Nigel began.

"Remind us where you got him from Nigel."

"I...um...got him from the RSPCA shelter. The one at Millbrook."

"Aha," Michelle spat, in a manner that implied a rhetorical pause rather acceptance. She looked at each of us in turn. "And who are these people? Why is that man dressed in Toby's blanket?"

Muscles across Nigel's body were tensing. Cords in his neck twitched. He blinked hard. His knuckles were whitening, the carpal bones under the skin seething in successive waves. He was about to speak when Michelle broke the silence.

"You didn't get him from the RSPCA, did you? Ask me how I know."

Nigel glanced at Yevgeny and signalled with a dip of his head that the Russian should take the rest of us inside while he dealt with this inconvenient family matter.

"Oh no you don't! Stay here. I want them to hear this, whoever they are. I called the RSPCA about getting our details put onto his microchip, and what do you think they said Nigel?

They'd never heard of him. Or you. So I took him down the vet and had him scanned, and guess what? Guess who he used to belong to?"

Nigel stood motionless. His fists were disengaged now, his fingers hanging loosely. He opened his mouth, closed it and then opened it again.

"It was my grandson's dog."

I didn't realise that I was the one who had spoken until everyone's eyes were turned on me.

"My grandson Trevor Long. He was murdered. It's been on the news."

Michelle was staring at me, her lips pursed in an expression of righteous anger derailed. She lifted a hand to point at me in a non-commital way. Her nail varnish was bright pink – not shocking pink, a little duskier than that. Her brow was furrowed. The lines hinted at the flawlessness of her complexion, the superfluity of make-up.

"You? Your grandson?"

She took a step towards me.

"Yes," I said. "I live in a care home and can't take a dog on. Mr Darwin kindly agreed to have him."

Nigel's face was changing - from alarm, through bewilderment and complicit cunning and was beginning to settle in gleefully wounded vindication. He put his arm around my shoulder and grinned a grin that was simultaneously sheepish and wolfish. I felt the weight of his arm pressing down hard on my bony shoulders.

"That's right. When I heard about the terrible things that had happened, I knew I couldn't stand by and do nothing. So I adopted this...ah...wonderful woman's dog."

"And he promised to pay Edith's fees at Fair Haven for the rest of her life!" Joan piped up.

Nigel's left eyelid fluttered, and for a split second his upper lip curled in frustration and anger.

"Err...yes. I did. And...um...that's why we're all here. To... ah...finalise the paperwork. On that..."

Michelle stepped towards me. As she did, Nigel released my shoulder.

"Have we met before?"

"Yes," I said. "You helped me pick my things off the floor in a café in Guildford."

"Did I?" Michelle scanned her memory, but was coming up blank.

"Cakey Boo Boo Num Nums…?"

"Oh yes! Of course!" Michelle clearly did not remember, but was visibly relieved and grateful for the escape line I had dangled her way. "How are you love? I'm so sorry for what happened to your grandson."

And then she embraced me.

My heart began to ache. Not just metaphorically, but also physically as my bad self diverted blood flow from limbs and major organs to my phantom penis.

"We'll take good care of him," she whispered in my ear - her breath like the warm breeze over a summer meadow. Keep thinking about summer meadows, Shaun. Noble. Romantic. Don't think about where your erection should be. Try to be good for once. Try not to be a scumbag.

Michelle released me and turned to her husband. She resumed where she had left off at "aha" earlier.

"Why did you lie about it?"

"I…" Nigel was taken by surprise.

"Why lie? You keep too many secrets Nigel Darwin. One day, it'll be your downfall," Michelle snarled as she stalked away. "Come on Soph."

Sophie finished typing a message her on phone. Putting her hand on Nigel's shoulder, she kissed him perfunctorily on the cheek.

"Bye Dad," she said without looking back.

As the two women disappeared around the corner with the dog, Nigel growled through gritted teeth: "Get them inside."

The ascent to the seventh floor was slow and arduous.

Joan managed surprisingly well, but I was struggling badly.

By the second floor, each breath felt like it was tearing a chunk of my lung lining away. My hands were going numb again and every few steps I was beset by a swirl of dizziness. Sandra and Yevgeny supported my arms as we climbed. Nigel paused a flight above us, looking down impatiently, before storming up another level to repeat the process, Keith at his heels. With each floor, he became angrier.

Sandra looked imploringly at Yevgeny.

"He's going to kill her, making her go up these stairs! She's ninety-seven for God's sake."

Yevgeny only grunted.

The stairwell was dank and sweaty, and it was a relief to emerge into the air-conditioned anteroom of the seventh floor. Nigel pushed the fire door open and we all trooped into the open plan, unfurnished office space. How long had it been since I was last here? The office block across the road - a carcass being stripped clean when we had spent our first days here - was now nothing more than a heap of concrete bones lying around a deep pit. But the camp beds, the desk, the freezers, the toilet tent all remained in position, as if nothing had changed. There was Ragnar on his perch, more dishevelled and morose than ever. On his chest there was a bald patch, picked clean of feathers and speckled with bloody pinpricks.

And sat behind the desk was Aleister Woodward the lawyer. He rose to his feet as we entered. Over his soft grey suit, he wore a long, black velvet stole. On it were embroidered red symbols which, even at this distance and with my eyesight unsettled me.

Yevgeny was still propping me up. "*Nechistaia sila*," I heard him whisper under his breath at the sight of Woodward.

"Sorry we're a bit late," Nigel declared airily. "Had a few loose ends to tie up before we came back and, well, as you can see..." he gestured towards Joan and myself , "the broken lift gave us a few headaches too."

"Not at all! Nothing to worry about," Woodward replied, coming out from the behind the desk. As he came forward, I could see another swathe of black cloth hanging over his right wrist. This one featured a red pentagram, inscribed within two concentric circles.

"I've just had a wonderful dinner at Gaston's. I really must recommend the *saucisse de Toulouse* to you. They were truly exquisite."

"Toulouse...?" Nigel sounded confused and appalled. "Is that...the arsehole sausages?"

"The...? Nigel, traditionally Toulouse sausages are pork, bacon, red wine and garlic."

"What are those other ones then? The sausages. Made from arseholes."

"I would imagine that you are thinking of *andouillette*. A specialised taste. Not one I have ever managed to acquire, but I do rather think you're doing them something of an injustice with your blunt description. Anyway...Mrs Sterckx, what a pleasure it is to see you again."

Woodward addressed me now, pushing his gold-rimmed glasses back up the bridge of his nose with his left index finger as he walked towards us. "Is that you Mrs Sterckx? Or is it your tenant, Mr Strong, to whom I am speaking?"

"Don't worry Shaun," Nigel murmured, the dead shark look plastered back across his face, "We'll have you out of there in no time."

I wanted to reply, but no breath would come when I tried to speak.

DEATH 2

7 I

I was dead before I hit the floor. I felt an implosion in my chest - a sudden pressure pushing inwards from all directions at once. My heart was greedily sucking all my blood into itself before it burst with a meagre pop. I dropped to my knees, gasping for air and waving my hands in front of me as if scrabbling for purchase on something nobody else could see.

Yevgeny stepped back and Sandra screamed as I keeled over forward and fell onto my face.

"Was that supposed to happen?"

Nigel's voice was the last thing I heard before everything went black and silent again.

***

And then it came back.

***

"No, it wasn't, but don't panic."

It was Woodward speaking.

"That's why we have a Plan B. Are you absolutely sure about this Nigel?"

"Yep."

"It's very difficult to undo once we go beyond this point. Probably not something I can help you with, in fact. Ha ha.

Conflict of interests, you could say..."

"I want it. I choose it."

"And you've got a suitable vessel?"

"I thought we could use the daft bird here. He'd appreciate the joke."

"The bird...? THAT bird? The eagle? Nigel, you do realise that for the ability to transfer to you in the way we discussed you will have to ... erm ... eat the vessel?"

"Yep. No use to me, is it?"

"I see. Well. I mean...you'll have to eat all of it. Beak, feathers, a *ndouillette* and everything."

"Not a problem."

"OK then. Funnily enough, it's actually easier to bind a spirit this way than trying to extract it from a host body. But we will need to hurry. Souls don't tend to hang about. Can someone flip her over please?"

I was observing the room from high above. I don't remember precisely when or how I began to see again. It occurred gradually, a picture emerging as the blackness came into focus. Nigel was rolling Edith over onto her back and Woodward had returned to the desk where he was inspecting the contents of a small black leather case. Yevgeny was standing near to the fire door, holding Joan and Sandra by the shoulder. They were all staring with mute horror at the scene unfolding in front of them. Keith stood halfway between the group at the door and the body on the floor, hugging the blanket round him and rocking back and forth slightly. His finger protruded from the neck of his makeshift cloak and was scratching at the damaged patch on his chin. Even Ragnar appeared spellbound, his wings half spread, yellow eyes locked on the dead body, blue nictitating membranes sliding back and forth intermittently.

Woodward walked slowly back, cradling something delicate between his hands. Nigel backed away at his approach. Standing up, he beckoned Keith towards him. Keith stepped forward as the lawyer knelt beside my corpse. He released the contents of his cupped hands over Edith's face and, using this thumb, drew a black shape on her forehead. He was chanting under his breath as he did so.

I was no longer above the room. I was back in it, perceiving things from just under six feet off the ground. The spot I had tended towards when I was doing The Thing. I looked down but saw no sign of any body. I tried to take flight but I couldn't move.

Woodward stood up and wiped his hands together.

"Did it work?" Nigel asked. He and Keith were skirting around the body towards the desk.

"Yes," Woodward replied. "He's not going anywhere."

"Can he hear us?"

"In a sense, yes. It's not 'hearing' precisely, but it's close enough."

Nigel carefully placed Woodward's leather case on top of the freezer, holding it at arm's length as if afraid that it could leap from his hands and attack him. Having disposed of the case, he swept the remaining paperwork strewn over the desk onto the floor.

"Shaun. Shaun, Shaun, Shaun. I thought that someone unique like you would be able to understand. But you've taught me a valuable lesson and I'm grateful for that. Do you know what it is? You've shown me that being exceptional, being above the herd - it's got nothing to do with what you are born with. It's about what you create. And the passive will never create anything. That's the real sin: passivity. Waiting on someone else to set the wheels in motion. You were a pitiful man Shaun Strong."

Nigel had moved up behind Keith now. He put his left hand on Keith's forearm and thrust his face forward over Keith's shoulder. Keith shuddered and shrank as he did so.

"Let's talk about Keith. He's your only friend in the world, isn't that right Shaun? And yet, what do you really know about Keith Pardew? Eh? What's his motivation? Where is this all going for him? Why do you think that the first thing he suggested when he found out what you were was blackmail?

What kind of a person does that? And where do you think the money you made is now? How much of it did you ever see? Any of it? Or none at all?

"You wanted me to catch you, didn't you Keith? Don't deny it. He saw what I had and - let's not play games! - he preferred it to what you had to offer. Sold you down the river just like that, he did. I've got your money Shaun. You want to know how I got it? He gave it to me! To 'buy his way in'! Can you fucking believe that?!"

Nigel burst out laughing. It was a harsh sound, like two bricks grinding together. He slid his hand down Keith's restrained forearm to the wrist and pulled it hard up into the small of his back. Keith cried out in pain and surprise, bending forward at the waist to compensate until his cheek was pressed against the desk.

"I'll say this much. At the start, I was impressed by what a cold bastard your friend here is. Not everyone would betray their mate like that. You have to admire the man's aspiration. But there's an important lesson I've learned from business. There's hard-headed determination and single-mindedness and there's ruthlessness too. But it's not always easy to tell the difference between those qualities and the state of being a spineless, snivelling shit. And the more I got to know our Mr Pardew here, the clearer which side of the line he fell on became to me."

"Ahem," Woodward cleared his throat and tapped on his watch. "We are on a clock here..."

With his free hand, Nigel reached into his jacket's inner pocket, drawing out a short, broad-bladed dagger, which he banged down onto the table beside Keith's face with an echoing open-palmed slap. Keith fell silent, the tension and resistance draining out of his body. Nigel put his other hand - the one with which he had just drawn the knife - on the back of Keith's neck. Keith's eyes rolled back and forth between the knife and Nigel's face.

"Nigel...please..." Keith choked.

"All you had to do was help me Shaun. We could have done amazing things together. Amazing things. But you chose not to. I respect that. All this…it's not for everyone. I get it. Your gift though…it's too rare and valuable a thing to let you waste it like you have done. And so I refuse to accept your choice. I choose not to! Nobody wants to serve in heaven these days. I gave you the chance to reign in hell with me Shaun, but I'm afraid that this is no longer an option. You will serve instead."

Looking over to Woodward, Nigel asked: "Does it matter how I do it? Anything I need to say?"

The lawyer shook his head. "Not really."

"You're the expert."

"It's the sacrifice that's the thing. It runs itself from here on."

"Right then."

Releasing Keith's head, Nigel reached slowly for the knife. Keith didn't move, other than to gasp spasmodically.

"Mr Pardew: sincere thanks for your help."

Nigel swung the dagger round in his hand so that the blade protruded from the bottom of his fist. In one swift movement, he twisted to the right, leaned back, raised his fist to head height and hammered the knife into the side of Keith's skull just above the ear. The pterion bone, I believe it's called.

Nothing moved. Nothing made a sound. Nigel stood back, leaving the blade in Keith's brain and the handle protruding to one side. Without realising I had moved, I was close up alongside Keith's face. His unseeing eyes stared into the space I imagined myself to be occupying before they filled with blood. The blood formed into droplets in the corners of his eyes which swelled up in size until they burst like red balloons, becoming rivers that mixed to become one with the streams of tears that had spattered Keith's face in his final moments. Then blood began to pour from his nose and he slid off the table, landing on the floor on his back, darkening blood pulsing from his face - slower and slower as his heart came to rest.

"Now what?"

"Just give it a minute…"

"I don't feel any different."

"These things usually take a little while...it's nothing to be concerned about."

I looked around the room. Yevgeny had quietly opened the fire door and was ushering Joan and Sandra out. Nigel was standing in a growing pool of blood beside Keith's body, his hands raised in a posture of aggressive questioning, facing Woodward. Woodward was looking directly at me. Not at Edith's body - me. The point from which I was perceiving all this. He winked.

"I think it's beginning now. I'm confident you can handle things from here now Nigel. Best I get off - busy day ahead of me and...well...my continued presence would just confuse matters, I think. Do you feel it?"

Woodward removed his glasses and wiped the lenses on the black maniple. He replaced them and then moved on to folding up his vestments.

"Yes," said Nigel. "I can definitely feel something happening now."

Woodward put the velvet cloths back into his case and snapped it shut.

"Super! Let me know how it goes. Enjoy your meal!"

I could feel myself fragmenting again. It was just like when I died the first time. I began to disappear.

LIFE 3

72

My eyes flicked open. Everything was red. The side of my head ached and my chin tickled. I could smell iron, nylon and body odour. Reflexively, I moved my hand to wipe my eyes clear. As I did so, the maroon veil lifted and I could see again. Carpet. Grey, soaked to brown. The metal legs of a desk. A tartan blanket. A scrawny white body, covered in scrapes and yellowed healing bruises. The body was only wearing a diaper, but I couldn't see its face because I was looking out of that face.

I tried to roll onto my back. My body flopped over, but something was sticking out of my head and it stopped me from turning my face up to the ceiling. I pushed myself into a seated position instead and felt around with my hand to identify the obstacle behind my ear. It was a rubberised handle. Touching it sent electrical blasts of pain arcing through my brain and along my spine. There was a horrible noise, like an angle grinder being applied to a paving slab. I sat up to see where it was coming from. The desk was still blocking my view so I pulled myself to my feet.

Nigel was screaming. He emitted the same, inhuman sound as I had seen him produce that first morning at his home. The veins in the sides of his purpling head throbbed. The sound went on, longer and longer - longer than a normal set of lungs should have permitted. When Nigel had finally expelled every cubic centimetre of air in his body, he pulled himself back up to his full height, trembling. He looked around with what seemed to me to be the first sign of uncertainty and fear I had ever seen cross that face.

I glanced in the window as I rose up and saw my reflection there: it was the gore-soaked body of Keith Pardew, a knife buried in his skull. Blood was dripping from my nose and mouth.

I reached up to the side of my head and grasped the handle. I pulled gently and after a little resistance at the start, it slid out easily. Trust Nigel to have used one of those commando knives with the grooves up the blade. I felt a warm tide flow down my neck.

"Well. This isn't exactly what I had in mind. Although if I tell the truth, I don't really know what I was expecting," Nigel said, smiling uneasily. He circled away from me as I walked around the desk.

I tried to speak, but a dollop of blood and fluids spilled out of my mouth instead. Spitting the last of it out, I hissed: "Nigel…"

Then I realised. Even now, I didn't know what to say. I was too self-conscious to say anything that the drama of the moment demanded. Even inhabiting the blood-drenched, reanimated corpse of my best friend and facing down the man who was responsible for my three deaths, I could not get over my own hang ups.

"Stay back!" Nigel fumbled with the webbing he had strapped around his chest, searching for something with his hands, never taking his eyes off my own. By the time he found what he was looking for, we had rotated to stand on opposite sides of the desk. Nigel was holding a gun and he was pointing it at me.

He fired and it caught me in the shoulder, knocking me over backwards. The plate glass window behind me shattered as the bulk of the bullet passed straight through. The shards exploded outwards into the Woking evening.

"My fucking window!" Nigel shrieked as a vast sound of rushing wind filled the room. "That cost a fortune!"

I rolled over onto my hands and knees. My shoulder was pumping blood now, but I was still holding the knife.

"Are you a zombie now? Is that what this is? What has that fucking twat Woodward gone and done?" Nigel's voice was getting higher and he was shouting faster. "Is it Keith? Or is it Shaun? Speak up you fucking zombie bastard!"

I crawled forwards, unable to get back up to my feet. My internal systems were depressurising quickly. I lifted my head and there in front of me was Ragnar.

"I have had enough of all this! Drugs…the supernatural… It's too much hassle! Too much bloody drama! As soon as I've finished you and those others off, it's blockchain all the way! Cryptocurrency, boys - that's where it's all happening!"

Ragnar's beak was open and he was hopping up and down on one leg. The leg that was tied to his perch with a leather jess. I looked at the eagle and he looked back at me. We both understood.

"Keith. Shaun. Whatever… It has certainly been an adventure, but I'm going to have to call time on this little escapade. Don't take it personally…"

Ragnar spread his wings to their full seven foot span and flapped them, slowly lifting into the air like a kite in the howling gale pouring in through the empty window. I lunged forwards, Grabbing the leather strap in one hand, I sliced it in two with the knife. The eagle pulled his wings in, dropped to the ground and then launched himself into the air again, swinging his body around in flight to bring his savage talons upwards into Nigel's face.

Nigel thrashed his arms around as he tried to escape the clutches of the frenzied raptor, which was clawing, biting and buffeting him with all of its strength. I pulled myself to my feet using the desk for support. The blood was flowing black from my gaping wounds and the room was spinning around me. Nigel and Ragnar careered past. I finally knew what I had to do.

So I did it.

I did it for Keith. I did it for Dr Claudius. I did it for Geoff,

Gabe and Jaz from SmrtHole. I did it for Trevor and Clare Long. I did it for the man who got fed to owls, if he really existed. I waited until Nigel and Ragnar were between me and the empty window. I spat out a mouthful of blood and mucus and charged at them.

I caught him low on the hip with my working shoulder, wrapping my arm around his waist and pushing forwards. He tried to tear me off when he realised what was happening, but his hands reflexively returned to his face to protect them from the eagle's raking claws. I pushed and pushed until there was nothing beneath my feet to push on.

We fell. Bellowing in rage and terror, Nigel snatched at Ragnar and at me as we fell. The eagle flapped his great wings, but it made no difference to our descent. Ragnar cried out, his yelp high-pitched and fragile. I pulled my hand free from Nigel's grip and plunged the knife into his forearm. He screamed as his hand fell limp.

The mighty bird broke free. Catching an updraft beneath his majestic wings, he swept between the office blocks and upward into the sky above Woking without looking back. He was really free at last. By the time we hit the ground, Ragnar was nothing but a speck dissolving into the setting sun.

DEATH 3 REVISITED

73

So that's it. That's how we ended up here, in the tunnel, Nigel and me. I don't think I'm coming back this time. It feels different. Definitely more final. And that's alright with me. Not that it's up to me, but you know…when it's fate, you've just got to accept it, haven't you?

One minute we were lying on the pavement. I could see Nigel's smashed body a few feet away from me. He looked a lot smaller once his skeleton had stopped propping his flesh up. His eyes were still moving as I crossed over, but the next thing I remember was being here and he was here with me.

Something relentless, something merciless, something without pity is trying to pull him away. For now, he's managing to hang on but it won't last. It doesn't. I feel his fingers lose their grip and he's sucked away wailing into the void.

Bye bye Nigel. I can't say I'll miss you.

What now for me? On towards the light, I suppose. Whatever I've got coming, I'll take it. I always do. No point worrying about it. I'm content. Just let it be at that.

So that's my story. Thanks for listening to it. Now, why are you here?

THE END

ACKNOWLEDGMENTS

Thanks to everyone who gave me advice and suggestions, everyone who listened to me go on about this book and everyone who encouraged me to keep going over the period of several years.

Special thanks go to Kate (my wife and editor) and my boys Evan and Rory for tolerating me while I was writing it. I couldn't have done it without your support and love. Perhaps one day we'll publish an edition of this book with Evan's illustrations in...

Talking of illustrations, massive gratitude to Karl Broome who drew the cover picture.

If you enjoyed "Projection" get in touch with me at:

alan@sea-cucumber.co.uk

None of the characters appearing in in this book are based on real people.
None of this happened to me.
I made it all up.

- Alan Boyce, 2020

www.sea-cucumber.co.uk